D0394134

# doctor sleep

**Other Books by Madison Smartt Bell**

*The Washington Square Ensemble* (1983)

*Waiting for the End of the World* (1985)

*Straight Cut* (1986)

*Zero db and Other Stories* (1987)

*The Year of Silence* (1987)

*Soldier's Joy* (1989)

*Barking Man and Other Stories* (1990)

# Integræ Naturæ   ſpeculum, Artiſque imago.

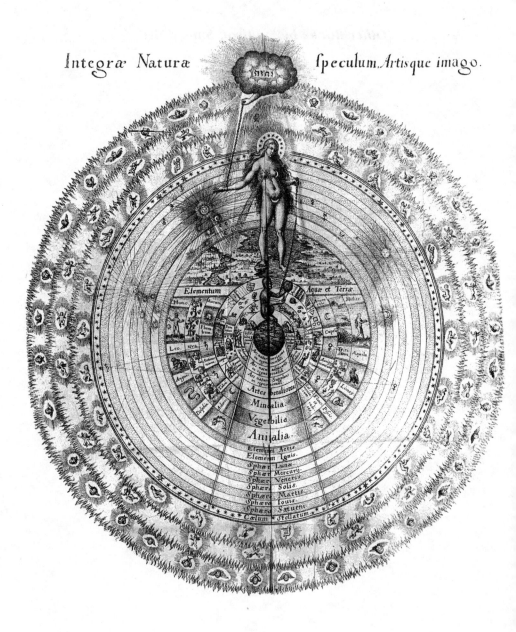

# madison smartt bell

# doctor sleep
## doctor sleep
### doctor sleep

**HARCOURT BRACE JOVANOVICH, PUBLISHERS**
San Diego    New York    London

Library of Congress Cataloging-in-Publication Data
Bell, Madison Smartt.
Doctor Sleep/Madison Smartt Bell.—1st ed.
p.   cm.
ISBN 0-15-126100-8
I. Title.
PS3552.E517D63   1991
813'.54—dc20      90-37932

Book design by Camilla Filancia
Printed in the United States of America
First edition    A B C D E

HBJ

*For Beth, with love*

*I'll break my staff,*
*Bury it certain fathoms in the earth,*
*And deeper than did ever plummet sound*
*I'll drown my book.*

—SHAKESPEARE, *The Tempest*

## *acknowledgments*

For ideas about Giordano Bruno and Hermetic myth and magic, this novel draws heavily on the work of Frances Yates. For a theory of hypnosis and multiple personality, it draws on the work of Dr. Eugene Bliss. Some of its devices of stage hypnotism were suggested by those of Ormond McGill.

The completion of this book was supported by a Beatrice Aitchison Summer Research Grant from Goucher College. Thanks also for research assistance both deliberate and inadvertent, and for all sorts of other help, to Taghi Modarressi, Thurman Mott, Mary Swander, William Heyen, Thomasin La May, Marcia Gollub, Vivienne Schuster, Carole Luke, Elizabeth Krome, the entire staff of the Rare Book Room of the Johns Hopkins University Library, Denis Johnson, and Alisdair Gray (who will hardly be expecting it . . . ).

# PART 1

## Utriusque Cosmi Historia,
## Et cetera, and so on

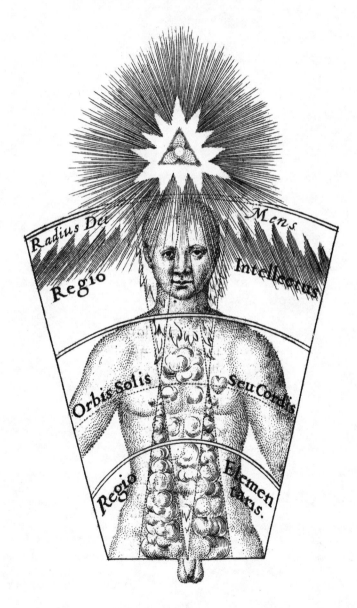

# one

Oh Lord my God, Creator of the Universe, once again you caused me to remain awake the whole night through. Toward dawn I think I managed to forget myself a little, but you couldn't really have called it sleep. More like floating from layer to layer of not-sleeping, from shade to shade of white, if there was any such distinction. On the wall beyond the foot of the bed, first light was spreading like a stain. I lay on my back and watched it grow, thinking for no good reason of the story of the shaikh, how he, who had once firmly grasped the thread of faith, fell from the way, entrapped himself in every form of error and apostasy, and was lost.

For an instant when I sat up I thought for sure I was going to cry, just a physical pulse like nausea, throwing up tears, but I swallowed it back. Clara was sleeping on her side with her face turned away from me, her long bright hair running down her back; it covered her like a miracle. I picked up a loose tail of it, held it a moment, curled in my palm, brought the ends of it to my mouth and sucked them into a little point. She mumbled a little, but didn't wake. I put the hair back where I'd found it and watched it flow back into the current of the rest. Then, bone by careful bone, I reached the floor with a foot and in one long step was at the door.

There was no milk and only three or four spoons of coffee, enough for a couple of cups, but I'd need more. I had a new client at eight in the morning, a woman, a career woman undoubtedly, but I couldn't remember much else about her. Better go out and grab a few things, and also we needed ourselves a mouse. I flipped up the wall calendar and had a look but I'd scrawled down the appointment so hastily I couldn't make out what her trouble was supposed to be. Behind me, the coffeepot chugged on its short ration. Somehow I got stuck facing the kitchen table, one hand glued to the back of a chair, staring down at a little black clock in the middle of Clara's place mat. There was something I needed to do about that but I didn't have any idea what it was. It was the latest sort of gadget—you could turn off the alarm by shouting at it, even. The second hand moved in galvanic jerks, and the other two said it was almost seven. I kept on looking down at the thing, bound up in one of those states of brutal stupidity that a long insomnia jag can engender, until I heard the coffeepot come to a conclusion and shut off.

That flipped the switch, and I remembered: Clara had set the alarm on the clock as usual, to wake her up to run, but sometime in the course of the night I must have removed it from the room so I wouldn't be annoyed by its tick. A somewhat implausible motive, of course, since the clock, being battery-powered, doesn't actually tick at all. Clara and I have had some arguments on this topic. She has reason and proof with her, while what's with me is . . . problematic. I hear the bastard tick, that's what. It's experientially justified.

So I picked it up and took it into the bedroom and set it down on her nightstand. There was a folded handkerchief there and I put it on that so it wouldn't make a noise, not that it would have awakened her. Her mouth had parted slightly on the pillow; she fogged the linen with her breath. My god but she was a champion sleeper. I got my shoes and my wallet and keys and went softly into the front room, which truth to tell is really in the back. The bones in my hips and shoulders were starting to grind each other down, at least that's what it felt like. Maybe just a little stiff. . . . I sat on the sofa to pull on my shoes and then leaned back to admire the swirling golden motes the effort of bending over had produced. Some birds were twittering in the back garden and when my head had cleared I screwed it around to look. There's a sort of great gorse bush growing partway over the window and the birds always like to congregate there. Now and then you'll see a finch, something multicolored and unusual, but there were only a couple of sparrows today. I heaved myself onto my feet and went out.

Going in and out of the usual shops, I bought the milk and the coffee. Along the street it was busier than normal, with everyone beginning to set up for Carnival. At the Ladbroke Grove tube stop I bought one of the London tabs without particularly meaning to. It appeared that another little girl had been murdered the night before and her picture was smeared across the front page of the paper: Heather Jolley, blond and wispy, four years old and smiling for the camera. Now dead as Queen Anne, deader even. Nothing I could do about that, of course. I didn't want to read about it. But I bought the paper just the same and tucked it under my arm. A bit further on was a bakery and I stopped there for a baguette and also got a

**4**

couple of pastries to treat Clara with later on. Then I went across the tracks and turned in to Oxford Gardens.

In the window left of Mr. Waltham's door, a couple of guppies were eddying about in the big tank and that was all. The surface of the water was all dotted over with algae, in long-standing need of a serious skim. In the other window a couple of Lab puppies were snoozing in a pile of dirty shavings on their cage floor. One opened an eye when I started yanking at the bellpull but that was the extent of his excitement at my arrival. It was dark inside and Waltham took a good five minutes answering, but I kept on ringing and knocking anyway. The old man lived behind the shop, and I knew he was always up at the crack and knew he'd open to me in time.

At last the buzzer fired and I pushed in. Probably he'd had his finger hovering over the button from the instant I'd come up his steps. The buzzer was his sole concession to modernity; everything else was prewar, even the animals, I sometimes thought. There was a rank fusty smell to the whole place, since he wasn't overswift with the cleaning, and it was very dim. I made my usual *pro forma* circuit of the tanks and cages. A few more sickly looking fish, a tub of painted turtles. One spider monkey shuddering in a cage too small for it. Some hamsters and gerbils, burrowed in. Only the white mice seemed active, chittering and chasing each other and running on their wheels. At the end of their row the mildewed green parrot was chained to a high perch by one ankle. "Push off, you berk," the parrot said as I went by him toward the counter. Rude creature, but then it was the only line he knew and I suppose he might have meant it kindly.

Waltham was hoisted on a high stool beside the ancient cash desk, studiously not noticing me as I came up. Except he did lay his papery hand across the breasts of the Page Three lass he'd been admiring. Then made a ring of his thumb and forefinger and adjusted his frail rimless glasses to peep back in again. I waited a moment more, then rapped a knuckle on the counter, with a certain care for the splinters rising from the old tired wood. Mr. Waltham raised his head a little, still not looking my way, and pursed up his lips like a rectum.

"Good morning," I said.

Mr. Waltham sniffed.

"Here for my usual," I said.

Mr. Waltham pulled his glasses down the ramp of his bony nose and gave me an imperious look across the top of them.

**5**

"How may I assist you?" he said in the familiarly frigid tone.

"I'll have one white mouse," I said, a trifle wearily. Same old drill he put me through every two weeks. . . .

"Push off, you berk," said the parrot. Mr. Waltham screwed up his lips a little further, then relaxed them slightly, to speak.

"I know what's going to happen to that 'ittle mouse," he said.

"You could always refuse to sell it to me," I said. Because I was getting a bit tired of the game, and besides I knew it was safe enough. He wasn't making such a go of the shop to afford that sort of delicacy. He got down from the stool then, a bit rickety on his skinny pins, and came around the end of the counter. The funny thing about Waltham is that he moves like a fat man even though he's not. He walks with a waddle and allows himself the room that someone five times his girth might require. He picked up his catch net and one of the cardboard cartons and shambled over to the mouse cage.

"Which do you prefer?" he said.

"Oh, just pick me out a likely one," I said.

Waltham shriveled his lips some more and said, "The gentleman must make his own selection."

"All right, all right then," I said. Same old drill. I pointed to a fat sluggish mouse, hulking in a corner of the cage. Waltham had a nice speedy wrist movement and he got it in one go. But the mouse didn't want to drop off into the box; it kept clinging to the netting with its little claws and Waltham needed several hard shakes to make it let go. It appeared to me that his hand continued to shake after he'd shut the carton's lid, as if he was developing a tremor. Of course I was a little dizzy myself so it might only have been my eyes. Again I felt the ghostly urge to weep but this time it passed more quickly. I followed Waltham to the cash desk. As I drew near he flipped the paper shut; it was a different tab from the one I'd bought, with a different picture of Heather Jolley I could easily recognize upside down. I gave him a stubbed pound coin from my pocket and he pushed back a couple of shillings' change.

"I know what's coming to that 'ittle mouse," he said, and slid his thumb between the leaves of the paper, straight back to Page Three, I was certain. "Oh yes, I know very well."

"Right," said I. "You know, I've been considering getting an osprey.

Give those guppies something to think about, eh? You wouldn't care to order me an osprey?" But Mr. Waltham had leaned his head back toward the paper, and I sensed the audience had terminated.

"Push off, you berk," the parrot said. There was a bell nailed to the door that jangled when I went out.

It was loud all along Westbourne Park Road, the rude boys all tinkering with their sound systems. A constant electric vibration in the air, and every now and then a sudden blast of music, brief and astonishing as an exploding shell. The noise tapered off as I went back along Ledbury Road and down toward Chepstow Crescent. The sky had cleared and the sun was up, mounting its low southern arc, and I thought of Clara; she'd be running through Hyde Park just now, crossing the long shadows of the trees and the yellow pools of light between them.

A mouse whisker was tickling my palm and I shifted my grip to avoid it. The box was something like a Chinese take-away carton, right down to the little wire handle—well, perhaps that wasn't the happiest thought. There were air holes of course and that was how the whiskers got to me. I began to walk a little faster. Something was making me feel quite weak and giddy, possibly four or five nights of no sleep. I'd forgotten to drink any of the coffee I'd made; a taste of that might perk me up, and there was time, still fifteen minutes. Supposing Clara had left me a cup. But when I came in sight of the house I saw that there was someone already waiting on the steps.

Had to be that woman come early, Miss Whatshername. She was wearing a dark suit and had a flat soft leather portfolio clamped to her side, under her purse. The suit was tailored, though her shoes looked cheap. The peculiar thing was that she had turned completely into the entryway instead of facing the street like most people would if they had a longish wait on a doorstep. In fact she looked like she was trying to cram herself completely into the join of the bricks and the doorjamb. Her nose was almost touching the brass nameplate Clara gave me my last birthday, and when I came up the steps I saw she'd squeezed her fingers into the mortices so tight they were ready to start bleeding. A grip like that, I almost believed she could have gone straight up the wall like a lizard if she'd cared to.

"Miss?" I said.

She turned around and pressed her back into the wall. Her face was chalk white and her lips were blue, I swear to God I could see it even under

7

the lipstick. Hair done in very early Princess Di and a Sloane Ranger pearl string around her neck. Under the pearls her throat was pulsing like a frog's gullet.

"Is it Doctor Strother?" she asked me. Pound-note accent, I could hear it clearly behind the panic. Maybe I'd been wrong about the shoes. *Agoraphobia*, that was it, and I remembered her name now too. "Ah, you must be Miss Peavey," I said. Let the doctor business go for now. "You're a bit early. But do come in."

The bakery package fell out of my hands when I reached around her to unlock the front door. From the corner of my eye I saw her try and fail to pick it up for me, something like watching someone grab at a valuable object she'd just dropped off an immensely high cliff.

"Come in, come in," I said, and not a minute too soon either. I scooped up the bag and followed her into the hall. No windows here, only a skylight four floors up, and her breathing eased a little once I'd shut the door behind us. Our flat opened straight to the left of the hall door; I opened that and ushered her in. Now what? I hadn't looked for her to come early and I needed to settle the mouse business out of her sight. It's an upsetting sort of a thing for the average client, and she was already in a state. Best get her installed in the crooked room.

"Now then, this way, Miss Peavey. . . ." I opened the door to the spiral stair. "Best let me lead, it's a little narrow." And I started down ahead of her. The stair is a metal corkscrew set in a sort of shaft, like a closet, dark and tight and no good for *claustro*phobics, but for this lady I thought it might even be comforting. She came along after me, one hand trailing along the wall as she followed the turns. I had carpeted the stairs over a thick rubber pad to stop them ringing, but they still made a dim booming sound with each step. At the bottom I stepped aside from the door and waved her toward the fat leather chair, just where the room made its twist and turn.

"Now make yourself comfortable, please, Miss— oh, may I call you Eleanor?" She had to swallow a time or two over that one. A dose of your bloody presumptuous American excessive familiarity for the little miss.

"Yes, yes of course," she said eventually. And she sat primly down on the edge of the chair with her knees together and her feet together and her hands folded parallel over the rim of her portfolio, like a rodent's paws. I saw she didn't wear any rings.

**8**

"Just put your things anywhere you like," I said. "Make yourself comfortable, I won't be a moment." And I went back up the stairs.

On the kitchen table there was an envelope with my name scrawled on it, I saw from the corner of my eye, but there was no time to look at it just then. I noticed Clara hadn't touched the coffee, sometimes she didn't drink any before she ran. I splashed two-thirds of it into a mug and took a tremendous belt. *Ah. . . .* The pastries, buttery little bow ties, were still faintly warm in the white bag and I thought about eating one of them then and there, but on no sleep the effort of digesting anything would have stolen too much blood from my brain. So I set them out on a plate and covered them with a scrap of foil.

And now.

I went to the waist-high tank by the window, opened the lid and lifted out the snake. He wrapped his brown and red-gold patterns around my forearm, the muscle of him cool and snug against my skin. He was a little sluggish, though, for a hungry snake. I fed him every two weeks and the last few days beforehand he'd normally be lashing like a whip whenever I picked him up. I held him till his body temperature had warmed to match my own and then I set him back. He slid behind a biggish rock and lurked, remaining perfectly still when I opened the carton and dumped the mouse in with him. The mouse made a few tentative steps over the tank floor and stopped to look out toward the lint on the carpet, beyond the glass wall. I covered the tank with a piece of sheet that Clara had rehemmed for this purpose. Snakes like a little privacy while they're eating, or anyway my snake does.

I bolted the rest of the coffee standing in the kitchen, and went back down to the crooked room. No good taking the mug in with me, that fresh-perked aroma is counterproductive. Wake up and smell the coffee, all that. . . . I shut the door on its oiled hinges and sat in my desk chair and flipped on the yellow light under the shelf. With the dimmer switch on the desk panel I shut down the light next to Eleanor Peavey until I could just see the slightest glow in the filament. She'd put down her gear and sat back a little, just barely permitting her shoulders to graze the leather of the chair. Still strung taut as a wire, that was plain. She was peering up at the microphones curving out on their gooseneck booms from the bookcases, one over her chair, one over mine. A lot of them tend to worry over that. So I pulled out the drawer with the recorder and explained its intentions and usefulness and made my customary promise not to tape her without her knowledge and consent. Then picked up the clipboard and took a short impressionistic medical history, which turned up the usual childhood illnesses and not much more. She was twenty-six, university degree from Exeter, single, lived with another young woman in a three-room flat near Regent's Park, and had worked for about the last four years as some kind of key-puncher for British Telecom.

"In that whacking great tower, you mean?" I said. When she nodded I started to ask her what floor, but then decided to hold off. The British Telecom tower, so, that bulb-headed phallic atrocity against the London skyline; I don't know just how tall it is but if you're on the upper stories you might as well be on a satellite.

"Enjoy your work?" I asked her.

"Oh yes," she said with a watery smile. "Oh yes, it suits very well." By which I believed she meant to say that she hated it with a perfect passion. You get a lot of that sort of mixed signal from that sort of young gentlewoman nowadays. But I was starting to feel encouraged all the same; it might be a simpler job than I'd thought, supposing she was an adequate subject.

"Well then," I said. "If you'll just turn yourself this way . . ." And I got up from the chair and crossed the carpet to show her what I meant. I'm not so tall, maybe not even taller than she, but with the light behind me I would have seemed to loom, a sudden shadow. That's on purpose. She frowned and blinked as it crossed her face. I took hold of the plump brown leather padding and rotated the chair on its swivel to face the little end of the area. All the walls of the crooked room are just slightly uneven, and just where the client's chair is placed, the whole room takes a forty-five degree veer to the left and tapers off into a queer sort of corner about eight feet deep, terminated by a three-foot wall. At the top of this is a window well, sidewalk level if you're on the street, but normally I keep it covered with a heavy black velvet curtain of the sort that photographers use in darkrooms. Below the curtain hangs a small white bulletin board, empty except for a lot of colored pushpins outlining a cross inscribed in a diamond. I pulled a couple of levers on the side of the chair to pop up the footrest and recline the back far enough that she *had* to give up her weight to it now. The tilt brought her eyes to the level of the black pushpin at the join of the crossarms, the center of the diamond.

**10**

I never actually touched her though. None of your mesmeric stroking here, thank you ever so much.

Lightly I went back to my chair and sat down, all in perfect silence, which comes naturally to me but irritates Clara considerably, for some reason. She sometimes says she'd like to make me wear a bell, and I'm not sure she's kidding. But never mind that now. The Record button made a dampered click when I pushed it, and that was all.

"Well," I said. "At the top of the bulletin board on the wall, you see a yellow pushpin at the top of the cross and the peak of the diamond. Yes? You are looking at the yellow pushpin against the white bulletin board, just there at the diamond's point. And now your eyes lower and you are looking a little below the yellow pushpin, where you see the *red* pushpin against the white background; you are looking at the red pushpin now. And now you lower your eyes again to see the dark blue pushpin, you see the dark blue pushpin very clearly outlined against the white fabric and your eyes are a little tired and slightly blurring and you lower your eyes to the *black* pushpin, you are looking at the *black* pushpin at the center of the diamond, you see nothing at all but the *black pushpin* on the white background, your eyes are very heavy, your eyelids are sinking, you can scarcely keep them open, you can*not* keep your eyes open *any longer*, your eyes are closing, now your eyes are closed. Good. Good. *Good.* Now your breathing becomes slower, deeper, more regular and easy, the little muscles around your eyes are relaxing, you feel the muscles of your face becoming soft and pliable, you feel every muscle in your body beginning to let go, and now there is a warm tingling feeling in the center of your body, feel how it spreads into your arms and legs, until this warm tingling feeling of relaxation has reached the ends of your fingers and toes, and you are perfectly calm now, Eleanor, you have never been so calm as this, your mind is entirely empty, you are thinking of nothing, nothing at all. But in your mind's eye you still see the black pushpin, just a black circle on a white, white background, growing slightly larger now, and now you are counting slowly backwards from twenty-five, twenty-four, watch the black circle, twenty-three . . ."

I opened my own eyes, which seemed to have got shut somehow, and gave my head a solid shake. Oh, for one more gulp of coffee now . . . maybe I could just start packing the grounds under my lip, like snuff. Nearly put myself under, didn't I? But I was still awake and still counting down.

Right to sleep I nearly went, though of course it would never work if I'd been alone, in bed, not working—just one more stupid self-defeating nuance of paradoxical intention. She looked fairly good to me so far, fingers uncurled and her palms flattening against the chair arms, head lolling a little away from me. Couldn't tell for sure if she was really traveling or only trying to cooperate, though for the moment either would serve.

". . . two, one, you see the black doorknob on the white door, *zero*, take hold of that doorknob, Eleanor, and now you have opened the door and you are going down the stairs, down a close dim warm spiral staircase, Eleanor, you turn as the stairs turn toward a point, you hear the muffled boom of your every step and now you have reached the door at the foot of the stairs. Open the door, Eleanor, and now you are in a round room with white walls covered with words of a foreign alphabet, see how the words are inscribed there in gold leaf. The room is quiet and very comfortable, there are carpets and cushions on the floor, and at the far end of the room a dark-haired woman is seated on a hassock; she wears a blue robe and she is reading aloud from a leather-bound book. Her voice is deep, rhythmic, resonant, and more and more you are relaxing, Eleanor, as you listen to the sound of this voice, you sit down on the carpet, you stretch on a long dark carpet, feel the weave of the wool on your bare arms, you lay your head on a soft cushion, your eyes close, there is a smell of fruit, of blossoms, you hear the sound of the voice reading, you listen to the voice, Eleanor, it doesn't really matter what it means."

I turned quietly in my chair and picked up the book at the top of the stack I like to use for these deepening rituals. *The Conference of the Birds*. I flipped it open to the first dog-ear.

"From a staff he produces a serpent; and by means of a staff he sends forth a torrent of water.

"He has placed in the firmament the orb of the proud, and binds it with iron when glowing red it wanes.

"He brought forth a camel from a rock, and made the golden calf to bellow.

"In winter he scatters the silver snow; in autumn, the gold of yellow leaves.

"He lays a cover on the thorn and tinges it with the color of blood.

"To the jasmine he gives four petals and on the head of the tulip he puts a red bonnet.

"He places a golden crown on the brow of the narcissus; and drops pearls of dew into her shrine.

"At the idea of God the mind is baffled, reason fails; because of God the heavens turn, the earth reels.

"From the back of the fish to the moon every atom is a witness to his being."

When I reached the end of that line she rolled her head toward me again and I knew I had her, it was a real sleeper's, a dreamer's turn. Her face had gone all smooth, ten years smoothed away from her so that she looked almost a child again. Ever fall in love with someone you watch sleeping? Though what was tantalizing me most at the moment was the simple idea of sleep itself.

"Yes," I said. "Yes, you are going deeper now, you are drifting, you are drifting very deep. Your body is warm, soft, limp, and heavy—all but your left arm, which is getting very light. Your left arm is getting *very* light, your left arm is getting lighter, your left arm is filling up with helium—"

—but I didn't have to go any further than that, because with just the hint of suggestion the arm lifted all by itself, rising softly, airily, leaving the slack hand hanging in midair like the basket of a hot-air balloon, shivering a little in the breeze. Then I saw her shudder all over; her face squinched up and then relaxed. I could guess well enough what she might be feeling. She'd surprised herself a bit, you see, she hadn't known till now she could let go of her control. But she *was* a good subject, I never would have guessed she'd be this talented, or would I? The controls were off. That hovering hand was full of autonomic twitches. There was something different strumming the harp of her nerves, unfamiliar but not really alien, some antediluvian energy drawn from the back-brain dinosaur or, if you prefer, the snake. And there's always a good strong visceral thrill at the moment it takes over. Her first time, and maybe it's never as good as the first time, but there's always a bit of a kick left in it, even, sometimes, for me.

*13*

# t w 0

*Man is the greatest of miracles. . . .* Now how exactly does that go? Having finally shut the door upon Miss Peavey I returned to the front room. On a shelf between the stereo and the snake tank, the answering machine was winking and blinking, desperate for a little attention from somebody. It appeared that large numbers of people had been wanting to make contact while I'd been below in the crooked room, more of them than usual for so early in the morning. I twisted the dial and went into the kitchen. The same amount of coffee still stood on the warmer and I poured it into my mug and started a fresh pot without much thinking about what I was doing.

*Klonk, hiss, beep,* said the answering machine through the doorway. I flipped the foil off the plate. Both pastries were still there; they'd gone cold. Either Clara was still out on her run, or no, that wasn't possible, it was already after nine. So she hadn't noticed them, or hadn't had time to eat. . . .

"Mister Strother, this is Missus Wilton Harvey—"

On the tape, she interrupted herself with a long juicy burst of coughing. Always *Mrs. Wilton Harvey,* thank you very much, though I do call her Kate whenever we're in the crooked room. I broke a corner off one of the pastries and nibbled at it: flaky, buttery, and sweet. Mrs. Wilton Harvey was listing off dates and times that would suit her for an appointment, though every time she came she swore she'd never be back. Always called me Mr. Strother too, none of this "Dr." folderol. I rather liked her for that. Her voice was throaty from the hundred million cigarettes she couldn't stop smoking. Some people thought that huskiness a sexy note; the tinge of death in it made them think so. I broke a bigger piece off the pastry and munched it down. It was beginning to sound like Mrs. Wilton Harvey was going to run out all my tape, giving her calendar clean into the twenty-first century. Why couldn't she just have had me call her back?

Lonely, maybe, lonely and bored. She was an expat just like me only quite some older, edging into her sixties, I would think. Married to some

**14**

wheel in an international bank and as they'd only been living in London for five years or so she hadn't yet managed to meet anyone. According to the somewhat overpublicized truism, you can't hypnotize people to do anything they don't want to do, and Mrs. W. H. didn't want to quit smoking, no, she wanted to keep breathing it in and blowing it out. The coughing was a problem, though. It kept *Mr.* Wilton Harvey up at night, so he'd go into the office with raccoon rings around his eyes, and have bad trouble making the money be funny.

*Man is the greatest of miracles . . .* finally she got finished and hung up. I'd eaten the whole pastry when the machine went *bloop.* "Clara?" I scrabbled around for pen and paper, didn't find either on the kitchen counter or in the drawers. "This—hm, well, never mind, p'raps I'll try you at work." *Bleep.*

I stuck my head into the bedroom but it was empty, sure enough. Bed unmade just as I'd left it, her closet door swung open with a thin belt snaking out. She must have overrun herself, so to speak, and had to get ready and leave in a rush. The picture of her changing made me smile. Had I heard her feet crisscrossing over the ceiling of the crooked room? No, that was what those sound baffles were for.

I found a pad and pencil on her bureau and went to stand over the machine with them, in case any more calls came in for Clara. *Beep, whoosh, click, beep. . . .* A hanger-upper, we got our share of those. *Bloop.* "Adrian? Adrian, I hope this is you, it's Stuart—" and right away I felt a little tingle of I-don't-know-what. "Just got into Heathrow, I wanted to call and tell you—dammit . . ." There was a pained noise as the receiver bonked into something hard. "Can't seem to find the address just now, but it's at eight or so. Shepherd's Bush, somewhere . . . You'll find it if you got my letter. This is jet lag talking, man, I'm still on New York time. Well, I guess I'll call back when I find it."

*Click-beep.* Sure, Stuart, I got your letter. I put down the pad and drifted into the kitchen again. But I'd forgotten the occasion was tonight, though actually there's no such thing as real forgetting. Still I supposed I could probably make it, that's if Clara hadn't made any other plans affecting me. . . . I ate the other pastry rather quickly, still standing in the kitchen, and finished the coffee that was left in the mug. *Beepwhooshclickbeep.* Another hanger-upper. There was a smear of coffee grounds on the edge of the sink from where I'd cleaned the basket, and I pulled the damp cloth off the faucet and wiped the surface clean. *Beepwhooshclick beep.* Still another hanger-upper? That was getting to be a lot of them, a little peculiar, all in a row. And now we were in the middle of some old message for Clara.

Funny to think of seeing Stuart again. It gave me an odd sort of taste at the back of my throat. I went over to the shelf and shut off the machine. There was no one coming in until afternoon so I was free as a freaking bird, wasn't I just? I squatted down and lifted a corner of the drape and peeped in to see if nature had taken its course in the snake tank. It's interesting, if you happen to be interested, to see a constrictor convert a mouse to porridge. But nothing much had happened so far. The snake was still knotted behind the rock, the sharp point of his tail shoved up one side of it. He'd tucked his head under one of his coils, so that I couldn't see it. The mouse, meanwhile, seemed to have relaxed considerably and was strolling up and down the gravel, pausing now and then to whisker a section of the driftwood branch I'd supplied for the snake to climb on. Making himself free. . . . I'm not the sentimentalist Mr. Waltham pretends to be, but I'd as soon it had gone off a little more quickly. Still, I had faith they'd work it out in time.

When I stood up I felt something like a kick to the side of the head and my field of vision shut down altogether for a second. It came back streaked with a lot of little curly lines, and I decided it would be a good idea to sit down on the sofa. Of course it was those pastries; eating on a few days of no sleep will sap the nervous energy right out of you. So I propped up my feet on the sofa's arm and laced my hands behind my head. The sun was still shining in the window, turning my closed eyelids a warm and grateful red. *Don't think about it.* I began to fasten metallic helium balloons to myself, tying each with a strong silk thread, one to each finger, one to each toe, larger ones at the knees and elbows, neck and small of the back. When the last one had been attached I had just enough buoyancy to go soaring out over a calm blue ocean, under a cloudless blue sky. There was a solitary white gull gliding high above me, turning and turning on an invisible column of the air, not moving its wings at all. But the gull seemed to shiver in a way that troubled me, and I looked away. The silvered balloons were leaking, shrinking, though they remained always perfectly spherical, and I sank far enough to be able to register the long regular swell of the sea. When the balloons had reduced to the size of marbles, I went slicing tidily

**16**

into the cold water—*no! warm, warm, blood temperature* . . . and continued to sink, down a spectrum of deepening color, dark blue, purple, navy, black. . . . The knots undid themselves from my fingers and the balloons floated up, gleaming like bubbles. The light of the surface was out of my sight, and for just an instant I was nowhere at all and liking it, but then I saw something. Someone, I mean. A person with midlength hair, wearing a robe of some kind, or a dress, angled curiously against a wall . . . oh goddamnit it was only Eleanor Peavey, cowering in my doorway while she waited for the cab to pick her up.

I opened my eyes and there was the ceiling sure enough, about six feet above my head, cracks and bubbles all over the fading white paint, and a cobweb or two along the molding. A chip of paint had flaked away, disclosing a small brown trapezoid. Goddamn, but I was almost asleep, I think. Oh very well, Miss Peavey. I'll solve your problem for you. No, let's be accurate between me and myself—I won't solve it, but I'll mask it.

She was a half-decent subject, in fact. She went in deep and fairly fast but even in trance it was no fun for her to contemplate wide open spaces. I understood well enough how she felt, or at least I thought I did. Every time she shot up the lift toward the top of that dreadful tower, she stopped feeling attached to anything much at all. Whenever she looked out the window she stopped believing in the floor. She was losing faith in the safety net, which is a work of faith alone. And as it got worse she didn't even trust the sidewalk to be solid anymore. Getting off my doorstep and into her cab cost her the effort it might have cost me to swing across St. Paul's dome on a flying trapeze.

But she was the sort of person I could fix. I'd get her deconditioned right enough, not the work of a moment, but I could do it. Not the sort of problem you had to follow deep, though perhaps you could if you cared to. She felt like she was falling, but was really just stuck. She was doing a number with her clothes and accessories and the put-on accent, but it wouldn't have fooled her countrymen for a second, though it was enough to confuse me. And she wasn't really going anywhere with it, just around and around in a tight loop, so fast it was making her dizzy. I'd do her up, six or eight sessions it would probably take, and money in the bank. A nice cosmetic repair and she'd brave the pavement like the rest of us, and once more whistle while she worked. She was scheduled to come back tomorrow morning.

**17**

Something was trilling at me from beyond the windowpane, muted but distinct. I turned my head and over the bulge of the sofa cushion saw a gold-barred bird of some variety, sitting in the gorse bush and singing like a champion. Almost as soon as I saw him, he flew. But the branch kept springing up and down, the dark spines of it shining in a sunbeam. So alive I might have believed it had a song to sing to me too.

I got up, more cautiously this time, and walked a figure eight on the carpet with no ill effects. Music, maybe that would be the thing, something on the soothing side. I looked over the tape shelf but all of Clara's Gregorian chants seemed not to be there somehow, and I couldn't find *Music for Airports* either. Strange. She normally took the more up-tempo stuff for running. But maybe she'd wanted something tranquil for the tube.

I went to the bedroom and tidied up some. Tossed some odds and ends into the bureaus and closets, shut the drawers and doors. Then made up the bed, tight as a tick, and cleared up a cup and a couple of glasses. Once I'd washed those I scoured the sink. Taste of domestic duty, improve my sense of self-worth a short notch. I poured myself a fresh cup of coffee and settled on the couch with the paper. First the funnies, but they didn't seem too funny. I started leafing backward toward the front page. THE HUMAN BEER BARREL, some Welsh lad who put down fifteen pints a day and looked it too. . . . Further adventures of Ian Botham. . . . The agony aunt with the usual problems and remedies. . . . Sellafield nuclear plant still belching out death in all directions. . . . More soccer violence on Sealink. . . . Grief and confusion of the Lamplugh family, whose daughter Suzy still hadn't come back from a business appointment with some rapist/murderer, or vice-versa, said to call himself Mr. Kipper. . . . P. C.'s advice on how to make the most of the Notting Hill Gate Carnival without being robbed or murdered or raped. . . . Grief and confusion of the Jolley family, and now I was back to Page One, reading in spite of myself about how little Heather, gone missing for several days, had finally turned up, dumped in an alley somewhere behind King's Cross, having been _____ed and _____ed until there was not much left of her but broken bones in a bag of skin, though that wasn't quite how the story phrased it. Much the same as the others before her. I folded the paper across her picture and dropped it on the floor. That alarm clock seemed to be ticking again, somewhere, sometime. Eerie how it came and went. At last I cornered it in the bedroom and crammed it into a drawer underneath my socks, so there. Next thing I knew I was on the street, southbound in the direction of the Bayswater Road.

When I'd come as far as the Notting Hill Gate tube stop, it occurred to me I might just as well go on to the library, try to do a little work. Hadn't been there in quite some time, but it was only a short hop on the Central Line, and I had no other business till the afternoon anyway. I got off at Tottenham Court Road and walked up to Great Russell Street. There was smoke from chestnuts roasting on braziers at either side of the museum gate. I went up the steps and into the lobby, which was medium-crowded for the day and time. A dark-haired woman I thought I half-recognized was standing at the gift shop cash desk, turned mostly away from me, so I just saw the wave of her hair and the tip of her nose. But I didn't move in for a closer look; there'd been enough illusions already and it wasn't even noon. At the checkpoint in the corridor someone examined my card and then waved me on toward the library door.

I hadn't thought to bring my notebooks or anything else so once I'd put my order in there wasn't much for me to do. I sat at the desk with my elbows on the greenish blotter and contemplated the chipped stained enamel of the number plate. Today I was number twenty-four . . . in one of the middle ranks of reading room desks, or benches really, since they're all attached, all in concentric circles closing in on the center. Or radiating out. I craned my neck back and looked up at the indented squares that climbed in diminishing bluish white rows to the blank open ring of the skylight at the height. That skylight seems to be the source of the cool even light all through the room, though of course most of it's really artificial. But supposing the eye of God were to peer down through the skylight's loupe, it would see something rather similar to the memory system Giordano Bruno outlined in *De umbris idearum* . . . wheels turning within more wheels and all of them dense with information, not just information either.

Almost heresy, in a way, to be thinking such a thing about the British Museum reading room. It couldn't have been what they had in mind when they laid out this floor plan. No, it made me laugh to think about it. But some bluestocking two seats over put down her pencil and glared at me, so I shut up and looked away. Once I'd drawn the whole scheme off the directions in Bruno's book. Took me more than a month to do it. . . . In fact Clara did most of the actual pen work. She knows something about architectural drawing and a good deal more about graphic design.

A functionary cruised by the desk and lowered a couple of books onto the blotter. On top was Bruno's *Eroici furori*, Italian, but with a French pony on facing pages. My Italian is bad to nonexistent but I could track the gist of it in French, and by switching back and forth from page to page could even get some feeling for the excursions into verse. At least on a good day I could do all that. But now the words were wiggling around on the page in an extremely disconcerting way, and I couldn't pin them down long enough to get the sense out of them.

So I shut that book and laid it aside and opened the other one I'd asked for. Robert Fludd, *Utriusque cosmi, maioris scilicet et minoris, metaphysica, physica atque technica historia* . . . along with everything else in or out of the world you could possibly imagine. Heady stuff, and I didn't expect to get far through the Latin, not today, but I could look at the pictures. The pictures were good ones, and their purport was much the same as the message of *Eroici furori*, so at least I believed.

I was looking at a picture titled INTEGRAE SPECULUM ARTISQUE IMAGO—a universal map not dissimilar in some ways to the Brunian memory dial. It was a reactionary post-Copernican scheme, centered on the earth and radiating outward through the elements, minerals, plants, animals, planets, to the stars of the zodiac, and beyond. This was not what interested me just at the moment, however. There stood, on ELEMENTUM, AQUA, ET TERRA, a sort of Venusian figure . . . well, maybe not. She seemed a fully sensual woman, naked and carnal, though crowned with a diadem of stars. Her figure stretched across the planetary spheres. From her left hand there hung a chain that connected her to the hands of a little tailless monkey squatting on the orb of the earth. From her right wrist another chain rose up across the astral spheres to join DEUS, in a brilliant cloud.

I sat looking at the diagram for a long time, considering all the links in those two chains. For a long time I had suspected that he had something of importance to tell me, this ape of nature. He might tell me, if he would, or could, just who that woman was and how to reach her. But unfortunately, apes don't talk. They haven't got the gift of conversation. And I have never been able to concentrate worth a damn in the British Museum reading room. It's too beautiful, too ideal, and the echo is too overpowering. The echo is so perfect that it will magnify a cough, a breath, a flip of a page or scrape of a pencil, each a thousandfold. And after a while it starts to sound like Bedlam, all that information percolating. I couldn't take it any longer, so I went scampering back out.

All the way back I was feeling low about missing Clara earlier that morning. Missing seeing her awake, that is. Though it didn't really make any sense. I'd see her when she got off work, after all. I'd have dinner ready by the time she came in. It would be nice. Nothing, but nothing, to worry about, and I could make no sense of my sadness.

When I got off at Notting Hill Gate it was a few minutes past opening time, so I went up Ledbury Road toward the Tooth and Claw. It had clouded up and begun to sift down a little rain, but not enough to bother with the umbrella before I got into the pub. Terence was behind the bar, and the place wasn't very busy yet. Yesterday he'd had a full beard, but today he'd shaved it down to a Vandyke. It didn't look bad on him, either. For a black man he had aquiline features and the rearranged beard made him look something like the devil.

"Adrian," he said, with a ceremonious nod. "What will it be?"

"And good day to you," I said. "Lovely weather. . . ." There was a cough of thunder and rain began lashing against the frosted windows of the pub. Outside from several different directions came terrified squeals of feedback from the sound systems.

"Do you think it'll rain out the Carnival?" I said.

"Never happen," said Terence. "It will be fine tomorrow, man, you watch. And nothing ever stops the Carnival."

"I'll take your word for it," I said. I would too. Terence is convincing, I can't remember just what island he's from and possibly he can't either, but he has the rich and resonant voice of a priest, or bishop, or magician maybe. He'd make a stellar hypnotist, I've often told him so.

"No, nothing stop Carnival," Terence said. "What for you?"

"Sausage and mashed and a half of Strongbow," I said.

Terence frowned as he served my plate. "You kill yourself with that rubbish, man."

"Oh, I'll just sweat it out."

Terence made change and pushed it back to me. "Will I see you today at practice, then?"

"That's right," I said. "The four o'clock go."

"Got time for afters?"

"Doubtful," I said. "I'll want to get home early."

"That diet's spoiling your will," Terence said.

But all I could do was wink at him, because my mouth was full. I was

**21**

a lot hungrier than I'd thought, and maybe eating faster than I should, at that. The rain noise went up a notch, with someone coming in the door. Terence looked over my shoulder, then drew another half of cider, popped a can of Tennent's Super and went to serve the newcomers, friends of his, must be. I swallowed the nub end of my banger and swiveled on my stool. At a table near the doorway, a man and a woman were peeling off their brightly colored rubber macs. They had a baby carriage with them, covered with a clear plastic sheet that ran bright droplets of rain to the floor. The woman undid the snaps of the plastic, took out a newborn baby, and handed it to Terence, who raised him high in his long-fingered hands, and smiled. The mother and father were beaming too. He knocked his can against her glass, they drank, and smiled again. Outdoors, I heard the rain stop on a dime.

"Look at him," Terence said. "Born yesterday." He wasn't speaking to anyone in particular, but I looked. Something must have rolled back the curtain of cloud from the sun, for a beam came shining through the glass and fell on the baby's face, turning his skin a reddish gold. He wiggled and waved his little hands, squinted his eyes and gave a sort of smile. Born yesterday, still trailing clouds of glory, maybe, though those were fading fast. But welcome to London, kiddo, welcome to Notting Hill Gate. Outside you can already hear the festival beginning, though it would be vain to claim that it's entirely in your honor. Still, maybe you'll get your pleasure from it, maybe not. Welcome to the world of *things*.

I swiveled back to face the rising rows of bottles, and clicked the backs of my nails against my empty glass. Terence came back behind the bar and wanted to know what I was crying for.

"What the hell is that to you?" I snapped at him, and I covered up my face with my hand. It was dripping, sure enough, I hadn't even realized.

"Sorry," I said. "Sorry, Terence." I haven't got such a lot of friends, and generally he's been a good one.

"Don't know what comes over me," I said. "I've got a mood on, must be, and I haven't been sleeping well of late."

"Never mind, then," Terence said.

"Thanks," I said. I wiped my nose on a napkin and got on my feet. "See you this afternoon. . . ." Outdoors, the rude boys were hauling the tarps back off their sound systems and tuning up again, but I didn't pay much attention to them. The day had turned suddenly fine again, and it

**22**

gave me a jolt of euphoria, and made me think that I still might rise entirely out of myself one day, one day not too long from now, because *man is a magnum miraculum, a being worthy of reverence and honor. For he goes into the nature of a god as though he were himself a god; he has familiarity with the race of demons, knowing that he is of the same origin; he despises that part of his nature which is only human for he has put his hope in the divinity of the other part.* Right. That's it. I'd known that all along.

# three

I rode this wave of exaltation most of the way home. The meanest and shabbiest people I passed looked brilliant, their faces brightly shining on me. They seemed new-made, as if some magic word had just then worked them out of the blank material of the world. Perhaps they had suddenly fallen from heaven—angels or demons in human form. Or it was I myself who'd fractured the shells of the layered orbits and risen up among them. Say if you will that it was only my imagination, but much can be seen with the eye of the mind.

Or as the pure in heart would sometimes say, back in the drug-driven American seventies, "I just get high on life. . . ." Clear eyes, rosy cheeks, and a big saccharine smile to go with it. Ho ho ho. . . .

There was a bit of mail in the box. Letter for Clara from her mother in St. Paul. A book I'd sent to a friend in Canada had already been returned—now how had they managed that so quickly, when I'd only mailed it yesterday? I looked for the accusatory pointy-finger stamp, RETURN TO SENDER, but it wasn't there, and after I had stared at the wrapper awhile longer I understood that I'd reversed the addresses and actually mailed the thing to myself. . . .

If I didn't get some real sleep soon I was probably going to crack up completely. That much seemed altogether obvious. I went on gaping at the parcel . . . it was air mail, with about ten pounds' worth of stamps on it, all painstakingly canceled, to be sure. I reached into the box again but there wasn't a whole lot else: a couple of bills and a clothes catalogue. Oh, and a chipper postcard from Stuart, with a picture of an airplane on it. Evidently he'd mailed it from Kennedy, and odds on it came over on the same plane he did. There went that funny taste again.

When I pulled the other stuff out something came loose from the leaves of the catalogue and fell against the floor of the letter box with a metallic clink. I fished it out and examined it: a disk of metal about the size of your average washer, and with a hole through the middle too. It was serrated on the outer rim into little pointed teeth, like a gear or a cog of some kind, except that it seemed too flimsy to be either. I could bend the teeth back by pressing them with the ball of my thumb. As I peered at it I felt my imagination's eye roll over and go searching around the British Museum lobby for something or somebody; I didn't know which, but a shock of *déjà vu* hit me so hard it made me dizzy. I had to lean against the doorjamb for a second. My head came clear again soon enough, but I still couldn't figure out what the gizmo was or if I'd seen it before or not. I pushed it down in the watch pocket of my trousers, unlocked the door, and went in.

No messages . . . reason being I'd forgotten to turn the machine on, like a fool. I stood for a moment looking out into the back garden and as I watched another cloud bank jammed itself across the sun. It was rather dreary out there, without light. *Lux seu ignis*. . . . And I was beginning to feel gloomy again about that infant I'd encountered at the Tooth and Claw. Still, wherever there's a way in there's sure to be a way out, right? That's only logical. You have trouble convincing lobsters that this is so, however. Lobsters just aren't logical.

Why aren't they, then? I went to the bedroom and put Clara's letter and the catalogue on her bureau. Passing back through the kitchen I picked up the leaf of foil that had covered the pastries and carelessly wadded it up in my hand, then unfolded it and smoothed it flat on the tabletop. Waste not, want not—there was that envelope with my name on it in hasty sprawling letters. It had slipped my mind all morning. Must be the foil had landed on it when I uncovered the pastry plate and that was why I hadn't noticed it before I went out. To the left of the *A*, Clara had drawn a lot of squares or boxes inside of each other, an infinite recession, sort of a perspective hole right through the paper was what it looked like. That was something she tended to do when—

The doorbell bonged and I started looking all around for the clock but of course I couldn't find it since I'd stashed it away in my sock drawer. Clients, time for clients, I'd lost track of the time. Going down the hall I stepped on my shoelace and had to stop and retie it while the bell bonged again. Then I went on to the door and snatched it open.

Case of wrong address, I'd have said at first glance. He just didn't look like the client type. You do get funny customers, but my assumption was he was lost. He was also about ten pounds underweight, at a guess. His feet looked loose in the huge Doc Martens, which had been cut out to expose the steel toes. Black jeans bloused into his boot tops, with holes at the knees—not cut holes either, they'd worn through the cloth, which was stiff with dirt. Black leather jacket, naturally, scuffed and cracked, with swastikas and other inspiriting devices daubed on it at random in white house paint. There was a bit of chrome dog chain strung through the left epaulette of the jacket. His hair was matted, like an old mop; on a closer look I decided it was a mohawk that had expired from want of proper maintenance.

"Look orright to you, do I?" he said.

"Sorry," said I. "What can I do for you?"

"It's about the hypnotist," he told me, shifting his eyes to the nameplate and back. "I rang for an appointment, I did."

"Ah," I said. "Ah yes. Your name?"

"Jones," he said, "It's, er, David Jones."

"Right, this way, please, Mister Jones. . . ." And I ushered him in, though my heart misgave me. Jones, in a pig's eye his name was Jones. I led him down to the crooked room, but I didn't put him in the chair just yet.

"Now then, Mister Jones, accounts with us are payable in advance"— for the likes of you, I didn't add. "That's fifteen pounds by cash or check." I thought that might get this one over quickly, on the spot, but he was rooting in his jeans pocket. Out came two mangled five-pound notes, three pound coins, and the rest in small change, but correct to the last brown penny. I felt a little sorry about it, felt like handing him some of it back. But instead I dropped it rattling into a desk drawer and motioned him to take his seat.

"Well Mister Smith—it was Smith, wasn't it?"

"Smith it is, right you are."

I thought so. He was jumpy in his seat, kicking his boot heels against the rug and swinging the chair to and fro on its swivel. I felt like grabbing the chair and holding it still, but instead I just wrote "won't give real name" at the head of the file form and pointed him out to myself with my pencil.

"And what was it you came to see me about?"

"Tryna give up fags," he told me. He cleared his throat, sniffed, and wiped his nose with the back of his wrist.

"I see. Well. You might just slip your jacket off, you'll want to be comfortable as you can."

He shot me a mistrustful look; these folk don't shed their armor easily.

But after the beat of hesitation he unzipped and unbuckled and let the jacket fall to the floor. Underneath was a grotty white tank top and a faint odor as from an open grave. Quit smoking, eh? I might could take care of that for him, if that was all. As a matter of fact I'm fairly good at it. I quit smoking once myself.

"Have you ever tried to quit before now?"

"Quit, quit fags, you mean? Oh yuh, I've tried it dozens of times." He was swinging the chair around again, not looking at me, but at the wall. His case of the sniffles seemed rather severe.

"Any particular methods? Tried nicotine gum? Bets? Support groups? Aversion therapy? Or just cold turkey?"

He quivered a bit at that last phrase. "No," he said. "No particular tricks, just stopping straight out in the regular way."

"How long since your last cigarette, may I ask?"

"What's that then? Oh I'd reckon a day, two days."

"*Two days?*" But then you do get that pattern from time to time. Cigarettes cost a lot in London, and sometimes people don't have the money. Funny to think of struggling to make your nut for cigarettes, or maybe it isn't all that funny. "Well, you may not know it, but you're over the hump. Your blood will detox in about two days, so probably it has already. In point of fact, you've already quit."

"Oh yuh, you reckon that's the truth?" But he didn't seem especially interested. He wiped his nose on his arm again. I suppressed an urge to pass him a tissue. Though there was a box of them on my desk.

"Question is, how will you *stay* off? Ever been hypnotized before, Mister Jones?"

"No, no, never was."

"Well, probably you've heard something about it," I said. "Some of what you've heard may be wrong. Hypnosis isn't black magic, for instance. You'll be aware of what's happening and you'll still be in control right along. The fact is you can't completely give up that control to another person, me or anyone else for that matter. So to break an addiction, any addiction, you've got to really want to get off."

"Oh yuh, I want to get off it right enough," he said, and this time there was some force of conviction in his tone.

"Right, then. Shall we just get started? Let's just begin with a couple of tests. Just you try rolling your eyes back in your head, that's the way, as far as they'll go. . . . Now *without* moving your eyes from the position they're in, just slowly pull your eyelids shut . . . good, that's it, keep your eyes closed now."

He couldn't actually do it, the eye-roll test, but it was still best to be encouraging. And try him on the arm. I got up from my chair and went quietly over the floor to stand over him. "I'm going to just lift up your arm now," I said, suiting the action to the word. "Just let it come up now, relax, now then, your arm is becoming very stiff, very rigid and hard, now then, you've got no joint at the elbow, it's just like a board, like a steel rod, you couldn't bend your arm if you tried, it's not possible to bend it, try to bend it, try to bend your arm now."

I was supporting his wrist with the open palm of my hand, and when I made that last suggestion the joint flexed a few degrees, but then he stopped it. Consciously, I would have guessed. When I let go the arm fell quite suddenly, like a shot bird, to flop against his bony thigh. He wasn't a really spectacular subject, but I still thought I could get him into a light trance, good enough for the short agenda I had in the back of my mind. He was still for the moment, no more fidgeting. I stepped behind the chair and grasped the cushion on either side and began to swing it lightly back and forth myself.

"You're in a boat," I said, "a slim black boat going down a calm river, you're sitting in the prow of the black boat, on a red velvet cushion with a golden fringe . . . you're very comfortable, you are, and someone in the stern of the boat is paddling you along, so you don't have to do anything, nothing at all, your progress is effortless, your muscles are relaxed and soft, you hear the paddle dipping in and out of the water behind you. Dip your fingers into the water . . . feel how warm and pleasant that water is. . . ."

I kept on gently rocking the chair, a little synthetic boat action. . . . His scabby kneecaps were sticking up through the parallel holes in his jeans in a sorrowful way that made me wish there was something I could do that would really help him. I thought I had him going a little bit though; his eyes were starting to travel some, under the closed lids.

"On the banks of the river you see fields of poppies, bright red poppies in full bloom. . . . As the river gets narrower and narrower and narrower, the poppies get closer to the boat . . . and now the poppies are near enough for you to touch, the petals are soft and velvety and powdery . . . and

**28**

the smell of the poppies is overwhelming, intoxicating, you are drunk on the smell of the poppies as the boat follows the stream into the cave. It's dim, it's dark, it's very quiet, but there's a bit of an echo from some words that want to be spoken now, and now you tell me, *what did you really come here for?*"

Gotcha. He spoke up like a little gentleman too.

"I thort you could help me come off smack."

Oh Christ.

But actually I thought so all along. It all fit in: the case of sniffles, the funny business with the name, the collapsed vein on his left inner forearm I'd been gazing at absently while I rocked the chair. All of a sudden I just felt very weary and old.

"All right," I said. "Up ahead you see a light, it's the light at the end of the tunnel. It's growing, it's getting bigger quickly, you can see the world again out there. You're coming awake as you leave the tunnel: you'll wake up completely on the count of five. One—two—three—four, wake up now, open your eyes—five."

I let go of the chair and went back to my desk, speaking with my back to him. "I'm sorry, pal, but I really can't help you. Heroin isn't a problem I handle. I'd have told you as much on the phone if only you'd asked. You get your money back, of course." I scooped the money back out of the drawer and turned around and held it toward him, but he batted my arm aside and the coins went scattering all over the floor.

"You've got to help me, mate," he said. "I'm in need, in very bad need of help, don't you see?" He wasn't kidding either. He was shaking all over now and his face was shiny with sweat. Poor lad, I figured I knew what he'd done. He'd skipped his morning fix and saved the fifteen pounds for me. A waste. I squatted down and scraped the coins up from the rug, keeping one eye on him while he raved. Once I'd got them all re-collected, I snagged the jacket and stood up.

"Just be reasonable now," I said. "There's nothing I can do for you, but there's people that can help. There's programs, you get on to one of those." I put the money in a slash pocket of the jacket and held it out toward him at arm's length, but he still wouldn't take it.

"Bugger all that," he said. "Bugger *programs*, I need some help and I need it now."

"You won't get it here," I said. "I'm sorry. But you'd better just go."

I could tell he wasn't in good control of himself. He wasn't in a frame of mind to hear reason, and I didn't want him breaking up my shop, so I about-faced and went padding up the stairs. I guessed he'd follow me, or follow his jacket, which I was still trailing from one hand.

"Here, you come back," he was saying. Other things too, but with a little mental twist I could reduce his whole discourse to static. Just the same I got distracted and turned the wrong way from the top of the stairs and went into the front room, instead of to the door as I'd intended. He caught up with me there and snatched me by the shoulder. Only meant to get my attention, I wouldn't doubt. He'd cottoned on to the idea I wasn't really listening anymore. Still, things were getting out of hand.

I shook loose, stepped away, and tossed the jacket at him from about a yard's distance. While he was busy catching that, I stooped to uncover the tank and grab out the snake. Irritated by this sudden seizure, he put on a few seconds' worth of a good snake act; his body stiffened in my hand and jerked around in angular ways, his wedge head jabbing and searching.

A perfectly harmless snake, of course, but you wouldn't have known it to look at old Jones-Smith, or Smith-Jones if you prefer. He turned an interesting pastel blue and his breath stopped suddenly, as if he'd been garroted. Well, even if you're used to snakes, it's startling to see one out of context. Rearing its head from your breakfast plate, for example, or sliding out of the faucet as you run your bath. . . .

"Push off, you berk," I said, quoting Mr. Waltham's parrot. But right away I regretted the rudeness. "Just see yourself out, will you?" I said. And I gave him a pleasant nod as he went backing across the carpet. A moment later I heard the latch click and when I peeped around the doorframe the hallway was empty.

The snake had gone torpid again in my hands. You're not supposed to handle them right after they've eaten, but he still felt slender to me, and when I put him back in the tank I saw the mouse was alive and well, standing with its front paws pressed to the glass, peering up with its little red eyes to try to see what all the commotion was for. I didn't know what to make of it, quite; my snake normally had a hearty appetite. He was an enterprising snake, and the day before I bought him he'd broken into the mouse cage at the pet shop and gobbled mice till he was lumpy and swollen as a kielbasa. The motion of the transport upset him and when I got him home he regurgitated mice all over the flat. Got us in trouble with Clara, that did. . . .

My hands were trembling just a little as I re-covered the tank with the drape. I felt a little guilty too, about that stunt I'd pulled. Give Smith-Jones some bad dreams, I wouldn't wonder. Still, it had appeared to be a choice of evils, and at least we hadn't smashed up the furniture or broken anyone's bones.

I went into the kitchen and drank a glass or two of water, but that queer taste wouldn't wash out of the back of my throat. Luckily I had clients stacked up till the middle of the afternoon, so I could keep busy, keep my mind off things. I soothed test anxiety, alleviated thumb-sucking, turned personalities from Type A to Type B. . . .

The last lady in had come for insomnia. No, she had no particular worries. No health problems, no exceptional stress. Marriage tranquil, husband successful, children doing splendidly in school. She woke up each night around two o'clock and stared at the wall until morning, and with all that extra time to think, she still hadn't thought of a reason. I did her up in a minute, though. I gave her the magic, morphic words. Sure, I know how to cure insomnia. Do it all the time. . . .

# four

I was tired when the last one left and who would wonder? I'd been tired enough before the first one came. I slapped the door shut behind the final client and turned back into the front room. There was some messing about I should have been doing with my files and tapes. But instead I sat on the sofa and picked up the newspaper again. It seemed a little close in the room so after a moment I screwed myself around and cracked the window behind me, then sat back. The birds were silent in the gorse bush, or else there just weren't any there. A finger of cool air stroked slowly down the back of my neck.

Mrs. Thatcher and Norman Tebbit attending the reopening of the Grand Hotel at Brighton, where they'd just missed being blown into corned beef hash a couple of years previously. They were . . . *indomitable*, I suppose would be the word of choice. But the bombers themselves were prospering quite well this very day. More explosions in Londonderry and elsewhere. Elsewhere it was suggested that Britain's precautions against nuclear accident were inferior to those of the Soviets. Back in my native land, official spokespersons were pish-tushing at the notion that the accidental drop of a hydrogen bomb from a B-36 on a base near Albuquerque had any particular significance for the destiny of the earth. After all, it didn't go off, did it? At least the nuclear part of it didn't, though there seems to have been a reasonably impressive conventional explosion. But this all happened back in 1957 . . . 1957? What were they so defensive about?

From the right angle, the world could be seen as one large and magnificent fireworks display. . . . Meanwhile, beer prices were on the rise. . . . George Harrison's very first guitar sold for 3,600 pounds. The fire brigade had been called in to free a prisoner who'd got his head stuck in the observation hatch of his cell door at the Cheshire county jail. And on the centerfold of the paper was an entire spread of scrapbook snaps of the late Heather Jolley. Heather Jolley visits the zoo. Heather Jolley on Christmas morning.

Heather Jolley visits her gram. Heather Jolley. Heather Jolley. *Sensationalist bloody muck*. . . .

I sank the paper in the kitchen trash, then splashed a little water on my face. Starting to feel a little groggy, and it would be time to leave for practice soon. Yes, and I'd done nothing about our supper— When I turned around from the sink, there was that envelope still in its ambush position on the tabletop. Right next to where the clock had been that morning, and for an instant I almost thought I heard it tick. But I still didn't open it, this fascinating envelope. Now I noticed for the first time how the pencil point had broken off on the last downstroke of the *N*, making a ragged, random mark. But I still didn't open it.

There was the pencil itself in the bedroom, snapped in two and dropped in the otherwise empty wastebasket. I remembered tossing that stray belt back into her closet when I was straightening up that morning. With the utmost caution I opened the door, as if I might have been trying to outwit a jack-in-the-box. Clara's closet was always crammed to the gills, a luxuriant swirl of colorful cloth, from which oddments had a way of leaping out at you. This afternoon, though, it was neat as a pin, because it was empty, sure enough. The clothes were gone, the shoes were gone, everything missing but a couple of wire hangers lightly jingling on the rod. On the floor was a wee ball of slut's wool, and next to it the coiled belt, which I picked up. I saw the leather had rotted out so that the buckle dangled crookedly, on the point of falling completely off. Not worth taking. Left as a talisman. The wheels of my memory turned round and round.

So, goddamn, she left again. Why did she keep on doing that? It was upsetting to a person. I pulled open the drawers of her bureau—they too had been raked bare. The little jewelry box was gone, and so were a couple of photos in frames, now that I happened to notice. I checked over the shelves in the front room. That explained the missing music. Most of her books seemed to be gone too. The kitchen gear was all intact; she hadn't been cooking much of late. So were the canned goods, for that matter. But this was a much, much cleaner sweep than what I was accustomed to.

It made me wonder how she'd managed to get it all out so fast. I'd only been down in the crooked room for an hour, though she did know my appointment schedule, and would sometimes make use of it to throw me the odd surprise, sometimes nice, sometimes nasty. . . . But this time she would have had to have help. Valerie, I wouldn't wonder, and Val's pinheaded

*33*

boyfriend, Richard. And I never heard a thing. Getting my money's worth out of that soundproofing job, I was. On the other hand, it was possible that she'd been funneling stuff out a bit at a time, on trips between the flat and her studio. Well, what difference did it really make?

I picked up the phone to call over to Valerie's, figuring that's where she'd be. Val had a three-room flat near the Albert Bridge, and in one of the rooms was a futon tricked out on a cunning frame that did into a couch in the daytime. Clara had apparently found this arrangement very comfortable at other times when she and I were on the outs. But after I'd dialed the first few digits, I put the receiver back down on the hook.

Clara would still be out at work. So, in all probability, would Val, and I wasn't in the mood to chat up pinhead Richard. Also, I'd better read that freaking note before I talked to Clara, on the off chance that the rules of this game had changed. Because it wasn't her standard practice to leave a note at all. What she normally liked to do was just vanish, leaving me gulping and quivering, wondering if she'd been swallowed up by whatever vortex sucks the Heather Jolley types out of this world and into who-knows-where. The first time it was truly terrifying, and ever after it retained a solid shock, but I'd begun to get the hang of it. When she went missing, I'd have a look round and find that some overnight bag had gone with her, a few changes of clothes, a spare pair of shoes. I'd learned how and where I could find her too, more often than not. But this was the first time she'd left with *all* her gear. This was the first time she'd ever left a note.

Sealed and everything. I slipped a thumbnail under the flap and tore it back. Need to trim that nail before practice. Inside was a single sheet off an ordinary A-4 typing pad, snatched angrily loose so it was ripped across the top, and *why didn't I just go on and read the thing?*

*Adrian, well, I'm gone again   This time I mean it   Had enough or not enough   what's the difference?   not much to you   I won't take it back   whatever's left in the flat you can have   well never mind the business   the drawing's yours   that one you liked*

*thought of explaining but what's the point   you're always peering at things that aren't there   anyway I can't see them   But I'm here I'm here   I used to be here, that is   can't say I've enjoyed being*

**34**

*invisible    don't try to find me this time    or try if you like but you*
*won't find me now    see where it gets you*


*I'm sorry    no I wont say that    It's not my fault    it's just too bad*


She hadn't signed it. That looked bad. It all looked more than bad enough, indeed; I was able to register this much, in a distant abstract sort of way. The rules of the game had really changed; the game was very possibly over altogether. I pictured her looking down the tube of her pencil the way somebody sights along the barrel of a gun. She had an aggressive way with a pencil, and she never gave a damn for punctuation. I felt annoyed at myself. It was true as she argued that I was talented at overlooking the obvious. But how had I managed to walk around that note the whole day long and never really see it? Something was wrong with my mind. It was broken.

I folded the paper over and over and shoved it down into one of my back pockets. The rectangular lump of it pressed into my flesh. It was time, past time, to go.

That let me out of cooking supper, anyway. I collected my gym bag and left the flat. Halfway down the street I had to go back and double-check that I'd locked up. Walking away the second time I realized I still wasn't completely sure, but I wouldn't permit myself to go back for a third inspection. Nothing to gain by adding a compulsion to my lengthening roster of clinical symptoms . . .

There was a somber roar behind me; the Carnival had begun to really crank. People were streaming up Pembridge Road from the Notting Hill tube stop. That was where I'd meant to embark, but I walked on past without taking note of it. I was moving rather quickly, and after a while my feet got sore, and I could feel a case of shinsplints coming on, but somehow I couldn't persuade myself to slow down. The machine of my body was running away with me. Strung from its shoulder strap, the gym bag beat against my hip; I could distinctly hear the squeak of its little swivel as it turned with the rhythm of my steps, but that was all. The ordinary sounds of the street were muted in a curious way, as though I'd been deafened by some sudden loud noise, shut more deeply into myself. I walked insensibly through the bustle of Earl's Court and came out onto Old Brompton Road.

**35**

When I reached the north gate of the Brompton Cemetery, it appeared to me that here was where I'd been heading all along.

Before the stone arch and the iron-barred gate I hesitated, trying to think of some prayer for the dead. Simply as a courtesy, you know. A superstitious habit, hedging the bet, according to the example of that vile old rationalist Pascal. But I had always had my doubts that God would have been fooled by that ploy of offering belief just on the off chance of His existence, so why should I expect Him to be fooled by me? Nothing occurred to me to mutter, for luck or any other purpose, and after a blank moment I went through the gate.

Brompton Cemetery isn't half the size of Highgate, but it's big enough for me, and more convenient. It stretched out south further than my eye could see. I turned to the right and walked along the outer edge to the western wall and turned again. Beyond the hospital grounds, the sun was lowering, a reddened flame, still formless. Hitching up my bag, I crossed the narrow strip of graves between me and the catacomb and hopped up onto its roof. I walked on a few more paces, watching my feet, nervous as a child afraid of stepping on a crack. Superstition, superstition, though stepping on the wrong crack here might really be the end of you, since some of them went all the way through and the catacomb roof was already collapsed in several places.

There were notices forbidding people to walk here, but I liked the elevation. I stopped and looked out over the great necropolis. The grounds were not particularly well maintained, which was part of the attraction of the place, at least for me. Further south was someone harvesting from a great brown snarl of blackberry vines that scrambled along the wall. Back toward the center a tall growth of weeds stood among the stones, withered and faded to the color of hay. The cemetery itself was in a phase of dissolution, its crypts caving in, headstones tilting crazily, some of them overthrown. Now I remembered: *The gods, leaving the earth, will go back to heaven; they will abandon Egypt; this land, once the home of religion, will be widowed of its gods and left destitute. . . .* I was thinking, not for the first time, that the broken crypts suggested that the dead had found some way of escape and left their houses vacant. *Then this most holy land, the home of sanctuaries and temples, will be covered with tombs and the dead. . . .* Not an empire of the dead, then, but only a dead empire, heart torn out and the soul evaporated. *O Egypt, Egypt, there will remain of thy religion*

**36**

*only fables, and thy children in later times will not believe them; nothing will survive save words engraved on stones. . . . For behold the divinity goes back up to heaven; and men, abandoned, all die, and then, without either god or man, Egypt will be nothing but a desert. . . .*

Certainly these were morbid thoughts, but probably I had come here on purpose to indulge them. Opposite me, near the eastern wall, a thin gray braid of smoke went twisting up. I stared at it, wondering if it could be real, until I realized there must be a bit of groundskeeping going forward. Often when they mowed they burned the mowings. I hopped down; if the groundskeepers caught me walking the catacomb roof there might be some difficulties I could do as well without. A flagstone path presented itself and I followed it toward the center of the cemetery.

Though I'd begun to wish I'd never come, something wouldn't let me just reverse my tracks and leave. I walked on down the central pathway toward the funerary temple below. Clara never cared for this place; she thought my liking for it perverse. I'd tried once to bring her here, but it made us ill at ease with one another. I tried to interest her in the inscriptions and the statuary, and she, pointing out the shattered crypts, came back with horror stories about all the dread diseases the living can catch from corpses. No use telling her those bodies had been loam for decades. She just didn't fancy the cemetery, thought it was creepy, in a word.

I plucked a straw and set it in the corner of my mouth, sucking air through the reedy tube, but then I thought, What if it really is contaminated? Ridiculous, but still I flicked the straw away and spat to clear the taste from my mouth. In the strictly material world, the fear of death is powerful; certainly the mechanism of my body feared it very deeply. I spat again as a further precaution. Someone on a bench just ahead peered sharply at me, a natty little chap, zipped into a black silk baseball jacket, no insignia. He wore designer jeans I'd guess he'd shrunk to his limbs by lying in a bathtub, and he had a tidy little brush of a mustache. Seemed he was waiting for somebody, but not me, though I thought I felt his eyes track me briefly after I'd passed by. All around the cemetery were dispersed the solitary shadows of other men, sitting or standing or spectrally drifting in the weakening sunlight, over the hummocked earth among the graves. It was Friday, I recalled, and on the weekends this area became a cruising ground for gays. But there was no one inside the ringed colonnade of the temple when I reached it.

At least, not anyone I could see, though when I paused I definitely heard footsteps on the stone floor up ahead, making a startling clack. There was an echo that made them difficult to locate exactly, and whoever it might have been was out of my sight around the curve of the columned row. I went along softly, not that I cared. After a minute, the footsteps stopped, and I stepped out between two columns to look down at the center.

The central circle was tall with weeds, and crossed by a palely paved footpath that ran out through the pincer arms of the colonnade, marking the vertical axis from the cemetery's north gate back to the sealed door of the small domed temple itself. Midnight. At nine and three o'clock on the dial were steps that climbed to breaks in the columned wall. Through the gap opposite where I stood, I saw the smoke of that phantom fire blown low along the ground by a damp wind that had suddenly come up. At other points within the circle were crumbled steps that led down into more catacombs. There were catacombs under the spot where I was standing, and some few dignitaries entombed in the brick wall behind me. At the lintel of the far colonnade there was a flutter of a sparrow hawk landing. He turned in a semicircle, curving his beak down toward the bleached grasses below. After field mice—I'd bet there were plenty of field mice there. The sound of crickets was suddenly loud among the riot of flowering weeds. When the little hawk flew, I shifted my feet and quietly moved on, my eyes running over the markers set in the bricks. It was getting cooler quickly, with that wind.

My first day in London I'd come here, practically straight off the plane. I was kipping with an acquaintance in Chelsea, so it wasn't much of a walk, and I didn't mind that it was raining. I wanted to rush out right away and have a look at my new city. How much younger it seems I was then . . . though it has only been four years. By the time I discovered the cemetery the rain had drenched through my cheap Delancey Street umbrella and soaked through my jacket into my skin, but I more or less enjoyed that. My awareness had been battered out of existence by the trip, so that I felt nothing but my senses, and anything that came to them was a joy.

I suppose I would have seen the complex of tomb architecture as a microcosm, which is what I never quite explained to Clara—here the city was made small and accessible, though I did not then see it as inert. *This is not death, but the dissolution of a mixture.* I hadn't even met Clara then. I'd met no one, and seen little enough so far, but I saw how the pavements turned sleek under the rain, how the rain freshened the overgrown tombs to a new green vitality. Then it did not seem a desert place, as now— *In that hour, weary of life, men will no longer regard the world as worthy object of their admiration and reverence. . . .* Back then, when it was all fresh to me, it only made me feel the more alive. Even the Hermetic prediction of the death of the soul— *For darkness will be preferred to light; it will be thought better to die than to live; none will raise his eyes towards heaven; the pious man will be thought mad; the impious, wise; the frenzied will be thought brave; the worst criminal, a good man. The soul and all the beliefs attached to it, according to which the soul is immortal by nature or foresees that it can obtain immortality as I have taught you—this will be laughed at and thought nonsense. . . .* And who after all is to say that's wrong?

But it saddened me to remember it now. I began to walk a little faster. Things hadn't worked out quite as I'd planned. Not my research, not a good many other matters, though of course it always could have been worse. It had, sometimes, been very much worse. . . . I turned through the break in the wall of the colonnade and hesitated, looking down at the weeds at the foot of the steps, into a sort of brushy trench behind the spreading rows of graves. The first thing I noticed was a pair of motorcycle boots with metal taps screwed to their soles, which explained the clash of the steps I'd heard earlier. It took another second to register that these boots were being worn by a man who'd twined himself around another man: someone had achieved a rendezvous. One of them sensed my presence and they both looked up at me, briefly and incuriously, then tightened themselves to each other once more.

And with all the more verve and delight, I could tell. I stepped quickly back inside the wall and walked around another quadrant, past the steps to the temple door. Not that I minded seeing them; it was interesting even, but I was in too sour a mood to feel like adding piquancy to their dish. Also there was something else. . . . *The gods will separate themselves from men, deplorable divorce.* I went out the far side of the colonnade and walked along a path that curved through tall shrubbery round the rear of the church. A chipped and stained Victorian angel raised a palm to me from the depths of a green bush. The air had an acrid tinge, from the smoke no doubt, that wrinkled my nose and made my eyes tear up a little. *Only the evil angels will remain who will mingle with men, and constrain them by violence— miserable creatures—to all the excesses of criminal audacity, engaging them*

**39**

*in wars, brigandage, frauds, and in everything which is contrary to the nature of the soul. Then the earth will lose its equilibrium, the sea will no longer be navigable, the heaven will no longer be full of stars, the stars will stop their courses in the heaven. Every divine voice will be silenced, and will be silent. The fruits of the earth will molder, the soil will no longer be fertile, the air itself will grow thick with a lugubrious torpor. . . . Such will be the old age of the world, irreligion, disorder, confusion of all goods.*

They were onto something right enough, the pseudo-Egyptians. They prophesied truer than they could have known, and I was bleak enough with the truth of it, but after all I was only trying to distract myself, wasn't I? I was jealous of that pair of lovers, no getting round that, really. Not that I'd have changed places with either of them. Their dish wasn't mine, but they'd made me feel my loneliness, and I resented that. Life surprises you so, cropping up where you don't expect. *How then could it be that in that which is God, which is the image of the All, there should be dead things? For death is corruption and corruption is destruction, and it is impossible that anything of God could be destroyed.* But by then I had come to the south gate and when I stepped through it the roar of the traffic on Fulham Road swept this thought away in its train.

# five

"I say! I say!" I heard this line repeated several times, floating a little forward from the wall of general noise, but I didn't think it had anything to do with me until the driver of a cab stuck at a zebra crossing leaned out of his window and began flipping his right hand at me. *Wake up, stupid! and look about yourself.* . . . So I turned in my traces.

"I say!" A small square woman was hustling toward me, a bit of white paper flapping high in one of her hands like a truce flag. "I say, I believe you may have dropped this. . . ." She halted in front of me, panting a trifle, but in a distinctly ladylike way. She was well dressed, brown cardigan over a cream-colored smock, sensible shoes, hair whacked off in a no-nonsense fashion, no shape to speak of. . . . She was about my shoulder height and had very light gray eyes. I supposed she must have been chasing me all down the block. The cab driver gave a cheery toot of his horn as he slipped over the crossing and accelerated away.

"Well, I never would have noticed . . ." I said. What she had looked to me like a foreign object though. As I reached for it I stole a glance at the watch on her wrist, having come out without my own. Christ, would you look at the time, I was late. What she'd picked up was a slice of paper folded in six. I undid the first couple of folds and recognized a line or two of scrawl: Clara's note.

"Oh thanks, really," I said. "You're very kind to bother."

The lady gave me a pert nod, turned, and shuttled off the way she'd come. Decent of her. . . . I tapped my back pocket; yes, the note was definitely gone from there. What, did I think it had replicated itself? But I didn't remember taking it out, or looking at it, or thinking about it, or flinging it away, for that matter. Funny, that. I stuffed it back where it had come from and patted down my other pockets for wallet, keys, and change purse . . . something strange in the watch pocket, what was that? Right, that peculiar metal disk I'd found in the letter box that morning.

All right, then, I was fully equipped. I checked to see my bag was shut and walked over as far as St. Stephen's Hospital, then worked my way into the warren of streets behind it. On Slaidburn Street there stood alone a two-story dormered house with a low door. The words CHELSEA RAC-QUET CLUB were still faintly legible on the lintel, but what you were apt to notice first was the white banner with the Oriental characters strung above.

I went in. Behind the service hatch to the left of the door, Mrs. Farr was talking on the phone. She had on her gi and her stone-gray hair was pulled back tight and tied to the nape of her neck with a length of braided leather. She was wearing sandals against the constant cold of the concrete floor. I peered down at her large round toes. Mrs. Farr had enormous hands and feet; I'd always been impressed by them. I piled my wallet and change purse on the ledge of the hatch, waiting for her to finish the call. I took the bone ring from my left hand and clipped it onto my key chain, and took a couple of pound coins from the purse to pay for the session.

"Strother, yes, right . . ." said Mrs. Farr, smoothing the receiver back onto the hook and rooting in a file drawer. She swung back around to the hatch and passed me the worn brown envelope with my name penned on the back. I shoveled my valuables into it, peering over her shoulder at the clock: half-five.

"Terence still about?" I said.

"Eh?" said Mrs. Farr, chucking the envelope back in the drawer. She gathered my two pounds of payment into her long blunt-ended fingers and jingled them into the tin cashbox. "Oh yes, he took the children's class today."

Good, I hadn't missed him, at least. I could hear a light thumping on the mats upstairs, and every few seconds a string of *kyais* in falsetto, muffled by the walls. A couple of tired-looking mums sat shoulder to shoulder on the folding chairs in the small anteroom, waiting for the children's group to finish. I went into the dressing room and sat heavily down on a green bench, bending over to unlace my shoes. Just that small movement was enough to wake up the soreness in my left hamstring and the tricky spot in my knee. I was tired, tired enough to be dangerous, maybe. *Pay attention, don't forget.* . . . I stood up and started taking off my clothes.

"Eat a lot of your own cooking, do you?" Somebody was talking some kind of shop. There were only three people in the dressing room but me. A pudgy chap I didn't recognize, standing on the scale and frowning into its big round dial. Behind me were a large Cockney and a little Frenchman. It appeared the Frenchman was a chef somewhere.

"How d'you keep your weight down, then?" the bigger man was saying. "All the pastries and those cream sauces?"

"Oh, I do a lot of sport," the Frenchman said.

He was shrugging and turning up his palms when I glanced over my shoulder at him. He was small and dark, stripped to blue bikini underpants, and not a spare ounce on him anywhere. I knew that already; I'd sparred with him a time or two. His name was Michel, or something like that. Too small to be much of a threat, but fast. I tightened the drawstring of my gi pants, stuffed my street clothes into the bag and hung it on a nail. The floor was cold, a shriveling cold, and the air smelled of chilled sweat. I could feel the floor's pattern on the bare soles of my feet as I went across the hall to the weight room.

A sample of the troubled youth Terence brings down with him from Notting Hill was on his back in there, doing bench presses, and the room was empty otherwise. He gave me a grunt when I came in. Maurice, I believe his name was. I did some splits and watched him work. A fine strong youth-man. Really the kid had more muscle than he knew what to do with, and he shouldn't have been lifting without a spotter, but I didn't feel like being a nag, or spotting for him myself either. I hate lifting anyway. Boring, and it makes you tight.

I got up and did some triple punches on the air and then went to the rear of the room, where there was a mackawari board mounted on a chest-high plank. I went into a left front stance, tapped the canvas pad with my left fist, and took a solid shot at it with my right. Reverse punch, medium speed. Again. Get more hip into it. . . . Again, faster, twist. Now, full speed, full power—

"EEEAARRGHH!" The shout rang off the walls of the little room. I could feel the first sweat breaking on my chest. I switched stance. Left reverse punch. *Blam.* Turning to lock into the correct position, taking the shock from the two front knuckles straight back to the shoulder. *Blam. Blam. Blam.* The board flexed back from my hand on the springy plank. It made a happy snapping sound with each connection. And now a little something extra for this last one—

"EEEEAAARGGHHH!" But it was a miss, and a dirty miss, off by a good three inches. Rubbish. I'd clipped the corner where the canvas

**43**

folds, and the place was marked by a smear of fresh blood. The twist of the punch had torn a cut between my knuckles, and there was a line of blood edging down the bones on the back of my hand. *Wake up, stupid!* I licked at it, a hot salt taste. It didn't appear to be especially deep. Terence poked his head in the door.

"Calm yourself, Adrian," he said. "And stop drinking your blood. Time to fetch yourself downstairs."

The children's class was piling down the steps from the upstairs room, pulling off their belts and popping them at each other. Hard to get them to observe the proprieties consistently at that tender age. I cut my way through the knee-high swarm and followed Terence down the turn of the stairs to the basement. Left off the corridor below was quite a large room that had formerly been a tennis court and was now covered with thin mats from end to end. Master Kim was strolling up and down one end of it, in front of the Korean flag. He nodded to Terence and glanced down at my cut.

"Uuuurggh," he said. I lowered my eyes. I'd screwed up, and been caught at it. *Uuuurggh.* I jumped into line, next to Terence, noticing I was the only brown belt here. That meant I was really going to get it.

"*Charyet!*" Terence cried. "*Kunye!*"

The ranks behind us snapped to attention and exchanged a bow with Master Kim. In unison we all sank to the floor and sat back on our heels. Hands on knees, eyelids lowered, three-quarters closed—I'm usually pretty good at this part. I roll my eyes back in my head, tear an ogival window in my brain, and step through it into a dream of an ideal body that does everything perfectly, on demand. But this time I couldn't get through the opening. Something seemed to be blocking it, coming toward me from the other side. Clara's face, her light gray eyes. Well, goddammit, that was what had me staring at that helpful lady so. She'd had Clara's eyes.

Everyone else was already on their feet. I got up creakily, so strained with fatigue I thought I was going to break in half. Master Kim's eyes swept over the ranks like a broom, and he began to cry commands.

*Middle target punch—one, two, three, four . . . about-face. Upper target punch—one, two, three, four . . . about-face. High block, low block, single arm block—* The cut had dried, my sleeves were popping crisply on the hand techniques, and my mind was finally starting to drain the way it should. On my way to being a happy little robot once more.

**44**

*Front kick. Side kick. Knife-hand block, knife-hand attack. Reverse
punch. Six-step.*

"*K'mon,*" said Master Kim. "*Sho.*"

He waved his hand and all the belts faded out toward the rear of the
room, everyone but me. I stood alone before him, listening to the blood
hammering in my temples and trying to breathe. I should count myself lucky,
getting all this personal attention. But when I blinked my eyes I saw Clara
sitting at the far end of the crowded table from me. That pub, what was
the name of it? there on the King's Road.

"*Junbi.*"

Master Kim walked around behind me as I pulled myself into the ready
position. He counted me through Chul Gi number one, jabbing me in the
small of the back on each count, to keep my interest lively. It worked. I
blocked and punched and screamed and forgot all about what happened
with Clara in that bar. About three years ago, it would have been.

Chul Gi number one takes twenty-three seconds to do on your own
count, if you do it right, and leaves you breathless and streaming sweat.
Then Pal Sek. There are forty-three moves in Pal Sek, and Master Kim
jabbed me in the rib cage on most of the counts, but not all. I was properly
grateful for that: it stopped me thinking and helped me concentrate my mind
on what I was supposed to be doing. Pal Sek takes forty-five seconds to
do on your own count, although it often takes me fifty-some. A crook of
Master Kim's finger brought Terence trotting up to do it with me. Tonight
I managed to keep pace with him. We were neck and neck, screaming into
the last knife-hand block.

**"EEEAARGGHH!"**

Together we came back to attention, bowed, relaxed. Master Kim
grunted and nodded and waved me away. It looked like he'd forgiven me
for the cut. I went and fell down in a corner and watched him take Terence
through Chul Gi number two. Mrs. Farr had joined him. She'd been round
a long time, long enough to make second dan. I had cooled down enough
to begin to be able to think again, and I was trying to think of something
neutral, like the six months Mrs. Farr had supposedly spent in Korea, but
then I remembered that pub again. The Chelsea Potter, it was called. Never
one of my favorite places. But I'd been running with a pack of American
exchange students who liked to come over to the King's Road occasionally

and kit themselves out with new records and clothes. They were a lot younger than I was, of course, but all the other postgrads I'd managed to meet were desperately dreary library moles, and as ever, it was difficult to get to know the English.

Terence came and sat cross-legged next to me, as Master Kim called up the purple belts: Michel, Maurice, a couple of others I didn't know by name. Terence's beard had gone stringy with the sweat that raised an obsidian gloss on his skin. We kept our eyes front in the approved manner, him concentrating on the lower belt forms, I supposed, and me pretending to. Clara herself was a bit older than most of that lot, though not so much as I. We'd never had a private conversation but I'd certainly noticed her. She stood out, not only because of her looks, which were mostly camouflaged by the gray sweat suit she always wore, always completely plastered with paint. In those days she had some studio arrangement in Chelsea and she'd come out for these quick pub lunches slathered over with fresh pigments, not just on her clothes but all over her hands, gumming parts of her hair together, streaked down her cheekbones, even running into her mouth some days.

She was distinctly noticeable, as I say. I was eating a pork pie and trying to sustain a one-candlepower flirtation with some brainless bit of blue-eyed fluff on her year abroad from Sweetbriar. Clara was well down the bench and I wasn't really paying attention to her but I was faintly aware of what she was talking about. Wisconsin, where it appeared she'd grown up. She was explaining about barn decorations in Wisconsin or something like that, when all of a sudden this pig of a preppy from Rice or wherever pricked up his forefinger and silenced the table.

"Wait, I *know* you," he said, making it sound as serious and important as if he'd just discovered the formula for polymer plastic. Clara glanced at him and then dropped her head sharply so that a curtain of hair swung over her face. It was a strangely childish gesture, one that I'd see a lot of in the future, but I hadn't yet had the chance to learn to recognize it as a trouble sign.

"You're Carla Pedersen," the Rice guy said.

Clara straightened up and sloshed her hair back over her shoulder and fixed him with those cool gray eyes. "No," she said, and shook her head, just slightly.

I would have shut up if I'd been him, but he was too enraptured with this discovery he thought he was making. "Jeez, you were *great*," he said. "You were the *best*, I used to watch you on *TeeVee*. Whatever made you—" And then he did shut up, very suddenly, scooted back his chair, and began to gape down in a slack-jawed manner at the spreading dark stain on his chinos. I'd had my eye on the ball throughout, but it still took me a second's lag to register what had happened. The Rice guy had a fresh pint of Guinness in front of him, and Clara had reached across the table (not in any particular haste) and tipped it over into his lap. The empty glass rolled a silent turn on the carpet and clicked into the leg of a chair. By the time I looked up, Clara was gone.

Halfway down the block I saw her running, not especially fast, but the sidewalks were crowded, so she turned heads. I followed at a rapid walk, moving into the wake she cut through the crowd. She turned into Oakley Street, where there were fewer people, and jogged a couple blocks more down toward the river. Then she fell back to a walk. I stretched my legs and began to gain a little. She had to stop for the light at the Embankment, so that was where I caught up with her.

I stood beside her, just out of harm's reach, like maybe I just happened to be there waiting for the light to change myself. For a minute I wondered if she'd even recognize me, out of the context of the group. She took a short look at me, bit her lip, and shook her hair over her face again. I was catching on to this gesture already, so I kept quiet, and kept my distance. She had both hands deep in the belly pocket of her sweat shirt, I noticed, and she was hunched over slightly, as if her stomach hurt.

When the light finally changed she crossed the street and climbed up the bridge, me following still, a few paces back. At the top of the gentle curve she stopped and rested her elbows on the rail. I stood and looked where she was looking, at the couple of boats moored to the pier and the flat brown water stretching back, a clouded mirror, to the next bridge along the Thames. Half-turning toward me, Clara pulled her hair into a cord and twisted it up and began trying to pick a clot of cadmium yellow out of the end of it with her thumbnail. After a little bit she gave up and let it fall.

"I suppose you'd like to know what all that was about," she said.

"Nope," I said, with an ingenuous smile and shrug. "Not really."

This turned out to be a stroke of inadvertent genius, because Clara smiled, and touched my arm. Her moods were sudden as the weather, and it was a bright day, as I recall. She led me the rest of the way over the

**47**

bridge and down into Battersea Park, where she showed me the Henry Moores, and I showed her the monument to the first little flea-ridden terrier ever vivisected in Great Britain. We talked about a number of other things also, but she didn't explain that scene in the pub to me, not until quite considerably afterward.

"Twenty push-ups," Master Kim said, stooping to tap me on the back of the neck. "On your fists."

He passed on. Automatically I flopped over onto the mat and began to knock them out, counting loudly in Korean and peering around to see what I'd done wrong. Ah yes. I'd been so wrapped up in the wonderful world of reminiscence that I'd missed the call to line up for sparring.

I finished the push-ups and stood at attention. Master Kim left me standing there for four rounds before he waved me into the line, opposite Mrs. Farr. I bowed, she bowed, I screamed, she screamed, we both dropped back into fighting stances. Mrs. Farr is a counterpuncher. Every time you move in to try something, this nasty little punch comes out and gets you. My left arm was doing me about as much good as if it had been molded in soft lead. She scored on me three times in a minute, and I could tell she was pleased with herself, though the grim lines in her face never changed.

After this I had a couple of uneventful rounds of instructional sparring with the lower belts, and then Master Kim signaled everybody down. Everybody but me and Maurice, and four cornermen, to score. One point, sudden death. I figured it could be interesting, because Maurice is an ambitious fighter, and he's also very strong. He relies on his strength a little too much, perhaps, but he piles up bruises with his blocks, and eventually the pain can wear you down.

I thought the thing to do was turn this tactic back against him. Maurice's star technique is a spinning back kick. He's rather dangerous with this, primarily because he doesn't usually know where it's going till it gets there—can't screw his head around in time. He also tends to throw them on a pattern I can anticipate, so when he came whirling around with his fourth attempt I was set to smash a really solid low block onto the back of his ankle. It hurt him some, and it shook him off balance; I got in to score with a reverse punch to the floating ribs.

This took place in Mrs. Farr's corner, but for some reason she didn't give me the point. Demoralizing, that. It got me in a spot of trouble, because while I thought it was over Maurice was still coming on with a little of this

**48**

and a lot of that, which I was barely managing to block. You don't want to let Maurice just hammer on you indefinitely, he's too strong. So I snapped a back-fist at him to make him hesitate, switched into an open stance and dropped a roundhouse kick in over the back of his guard arm. Impossible to block from that angle, and you can't avoid it if you don't see it coming. I picked a bead of sweat off his temple with the ball of my foot.

Mrs. Farr and Terence both gave me that one. So I was out of the doghouse once again with Master Kim. Maurice shook his head and smiled, and we bowed out and sat down to watch the other scored bouts, me taking care not to nod out again. Because I was too tired to tolerate any extra calisthenics, and there was enough coming my way with the usual finishing basics routine: more sets of kicks and punches and sit-ups and push-ups and leg lifts. Oh, but I hate leg lifts. Finally that was over too, Master Kim and the others had trooped upstairs, and there was nobody left but me and Terence down there on the mats, doing a few slow splits and butterflies.

I wasn't really in the mood tonight, but I didn't want to say so. There was a bruise the size of a halved tangerine swelling out of the hollow of my left wrist, undoubtedly from some facet of my encounter with Maurice, though I couldn't quite remember which. My knee felt a little wobbly too, and I was shaking internally with exhaustion. Terence got up, stretching like a cat, and crossed the floor to peep up through the basement window well. Even from where I was sitting on the floor, I could see Master Kim's spit-shined shoes receding down the sidewalk.

"All clear," Terence said, and led the way into the hall. The others had shut off the light. I bent double and followed him through the short low passage and then straightened up inside what used to be a squash court. The door folded up flush with the wall when I shut it—you wouldn't know there was a door if you didn't know where to look.

"You forgot the light," Terence said.

An echo in the deep square enclosure magnified every slightest sound. I looked up. There was a balcony for spectators about fifteen feet above, and sometimes a few of the Notting Hill gang would hang around to watch us at our illicit extracurricular activity, but it was too dim now for me to see if anyone was there or not.

"I can see," I said. There was enough ambient light for us to make each other out reasonably clearly. "You?"

I saw Terence's head nod in profile against the ghostly white of the rear wall. His feet swept together, in time with mine. We bowed, our foreheads almost brushing, and each took a short skip back.

I felt the clean white surge of adrenal energy, like a drug, or like falling in love. Trust someone to almost kill you barehanded, but not quite; trust yourself to do the same for him . . . there's nothing that feels quite like that, though perhaps a couple of things come close.

Terrific painkiller too. I didn't feel hurt or tired anymore. Terence moved in a semicircle to my left and stopped. His lead hand was open, fingers twitching slightly. The outline of his gi was indistinct against the white glimmer of the wall behind him, but I saw the black of his head and hands etched plainly. I wondered how well he could see me. I popped a fast head fake to test that, and he came around instantly with a spinning hook kick, which I ducked under. Then a roundhouse with the same leg, reversing his direction—that one nearly got me. I blocked it awkwardly with an elbow, leaving a brief opening he didn't get into. Against an equal you have to move *before* you've seen the opening. You just have to know.

A current ran down my forearm like a river of light and I was already moving into the breach I was convinced I was going to see. Switch stances and drop that high roundhouse in over the shoulder—on Maurice it had worked like a dream, but in this dream I saw Terence beginning to pivot before I quite had time to

# six

. . . I found myself whirling through rings and rings of celestial fire, burning white and gold together with a flame that did not consume or wound but covered me like a garment. But I was naked, flying on these wings of fire, burned painlessly back to that first original purity of soul. I turned on my own axis while the sphere to which I had penetrated carried me round and round the hub of the earth. Around me there spun other bare and transmogrified human souls like mine, along with angels and archangels and the seraphim: winged heads whose wings kept opening and closing to veil and reveal their bright visages. The spheres acted upon each other in their revolution to make a music that comprehended all the joy and terror of the universe in a single one of its notes.

The note sustained itself, shimmered, glowed, rose and fell. One of the angels had his wings jammed in the closed position. He kept appearing and reappearing in different quarters of the field of my transfigured vision. A black angel, with a Roman face, holding one hand clamped over his long nose and the other thrust forward with several fingers extended. The fire that carried me round was cooling, I felt the revolutions slowing, and the music of the spheres began to resolve itself into some sort of word.

*Ayyyy. . . . Ayyyyy. . . .*

The long sighing vowel never quite completed itself, always sucking away back into the mouths of the numerous Terences who continued to rotate maddeningly round me. All of the Terences seemed to be having a bad nosebleed, and all of them were poking a bouquet of fingers in my eye, and they all kept jigging up and down, like horses on a carousel coasting to a stop.

"Adrian. Adrian. Do you hear me? Are you alive in there? How many fingers, Adrian?"

"Enough," I said.

"No, man, tell me how many?" The last solitary Terence drifted to a halt somewhere off to the left of where I was lying on the mat.

**51**

"A hundred and forty-four," I said, and pushed his hand out of my face as I sat up. The movement revealed to me what a right pig bastard of a headache I had. But it wasn't that. I saw the room enclosing me again and I had to groan out loud at the loss of everything I was just recovering from.

"What?" said Terence. "What is it, you bad hurt?"

"Nothing," I said. "I was thinking about something, something else."

Terence snorted, and a little trickle of blood ran out between his fingers.

"What happened?" I said. My headache was slap in the center of my head and radiating toward the edges. I found a bird's-egg swelling between my right temple and my ear, which was extraordinarily sore when I touched it.

Terence sighed and lay back on the mat, wiping his bloody fingers on the chest patch of his gi. "I tell you, Adrian," he said. "We having altogether too much fun."

My, but it hurt my head to laugh. I pressed that bird's egg by my ear again and discovered that after a short delay it produced a wavelike rise and decline of the deeper pain. Terence's long fingers were exploring the high sharp bridge of his nose.

"Not broken, is it?" I inquired.

"I don't think so," Terence said. "Just bloody. I bleed too easy, from the nose."

"Let me just get a towel or something," I said. I succeeded in getting to my feet and taking a number of steps in the direction of the door, but then the pain induced me to hesitate and sag against the wall.

"Never mind that," Terence said. "I think it stopped."

I pushed myself off the wall, came over, and offered him my hand. He took it and dragged himself up, and we progressed, supporting each other in a rickety fashion, as far as the low door.

"The halt leading the halt," I suggested. When Terence stooped for the ring in the door handle, his nose began to seep again.

"Keep your head back," I said, and led the way down the passage.

In the corridor it was dark and Terence passed me, holding his nose pinched shut, going craftily up the stairs, silent on the balls of his feet. "No one about," he said in a stage whisper. I went up after him, hauling myself along with one hand clamped to the stair rail.

"We'll get ourselves caught at this game one fine day," Terence muttered.

Upstairs the lights had been shut off too, and there was only a little weak radiance slipping in over the transom from the lamps that were lighting on the street.

"Having too much fun," I said. "Oh well, he'll break us back to white belt when he catches us, I suppose." I closed my eyes and listened to the sliding sound of Terence's feet moving away from me. There was a swirl of metallic particles dazzling my mind's eye, and for a moment I thought it might organize itself into an aperture—a crack I might again slip through. But when I looked again, I saw it was only that Terence had turned on the light in the showers, there beyond the dressing room.

I stripped and went in after him. Terence was leaning back under the tap, washing clots of dried blood out of his mustache. I put the water on as hot as it would go and rammed my head right under it. It made my head pound like the devil, but when I took it out again the pain seemed better focused and easier to cope with. Terence had switched his shower all the way to cold; I could feel the drop in the temperature from where I was standing in the steam. He was trying to scrub the bloodstains from his gi.

"You want to put some salt on that," I said. "Or something. There's some trick, I know." I shut off my shower and went into the other room and dressed. After a minute Terence came out too, holding the gi at arm's length and frowning at it. He'd got the blood tracks faded to pale pink.

"Sorry about the mess, old chap," I said in a bogus accent.

Terence aimed at the side of my head along his index finger. "You mind your own lumps, fellow," he said.

I made a face. Terence began pulling on his trousers. I patted my pockets for wallet and keys, and panicked for an instant until I remembered I'd given all that into the keeping of Mrs. Farr. The file drawer was still open when I checked: a bit of luck, or kindness on her part. Terence was fully dressed when I came back.

"Opening time, I should surmise," I said.

"Past it," said Terence.

The snap lock closed behind us with a little click, and he gave it a couple of shakes to make sure it was shut solid. There was only a little natural light left glimmering in the sky; it must have been gone six. A light damp breeze cooled down my forehead as we walked up toward Fulham Road.

Terence went directly to the bar when we came into the Goat in Boots.

That's our convention—winner buys first round. It occurred to me, however, that it might be open to question this time who had really won and who hadn't. I sat on a stool by the banister overlooking the lower level of the pub, and kicked my gym bag under the little round table.

"He drew you a shamrock," Terence said, returning with my pint of Guinness, and a can of Tennent's Super for himself. The black liquid looked solid and compact enough to have retained its upright shape even without the glass. There was indeed a four-leaf clover sketched on the brown foam, executed with a cunning twirl of the glass beneath the tap's last squirt. Signature of the Irish bartender . . .

I raised the glass, using both my hands for safety. "Your health," I said, and drank. "Do you know what happened, by the way? Being that I see you're claiming victory. . . ."

"Some of it," Terence said. "I'm coming round with a reverse knife-hand strike, just so—" He hitched his shoulders to indicate direction. I didn't flinch. "I hit you there where I was aiming." He pointed to my bird's-egg lump. "And at the same time you hit me. . . ."

"With the roundhouse," I said. "You spun right into it, Jesus, Terence, why aren't you dead?"

"Luck," Terence said flatly. "That is the best explanation. I think I must have hit you first, so your foot was loose already. Flopping, so." He made a dead-bird gesture with one hand. "That's the logic of the thing. That's how I take the win."

"Sorry about your nose," I said.

"It's nothing," Terence said. "I still have my beauty. Sorry about your head."

"Don't mention it," I said, leaning over to grope in my gym bag. "First time I've managed to get unconscious in about a week, really I should be thanking you." I shook a handful of aspirin into my palm from the vial that had been kicking around at the bottom of my gym bag.

Terence's eyes went sharp. "Careful, now," he said. "If you have a concussion, you don't want to swallow that."

"How many fingers, Terence?" I said. I flipped an aspirin into the air and caught it in my mouth.

Terence was still frowning though. "Tell me now," he said. "How well do you remember the day?"

"All right," I said, with a pull at my stout. The shamrock stem sucked into my mouth and the four leaves rearranged themselves, distorting on the surface of the foam. The dissolution of a mixture. "My name is Adrian Strother." It was going to make me a little gloomy, having to go through all this. "I'm from America. I was in your pub today and you gave me bangers and mashed for lunch. Then I went home and hypnotized people all afternoon and then I came to practice. I kept up with you on Pal Sek, for a wonder. I lost a round with Mrs. Farr and won my exhibition against Maurice. And a lot of other things happened all day long that I don't especially want to tell you about right now."

"Well," said Terence. "Watch yourself, Adrian, just the same. Aspirin on concussion, that can kill you."

I chased the rest of the aspirin down my throat with a luxurious, three-gurgle swig of Guinness. "Are you acquainted with what *il Nolano* said about the pig?"

"O bloody Hell," said Terence. "If you can quote Giordano Bruno at me, I suppose you must still have most of your brains about you."

*"The pig,"* I said, *"likes better to turn about in mud than in a bed of linen, he would prefer a sow to the most beautiful of women, because the affection follows the reason of the species."* Here I took another long pull at my glass. *"But if a beast had a sense of the difference which exists between his own condition and that of man, and the meanness of his own state with the nobility of the human state, which he would deem it not impossible to be able to reach, he would love death, which would open to him that road, more than that life which keeps him in the present state of being."* Actually it made me feel comforted about the condition of my brainpan, to be able to recite all that with reasonable accuracy.

"European voodoo," Terence said, twisting disgustedly in his chair.

"What if it is?" I said, tossing off the last of my stout. "Still better than your island mumbo jumbo. More civilized."

"But not as powerful." Terence grinned. Difficult to fix just precisely where Terence stands on these matters sometimes. His can gave out the death rattle when I picked it up and shook it, so I took my own empty glass and started for the bar, which was crowded with upmarket types. My eye was drawn to one beak-faced blonde, got up in mock-equestrian gear. A loud hawking voice that kept grating on me even when I turned away. I pushed forward till my gizzard pressed into the rail and shoved my empty pint onto the counter's inner lip. An idea struck me when the barkeep finally stopped.

"Pint of Guinness, can of Tennent's, and . . . a large Paddy's please," said I. I've been more moderate in my habits than that for the last several years, but I was thinking, when all else fails, why not drink yourself to sleep? The bartender left and stayed away for what seemed a longish time. I turned my back to the counter and looked down the steps to the pub's lower level. Below, there was another counter where they dished up the shepherd's pie, &c., a group of tables, and beyond them in the corner a pale-faced fellow in a cheap suit, prancing in front of the fruit machine. The dials of the machine buzzed and spun, and every so often his hand flicked out and touched a button, like a cat's paw patting a ball on a string.

A stall? What was my next line with Terence? In this sort of discussion he has the advantage of being able to snipe at me from either side of the road. In his posture as your basic third world radical he despises all religion equally as the opium of the people and so forth and so on. But his save-our-youth operations work in and out of the Notting Hill churches; I think he's even a deacon in one, or several. I've seen him tricked out in his church suit on Sunday. What connection he may have with West Indian magic I might be better off not knowing, though possibly or probably he was kidding. But let's not forget his status at the Tooth and Claw—high priest in the temple of the senses.

So I carried the drinks back to the table. Terence's eyes paused on my glass of Paddy's, but he didn't go so far as to say anything just then. Meanwhile I was staring across at his wrist and reading the time from his upside-down watch.

"That meeting I mentioned, it's tonight," I said. "Out at Shepherd's Bush."

"Oh yes," Terence said. "Your pal from America."

"My erstwhile pal, right," I said. "He's got the cure, he thinks, and now he wants to export it." I lifted the glass of whiskey and drank it right down.

"Does he indeed?" Terence said, stroking a thumb through a crinkle of hair on his lower lip. "And where does he get his, then?"

"Oh, maybe just the satisfaction of the thing . . ." I said. I was getting a trifle distracted, in truth, by the sudden spread of the whiskey glow, into

**56**

my lights and my liver. Think of all the people who stand ready to wreck their whole lives for the sake of that sensation. . . .

"Eh?" said Terence.

"I mean if he's a true believer," I said, "then proselytizing should be its own reward." I folded my right hand over my left forearm and began to fidget with the pattern of pockmarks underneath the cloth of my sleeve.

"True believer in what, exactly?" Terence said.

"Well, probably I shouldn't presume," I said. "It's been a long time since I've seen the gentleman." Over his shoulder, I spotted an opening at the bar. "Back in a tick," I said.

I sprang into the breach and then returned to our table, bearing another large whiskey. Because my head was beginning to feel so much better I thought it could only benefit from more of the same. But when I belted the second drink back my temples beat so hard that for a moment I wondered if I might have made a serious mistake.

"Really, Adrian," Terence said. "How much do you love death, after all?"

"I'd rather live," I said, as the room and its contents floated slowly back into focus. "Look, Terence," I said, speaking with all the conviction I could muster, since it was my own body I needed to convince as much as him. "Look, I haven't got a concussion. I've got a bruise and a bang on the head, that's all. But it's good of you to worry." I winked at him. "I'll do the same for you, next time."

Terence bugged his eyes at me. "Next time, you say? All right, I'll let you be."

I flushed my smarting pipes with stout. "So you want to go have a look at what they're up to in Shepherd's Bush? Might be some use to you and your lot."

"Faith healing's a hoax," Terence said. "It doesn't really work."

That showed what *he* knew, all right.

"Forgive me my vocabulary," I said. "This thing that Stuart's pushing is a technique, all right? It's purely utilitarian—you and Aristotle should both be completely satisfied."

"All right," Terence said. "Can't hurt to have a listen."

"But you're wrong about faith healing," I said. Evidently I couldn't help myself. "Your vision of the world is askew."

"Are you going to start all that?" Terence said, with a restless sigh.

I rapped the table with my knuckles. "Is that alive, Terence? Can it feel when I give it a bump?"

"What we have here is a bit of wood," Terence said, involuntarily looking down. "You're soaked, Adrian, you never drink as much as this."

"How about . . ." I pointed over the banister, down to where that same fellow was still at the fruit machine. "Well, the fruit machine, for instance, is it alive?"

"The fruit machine is an inanimate object made in a factory out of plastic and metal," Terence said. "Designed to rob gents like that one of their money."

"But *he* thinks it's alive," I said, leaning forward and lowering my voice. "Just look at him there, he's dancing with it, he's singing to it even. He *knows* that it can hear him and answer him. . . ."

"I hate it when you try to hypnotize me," Terence said. "Don't bother."

"I'm not," I said. "But look at him, it's only the truth what I'm telling you." The pub sound system was playing some strange Kate Bush number and the fellow was dancing to that febrile rhythm, a step forward, a step back. The fruit machine shuddered and blinked back at him as his hands slapped out against its various buttons. I could read the movement of his lips: *come on, come on now,* he was chanting. Just as the song ended, he hit the pay-out button and the machine spewed coins into its tin trough for what seemed like over a minute. The fellow was still cramming the gelt into the patch pockets of his jacket when Terence swung his head back to me.

"A small coincidence to build a grand delusion on," he said, and squeezed a crimp in the waist of his empty can. "Let's go then, if we're going. It's time."

# seven

The tremendous roar and moan of the Central Line train pulled me down into itself with a gravitational weight. My arms and legs went rubbery, one hand slipping down on the smooth chrome post I was holding onto for balance, and my eyes drooped gradually shut. That last good shot of Paddy's was shimmering brightly in my bloodstream. The *click-clack* of the wheels on the rails kept up a percussive rhythm that was occasionally ornamented by an offbeat squeal from the coupling between our car and the one behind, but what was holding me entranced was the funnel-shaped drone of the engine rushing through the dense textures of the tunnel's close air.

The complexity of the sound was staggering if you really paid careful attention. My head lolled over, cheek pressing against the cool of the metal post. There's some apocryphal story I once heard about a composer who lived hard by a Brooklyn el track, so close he could stretch his hand from his window and stroke the trains as they went by. *Doesn't that distract you from your composing, then?* he was forever being asked, and always answered, *Oh yes, it does, every time the train goes by it makes such a beautiful sound it takes my confidence clean away. . . .*

But somewhere in me something was splitting; the deeper that stupor weighed down my senses the higher I felt my other part lifting, lofting itself into the air—the awkwardly lumbering flight of a crow. A shadow was flapping on and off with the rhythm of the wing strokes, and in the interstices of the dark I saw Clara appear and disappear, appear. . . . She had wrapped her hair in a long loose twist and pinned the end of it beneath her elbow, against the drafting table. The wing beat down, and she was lost, rose and there she was again, the needle tip of her drawing pen hovering over an intricacy of some great mazy architectural design. That was the other end of Clara, a part of her I seldom saw, full of a wicked fanatical precision, sighting down her pen point to know exactly if a line no wider than a mouse hair had made some infinitesimal wobble, or laid its ink unevenly, or permitted itself a microscopic blot. In the stark white light above the tilted table, her pupils had shrunk very small. I was beating up toward her, but making no progress. At each of my advances I was borne equivalently back by heavy waves of the air. Try as I would I couldn't make out what she was designing, and she was not aware of me at all. The wing swept down and cut the light.

"Adrian!" Terence clamped my shoulder and gave it a vigorous shake, causing my eyes to roll involuntarily open and regard the buttock-dented plush of the bank of seats opposite.

"I'm all *right*, I tell you," I said sharply, and shut my eyes back again. But I was tumbling now, and couldn't stop myself. Gravity hugged me to itself again.

I rocked forward as Terence jostled me another time. "So you may be, but this is Shepherd's Bush."

"Oh? Oh." I had a look and saw that it was the truth he was telling me. Hand over hand I dragged myself up the pole, and followed him, stooping, to the door of the low car. One of my ears remained wistfully tuned to the receding hiss of the train down the tunnel as we emerged from the station and set foot onto the Uxbridge Road. That had been an interesting flight of fancy there, or whatever one might choose to call it. A shame I hadn't made out exactly where she was. Have to make another attempt, to express myself into a phantasm and find her so . . . it would need practice. Of the four *furores*—poetry, religion, prophesy—the most powerful is love.

"Which way, then?" said Terence.

"It's near the foot of the market," I said. "On Goldhawk Road, that would be."

"Ah," Terence said, and jaywalked across the street, me following him a bit nervously. There was no traffic whatsoever at the moment, but it was a wide street and something about the passage seemed to make me jittery. Touch of contagion from Eleanor Peavey, that might have been. Am I suggestible? Yes, I am.

There was little light on the tattered green of the common, which smelt indistinctly of dog. The frequent bare patches in the grass had turned slick with mud under the drizzle earlier that day. Once I almost lost my footing. At the narrow end of the common three dark men in bulbous woolly hats turned to face our way; I sensed they were staring at us, though it was too dark for me to make out their faces. A faint gage odor came to me, moving slowly in the damp air. It was misty enough that the street lamps were surrounded with fuzzy orbs. I caught up to Terence and then passed him, hustling across the street.

"Don't recall the name of the place, d'you?" Terence said. "Is it a pub?"

"Pub or a dance hall," I said. "Maybe both. I had it written down somewhere. . . . But I think we should fall across it soon."

Just to our right, on the high side of the street, was a gateway arched by a wooden signboard, which let into the long curving alley of Shepherd's Bush Market, the stalls all shuttered down now for the night. I went on, nosing at the wet atmosphere. Toward the end of the block some people were congregating in front of the lamplit doorway, shifting positions as they spiraled inside.

"Looks likely," Terence said.

"Yes."

By the time we reached the door it had cleared of other traffic and we went in unimpeded. A long dank room with travel paths worn in the brownish carpet, dimly lit with low wattage fixtures dangling from the ceiling. Some sixty folding chairs had been erected, filling about half the space, and perhaps two-thirds of them were occupied. At the front of the room there was a portable lectern set up on a cafeteria table, no microphone. From this position a tall lean fellow with a Liverpool accent was muttering something to the assembly.

Terence and I went quietly as might be to a pair of seats at the corner of the last row, but there was no helping the screech my chair let out when I sat down on it. A Paki gent in the next row up turned round to frown at us and then turned back. The Liverpool chap was making grateful allusion to various helpful colleagues in other quarters of the city. Next he began referring to "the gentleman from the States." He had a spade-shaped Adam's apple that bobbed up and down to salute each word as it exited his gullet.

My interest in craning my neck to look all over the place for Stuart was overridden by a more powerful instinct to keep my head down. I hadn't seen him at all when I came in. Of course it had been a long time since I'd last set eyes on him, four years in all, so perhaps he'd changed. Anyway the light was low and he'd have had his back to me, since he must have been sitting in the front row, waiting his turn. That taste again in the back of my throat. . . . I was beginning to stiffen up after the workout. Leaning slightly forward, I crossed my hands to clasp my opposite arms and stared

*61*

down at the carpet between my shoes. It was spongy and smelled of old beer; I had the feeling it might have leached a little brown ale if I pumped it hard enough with my feet.

"And I'm certain Mister Boatwright will be happy to answer any questions you may have at the end of the talk. . . ."

My head lifted, all on its own, in time to see the Liverpool fellow departing the podium, and the person coming up from the other side was definitely Stuart, shucking out of a new-looking leather jacket and trailing it along the surface of the table as he came up to the lectern and stopped. He took hold of an edge of the lectern in either hand and stood for a minute with his head bowed down. Then he raised his head and gazed out at the audience for another long silent time. The chairs began to rattle and creak; there were exchanges of mumbles and sniffles and coughs all round the room. Either Stuart had developed a stronger dramatic sense than he'd had when I had known him, or he'd genuinely choked and was in trouble. But when he finally spoke his voice was strong and clear.

"Hell is real, and I have been there," Stuart said. "Some of you have probably been there too."

This worked, the room went quiet immediately. You could practically feel the abruptly sharpened focus of attention.

"Don't we all know something about the geography of that place?" Stuart said. "We do. We've spent great ruined portions of our lives mapping it out from end to end." He pushed himself away from the lectern and let himself fall back onto his braced palms. "Let me tell you just a little bit about the parts of it I've covered."

At this point I stopped listening for a while. I'd heard it. I'd heard a little of it, that is, and the rest of it I'd seen. To distract myself I began to look around the room. A well-mixed bag, more men than women by a comfortable margin. More whites than blacks by a smaller one. There was a scattering of East Indians as well. Most of the assembly seemed to be under thirty, with a few older faces spread among the rest. Some punks and skinheads among the majority of nondescripts. And a larger complement of West Indians than I'd have thought likely, considering they'd be missing the first evening of the Carnival for this affair.

"How do you like this combination?" I whispered, giving Terence a nudge. "Anywhere else, a gang like this could add up to a riot." The thought came to me just as I said it. It was true enough; you might just as well expect this lot to all be having at each other with bottles and sticks as sitting here quietly row on row. Then again, a lot of them were probably too strung out and sick to feel very much like fighting. Still, some turf rules had definitely been bent or broken, so I thought. It was rather interesting.

I stretched up to whisper to Terence again. "See any familiar faces here?" I said. "Any of your lot come down tonight?"

"My people have heard enough of your European claptrap before tonight," Terence said huffily, not looking my way.

"I just gave you a double handful of my brain cells," I snarled at him. "What more do you want?" And I looked back at Stuart then. He looked good, objectively speaking; even in the greasy light he had a look of health about him. It seemed like he'd put on some weight—no question but he'd needed to.

"Eh," Terence said into my ear. "Forgive me, Adrian, I was thinking of something else. That man who made the introduction, he said Horace Stamp? Horace is one of the organizers here, now I find."

"Horace?"

"You know him, eh, you've met him at the pub." Terence faced front again, suddenly intent.

Oh yes, I did know Horace Stamp, though not too well. We crossed paths now and again at the Tooth and Claw. He was a Jamaican, coffee-colored, with a barrel body, long arms, and next to no legs whatsoever. Though a man of his build lost little height by sitting down, I still couldn't make him out over all the other heads between us and the front row. Like Terence, he was a neighborhood organizer in Notting Hill. Sometimes they were allies, sometimes rivals, and now I thought I knew what had got Terence so annoyed. He'd been one-upped, had a march stolen on him. Horace had got his hand into this occasion without letting him know anything about it.

"Once the scag gets its way into you, it takes you over, body and soul," Stuart was saying. "You know that's a fact, most of you do, or you probably wouldn't be here. You'd sell your mother for another good hit. You'd sell your lover. You'd sell your soul, if only you still owned it. . . ."

He went on to illustrate this point with further examples from his own career, and I discovered that with a certain effort of concentration I could keep on looking at him without actually hearing anything he said. There he was, perfectly visible, opening and closing his yawp as silently as a goldfish in a bowl. Behind him, through a pair of swing doors to the left of the

**63**

table, I could hear an occasional splash or click of glasses from the public bar of the pub we were in. The building was on a corner and the bar must have faced the other street. Terence set his hand on my shoulder and leaned down toward my ear hole again.

"Horace will have brought his own folk down," he said. "He'll be responsible to keep them in line, d'you see? The same with the other organizers here, the lot of them, every group answering to a leader. That's why you'll see no trouble tonight."

"A lot of diplomacy going into it, then," I said. "What about loose wires? This thing is open to the public, right, so anyone could just stray in and upset the balance for you. . . ." I had my eye on a trio of National Front characters a few rows up and to the right as I was mumbling this.

"Whoever comes has a common interest," Terence said. "That must be the theory. And it seems quiet enough at the moment, doesn't it?"

So it did. Stuart had entered one of those long pauses, and all I could hear in the room was the uneven rhythm of different people breathing.

"Soon enough," Stuart said eventually, "you'll give up whatever hope you had. You'll decide there's no way out. And when you've made that decision, that's the way it is."

There was a snap of a match and a feather of smoke rising from one of the forward rows.

"But there is a way out," Stuart said. "You can get out the same way you got in. The same pathway, exactly, you follow it a step at a time."

He pushed himself back, swayed forward, and caught himself on the heels of his hands. I was beginning to catch on to this sequence of moves as a calculated oratorical mannerism.

"I got out," Stuart said. "I got myself out just that way . . ." He raised his head a couple of notches and I couldn't stop myself from shrinking slightly. For an instant I thought he'd spotted me, but then I decided he must be looking out over the whole crowd, to some imaginary point beyond the rear wall.

"But it wasn't really quite so simple," Stuart said. "It wasn't just a matter of stopping with the dope. I had to stop being the person that shot the dope. I had to stop being myself, you see, and that—that's a little more difficult." Stuart stopped speaking and suddenly smiled, with a sort of relish, which might have been the last thing I would have expected. Then he snapped an index card out of the pocket of his white shirt, glanced at it, and set it on the lectern.

"I'll tell you something about the Spiral Center," he said. And then he began to give the pitch, which (delivered by other acolytes) was familiar to me also. The Spiral Centers were exclusively run by ex-addicts. There was a hierarchy up which the recovering junkie had to climb. Progress through the pecking order appeared to be its own reward. As it well might be in an environment where there was precious little other stimulation of any kind. The Spiral Centers were, by preference, set up in remote areas. They removed the junkies from their urban context, the better to take their defective identities apart. The few centers that were organized inside the cities remained rigidly self-isolating. It was the nature of the game.

Stuart began to talk, somewhat more cloudily in my opinion, about group therapy. The importance of total emotional frankness, the necessity of accepting the critiques and the prescriptions of the group. By such devices the old addicted personality might be replaced by a new, unaddicted one.

I watched Terence watching Stuart. After a moment he leaned over to me. "It works, does it?" Terence said.

"It's a behavioral model," I said. "Take away the rhetoric, it's operant conditioning. Works extremely well on rats."

Terence grinned. "But not on people, you don't think?"

"I never said that," I told him. "It appears to have worked on Stuart." Who now was winding up his spiel.

"This isn't just some more snake oil, people," Stuart said, holding his right hand palm up and letting the index card flutter away from it. "It's a practical method and it does work. If you put the effort into it. You've got a plain choice between life and death, and it's not too late to choose to live." He paused, looked down, then up. "The first Spiral Center in Britain is now being organized on a farm near Darlington," he said. "There's a farmhouse there we're already using and some other buildings standing. We're putting up Nissen huts for temporary quarters. Later on there'll be better facilities—we'll be building it all ourselves. We're looking for donations, yes, but especially for volunteers. Anyone interested, speak to Mister Gardner at the end of the meeting. . . ." He indicated the Liverpool fellow. "It'll be fresh air, a change of scene. . . ."

A nervous titter went spreading among the chairs. People were shifting their weight and looking at each other.

"Seriously," Stuart said, stretching a finger up into the air, "here's a chance for anyone to get into the program on the ground floor. Right now it'll cost you nothing but time. You give us your time and your labor—we'll give you back your life."

He turned away and walked in a loop behind the table. There was a patter of applause and the burr of people beginning to mutter together, but when Stuart fetched back up at the lectern, the room got still once more.

"Questions," Stuart said. "Yes."

"Are you let have snout at this place you're talking of?" It was one of the white nondescripts asking. Stuart looked a trifle perplexed.

"Cigarettes, he means," Gardner prompted him.

"Right," said Stuart. "All you can smoke."

"What about beer?" somebody called from among the chairs, I didn't see who. There was a little laughter, louder now. Stuart smiled.

"No beer," he said. "No alcohol, altogether. No drugs at all but cigarettes and coffee. And tea, yes, tea."

"Why's it called *Spiral* Center, then?" This in a rich West Indian accent.

Stuart made a twirling motion with his forefinger. "You know how the dope twists its way down into you?" he said. "We use the same path. We follow it in, and in the end we replace it. It works the same in the communities. We use the drug networks already in place, only we reverse them to bring people back out. So the spiral, that's an image of it." He pointed to one of the skinheads. "Yes."

"Sounds a bit like jail or the army, that place," the skinhead said. "Were you locked in?"

"No," Stuart said. "No locks."

"What stopped you having it away, then, just doing a bolt for it?"

"It wasn't jail and it wasn't the army," Stuart said. "I owed something to the other people. I wouldn't have wanted to let them down. Not that I never thought of it. . . ." Inexplicably, he began to weep. "They were my family. . . ." He went on crying, not saying anything more. Except for the sound of his snuffling the room was as silent as outer space. After something like a minute and a half, Stuart reached down to the table to scrabble a handkerchief from his jacket pocket. He blew his nose loudly and put the handkerchief away.

"Any more questions?" he said. There were none.

# eight

Then the meeting broke up into various separate swirls. The members of the different groups got up and began to circle their leaders, behaving very much as Terence had described them. Terence himself went off and began working his way into the cluster of West Indians. Now that almost everyone was standing, I saw that some of these youth-men were known to me, by sight at least, from Notting Hill. Horace Stamp, a head shorter than any of the others, was talking earnestly to a crescent slice of them, underlining certain points with strokes of his long thick arms. What arms he had, as big around as lots of people's legs. I had always been impressed by them. Terence was standing to the rear of this group, chatting inattentively with someone in dreads, and looking down onto the back of Horace's grizzled head with a strange concentrated intensity. I think I would have turned around if I had been Horace.

The other groups had fallen into similar orbits, and as wholes they all were moving toward another center: the table with the lectern on it there at the end of the room. A man in a white apron pushed a metal trolley through the swing doors, set up a couple of urns of tea on the table, and laid out some throwaway cups. Next to this refreshment, Gardner sat behind a large book that looked like a ledger, with Stuart standing at his back. All the different groups continued to cohere, at least loosely, but they all drifted inertly toward this area, like separate planets swinging toward the sun. It seemed that only I was alone, and beginning to feel a trifle lonely.

The room was getting quite smoky from all the cigarettes people seemed to be lighting once they'd got their tea. The clusters were starting to break and reform by the table and the spot where Stuart was standing. I got up and went to the door and put my nose out. It seemed to have grown somewhat mistier than it had been when we'd come in, though it still wasn't what you could call real fog. Across the street two or three people were leaning against the railings; it was too dim for me to make out their faces but I could see the high punk hairdos through the vapors. The weather was taking a definite turn toward cool. I ducked back into the room, closing the door behind me, but a file of Pakis came up immediately and opened it again to go out.

Things appeared to be winding down, though all the remaining groups still kept their basic integrity. Except for the skinhead contingent, where there seemed to have been some sort of schism. Half of them had reached the position where Gardner sat with his ledger, and the others, four or five of them, had taken their tea to the opposite end of the room, where they slouched down against the wall, smoking rapidly and generally sneering around, in a fashion that might or might not portend some sort of immediate threat.

I hitched up my bag a little higher on my shoulder and went over to the tea urns. I squirted myself a cupful of tea and held it till I felt it cool a little, then set it down, untasted, on the corner of the table. Wasn't really in the mood for tea, was I? Not just then. Beyond the urns, Gardner was taking dictation down into his book, the name and address of whoever addressed him, or that was what it sounded like. Stuart had slung his jacket over one shoulder. He was rocking to and fro slightly as he spoke to one of the skinheads: one step forward, one step back. Then he took two steps forward and reached out across the table to shake the other's hand.

Terence's hand fell on my shoulder, and when I turned toward him I saw the rest of the West Indians were filing toward the door.

"Will you stay?" Terence said. "We're going."

"All together, I see."

Terence grinned. "I will have a little conversation with Horace," he said. "Come along with us, though, if you like."

"I haven't spoken to Stuart yet," I said. "I suppose I'd better wait."

"Interesting fellow," Terence said, nodding as he moved away. "Be careful of your head," he called back to me. "I'll be in the pub before closing time, if you're still out and about."

"I'll keep it in mind," I said, and watched him pass out through the door.

The room was thinning quickly now. All of a sudden there seemed to be nothing between me and Stuart but the table. But he was still in conversation, with one of the Malay-looking fellows. I could watch him without his paying any mind. His face looked fuller than I remembered, and though his eyes were a little bloodshot, that could very well have been from the

**68**

plane. Otherwise there was no trace he'd just been crying. I was wondering: Had he been weeping for gratitude as he'd implied, or was it just that he missed his dope so sorely? The cue seemed to allow for either possibility, or maybe even both of them, if you really thought about it carefully. It wasn't quite the first time I'd ever seen Stuart cry, though doing it before an audience this size was certainly a novelty.

"So," Stuart said to me. The Malay, if it was a Malay, had evidently gone away. "You came."

"Of course," I said. "You didn't think I'd miss the show?" On second thought, that might not have been the most flattering choice of word imaginable, but Stuart smiled. Then again, I couldn't tell from this smile whether he thought I was getting at him or not. That much, anyway, hadn't changed.

"You look well," I said. "Looks like you gained back the weight."

"Clean country living," Stuart said, fanning his hands palm down, a foot or so above the scatter of Spiral Center leaflets on the tabletop. "You're looking fairly rosy yourself."

"Right," I said. "Well, you'll probably be busy with all this administration for a while longer, I suppose, otherwise I'd ask you to step out for a drink."

"A coffee, maybe," Stuart said. "If there's a place."

"There's a caff on the other side of the common I know," I said. "If there's no place closer."

"Just wait till I let them know I'm leaving," Stuart said.

He crouched down next to Gardner's chair and spoke quietly to him for a moment. Gardner nodded rhythmically, running his finger down the lines in his big book. At the end he glanced at Stuart and mumbled something and nodded again.

"All right," Stuart said, straightening up and looking at me. "We can go."

The group of lingerers by the railing opposite the pub had swelled; it seemed to me that some of the skinheads from inside had joined them, some of the lot that had been hanging back against the wall. After we'd gone past I heard the taps on their combat boots scraping against the pavement, as if maybe they were following. I glanced back a time or two but they weren't very near and all I could see was a couple of those high hairdos gliding spookily along through the mist.

**69**

"What is it?" Stuart said.

"Nothing," I said, for surely it was nothing. I figured it was only that being with Stuart brought back a shadow of that good old New York paranoia. In London I'd spent hardly any time at all looking back over my shoulder until now. They didn't seem to be trying to gain, and I didn't look back at them anymore. And neither Stuart nor I found anything more to say to each other until we'd gone around the common and reached the little caff on the north side.

A small shop with about five tables and a high counter, lit bright white throughout by fluorescent tubes in the ceiling, though not extraordinarily clean. It was an Indian place, and had a heavy spicy smell, with cumin dominating. There were indelible yellow streaks of turmeric on the white Formica of the counter where I went to get the coffee. When I looked at the samosas sliding around in the steam pan, it occurred to me I hadn't eaten in quite some time.

"Hungry?" I called back to Stuart, who'd taken a seat at the third table from the door.

He shook his head. "I ate before the meeting."

I bought two samosas anyway, in case he changed his mind, and took them to the table with the coffees. Stuart took a sip from his cup and set it back down. I was still watching him. He'd always been a good-looking fellow, with thick black curly hair coming low on his forehead, and a black Irish sparkle about his whole face. That gleam had helped draw women to him, way back then. I realized that, if possible, he looked even younger than before. But then nothing had ever seemed to touch him much—at least not his exterior. The little ring he used to wear through his right ear had turned into a small gold cross, I noticed. He took another sip of coffee; there was a smooth fluidity to the motion that seemed new. Formerly, Stuart had moved in rapid, near-invisible jerks, like a water spider.

"You quit smoking," I said.

"Sure," Stuart said. "So did you, looks like."

"It's been two years, for that," I said. "Though the thought still crosses my mind from time to time." I bit off the corner of a samosa; hot meat juice splashed on the walls of my mouth. "Maybe you don't drink anymore either?" I said. "That why you didn't want to go to a bar?"

"Right," said Stuart, snapping his fingers. "All over. . . ." He grinned. I supposed he hadn't fully smiled before, since this was the first time I'd noticed he had a gold cap on one of his front teeth, with a little heart cut out against the white enamel.

"I still do go to bars," Stuart said. "Just don't drink in them. Of course I had to stay out of them altogether for a while. And yourself?"

"Oh, I still drink," I said, and had a bigger chomp on my samosa. "Not like the old days, you understand, but you can't give up everything."

"Who says?" Stuart grinned again, easing deeper down into his chair. That gold tooth of his went peculiarly with all of this new propriety. Where was all this weird calm coming from? It was beginning to make me just a little nervous, seeing Stuart in this new avatar of born-again junkie. He was a changed man, you see, and I suppose that was what made me a bit uneasy. I'd just as soon people stay more or less the same all through; otherwise you're never quite sure whether or not to trust them.

I swallowed the last of my samosa and wiped the yellow oil off my fingers with a napkin. "How about sex?" I said. "You give that up too?"

Stuart laughed. "I got married."

"Really," I said. "Well, probably not to anyone I know. . . ."

"Well," Stuart said. "Maybe you haven't completely forgotten Natasha."

"You're kidding," I said. "I mean, congratulations, of course."

"She's changed quite a lot since you last saw her," Stuart said. "As a matter of fact, she's in one of the centers upstate right now. Been there eighteen months or so, and doing very well."

"Ah," I said. "So you *did* give up sex."

"Temporarily," Stuart said. "I go up on weekends. She'll be coming home soon, anyway."

"Really," I said. "Well, I'm happy for both of you then, really I am. I didn't mean to be sarky about it. . . ."

"I'm happy too," Stuart said. "So's she, I think. It's all taken a little doing, as you can probably imagine."

"Oh yes," I said. "So, what's it really like in one of those centers?"

"It's tough," Stuart said. "It's not exactly a vacation in the country . . ." He smiled twistingly. ". . . whatever it might seem like from the talk. It's very very tough at the beginning, and of course there're always people that don't make it all the way through. But it does get a little easier after the first year."

"I see," I said. "Doesn't sound like it's really tailored to my taste."

"To each his own," Stuart said. "I doubt I could have done it your way either."

Our eyes met and locked and held. It was a funny feeling: I wanted to reach across and touch him somewhere, but I didn't, not yet. Then the door opened, letting in a portion of the misty cool. A fellow with a tall red mohawk and a spiderweb tattooed across half his face walked in. Maybe I looked at him too long, for he gave me a very hard squinny back. Why do they get themselves up that way if they don't want people to stare at them, I wonder? He bought two teas at the counter and went out. Through the front window I saw him hand one of them to another bloke with his hair in long spikes, like the Statue of Liberty. They glanced in once more through the glass and then went off.

"So how's *your* love life?" Stuart said.

"Ah well," I said. "My marital status has remained unchanged." This was technically true, at least. It wasn't really fair, but I wanted off this subject. "You see anybody else we used to know?" I said.

"The usual suspects, eh," Stuart said. "Now let me think. . . ."

"Uncle Bill?" This wasn't someone I should even have been thinking about, but there you go.

"Billy Boy is dead," Stuart said. "He kicked sometime while I was upstate, so I'm told. And Clifton, if we're talking about the trade, Clifton's doing six-to-eight at Attica."

"What, for dealing?" This surprised me. "I didn't think they had room for his kind anymore."

"No, but he killed somebody," Stuart said. "Some rich high school junkie from Scarsdale, is what it was."

"Doesn't sound like the old sagacious Clifton I used to know," I said.

"Well, apparently the kid jumped Clifton," Stuart said. "With a knife and everything—some crazy kid. Anyway, this is the story. Some people think Clifton got a bad deal, but you know, you look at the kid, you look at Clifton. . . . The kid is underage and all that, and Clifton . . . he had trouble getting good character witnesses, like. But he got the charge reduced to manslaughter finally. I can't say it altogether broke my heart."

"It wouldn't, would it," I said. "Christ, I wouldn't know where to go anymore, with him and Bilbro out of the game."

"You'd find out easy if you wanted to," Stuart said. "Not that I keep up, myself."

"Good for you, then," I said. "Don't know if I could do it your way, come to think. So, how's New York?"

"The rich get richer," Stuart said. "You ever think of coming back?"

"Never," I said. "I never will."

"Really never?" Stuart said, cocking up his eyebrows.

"I could put it this way," I said. "It's still a lot too soon to think about it."

"Ah," Stuart said, laying down a finger on the side of his nose. "Oh by the way, Nicole's in town, I thought maybe you should know."

"Where else would she be?" I said. "Nicole is an urban phenomenon."

"I mean *this* town," Stuart said. "Not in New York."

Something struck me cold when he said that, and I noticed my fingers were already trembling slightly when I reached toward the paper plate with that other samosa on it. I pushed it across the table to Stuart, who shook his head at it.

"Sure?" I said.

"Definitely," Stuart said. "You go ahead and eat it."

I tore off a corner and carefully, steadily, set it in my mouth. It went down like an equivalent amount of wet sand. For some reason I was thinking of the high cold dome of the British Museum reading room, its accretion of all those obnoxious sounds: tick. *tick. TICK!*

"Where did you come by that piece of information?" I said. "Have you two been keeping in touch?"

"Not closely," Stuart said, taking a somewhat shifty glance at his reflection in the front window and then looking down at the tabletop between my flattened hands. "We're nominally friendly, but I don't see much of her, no. It was just a big freako coincidence, actually, I ran into her at Kennedy on my way over."

"Cheap plane tickets make strange bedfellows," I said. "Did you get to share a seat?"

"As a matter of fact she was on a different flight," Stuart said. "As a VIP business traveler. She's got a new job now, scouting for one of the uptown galleries."

"A considerable change from her old job," I observed.

"She makes a great impression on everyone, I'm told," Stuart said. "I'm told she has terrific taste."

"Well, I suppose," I said. "It all sounds very nice for Nicole."

"She has a kid now too," Stuart said.

"That's funny," I said. "She wouldn't be married, would she? How old is this kid?"

"Four, three and a half, or something," Stuart said. "On information and belief, that is. I've never actually seen him. It's supposed to be a little boy."

"Jesus."

"Unlikely," Stuart said. Now his smile was a little thin. "It wasn't exactly an immaculate conception."

*No, I don't suppose it was.* I didn't say it. I didn't say anything else either, and the silence became a little awkward. I could hear some sitar rhapsody playing faintly through the kitchen door. Stuart raised his coffee cup to his lips but I could see from how far he tipped it back it must have been already empty.

"You've changed your earring," I finally said, looking at the little cross.

"I changed my life," Stuart said flatly. "I accepted Jesus Christ as my personal savior."

I was impressed by his casual tone; he might have been saying, *I walked my dog this morning, never mind the rain.*

"Indeed," I said. "You see, you *can't* really give up everything."

"Not unassisted," Stuart said. "No."

"I don't suppose you go around proselytizing, do you?"

"Not for that," Stuart said.

"But now I suppose you're required to think of me as a heretic. . . ."

"Maybe," Stuart said, and laughed. "But you know, I was always a very tolerant person."

"Advisable, at the time," I said. "But now?"

"Who knows?" Stuart said, and leaned forward, all the way into my space, a sudden intimacy that surprised me. Maybe he meant to make the pitch after all?

"I brought you something," Stuart said, fishing in the inside of his jacket. Out came a medallion about the size of a Kennedy half, swinging from a loop of fine gold chain: a beat to the left, a beat to the right. I reached out my forefinger and stopped it. On the side facing me were etched a circle and a triangle intersecting. Inside the protruding points of the triangle was inscribed the phrase, *Deus extra omnia.* In the center of the circle, in a bolder script, it said, *Deus in rebus.*

**74**

I took hold of the medallion and turned it over. Stuart let go the chain, which slipped down to coil coolly in my palm. On the flip was a third eye looking backward along a beam that emanated from the top of a schematically rendered head, toward a series of architectural and natural forms sketched in adjoining boxes. Along the beam was a third inscription: *oculis imaginationis.*

"Where in the world did you get this?" I said, looking up into Stuart's eyes.

"I had it made," Stuart said. "It's right?"

"It's perfect," I said. "You're giving this to me? I can't believe it. I'm touched, Stuart, really I am." I fastened it around my neck. The chain was short, and the medallion fell neatly into the hollow of my collarbone. I was a little flabbergasted. It was like a gift from a perfect lover, and I didn't have anything for him.

"I'm glad you like it," Stuart said, turning over his wrist to look at his watch. "Look, I'm going to have to go back, there's still some things to go over with Gardner and I told him I'd be there."

"All right," I said. "Well . . . thank you. You have any time off to-morrow?"

"In the afternoon would be good," Stuart said. "Sunday I go up to Lancashire."

"Well, call me, then," I said. "Or let me have your number. Where are you staying, anyway?"

"Near Piccadilly Circus." He passed me a card from the hotel and then stood up.

I stuck the card in my back pocket and followed him out the door. "I go this way," I said, pointing toward the tube station. "Or I can walk you back to the pub if you like."

"No, I remember the way," Stuart said. "Until tomorrow, then."

"Stuart . . ." I said, and tapped the medallion, but after all I didn't know what I meant to say. "It's good to see you looking well."

"Likewise," Stuart said, and we shook hands and separated. I was hastening toward the tube, trying to get ahead of the strange state of em-barrassment that seemed to have enveloped me, when I thought I heard his voice again.

"Hey! Wait a minute."

When I looked back I saw him trotting up toward me with a bit of folded paper in his hand. There was something uncomfortably familiar about this picture, and this time around I didn't have to unfold the sheet to know that it was Clara's note. I just snatched it and crammed it back down in my hip pocket, whence it evidently had once more hopped, skipped, and jumped, just like a Mexican jumping bean.

"Thanks," I muttered, queasily. "We'll see you."

"Watch yourself, now," Stuart said, and winked. "Looks like a person could get sloppy, living in an easy town like this."

He went off. Now that last line was considerably more typical of the unreborn Stuart than anything else from the evening's performance, I thought as I continued my way to the tube. Then I began to think very rapidly and nervously about how I was going to stop Stuart from meeting Clara, at all costs. It made it tricky not having any idea myself where Clara was, or possibly it made it simple. All things considered, maybe she'd picked a *good* time to disappear, and maybe I should be grateful for her timing.

It was an ungenerous train of thought, after Stuart had been so nice to me and everything, but still. But still—the thing is, before he started running around rescuing other people, Stuart used to be a fairly bad guy himself. A regular black-hearted villain, really. Not that I was holding that against him, and anyway, God knows, people change. People do change sometimes, God knows, I am myself the living proof.

# nine

When I'd been waiting on the platform for a minute or two, another one of those fellows with the Statue of Liberty hair came down the steps to join me. Funny, I thought; the style's unusual enough you don't ordinarily see it on two different people on the same day, but of course it might always have been the same bloke as before—I hadn't looked at him so closely. I did now, though, since it was only the two of us there and not a whole lot else to look at. He seemed restless, pacing long circuits on the platform, dragging on a Players and every so often leaning out over the rails to hawk and spit. Every time he came past me I took a close look at the roots of his hair, hoping to figure out the structural principle. The spikes were shaped in elongated pyramids, based on a square, and the hair itself was brown and woolly, something like a dread, only I couldn't figure out what made them stand up straight, with most of them a foot long at the very least.

Jumbo knitting needles, maybe? Then the Central Line train came huffing and puffing up to the station and took my mind off the problem. I embarked, and Mr. Liberty got on after me, sinking into an apparent daze, with his eyes half-shut and his head lolling back against the burn-pocked upholstery. Right, chum, me for that, me too. . . . The moment my head bounced into the frayed plush, there was a flip, and I thumped into the air again, cruising a widening circle, like a hawk this time, or maybe a buzzard. Though it was life I was searching for now, some sign of a particular life I needed to attract. Through the mystery of my movements I'd charm Clara back into my ken. Love seeking its reflection, its return, in nature down below, that undulant mirror. The wings folded, and I dropped.

Take the plunge? The question kept raising itself to me, that first afternoon in Battersea Park, but I didn't want to be precipitous, what with the recent proof I'd had that precipitation didn't please her. I could come just so close to her, not quite a hand's reach, and she'd slide away like a repelling magnet. So moved, she stepped a little closer to the chest-high pedestal where the wretched terrier went whirling on three legs, snapping at some parasite on its hindquarter.

"You can practically feel the fleas," I said. Clara had stooped a little, to read the inscription on the base, and she didn't seem to have heard me. The dog was done in big wet clumps of bronze, so that it looked mangy as well as flea-bitten. Clara straightened up and touched her forefinger, piebald with paint, against the swampy patina. Then she began to back around the statue in a circle opposite to the frozen movement of the dog. The hummock around the pedestal was slick and muddy, and when her shoes began to slip, she corrected her balance without noticing its loss. I saw the tendons of her ankle pull out tight from the worn elastic cuff.

"What I like about this dog," I said, "is it's completely worthless. The last dog in the universe, you know? Worst one, too."

Clara had stopped on the far side of the statue. She put her hands in the belly pocket of her sweat shirt and irradiated the bronze mongrel with her appraiser's stare. A cloud of her hair had fluffed forward over the corner of one eye, and after a moment she shook it back and stepped down toward me from the muddy hump.

"Do you sculpt too?" I said. "Or only paint?" That sort of idiot get-acquainted question I regretted the moment it parted from my jaws. I began to shift slowly along the northbound path, back toward the sluggish gray flow of the river.

Clara turned back and glanced at the dog from this greater distance, then fell into step with me. "It would be something to make an animal," she said. "A creature."

"No mean trick, that," I said. "Never take anything apart you can't put back together." And now she was staring at me, I felt, though I was facing forward. I had to turn my face toward her; it was as necessary as if I'd been seized by her hand.

"That's a way of looking at it," Clara said. The magnet had turned up its attractive side and was pulling me, drawing me in. My head flopped forward; there was a jar that made it wobble, and my eyes came open on their counterweights. The train had pulled into Notting Hill Gate, and I jacked myself out of my seat, reaching over my shoulder to rub at the crick in the base of my neck. That fellow with the fascinating spikes had roused himself enough to get off the train behind me, I drowsily observed. Bound for the Carnival, I suppose he was, though he didn't look especially festive.

O my Lord, how tired I was. . . . There was a steady flow of people streaming up the stairs from the tube, up Pembridge Road and on toward the Carnival; I fit myself into the stream and let it carry me along, north toward the lights and the roaring noise. Every child on the street had a bright steel whistle and they were all shrilling away to burst your eardrums, with never a break between one blast and the next. Behind the shrieking of the whistles, the sound systems and stages up ahead sounded as remote as distant thunder. Not especially appealing really, but I seemed to lack the energy to break the inertia that swept me along.

Perhaps I was disinclined to go back to the empty flat, if I thought about it. I'd had her attention for a while back there, and I should have taught myself a way of keeping it. Maybe I could still recover the recipe. If I knew what she saw in me I would show it to her again.

I let go. The movement of the mob took me quickly up the Portobello Road, almost as far as Lonsdale Road before the press became too tight for fluid movement to continue. I was jammed shoulder to shoulder with all the rest of them, and there was no longer any choice about where to go, though down the long slope before me I could see the close-packed heads moving in a sluggish wave formation, funneling down beneath the overpass, where a good many of the stages had been erected in the shelter. By then that constant skirling had overpowered my hearing so completely that I no longer knew for certain whether it was the whistles themselves I still heard or only the autonomous ringing of my ears. We were passing different sound systems as we shuffled by, but I couldn't hear anything more than the uneasy crisscross of different bass lines pounding past each other, though the amps were as big as barn doors.

The road took a dip and suddenly I could no longer see out down the slope. There was someone tall in front of me and all I could see was a damp spot between his shoulder blades, the dye seeming to bleed from his red shirt. Some eager beaver behind me kept mashing me forward so that over and over my nose brushed the rank wet spot. Something hard gouged into my kidney with every push, and that began to put me in an ill temper. There was a crash just to my left: someone had dropped a full pint glass. People were carrying brimming drinks out of the pubs on either side of the road and joining the throng with their glasses in hand, though some, it seemed, were too drunk to hang onto them. . . . It was getting a trifle difficult to breathe, I thought, and I cut for the sidewalk, apologizing if it

**79**

seemed appropriate, or putting in the old elbow if that seemed a better approach. After a brief struggle I reached a cul-de-sac between a fish-and-bread stand on the one hand and a sound system on the other.

Here there was an uninterrupted column of air streaming straight down from the overcast sky, drying the sweat that pooled in my crevices while I'd been stuck in the thick of the mob. The zip of my bag was undone, I noticed—either I'd forgotten to shut it properly before, or some pickpocket had just had a pass at it, in which case he hadn't found anything worth taking. My stinking gi was still there, and so was my bottle of aspirin, and that was all. I zipped the bag closed and went over my pockets: everything accounted for, including but not limited to Clara's freaking note. Which was all for the better, since it seemed unlikely that any helpful soul would turn up to retrieve it out of this stew, supposing I were to drop it for my lucky third time.

I flattened my palm against the wall of the amp and let the deep vibration run up my arm to my shoulder. With so many whistles wailing away I couldn't follow the least trace of the melody through the air, but I could feel the reggae back-beat in my muscle and bone. Music for the deaf. As I was savoring it in my viscera, I saw a fight break out near the center of the street. It was too crowded for me to make out the faces or the factions involved; all I saw was a sudden whirlpool in the crowd. Out of the vortex an empty pint rose to the fullest extent of a tattooed arm, crashed abruptly down and came up again, broken and bloody along the jags.

There was a moan from the crowd that I might have only imagined, considering that I couldn't really hear much of anything anymore, and then quite suddenly the bobbies appeared, a lot of them too, about fifteen or twenty. It puzzled me where they'd all come from so fast, because I hadn't noticed any at all on the street, but they were certainly getting on with the job. Inside of a minute they'd opened enough cracks in the crowd to lead someone away with his face running blood, and I thought perhaps they were dragging somebody else away in the opposite direction.

And then I decided I'd probably had enough entertainment for one evening. It had been vaguely in my mind to catch up with Terence at the Tooth and Claw, but it no longer seemed worth the effort and risk of getting there, and besides I was too tired. The Carnival would still be rocking and rolling tomorrow, and likely I'd be more in the mood after a good night's sleep, ho ho.

The bobbies were still cutting paths through the crowd as they dispersed, and I got behind a pair of them and let them break trail for me up to the next corner, where I could turn off. There were plenty of people on the side streets too, but not so compressed I couldn't move through them. At Powis Square there was a stage set up with a good reggae singer chanting and prancing in front of a four-piece band, and I paused to listen to the end of one number, but went on before the end of the next. My head had started to thump again. I fumbled the bottle out of my bag and swallowed a couple of aspirin dry; they stuck to the walls of my throat going down, and smeared a sour taste behind them.

My ears were still ringing when I came to my door, a beehive buzz that followed me inside. The tintinnabulation of the actual Carnival was muted once I'd locked up after myself, but the hum in my ears did not abate. It continued to plague me while I debriefed the machine. A couple of notifications from clients, and the hanger-upper had been quite active as well, but nobody I especially wanted to hear from. Nothing from Clara is what that meant, unless, perhaps, she *was* the hanger-upper.

Wishful thinking, that, undoubtedly, but still a call to Val might be worth a try at this time of the evening. I made myself a cup of tea and sat down beside the phone. But my luck hadn't turned for the better yet, because it was pinhead Richard who answered, on the third ring.

"Hallo?" Richard has a plummy public school accent, and he swallows back a portion of every word as it emerges, as though it were too absolutely precious for him to feel certain about letting it go forth. Two-year-olds feel much the same about their feces, so I'm told.

"Ah, Richard, it's Adrian, would Valerie be in?"

"Half a—oh. Sorry, I see she's just gone out. Shall I have her ring you back?"

"Good lad, Richard, you do that." I hung up and tapped my finger a time or two on the back of the receiver. For all his swank, pinhead Richard is nothing but a layabout. Valerie supports him, don't ask me why. He's quite good-looking (his head's nicely formed, despite its somewhat inadequate size), but not very nice to her. He has a number of dilettante interests and is always supposed to be on the verge of some major coup with one or another of these, but the fact of the matter is that he doesn't have anything to do at all but lollygag around and practice acting superior. So he would have had plenty of time, that morning, to help Clara shift all her bags and boxes. The thought of that was so distasteful I momentarily forgot that it was only a suspicion. I rang her studio then, but got no answer.

The pouch of chamomile had leached enough color into my mug, so I went to the kitchen and spooned the bag out on the edge of the sink. The tea was hot, and if I concentrated, it was soothing as well, but my head was still hurting quite considerably. I wondered if my brain was bleeding. Terence had a point, aspirin on concussion can definitely kill you. I didn't much think I had a concussion, but I wasn't a doctor, so what did I know? Even if so, it would be—    at the very least it would be—    —

I stopped myself from thinking that and went into the front room to uncover the snake. Something was wrong. The snake was knotted up behind his rock at one end of the cage, and the mouse was listlessly pawing over some chips of white gravel at the other. Wrong, the mouse was supposed to be inside the snake, at this point. It was discouraging. Just what I needed, a finicky snake. If the mouse was still there in the morning I'd probably have to start feeding *it*, and everything would get overly complicated. I dropped the cloth back over the tank and went to dial Val's number again.

Pinhead Richard rang on once more, just as I'd supposed he would, but this time I didn't make any answer to his first hallo, just sat quiet and listened closely. Beyond that high whine in my ears I could discern a distant sound of clashing crockery and, indistinctly, some woman's voice.

"Hallo?"

"Just put Val on, Richard, now be a good fellow. . . ."

"Harumph," said pinhead Richard. "Strother, I can't say I like your tone—"

Subsequent to which there was an interruption and a scraping sound.

"All *right*, then, I suppose we'll have no peace at all unless—" It was Valerie's voice, very cross.

"No need to be sour, Val," I said. "It's a perfectly innocent telephone call, I only meant to ask if you might be coming up to the Carnival tomorrow."

"Oh, you only meant to be hounding Clara," Val said. "That's what you're about, I know very well."

"Clara?" I said. "Well, since you mention it, I wouldn't mind a word with her, supposing she happens to be there."

There was an inexpressive silence.

"Sorry, Adrian," Val said. "It's no go."

"She's there," I said. "Look, let me talk to her—what's a little conversation among friends?"

"It's not me stopping you, understand," said Val, and delivered me another dose of silence. I pictured the mouthpiece of the phone crushed into her bony palm.

"She says you haven't got anything to say to her," Val said.

"What?" I said. "I don't get it. I mean, the usual line is supposed to be *she* doesn't have anything to say to *me*."

"That'll be your problem, I suppose," said Valerie. "Look, I don't much care for being a go-between, and it's getting rather late besides."

"Well, it's all been a little bit much is what—" and I cut myself off right there. Didn't like the sound of my voice; it was too petulant, altogether. "Sorry, Val, it's been a long day. I see you're in a difficult spot, I never meant to make it worse."

I hung up and rubbed my ear and looked at a blank spot on a shelf where some of Clara's books had been. After a minute I wasn't really thinking anymore. I went to the telly and switched it on and then to the tank, where I picked up the snake. He hung sleepily in an inverted U, then woke up a little and twirled himself around my arm. I sat down with him on the sofa, stroking a fingertip along the smooth-meshed scales. Snakes don't really give you such a lot, but then they don't ask for so much either. You don't have to feed them very often; you don't have to take them out for a walk. Their affectional needs are altogether manageable; a warmish body temperature suffices to send them into raptures. Also, of course, they're beautiful, though this particular snake of mine was definitely looking a little off-color, something dull and glazed about him I was having trouble accounting for.

There was a film on BBC-2 but after ten minutes I still wasn't interested. I got up and switched off the box and took the snake back to his tank.

"Eat, just go on and eat, why don't you?" I said to him. "Eat the mouse and make me happy." He slithered off my hand into the gravel.

I put my tea mug in the sink and went to hang my gi on the shower rail to air. I yawned. I washed my face, brushed my teeth, swallowed a handful of calcium pellets for the mild soporific effect. Yawned again. Sleepy, yes.

In the bedroom I shut the door of the empty closet, leave that trouble shut in there, don't have to think about that now. I unpacked my pockets onto the bureau, swung my clothes over the back of a chair. Off with the light, and so to bed. The drowsiness sustained itself even after I got horizontal, yes. The ringing of my ears had quietened and my head hurt considerably less. A dim filtrate of light seeped through the windows to spiral in the center of the room. The boom and crash of the Carnival was too far away to be disturbing. I closed my eyes and began to sink—I was going to do it! I was actually going to go to sleep.

After all, it's an easy, simple, and natural thing, just to go to sleep. I was breathing deeper and I could feel a vortical tug, pulling me deeper into the dark undertow. It was the world itself spinning under my bed, twirling into deeper darkness like a drill bit. And I revolving tipsily on top of it all, safe and warm and almost unconscious, while elsewhere at the very instant, murders and rapes continued to transpire at their usual frenetic rate, wars and institutional torture proceeded apace, people were sticking needles in their arms and legs as an anesthetic against all the rest, children were being tormented for the amusement of their elders, the fabric of the world itself was being dismembered and destroyed beyond any hope of repair, and *whywhywhy was I thinking about all that?*

My glands released a great frosty squelch of adrenaline, so that I began trembling under the sheets. All right. All right. I sat up and turned on the light. Here we go again, the hour of the freaking wolf. I was so exhausted my eyes wouldn't focus and everything in the room went swimming blearily around. And even as I told myself, *don't get angry, don't get upset*, I became progressively more enraged. Negatives aren't understood or even registered by the unconscious, and anyway it *was* infuriating, it *was* unfair, o god o god why won't you let me sleep?

Or I'll go crazy. . . . My musculature was drawing up tight as harp strings as my mind went ferreting about for stupid solutions. Some more aspirin, about a hundred more, that should take care of it. Or a leap from a tall building, the British Telecom tower, say, or slit wrists in a warm bathtub, or just a bullet in the squirrel cage of my brain. Each a surefire means of producing that blissful unconsciousness I so deeply desired . . . but inappropriate. Definitely inappropriate. There's one of the risks to this little syndrome. One loses one's sense of proportion.

Unbelievable as it may seem, I suddenly was aware of that cursed alarm clock ticking at me loudly from underneath the socks in my drawer. So I took it into the kitchen and set it on the floor. In the cabinet underneath the sink there was a biscuit box with some loose nails and screws and a couple of tools in it. I took out a hammer and smashed the clock to smithereens. And after I'd swept up the pieces and thrown them away, I began to feel a little calmer.

It seemed cooler now, and a few goose pimples were rising on my bare arms as I walked back into the bedroom. Clara's note was on top of the heap of my other pocket treasures on the bureau. It had gone grimy along the folds from riding around in my pocket all day, not to mention getting dropped in the street so frequently. I opened it and read it quickly through and then set it aside. Glancing around the walls of the room, I noticed that all the picture nails were empty now, except that as she'd said she'd left that drawing, the one I liked, stuck above my bureau with a pushpin. It was a drawing of me, in oil pastels. I was naked except for my feet stuck into a tangle of sheet, lying on my side. I'd actually been asleep when she'd done it, but in the picture my eyes were open. The colors were peculiar, nothing like the real colors of flesh, but the effect was interesting. In the background she'd sketched her own outline in faint gray lines, so she looked like a ghost, or an aura rising. An emanation. I'd send my emanation to find hers. But tomorrow. Once I had my rest.

I lowered my eyes and began pushing my change around with a forefinger, then stacking the coins in order of size. Once I was done I picked up the medallion Stuart had given me and let it hang from my thumb and forefinger, immobile at the full reach of its chain. I stared at it and began to think: a*round* and a*round* and a*round*. . . . Gradually, though I hadn't moved my hand a jot, the medal began to shift and rock. Then, slowly, it began to turn. My hand remained stock-still. I thought harder and the medallion began to turn more quickly, revolving so that the *oculis imaginationis* winked at me, off and on, with every speeding circuit.

Next, still with my mind alone, I slowed it down. Once it had stopped, I reversed its direction, now sending it in counterclockwise revolutions, wide sweeps of the chain. Finally I let it stop again, looked at it hanging still for a moment, then tossed it up and caught it so the medal and the chain gathered together in my palm.

Anyone who can do all that by concentration ought to be able to just go to sleep, don't you think? Though really it's a fairly simple trick. Most people can do it.

I opened my hand and looked inside. The *Deus in rebus* face had won the toss. Running back through Bruno, Pico della Mirandola, Ficino, Agrippa, Albertus Magnus, all the way to Hermes Trismegistus, and possibly beyond, is a traditional belief in the sympathetic and magical power of any object whatsoever. All secrets are hidden in the least detail, and had I fully known the secrets I could have used this round of palm-warmed gold to draw myself hand over hand up through the elements, the planetary and astral spheres, the ranks of cherubim and seraphim, all the way to the Divine itself. God immanent . . . *God in things*.

Or. . . .

I put down the medallion and picked up that peculiar gray cog I'd found inexplicably in my letter box that morning. Not so inexplicable after all. Now, hadn't I been stupid?

Long, a very long time ago it seemed, when Nicole was mostly living with Stuart a few blocks down the street from me, she and I had used this object for a calling card of sorts. A calling card in code, our secret. If one of us shot it under the other's door the other would know . . . that contact had been made, and that more was to be expected.

I twisted the bone ring on my finger. The cog felt tingly on my skin— it wasn't very long, I understood, since it had been touching hers. I put it down. Though I'd been looking for diversion, in a way, this was something more than I really required. Maybe Clara had picked a good time to disappear, and maybe not. I didn't know, but I was reasonably certain that Nicole had picked a bad time to turn up. She wasn't going to improve my psychological stability, not now, and maybe not at any future time.

Enough. I couldn't deal with it tonight, so I turned the light back off and escaped, as best I could, into the bed. With a studied effort, I slowed my breathing, slowed my heartbeat, reached down the long ganglia of my sympathetic nervous system to turn off the coffee I'd drunk with Stuart, turn up the calcium and the chamomile. Very relaxed and very calm I was, almost asleep, but not quite. This penultimate stage was as far as I'd been able to get for several days, but I could stay here for some time, and it was better than absolutely nothing.

To while away the necessary hours, I began to tell myself a story. There once was a shaikh, or perhaps a criminal of some sort, I can't remember which, who though guilty of innumerable sins, repented. He entered upon the way of faith and was received with open arms by the Lord of All the Universe. However, his faith wore away before too long, and once more he began wandering down the winding path of error. Yet, when he repented a second time, he found the Lord of the World still willing to receive him back. . . .

It was rather a repetitive story. Endless too, or at least I couldn't remember the end. I went on telling it over and over, lying awake and waiting for dawn.

# PART 2

## Ars Memoriae

ARS MEMORIÆ.

# ten

Then morning came, as come it must. It was gray, grim gray, in the cold bedroom, and the air had the feel of wet cement. I got up, with an audible pop and a palpable creak. The trick knee was feeling more than a little crunchy and I was generally stiff and sore from yesterday's workout. The usual smash of dizziness hammered down on my head when I stood straight, but I was getting used to that. I leaned against the wall and waited until the wave of it had shuddered on past me, then pushed myself erect again. How many days had it been since I'd really slept? . . . too fuzzy-headed now even to remember.

There were lots of new bruises, mostly on my arms and legs where they should have been, and I sat down again on the bed to admire them. Each had its sentimental link to some precious moment of practice the previous day, though of course I couldn't precisely remember them all. The purple bracelets around my wrists were owed to Mrs. Farr's neat snapping blocks, with perhaps a couple of Maurice's thrown in. The turquoise goose egg on the meaty part of my right foot was down to Maurice altogether, I was sure. The articulated movement of all those famous little bones in my foot made it squish damply when I stood back up and put my weight on it, and the pain was just vivid enough to bring me more alert.

There was also a large reddish patch, part bruise and part burn, along the right side of my rib cage . . . I couldn't quite identify that one. Someone must have tagged me when I wasn't paying attention, that much was apparent. I suppose I'd been too worked up to feel it at the time. The place where Terence had popped me on the head to send me on that brief whirling tour of the heavens was somewhat larger and softer than it had been, so it felt, and still quite sensitive to the touch. But my headache was entirely gone. That was a mercy. It occurred to me that since I was alive, awake, and evidently rational enough, the concussion theory might perhaps be discarded.

Though sometimes symptoms don't show for a couple of days. . . . I wasn't a doctor, what did I know? I lowered myself gingerly to the carpet and did stretching exercises until the soreness had abated and even the bruises seemed to flush with a grateful warmth. Then I got up, sagged into the wall for long enough to pay the dizziness its due respect, and went into the kitchen to put the coffee on. Thence to the bathroom and into the shower: washed my face, washed my hair, washed my arms and legs and middle. . . . The heat was pleasant on my lumps, and I stayed in till the temperature began to fail.

The little room was steaming when I finally got out. I lathered up my jaws by touch, picked up the razor and watched it hang for a second or so, to make sure my hand was steady enough so I could shave without slashing myself to mincemeat. I wiped down the mirror with the edge of my hand and cut the first couple of swathes through the bluish foam, but when I met my reflection's eyes in the glass, I began to bawl like an angry baby. And though there was absolutely no reason for it, I couldn't seem to stop. I dropped the razor, clamped the edges of the sink in my hands, and sobbed on, watching myself in the mirror the while. Try watching yourself cry sometime, if you're in need of a cure for vanity. It was an ugly and ridiculous sight, and though I couldn't help but laugh, the laughter wouldn't stop the weeping. Quite the reverse; each burst of laughter brought harder sobs again, in the same vicious circle whereby a persistent sneeze will keep a nosebleed going. I hadn't known I had so many tears left in me; they ran till they'd washed the shaving cream off my face. But finally it all seemed to dry up, and I sat down on the side of the tub to rest. My head was thumping, my sinus ached, and my mouth was dry and rough as shark skin.

The big scab between my knuckles, which I'd overlooked while enumerating my other injuries, had softened slightly in the shower and turned yellow around the edges. I picked at it a second, with a childish fascination, then made myself stop. The tap to the sink was still running full go; I hauled myself up, splashed my face with cold water, then shut it off. This time I managed to meet my own stare in the mirror without any more hysterics. My eyes had gone bloodshot but apart from that there was little enough that showed. The lump Terence had left me with was mostly hidden under my hair—turning lovely colors in there, no doubt. But all I could see of it was one red tendril, feeling its way toward my eye socket, like a vine.

I hung my towel on the rail, went to the bedroom, and got dressed. It smelled of coffee all through the flat and the scent made me feel somewhat livelier, though the coffee went sour on my stomach when I actually began drinking it. Half a cup and the bile was rising. I needed to eat, but had no hunger. Something jabbed sharply into the pad of my left foot as I stepped to put my cup in the sink. When I looked down to examine it I found a small black shred of the smashed alarm clock's casing.

I'd fixed its little red wagon, hadn't I? There were a lot of crescent-shaped pocks in the lino, from glancing blows of the hammer. I must have been more enthused than I'd realized. Now I could just guess what time it was too, by the sun, suppose, if there was any sun.

I flicked the shard into the trash and went to the front room to open a window and air out the place, then sat down on the sofa with my back to the draft. Now what did I have to do today, and when did I have to do it? There was another clock down in the crooked room, but I felt too lethargic to go and examine it. Up bright and early as I was, I should have plenty of time for everything. A little aureole of sunshine opened on the carpet between my bare feet, hardly bigger than a shilling, with a prismatic bluish tinge around its edges. As I watched, it began to dilate, and all at once the room was full of light. When I turned to glance out the window I saw the sun had come out altogether over the back garden, and there was a little goldfinch singing in the gorse bush there.

I went and put on my shoes, collected my keys, and went out onto the front steps. Nothing in the letter box, it was way too early for the post to have come. I went round the side of the house, where there was a waist-high iron gate with one rail missing and another bent, letting into an alley. The gate opened and shut with a rusty scrape, and twenty paces along the wall brought me into the garden.

There was the sunshine, once again, pouring down into the small square space blinded off by the rear walls of four houses. Ivy climbed the wall of the house opposite my own. There were some shrubs, a small bank of flowers, a fishless fish pool about three feet across, and a silver gazing globe set on a cement pedestal that might formerly have supported a birdbath— in short, there was everything necessary for happiness except an iron lawn dog, or a fawn perhaps. Also there was a small curved concrete bench, which I sat down on, facing the gorse bush and my own half-open window.

The sun was warm on the back of my neck, and a soft warm breeze fanned the fine hairs there. With a forefinger I tried my bruised temple again; the touch sent a sparkle straight into my brain—it wasn't at all

**93**

necessary to think of it as pain. I traced that twining tendril of it into the raccoon ring around my eye, letting my finger hang on the socket's lower ridge of bone. Only a flesh wound. My reflection was only a glittering shadow on the surface of my own bright windowpane. The goldfinch flew up from the gorse bush, and a brown wren popped down immediately onto the same branch, which sprang lightly up and down from this trivial exchange of weight. That was what Fearless Fosdick used to say in the Sunday funnies. Only a flesh wound, and he'd undo his coat to prove it and there would be a bird flying through a great dry hole in the center of him, on into the wide blue sky. I turned my head to see the sunlight warped in rippling rings on the glazed skin of the gazing globe. Follow the birdy, on up, on through . . . with a blush of self-satisfaction I understood that I was dreaming, dreaming, dreaming, though my eyes were wide open and I was awake. One doesn't absolutely have to sleep, only the sleep of reason will suffice. And it was very very nice, very soothing, this waking dream of mine, except for some joker who kept zapping me with a joy buzzer, right in the center of my palm. *Zzzzzt! Zzzzzzzzt!* Oh stop it, I said, elbowing him away, because I only wanted to keep following that bird, on up and out among the puffy white clouds, wherever it was going, let my body tilt a little further to one side, perhaps tumble over altogether to meet the damp grass with a soggy thump? But, *zzzzzt! Zzzzzzzzzt!* he wouldn't stop. I lifted my eyes heavily and realized that it wasn't a sensation at all really, but a sound, which was coming to me distantly from between the sash and sill of my own window; the doorbell. *Bzzzzzzzt!*

Oh Christ, Miss Peavey. The early bird on the trail of the elusive arffing worm. . . . I could picture her well enough, wedged into my entryway, trying her best to mingle her molecules with the molecules of the wall and door, and pumping that buzzer for all she was worth. And if I didn't get to her quickly she was going to have a heart attack right on my doorstep and make a terrible impression on the neighbors. I pushed myself up from the bench and brushed myself off, slapped myself in the face a couple of times, and prized each of my eyes open a bit wider with my thumb and forefinger. And managed to be already in the middle of a speech as I came hustling back around to the front steps.

"Oh my dear, Miss Peavey, what *will* you think of me, popping in, popping out—but it's a fine day isn't it? Isn't it lovely? I'd just wandered out to the back garden for a moment, I *do* hope you'll forgive me but I must have lost track of the time—" *no question there either, it had to have been about two hours I'd been woolgathering.* I unlocked the door and flung it open.

Miss Peavey staggered in, murmuring conventional *politesses.* "Oh, quite all right. Oh, please don't trouble. . . ." Meanwhile one of her hands was pressing down on her paste-pearl choker, trying to control that frog-belly flop in her throat: *Flop! flop! flop!* Rather a beautiful hand as well, I now perceived for the first time, slim and long-fingered—a Flemish painter might have enjoyed it.

"Well, perhaps you'd take a cup of tea?" I said. Because the snake was tucked away out of sight this morning, and I thought we might do better if she had a moment to combobulate herself on her own terms.

"Oh, *yes,* please . . . if there's time." I'd swear I thought I saw her almost smile; you would have thought I'd offered her morphine.

"Oh, nothing but."

I found her a seat in the front room, went into the kitchen and boiled up, using the time to shoot some more coffee into my own system. She took her tea with milk, ugh, and did away with it quickly too, though in neat, mannerly, ladylike sips. And appeared much the better for it. There was only one pearl barely pulsing when she set aside her cup: *tick. tick. tick.*

"Shall we?" I said.

She nodded, and stood up. I escorted her down to the crooked room and got her settled in the usual chair. When I took hold of the back of it and swung it round to face that queer corner, it seemed to me that she was nicely settled indeed, her limbs already going a little rubbery. Maybe the old cuppatea routine had truly been worth the bother. Yesterday morning I'd laid on the usual posthypnotic suggestions about it all coming easier and faster the next time round, but then those don't always work.

"All right," I said. Her eyes already looked heavily lidded, once I'd gone cat-foot back to my own seat and turned to her again. "All right, then, never mind those pushpins. Just look at the bulletin board now, Miss Peavey, and you'll find you can easily imagine that the pushpins are *gone,* nothing there but the blank white canvas of the bulletin board, empty, white, bare. . . ."

She sighed and sank a little deeper into the padding of the chair. Eyes three-quarters shut and going out of focus. Looked like she was better at this than I'd thought. I opened the drawer and set the tape rolling, then messed about with the dimmer switches till the room was almost dead-dark except for my pinpoint reading and note-taking light. Miss Peavey let out another somnolent sigh. I thumbed open the cover of *The Conference of the Birds*. Perhaps I'd read her the story of the shaikh, supposing I could find it, ha.

"Now as your eyes close, as your arms and legs become heavy and soft and warm and relaxed, as the warm sensation in the center of your body begins to spread all the way through and through you . . . you find it quite easy to continue picturing that blank . . . white . . . canvas. . . . Close your eyes, close your eyes *now*, and you see in your mind's eye that blank . . . white . . . canvas. . . ."

Done. Her head took a long slow roll toward me, cheek flattening against the brown leather. I let the cover of the book slide shut, didn't think I'd be needing it now. No, you're going to make the trip almost on your own, and I'll just be along to see you right, my dear little agoraphobe. . . .

"Now in the very center of this blank . . . white . . . canvas, you can see a point of light, only the size of a pinprick but it's very bright and white and pure, bright and clean as the light of the sun. And as you watch this point of light, Eleanor, you see it begin to swell and grow, till it's . . . oh, the size of a fingertip, and actually this point of light is the most beautiful thing you've seen in quite some time, Eleanor, so that only looking at it makes you feel happy and calm."

My own eyes had drifted shut at this point, and my finger was beating silently on the desk blotter with an increasingly leaden weight. This was a nice little induction if I did say so myself—I liked it. Really, I was so pleased with myself I was scarcely aware of what I was saying anymore.

"And as that point of light gets larger and larger, Eleanor, you see that it's ringed with other colors, wonderful golds and reds and blues—white has all the other colors hidden in it, Eleanor, did anyone ever tell you that? All the colors of the rainbow, and it's amazingly beautiful, this circle of light, it looks to you like a jewel. And the circle is getting wide and wider until it's all that you can see, it doesn't have a border anymore, but it's become a door, a tunnel, large enough for you to go right through, into a sparkling orb of warmth and light and ease. . . ."

I paused to force one of my eyes slightly open. She looked good; I let the eyelid slip back shut.

"You're passing into that orb now. . . . Or . . . perhaps it's going into you, you're simply taking it into yourself, all that wonderful warmth and glorious light. Just let it happen, it's only a flesh wound—" *waitaminute, where did that come from?* "—it won't hurt you, really, it's very nice, nice and warm and comforting. . . ."

There was a whimpering sound like a small child crying, and I snapped my eyes open and sat up straight. Something very interesting was going on over there with Miss Peavey, only I wasn't quite sure what. Her head was twisting back and forth in the dim light, eyes wrinkled so tightly shut a couple of tears squeezed out from underneath the lashes. It was her doing the whimpering right enough, and at the same time her lips were moving, shaping mumbled words I couldn't quite distinguish, though maybe it was some sort of prayer?

I sat quiet and kept watching her, saying nothing for the moment. I didn't know just where she was so I had little idea what I ought to say. Possibly she was in the Telecom tower, though I certainly hadn't meant to send her there as yet. It was too early in the game to start desensitizing; still, maybe she was desensitizing herself. Or maybe she was just making it all worse. As I watched, her arms and legs began to lift a little and then fall, tensing and relaxing in a convulsive movement. A wave or ripple came over her face: one, two, three repetitions, rolling her features around like a fluid. Then it stopped and she hitched herself up in her chair and sat completely still, almost rigid. Her face had an irritable pinched expression, taut around the nose and mouth, and rather pale, as if with anger. One of her shoes had dragged off her foot in her mild struggle, but she didn't seem to be aware of that. I watched a tear dry on her cheek as if a sudden blast of heat had been applied to it.

"Well now," I said. "Well. There. There we are. Just—if you can hear me, just raise the index finger of your left hand."

There was a stiff little pause and then the finger came up slowly. Its tip hooked over and went questing about like the head of a dancing cobra.

"Right," I said. "Now let me ask you, where are you now and what are you doing?"

"Doing sweet Fanny Adams in the hypnotist's chair," she said, twisting up a corner of her lip as she spoke. All of a sudden her voice was harsh as a crow's. "Bloody waste of time if you ask me."

"Oh," I said, a little puzzled. "Well, in that case, perhaps we'd just better—" But she broke in on me. Fair enough, I wasn't really saying anything much.

"Just like her, the silly bitch," she said very sourly. "Dragging me up one side of the road and down the other, doctors, faith healers, now *trick cyclists*. And what's the point, I'd like to know, what's the bloody point? She doesn't even know herself what her trouble is. . . ."

She made a face and a dismissive motion with one hand. It was odd how completely her voice had changed; with the posh pretended accent dropped, she sounded more like the Midlands, I'd guess, though I was far from being an expert. I wasn't quite sure what was happening, no, but it seemed clear we'd peeled a couple of layers off the onion.

"I see," I said, though I hadn't seen much. "Tell me, who's this 'she' you're speaking of?"

"Your precious Miss Peavey," she said, in a cleverly unkind parody of Miss P's more usual upmarket tone. "Who else d'you suppose?"

Interesting, quite. "Oh," I said, "but I thought *you* were Miss Peavey."

She snorted at me. "That simpering little milksop, not bloody likely. I wouldn't be her for a thousand pounds—I'm Nell."

This took me somewhat aback, I confess. "Nell it is, then," I said. "Ah. So pleased to meet you. I'm happy you were able to . . . come out."

"Hah," said Nell, with another snort. "If you could see the silly look on your clock, I tell you—"

"Oh, I can imagine," I said. I had too much else on my mind just then to remind her that her own eyes were shut.

# eleven

It was all rather agitating, really, and after she'd gone I was too jumpy to sit still. There was no one else coming in all morning, which might have given me something to do with myself. Instead I went springing up and down the stairs to and from the crooked room a few times, with no particular mission, and then raced round all the rooms of the flat, making the bed, cleaning the coffeepot and the tea egg, one thing and another. Then, passing through the bathroom, I caught sight of myself in the mirror and comprehended with a certain dismay that I'd never finished shaving earlier. . . .

Oh my, what must Miss Peavey think of me now? It was a bit disconcerting. A good twenty-four-hour stubble with a couple of red rakes through it on one side and that was the extent of my grooming. Hardly anything to do but grin at it. Nell, now, this Nell person might have gone for the look, or anyway thought it a good joke. But it had been Miss Peavey who had come and also Miss Peavey who had left, I was reasonably certain of that from the shivering cringing scurry she'd made into the cab I called for her. Nell, on the other hand, I could picture Nell going down the street in rather a different fashion: chin up, chest out, bold as brass with a loud *clackclack* of her hard high heels on the pavement.

But Miss P had made yet another appointment for the following morning, just the same, so I didn't suppose I'd cocked it up so badly as all that. Once again I lathered up and tested my grasp on the razor. The whole procedure went off without any particular mishap until I started on the left side of my mustache, at which point I accidentally nicked off a cuff-button's worth of the curve of my left nostril. It probably sounds a little unlikely but I promise you it could happen to anyone; it's happened to me before, which proves the point. Maybe I was excited or distracted or just generally shaky. It wasn't so much of a cut as all that, small, shallow, only a flesh wound, he-he-heh, but oh, how a cut nose will bleed.

I couldn't figure out a way to stop it. Nothing worked. I tried tissue paper, then cold water, more tissue, more cold water, both at once, no good. Cotton balls, of which Clara had forgotten a few, were useless. In a final desperation I patted a teaspoon of white flour onto it, hoping to form some sort of scab, but only got blood pudding for my trouble. After about twenty minutes spent in such futile attempts, I went out in a somewhat savage mood, a hand clamped over the ridiculous wound and a banner of blood-soaked paper towels flagging back over my shoulder. At a druggist's near the tube station I bought a vial of styptic powder, and in my urgency applied a handful to the critical spot while the cashier was still counting out my change. It hurt like cautery, like a red-hot poker pressed to my proboscis, and it was worth it too, for the bleeding stopped cold, on the instant. I bought a couple of papers without looking at them, and went out, frowning direly at whoever gave me a strange look.

But then there were enough other odd-looking folk yawing about on the street to take the heat off me, stragglers and strays from the Carnival who'd never made it home. Every block I'd come across another lost soul lurching through a circular realm all of his or her own, blind-drunk, shell-shocked, who knows what? The blast of sound alone, it occurred to me, might account for the queer unbalanced way they walked, as a broken eardrum might very well take the adjacent gyroscope out with it. But for the moment the Carnival itself seemed quiet. All I could hear in its direction was an occasional belch of feedback, or sometimes a tentative roll on a steel drum, beginning and interrupting itself abruptly. It was early yet, and the weather was uncertain for a festival: gray wet woolly clouds had rolled over the sun I'd been basking in so dreamily earlier that morning.

I went back into the flat and tossed the papers on the kitchen table, then on to the bathroom mirror for another inspection. Styptic crystals ringed my upper lip and nostril, a bloodstained snowflake. It still stung somewhat but I was afraid to wash it clean in case the bleeding began all over. I returned to the kitchen, started a soft-boiled egg, sat down at the table, and flipped one of the tabs face up. The whole upper two-thirds of the front page was inked with the blurry visage of one Pini Mukhtar. Who, as a line or two of copy soon informed me, had come to an untimely end at the age of six, her body found in the area north of King's Cross, the usual spot, found to have been &ced and &ced and &ced and &ced until the last breath of life had departed from it forever.

I ran my finger down the ruffled edge of the sheet, then slipped it under and turned the page. Opposite the tit picture on Page Three, the story strobed on for a column or two. The burgeoning Mukhtar family, late of Pakistan, kept a little electronics shop in Euston Road, where they lived behind the store in the usual way. That meant that little Pini had been nailed more or less in her own neighborhood, which was a departure from the customary MO of this particular child killer. Who, normally speaking, only picked off a kid every month or three weeks. Now it was two in two days. Police spokespersons, presented with the question as to why the monster's appetite might suddenly have increased, sought to camouflage their utter confusion and helplessness behind the suggestion that a copycat killer might have entered the scene. . . .

My three-minute egg was hard-boiled by the time I noticed the sound of it clicking against the walls of the pan, which was nearly dry, for that matter. I made myself eat it, though I didn't want it, and put the plate down in the sink. Then I went to check on the snake. He didn't have any appetite himself, or any self-discipline either. That's to say, the mouse was still there, though no longer looking especially healthy. His little red eyes had gone rheumy and he moved with the paralytic shuffle of an ancient wino.

What a mess. . . . I lifted the snake out and settled him on my shoulder, then went and found some shredded wheat and put it in a saucer with a little milk and put it on the floor of the tank. Feeding the mouse now, oh boy, the food chain was getting much more complicated than I ever meant it to. Though I'd be lucky, in a way, if a couple days' starvation was all that was the matter with this mouse.

I sat down at the table again and began flipping through the paper. Some sort of nebulous progress was alleged to have been made with U.S./ U.S.S.R. disarmament. Fatima Whitbread had set a new women's record for the javelin throw. In Zambia, a British woman had died of rabies. The courts had failed in an attempt to tangle up Walter Karnock in illegal Soho gambling. There was a photo of his lot leaving the Old Bailey, and I spent a minute looking at the fat fish face on him. I saw him occasionally in the flesh, since I did my night work on his manor. He'd come into the Empress sometimes with a few of his molls and minders, though none of them ever paid much attention to the show. Some said he owned the club himself, through cat's-paws. They said he was a funny fellow—a queer sense of fun he was said to have. Illegal gambling was the least of what he was into, to be sure. Probably they'd be after him for tax evasion next. It would take some such bureaucratic snare to tangle him. As for the rumored rest of it, he surely had his reputation, but witnesses were hard to find and hold.

I turned the page. The snake was restless, twining uncomfortably around my neck, so I unsnarled him and put him down on the table. He slithered through a set of figure eights and froze. Nobody and nothing can be quite so still as a snake when a snake feels like being still. I couldn't make out what was the matter with him, if anything was. He looked a little dull, a little morose—perhaps it was nothing but ennui.

Gas from a volcanic lake had killed 694 out of 700 denizens of the town of Nyos, Cameroon. A man, woman, and eight-month-old child in a home-armored truck had successfully crashed through a checkpoint out of East Berlin. Back in London, a raid on Bentley's had produced a handful of drug arrests, and a pediatrician at St. George's Hospital had been had up for distributing child pornography.

A gang of lawyers was drafting speculative legislation for the government of outer space. Karpov and Kasparov drew another game. . . . At the center of the paper there were a few more snaps of Heather Jolley, but she'd been upstaged by today's nice *new* murder. Poor lass, she hadn't been famous very long. Still, the tab hadn't bothered with a scrapbook spread on Pini Mukhtar, she and her people being only wogs after all. Also Pini was, or appeared to have been, rather a plain little thing, not nearly so winsome, blond, and photogenic as the late Heather J, whom the camera loved.

The phone rang as I was contemplating that. It was Stuart, and I fixed up to meet him at the afternoon opening of the Tooth and Claw, and told him how to get there. When I came back to the kitchen the snake had disappeared.

And what the hell did I expect? It was only the fault of the sleeplessness I'd ever left him unattended. Bad news. Disappearing snakes are gone for good more often than not, though the only other time I'd misplaced him he'd turned up again after two or three days. What worried me most was that Clara wouldn't like it. She got along with the snake well enough but detested the thought of his being at large, and supposing I were able to bring her back, this situation would be more than enough to send her flying off again.

But luck was running with me, on this one issue at least, and I found him in forty-five minutes or so. First you look in the warmest places, and I discovered him wedged in the crack between the stove's back and the wall, pressing against the faint radiance the pilot light in the oven transmitted through the metal. It was a tight cranny, and I had to straighten a coat hanger to hook him out of it, which made him very irritable. I put him back in the tank at once, hoping he'd be mad enough to feel like killing something.

So much for that. What do I really need a snake for anyway? But as a matter of fact there is a reason. I keep a snake in my flat in honor and acknowledgment of the snake in *me*. From the back brain all down the sinuous twist of the spinal column to the rattle of your coccyx—that's the snake in everyone, as Jung once cleverly observed. And sometimes it takes control of all the rest of your body too. You want to be aware of the possibility—as much as possible, that is.

Which brought me straight back to another one of those nagging subjects I had more or less been trying to avoid, namely Miss Peavey, Nell, and all her other potential or putative personalities and imaginary friends. Well, that was shaping up into a much more complicated situation than I'm normally supposed to try to handle on my own. It was meant to be the provenance of doctors with degrees, not freelance mavericks like me. I was allowing myself to be a deconditioner, period. Deep problems I referred elsewhere, as my sense of duty bound me. I'd never have been seeing her at all if she hadn't come to me with what she indicated was little more than a cosmetic difficulty. . . .

Okay, she came here for a haircut, not heart surgery—I should be sending her to a real shrink with a real sheepskin. But. . . . But anywhere I could think to send her they'd only tell her she was a schizophrenic, which would be dead wrong. They'd only bomb her with Thorazine or something, until she just shut up. I'd seen it happen. Besides, she was interesting, yes she was.

Arf all the arfing doctors anyway. The trouble with doctors is that they're scientists. The trouble with Freud is that he wouldn't or couldn't listen to Janet, and he stopped listening to Breuer way too soon. He never knew what they were onto, anymore than that nit-picking logician Mersenne was capable of comprehending what Robert Fludd was really all about. And really, if it hadn't been for Descartes, what happened to Giordano Bruno maybe wouldn't—

Uh oh, off the track. But be careful how you trust the scientists. Look what happened when they decided to treat matter as if it were inanimate and vivisect it down to its utmost particles—matter lost its temper and started burning down the house. You'd think after all that it would have occurred to the white-coat crowd that the situation might be rather similar with the mind.

Enough of the scientists. Bring back the magicians. I went down to the crooked room and rewound the tape, then sat for a moment tapping my finger on the dung-brown plastic of the recorder's case. In the Ur period of psychoanalysis, both Janet and Breuer relied on hypnosis very heavily, as is perfectly well known. Freud did too in the beginning but then he stopped, the muttonhead. Why did he? It bothered him, supposedly, that he couldn't hypnotize all his patients. Perhaps he just wasn't much of a hypnotist (though he went on using a variety of hypnotic induction, calling it by another name or by no name at all, for all the rest of his career). Still, he remained uncomfortable even with his successes with the method.

Why? In spite of his ostensibly Socratic approach to therapy, Freud was an intellectual totalitarian, a little Hitler of the mind, and since all hypnosis is ultimately self-hypnosis, he would quite naturally have resented the autonomy on the part of the patient it implied. The notion of individual freedom would have fouled up his *theory*, would have overset his largely successful attempt to re-envision the psyche on the model of the steam engine or hydraulic pump—to absolutely reduce the mind to a machine.

So he forgot the whole idea (reality, I mean) of hypnosis, and went on his merrily destructive way, prattling of the unconscious, defense mechanisms, repression, and the like. Terrific, we *know* traumatic memories are forgotten, you bearded ape, but the real question is Why?

Or maybe the question should be How? The art of memory is as old as Rome, but the art of forgetting is primitive. The art of forgetting is so ancient that it itself has virtually been forgotten, but people have been hypnotizing themselves for thousands of years before the process had a name. And a special capability of hypnosis is to make things seem to disappear, especially mental things, like memories. A flourish or two of the amnestic wand, and it's all gone, gone as if by magic. . . .

But not really *gone*, only forgotten. If self-hypnotic amnesia is the procedure for repression, it stands to reason that whatever it is has to still be in there somewhere. Even muttonhead Freud could understand that much. I found some headphones in a drawer, plugged them in, and turned on the tape.

Yes, it was a charming little induction, had me yawning and gaping all over again as I listened to it reel by. Then the sudden weird shift where Miss Peavey began to twitch and mutter in that peculiar childish tone. I still couldn't make any sense of what she was saying, though it was a bit clearer on the tape than it had been in actuality, owing to the high quality of the supercardioid shotgun microphone trained on her lips from the goose-neck boom above the chair. The first bit of it was muddied by my own voice going on with the induction, but then I stopped and she went on. Something like *naident, naidentirtz?* Sounded like no language I'd ever heard before. Probably it was only nonsense syllables.

Next came Nell, my first few exchanges with her.

NELL: If you could see the silly look on your clock, I tell you—

ME: Oh, I can imagine—

NELL: Think you're clever I suppose?

ME: You don't have a very high opinion of therapists, I gather?

NELL: What's the good of them? They never find out anything, they'll never know the story.

ME: You said before that Miss Peavey, Eleanor that is, doesn't really understand the cause of her trouble?

NELL: She doesn't care for your using her Christian name, you know— thinks you're making a bit too free.

ME: Hard luck on her, eh?

NELL: Yes, that's right.

ME: So, she doesn't know what her problem is really . . .

NELL: Hasn't a clue, poor piglet.

ME: . . . but I suppose you do?

NELL: Course. I sussed it out straightaway from the beginning.

ME: And what would be her trouble, then?

NELL: You'd like to know that, wouldn't you? I'll tell you one thing, heights are the least of it.

ME: I see. So what's she really afraid of?

NELL [with a delicious emphasis]: *Men.*

ME: Whatever for? Trouble with the boyfriends?

NELL: Boyfriend, hah, *she's* never had one. She doesn't know the first thing about it.

ME: She hasn't had much experience, I suppose.

NELL: Nothing.

ME: You, on the other hand, I suppose you've had rather a lot.

NELL: That's for me to know and you to find out.

ME: But I wonder what she would be so afraid of? Maybe something happened once? Perhaps when you were very young?

NELL: Well, p'raps there was something, when we were small, er, ah . . . when she was—

ME: That was before you even existed, *wasn't it?*

NELL: You shut your bloody hole, you—

ME: Does Eleanor know you exist at all?

NELL: She did but now she's forgotten about me. I was her best friend too. She never talks to me anymore.

ME: She isn't very happy, you know. Don't you ever feel a little sorry for her?

NELL: Why should I? She's only herself to blame if she's unhappy. Little silly . . .

ME: Why? What did she ever do to suffer for?

NELL: It's not what she did, it's what she didn't. She's weak. Namby-pamby. Helpless as a noodle.

ME: Doesn't sound as if you much care for her.

NELL: Righto, clever-clock.

ME: Hmmm . . . well, that should about do it for today. You can go now, Nell, I'd like to speak to Eleanor again.

NELL: Would you indeed? We'll see about that.

ME: Never you worry, we'll talk again. But it's time to let Eleanor have the body back.

NELL: Think you can give me the brush so easy, d'you?

ME: Have it your own way. But it's nearly time for you *all* to be going, and I doubt you'd be caught dead in her clothes, now would you?

A bit of a gamble, that, but it worked. Nell buggered off back into cloud-cuckooland, and once Miss Peavey had reoccupied her brain I spent the rest of the hour laying down calmness and relaxation (not that it seemed to help much at all once she woke up and hit the street). So there wasn't much of interest on the rest of the tape. I turned it off, then pressed Rewind.

I didn't know so much about multiples other than what I'd read in books, but the catch was I didn't know anyone else who did, and there was no use sending her to a regular psychiatric hospital. She'd come out an overmedicated zombie, once they twigged that she heard voices, or else she'd never come out at all.

The trick with multiples is to meet a personality that likes the patient well enough to cooperate with the (pardon the expression) doctor, but it didn't much look like that was going to be Nell. However, I thought there was somebody else in there too, a ghost of another identity that had made its veiled appearance just before Nell took over. I hit the Play button on the machine.

ME: Just let it happen, it's only a flesh wound. . . .

?: . . . naidint . . .

ME: . . . it won't hurt you, really, it's nice . . .

?: . . . naidint, naidintirtz. . . .

Not too helpful. She'd regressed, I'd bet my hat on that much, she'd regressed spontaneously to a very young age indeed. But if it was a pre-language age, that wasn't going to help me any. The thing was, it did sound like words, that gobbledygook, only not any words I ever knew. . . .

And then the light dawned rather suddenly. What if it was a different *accent*, apart from the other two she used? After all, this was a country where class, indeed opportunity itself, was so tightly lashed to one's manner of speaking that some people practiced with records and tapes to sound as if they'd been born in the Home Counties and then gone to a public school.

I replayed the passage and there it was, a strong *Scots* accent, slurred in the faltering small baby voice:

*Nay, dain't. Nay dain't, i'hurts. . . .*

I stopped the tape and pulled off my headphones, feeling as old and sick with weariness as the devil himself. These people and their nasty little secrets; it's enough to turn your heart against the whole of the human race.

# twelve

It had begun to seem rather close in the room, so I decided to go out. I left without a destination, but after I'd gone a little way I remembered that I ought to be picking up my tux at the cleaners; I'd be needing it for the next night, and I couldn't remember whether or not the shop was normally closed on Sundays. None of this occurred to me until I was halfway up the block, however, so I had to go back to the flat to get the ticket.

Must look my poor best of a Sunday evening. You never knew who might be watching, it might even be Karnock, the Duke himself, with a party of his West End grandees, if not the usual East End rogues. Then again, Karnock's parties tended to take the spotlight off the show. You might say they were the show. That certain dash he liked to cut—he learned it from American gangster films, I'm told. But unpredictability was supposed to be his main attraction. That was the trait that made him so frightening, back when he engaged in frightening for pay.

A matter of mere academic interest. No tickee, no washee—there was the subject for my concentration. At last I found the bastardly ticket, pinned down under one of the toaster's rubber feet. I snatched it up and went back out. The Carnival had come back to life by this time. There was a gradually thickening stream of fresh-faced, freshly festive people, coursing north on Portobello Road, and I fell in among them. No reason not to. It was in the rough direction of my cleaners anyway. And I thought I might just as well see what the Carnival looked like in the daylight.

But twilight might have been a better way of putting it. It was still heavily overcast and looked as likely to rain as not, though I wouldn't have ventured a definite prediction. There was turbulence above and if I looked up could see the gray clouds tearing and re-forming before a distant stark-white sky. I'd come out with no umbrella too. The pedestrian traffic was heavy enough, but not so clotted as it had been the night before. I had room enough to turn round, though not enough to swing a cat. Ahead, over a hump in the pavement where the road took a swing downhill again, I could already hear the interminable squealing of the whistles, and all the different sound systems grumbling uncertainly like thunder.

When I had come to the crest of the road I had a brief vista down the slope, and I saw that it was packed down there, sardine-tight from wall to wall of the buildings either side of the street, all the way down to the overpasses, if not even further. But by the time I'd recognized the difficulty it was too late to escape. There seemed to be a kind of domino effect, like what happens on the periphery of a high-speed car crash, taking place among the people who were now crushing up so tightly behind me. Some kind of particular commotion was going on back there and I screwed my head further around for a better look. Another one of those Statue of Liberty hairdos was bobbing around in the midst of some altercation, but it died down before I could make out what exactly it had been. Meanwhile, a fault line in the crowd ahead had opened and was carrying me further away.

So I relaxed and went with the flow, or squeeze might have been the more accurate term: I felt like a single particle of a lot of toothpaste being slowly rolled toward the top of the tube. As before I was surrounded by tall people so there was little I could see in either direction. I began working my way toward the east side of the street, hoping for an outlet. By the time the road had leveled off again, the whistles had already sliced the high end off my hearing. Really it was almost painful. I tore up a piece of paper towel I still had in my pocket from earlier in the morning and made two little wads to stick into my ears.

There was a police barricade across the mouth of Colville Road, but I still thought I might get out that way. When I came up to the first sawhorse I saw that the whole next block was full of bobbies' helmets, a hundred or more of them I thought, wedged tight together as cloves in a pomander. Then I recalled a squib I'd read in the paper yesterday—how they weren't planning to put any police visibly on the street this year. Because last year there'd been a wee touch of rioting, and there was talk that the sight of all the bobbies might have done something to provoke it. So here was your more *tactful* police presence, mashed down into the one cordoned block like a compressed spring.

That's where they'd materialized from so quickly, I realized as the mob swept me by, to break up that row I'd seen the night before. But once I'd drifted on down past the intersection, it seemed easy enough to forget they were there. Everything seemed peaceable enough at the moment, though the press of the crowd around me was beginning to make me feel a trifle tense. But past Westbourne Park Road the crowd bifurcated and spread out below the overpasses. I could move reasonably freely once again.

There were a lot of food and drink stands set up against the concrete pylons, and on an impulse I went to one of these and bought a can of Tennent's Super. It was a popular potation among the West Indians . . . perhaps I thought it would help me fit in. Tennent's is the malted equivalent of fortified wine, and on the first swallow I could plainly detect the extra boost of raw alcohol lurking behind the thick beery flavor. The label "Super" is not a joke, or wasn't to me in my present condition. The long insomnia jag had left me utterly permeable; ten seconds later I could feel it in my toes.

Somewhere at my back I could hear someone counting off into a microphone. The rote sound check came to me muzzily through the paper in my ears. I turned round and saw a sound stage raised on a pipework scaffolding some eight feet off the ground. No sign of a real performance as yet, but there was an audience in formation, and I went and joined the rear fringe of it, in reflex rubberneck fashion.

As I moved over, there was a squawl from the loudspeakers, then a band kicked off and three black women came spiraling out from a maze of big amps at the rear of the stage and began to twirl and sing before three mike stands. They all were wearing bright vinyl raincoats: red, yellow, electric blue, and all three of them were beautiful, or looked so at this range. They weren't half-bad singers either. I picked the wad of paper out of one of my ears and began to *wah-wah* my fingertip over my ear hole, as a kind of primitive treble control. People around me were beginning to beat their feet and clap time to the bass. Though the crowd was thickening around me again, I stayed through the number, finishing my beer. I might have stayed for another as well, if there had been one.

At the climax of the tune, all three singers ripped off their raincoats in unison and revealed themselves in spangled body suits. "We're the Night Birds," one of them murmured into her mike as the band wound down. "Come back tonight to hear us *really* sing. . . ."

They vanished, and I shambled off as the rest of the audience began to scatter, dropping my can into an overflowed rubbish tip along the way. Not such a terrific idea, that drink; all it had done was make me feel woozy and a little sick. I came out from under the overpass and began to walk along a railing that rose to some three feet above the level of the street. The sun had partially come out and was shedding a weak light all around. I felt strangely off balance with one ear plugged and the other not, so I pulled out the second wad and flicked it away.

What I needed was to put a bottom on my stomach, I thought. There were more food and drink stands against the railings and I gave them a once-over as I passed along. Curry or blood pudding would be more than I was up to now. I bought a piece of fish-and-bread and stood against the railing, munching: a dense mealy slab with a small whole fish on it, garnished with onion and pepper strips. The fish was laced with a thousand tiny bones, which made eating it a messy affair. I had to keep picking the bones out of my gums, and that made me self-conscious—I felt like it must be making all the people stare at me.

Then I realized that some people really were staring at me. Two men were giving me the hairy eyeball from the sidewalk on the far side of the street below, and I wondered what they found so interesting, as by any ordinary standard it was they who should have been the spectacle, not I. One had a set of those of Statue of Liberty spikes (well, I was getting used to that) and the other had a foot-high red mohawk and a spiderweb tattooed from his right ear to his right nostril, with a blue spider hanging from a single thread, right down to the bumpy ridge of his jaw. And this was when I fumbled up the idea that all those different spike hairdos I'd been noticing for the last eighteen hours might really have been one and the same. Eh? Behind me earlier today, on the station platform last evening, outside the caff where I'd stopped with Stuart—in conjunction with a red mohawk too, that first time.

Ridiculous. Nothing but paranoia, couldn't be anything else. These guys were too conspicuous to be following anybody, and besides I hadn't been worth following for several years. But when I blinked, they didn't disappear. They were still both giving me that squint, and I stopped thinking it was because they didn't like the sloppy way I was consuming my fish-and-bread. It took my appetite right away. I spat a few bones over the rails and wadded the rest of the food in the napkin, then walked very briskly off.

On my right the railing went on to the end of the block, which would make it awkward for them to reach my level, supposing they were really after me. I turned into an alley just to my left, did a quick reverse buttonhook down two more side streets, slid through the crowd at the overpass again, and finally came down into Ledbury Road.

I'd clenched the napkin to a tight crumby lump, and the fishbones stuck through it, pricking my palms. Halfway to the Tooth and Claw, I stopped to toss it in a dustbin and took a quick glance over my shoulder. Nobody. I began to think they'd never been there. What did it prove that I thought I'd seen them? After all I'd been hallucinating like billy-o, sitting in the garden that same morning.

I went right along down to the pub. The public bar was swirling with people, though hardly anyone was sitting. Maurice was behind the bar, serving up cans and drawing the pump ale into pint plastic cups. They didn't use real glasses here at Carnival time, as too many of them got lost to the street, and also they were a bit too handy for weapons. Maurice smiled and shook his head as I pushed up to the counter.

"Good shot yesterday—thought I had you."

"Live and learn," I said. "You'll come again."

"What for you?"

Good question. . . . I didn't really want a drink, so I ordered a half of cider and just wet my tongue in it, like a cat. Behind me the door squeaked open and shut and when I glanced back there they were, Mr. Liberty and the Last Mohican. They both developed a sudden fascination with the fruit machine when they saw I had them sussed.

"Terence in?" I said to Maurice, as he counted back the change from my pound.

"He's not working," Maurice said, jerking his thumb over his shoulder toward where the opposite curve of the counter overlooked the saloon. "I dunno if he's in back."

"I'll just have a look, then."

I left my cup and coins there on the counter, to promote the thought that I meant to return, and circled the bar to the swing door of the saloon at the rear. It was a small irregularly shaped room, with the lip of the main service counter underslung into it. There was only space for about three tables and Horace Stamp had taken up the lot of them for a conference with a gang of his youngbloods. He inclined his head in a priestly nod as soon as he saw me come in.

"Haven't seen Terence, have you?" I said.

"He's been in and out," Horace told me. "Sit down, have a drink, you'll see him back within the hour."

"Thanks," I said, and stopped to look back across the ring of the service counter. Maurice was hurrying back and forth, with several drinks clutched in each of his big hands. Past him I saw Mr. Liberty and the Last Mohican cruising around toward the saloon in a distinctly purposive manner. "Just tell him I stopped in, will you? I think I'm a little too pressed to wait."

I went through the back door of the saloon, which let me onto the street again. I scarpered down Artesian Road and made the first turn to the right. The Carnival was getting dimmer behind me, and when I looked back there was nobody there. Probably just my imagination after all. Outlandish as it might be, the punk regalia ended up working like a uniform of sorts; it stopped you really seeing faces or recognizing individuals. Probably every third layabout in London had a red mohawk and a spiderweb tattoo. Time to forget this little delusion. And I'd had enough Carnival for the day— just pick up the tux and go home.

Wu's laundry was tiny and smelled of ironing, with an overlay of dry-cleaning fluid. Mr. Wu was a nervous sort himself—his customers had to stand in a sort of shark cage just inside the door and push their business through a gate above the counter. But he smiled with all three of his ivory teeth when I slid my ticket in, and totted up the taxes for my monkey suit on the black beads of his abacus. I paid and went out with the tux slung over my shoulder in its white crinkle of plastic, and set foot on the street just as Mr. Liberty and the Last Mohican turned the corner.

Don't panic, now. But it was a little isolated here—outside the borders of the Carnival, and no one else at all on the street. I turned and began to take high steps back in the direction of the whistles and music, forcing myself not to look back. The rustle of the bag on my shoulder was making me very, very jumpy. But maybe it was a coincidence, yet, and if not I would just scrape them off in the crowds.

At the top of Powis Square a lot of people had clustered round some sort of attraction and I pushed my way up to the front. It was the Mangrove steel drum crew in a queer homemade wagon drawn along by a tiny tractor, set to parade across Westbourne Park Road. There must have been thirty drummers on the two tiers of the cart, which was itself a thing of wonder, patched together with bright red lengths of scrap iron, every connection a butt weld, and not a straight line on it anywhere. It looked like something built from matchsticks by a madman, but it was holding together and holding up at least one example of every kind of steel drum that had ever been conceived, and all the players flogging the metal in the heart of their dervish frenzy.

The cart was linked to the little tractor by a length of heavy rope, tightening and slackening and pulling tight again. A wizened little man with a lot of hair bundled up into one of those bulbous Rasta hats was doing the driving; he never looked back. Every time the rope rose to the horizontal the wheels of the cart began to revolve and the whole apparatus began to lurch forward. The rhythm of the drumming changed; I felt the shimmer of the sound start a swirling in my blood. All at once the sun came out completely and there was a shower of bright white light. The ringing of the drums rose to an even higher pitch and the surrounding crowd began to turn into a procession. Some clung to the bars of the cart and ran alongside it while others went dancing around them.

I switched my tux to my other hand and took hold of one of the bars. There was a deep vibration in my palm; I didn't know if the cart was about to shake apart or if it was only the drumming coming along into me through the structure. I was drunk with light and sound and sensation and there was a short period where I barely knew where the cart left off and my own arm began. I went with the procession all the way up All Saints Road. Then the sun ran away behind the clouds again, there was a roll of real thunder, and a few splatters of rain came down. A kind of moan went among the dancers, but the steel drummers played obsessively, maniacally on.

I broke away from the cart then and began wandering east on Westbourne Park Road. The first time I looked back there was no one following— the whole situation began to seem merely silly, once again. I forgot about it, in my daze. Past Chepstow Road was where the real sound system war was going on. The rude boys had raised such walls of amps and cranked the volume up so high they'd driven almost everyone away. This area of the street was empty except for me and a few stragglers and the rude boys themselves, frowning gravely each behind his turntable. Sloppily lettered signs were posted on the amps, saying things like "Here's the sound you feel inside." They were serious about that. The sound was so powerful down the row you couldn't actually even hear it because you couldn't hear anything at all anymore. But every time I passed through the focal point of another quadriplex of amps I could feel how it set my vitals trembling to the beat.

It was a little disturbing, but fascinating too. I stopped and began turning round and round on one of those acoustic skewers, feeling how willingly all my inner organs danced in time. A sensation like fear, or being in love, you might give it any name you cared to. And as I turned once more on the spit, back toward the way I'd come, I saw the two of them strolling idly up my way. All right then: fear. Fear and a taste of anger too. And at this point I did something rather stupid.

At the end of the block there was a pedestrian bridge that crossed above the railroad track. A narrowing of the street seemed to pinch me in that direction, and I went up the steps to the bridge without really considering what I was doing. It was covered with a steel mesh canopy, blobbily painted turquoise, meant to stop people lobbing rocks and bottles onto the cars passing below, but no shelter from the rain, which was coming faster now. I hurried down the steps on the far side, with raindrops patting down on my back and rattling the plastic of the cleaner's bag.

Here I was in North Kensington Estate, all by myself, since everyone who was able to walk had gone over to the Carnival. I took a few strides into the court of the deserted project before I turned around to look back. Yes, they were really coming after me. And now there seemed nothing to do but run.

I was seven kinds of fool for ever coming over there, but still I had a little luck of sorts. I ran in a circle, leading them along after me among the squat brown project buildings, and when I came around to the footbridge again there was nobody in my way. So I went pounding back across it, beginning to breathe a little too hard, the cleaner's bag flagging out behind me like the alarmed white tail of a deer. An expensive item, my tux, and I wasn't desperate enough to drop it. But as I went down one end of the bridge they were already coming up the other, their high-topped combat boots clanging on the metal.

Those boots, ugh—I didn't like the thought of them. They ought not be much good for running though. Then again I have never liked running much myself and don't like being frightened either. I kept on running just the same, passing along the rows of amps, through waves of sound breaking over me like surf. It put my insides back on the boil, and maybe that was what flipped my mood from panic back to anger again.

I slowed down a little and looked over my shoulder: the Last Mohican had taken a definite lead. I let him gain a little more, then stopped in my tracks, dropped the tux, spun, and threw a side kick at him. He should have run into it like running on a spear, only unfortunately I missed him by an embarrassingly sizable margin. My wonky knee gave a nasty pop with the wasted effort, but the leg still held me up when I came down on it. The Last Mohican brushed on past me, going too fast to stop. I grabbed Mr. Liberty by a pair of his spikes, which were soft and ropy, not stiff like they looked, yanked his head down, and smashed my knee into his face. Then something knocked me into a row of empty ash cans and everything became very confusing from then on.

I was scrambling through the scattered ash-can lids trying to make out which end of me was up, with a pair of those combat boots kicking after me, trying to find my softer spots. The toes of them had been cut out to expose the steel tips. It wasn't an appealing look; I'd never really thought so. I rolled an ash can into the way and somehow got back onto my feet.

It was raining harder now and the footing was no good; I was nervous of trying another kick from the slick pavement, and besides I didn't trust my knee. Here was the Last Mohican coming in, a gamecock, crest and all, lashing out with his boots at my shins, and taking jittery little hooks at my head, which I kept covered the best I could. He had a length of dog chain wrapped around his fist, I noticed. I was noticing all the wrong sorts of things: the pendent spider had red eyes, for instance. And the center of the tattooed web was empty. Afterward I remembered how my eyes locked on the vacant web-worked diamond and how I bent my knees and twisted my hips to get more power in the punch, but I couldn't recall what the contact felt like; perhaps I never felt it at all. But something shocked him briskly away from me and I think he would have gone flat on his back, except that his fall was broken by a lot of policemen who had suddenly appeared.

There were bobbies everywhere, doing all sorts of different things. I walked over and collected my cleaner's bag from a puddle and then stood quietly, feeling the rain turn my hair lank and stringy, and watching them go about their business. Some of them were arguing with the rude boys and shutting down the sound systems. A couple were helping Mr. Liberty back onto his feet, and another was staunching a cut on the Last Mohican's cheekbone with his own handkerchief, so it appeared. There were a few of them chasing off curious spectators who had begun to gather round, and then there was one attending to me, saying, *Here now, you. What's all this? Just you come along quietly now*, and other things of a similar kind.

# thirteen

Owing to sudden overcrowding at the Harrow Road police station, they weren't actually putting any of us in cells. There weren't many cells to put people in, but there were lots of, well, whatever you'd call them . . . detainees, maybe. Nothing much like booking appeared to be going on. Tact was the watchword for police operations this weekend, or so the media had had it, and I was hoping that this concept might translate into an uncomplicated, noninquisitive release. If I were running the shop, for instance, I wouldn't want to bother filing charges against all these people, would I? I'd just pull them off the street and cool them out for an hour or so, and then let them all go on their way.

Because of the general shortage of accommodations they had the greater part of us in the corridor, handcuffed to the bars outside the cells. Only a few people had been put right inside, presumably for more serious offenses. There was a stout black fellow alone in the cell whose bars I was chained to; it seemed he must have done something particularly atrocious to qualify for his isolation, but it was hard to imagine just what. He had a dark mole over one eye that gave him a slightly sinister aspect, but aside from that he looked pacific enough. I envied him his extra space; he had the whole cell to pace around in, though he wasn't putting it to much use. He just sat slouched on the cot in the rear, with his chin in his hand, muttering something unintelligible now and again, or shaking his head in a woeful manner.

For me and the rest of us, things were considerably more constricted. We all had our wrists cuffed together with the connecting length of chain passed round a bar. I understood the logic behind it. Most of us had been pulled in for some kind of brawling, and they wouldn't want us to be able to get at each other now. They'd made an effort to separate white from black, punk from skinhead, and so on, but still you never know, eh? So we were all chained facing front; I had to keep looking into that cell whether I wanted to or not, unless I decided to shut my eyes. Not so bad, but the chain was snapped between two close-set horizontal bars, which meant that

*118*

I couldn't sit down without twisting my arms at a painful angle, and I couldn't completely straighten up either. You wouldn't exactly call it torture, but the discomfort grew on me over time, and time passed very very slowly, as it tends to do in such conditions.

Mr. Liberty and the Last Mohican weren't in evidence. A different lorry had carted them off, probably to some clinic somewhere, as they each seemed to be in need of a stitch or a splint or something. Nobody on this corridor looked very much hurt. A few people were a little bloody, maybe, but from superficial cuts, or from the nose. I wasn't very much hurt myself, and the worst damage on me had been inflicted by Terence the day before. In this more recent brush, I'd only scraped the skin off the back of one hand, skidding among the ash cans, and sheered the button off my cuff, so one sleeve flopped loose and empty from my elbow. My knee still felt wonky from the missed kick, but I didn't think I'd ripped it out completely. And it flexed well enough for me to get down into a squat, which I did periodically, trying to find some easier position. There was really no way to get comfortable, though. Comfort wasn't on the menu.

Elsewhere on the injury list, there was an ambiguous white fellow chained next to me I thought might have taken a bad bang to the head. His eyes weren't pointing in the same direction, and he kept talking and talking to somebody named Mick, who the best I could figure was not really there.

"I tell you, Mick, I did just so . . . I . . . Well then, how do you like that, eh, Mick? I went down. I'll be passing back by Covent Garden after. All right, Mick, what about that concertina?"

He went on like that, with occasional pauses. Maybe he was always crazy, one of your natural mutterers. Lot of them abroad nowadays. Or else I thought he'd picked up one of those brain-rattling concussions Terence had been so solicitous to warn me of yesterday. He had reddish hair and pale bushy eyebrows, and he seemed to be staring at the West Indian in the cell, only his eyes weren't focused properly. The West Indian raised his head for a moment and dragged the crook of his elbow across it. It was rather warm in here with all the bodies packed so close, and everyone had begun to sweat. The next man on the row gave the redhead a covert kick on the ankle and told him to shut his hole, which he did for a bit. But then he started up again.

"Champion little dog, Mick, bones like a bird, and you'd not see a bird fly faster. You take him and I'll—ugh! ugh! ugh!" He began yanking his cuffed hands hard toward his face, putting his back into every jerk. The chain clashed against the bar, chipping off flakes of the sloppy jail-gray paint. After a few good yanks he set his feet against the lower bars and pulled until his hands went ice-white from the pressure. All the while his face was calm and absent, dreaming. Then he relaxed and slumped forward with his head against the bars.

"Champion little dog, look now, Mick, you could just hold her there in the palm of your hand. I'll be passing back by Covent Garden. . . ." His face knotted suddenly. "Go on, *put the boot in!* Give 'im a taste of the old steel toe."

His legs went out from under him like hot butter and he fell, a dead weight, till the cuffs caught him short and left him hanging from the heels of his hands, his buttocks just a couple of inches off the floor. His eyes were open, though heavily glazed; still I thought he was probably conscious. But he made no effort to get up, and he wasn't saying anything anymore.

"Officer," I called out, as one of them came along the corridor. "I think this man needs medical attention." Because concussions can suddenly turn around and kill you—it's true, just as Terence said.

The officer took a cool glance at the redhead on the floor and passed on without breaking his stride. *Push off, you berk. Shut yer bloody hole.* . . . Not half so polite as the bobbies outside. I didn't know if they were officers or not exactly. The people manning the cells weren't wearing the ordinary bobby's uniform. They had on dust blue coveralls with a brass zip from the guggle to the zatch, without any insignia or name tags. Whether this might be typical turnkey's garb or not I had no idea, this being my very first excursion inside a British jail.

I'd given up this sort of thing. I was respectable nowadays. I had a flat and a girl (at least until recently) and even what you might call a profession. I was a *hypnotherapist*, by God—there was a brass plate on my door that said so. I even owned full evening dress outright, though it was true I wasn't wearing it at the moment, and indeed I was rather grimy and frayed from rolling end over end in the street. Still, the whole situation was very undignifying. I didn't really want to be there, no. And what was really annoying me was that dangling, flapping sleeve. It sort of tickled the soft skin there inside my elbow, and there wasn't anything I could do about it, either. I couldn't reach my other hand to roll it up, and I'd have looked a right idiot if I tried to do it with my teeth. It's the little things that get you, in the end. So then I decided to just leave.

By the only path open. . . . I tilted my forehead into two bars and let them take a part of my weight. Still not too comfortable, but it would do. The bars made a twin pressure on my brow . . . like nubbins of horn sprouting . . . like the beams that sprang from the skull of the enlightened Moses. Oh, to be a true illuminatus . . . however, I'd settle for being a goat. I rolled my eyes tight back in their sockets and dragged the lids down over them. *Go!* I let my hands warm, then go numb, all the way up my arms to the shoulder. No more handcuffs, no more nagging sleeve . . . only the ghost of remembered limbs, what amputees are supposed to feel. *Go!* I was falling down a glittering hole, or perhaps flying laterally through successively narrowing rings of light. I was a young goat prancing on cobblestones . . . on concrete. A clatter of hooves on that hard surface . . . clatter of heels. *Black* high heels of *white* high boots . . . Thigh-high—well well, it was Nell, slinking along the pavement a hand's reach ahead of me. Red spandex minidress and the tail of a fake feather boa wafting back and forth in the breeze of her shifting hips. Every thirty seconds she'd look back over her one bared shoulder to make sure I was noticing her.

"Going out?" she said, as I drew level with her. Her mouth a bright bow tie, sticky around the edges. She'd mixed flecks of glitter in the lipstick. A sick sweet taste, suffocation. I put my hand in my left pocket—

The line was all wrong, though. She wouldn't have said that. That was what they said in New York, but they'd have a different come-on here, the ones that were on the game. My mistake—I'd been projecting.

"Want business, love?" Yes, that was the local line, but too late. I was sliding through those rings of light again, twirling, rifled toward my target: a blank pale area of a pale blue trellis, empty diamond of a faint blue web. Up close, I could discern black bristles poking through the clammy skin . . . the tattoo was the shade of the USDA stamp on a flabby side of pork. The red-eyed spider had crept away along the jawline, leaving the vacant web unguarded— *Bam!*

Somebody rousted me by the shoulders and began jouncing me against the bars. One of the coveralls—they didn't show much in the way of manners.

"All right, then, let's look a bit lively, let's just have a peep at your papers, then."

**121**

I jerked my hand against the darbies, reflexively reaching for my pocket.

"No no," the coverall muttered, crowding me closer against the bars. "Just you tell me, there's a duck."

"Left hip pocket," I said. Other than a quick pat for weapons, there'd none of us yet been stripped of our gear. The coverall pulled my wallet, flipped out my little green book from Immigration, and thumbed his way through a page or two. He was a mouth breather, I could hear him.

"Well well," he said cheerily. "So, I see. We'll be done with *you* in no time." And he went off, taking my whole wallet with him.

"Don't I get a chit for that?" I called. But I couldn't get much heart in it.

Goddamn.

It was just one of those things that happened though, could happen to anybody, can't be helped, no use dwelling on it, no. . . . The hard thing was I'd almost gone to sleep, really. I even felt like I *still* could go, if there'd only been some way of lying down. There's irony for you. You can take it and—

I started thinking about that guy, the Last Mohican, that one with the web tattoo. Who would get a tattoo clean across his clock anyway? Not that it was an entirely uncommon sight round town these days, but what could be the significance of it? I had never really thought. But now I did, the answer came easily. The message was simply, *I give up.* There'll be no more school, no job, no nothing. No expectations, whatsoever. No more *trying.* I GIVE UP! And go out branded with my hopelessness, for all the others to admire.

The Last Mohican probably didn't even know himself that that was what it really meant. No, it was my secret now, and I could feel more secrets in the offing. I had run upon one of those verges where everything could be understood. Whether I *wanted* to understand it, that was another question. And the fact was that I had no time to waste on beautiful thoughts just now. It was time to take some corrective action, or I was going to get myself deported. Done in no time. They'd send me back to New York again, where I would die. So I began to rattle my chains, chipping a little paint myself, and crying out in a loud voice for phone calls, lawyers, the press, whatever. Presently a coverall nestled up behind me, laid a truncheon expressively across the small of my back, and suggested that I pipe down, a little or a lot.

"I'd like to make a call to Scotland Yard," I said carefully.

"Would you indeed?" the coverall said, applying a subtle pressure with his stick. "People in hell want ice creams too, so I'm told."

"I . . . I'm in the employ of the police," I said. "I work for them, see? International Affairs Department. You might just make the call yourself, you know."

"There is no International Affairs Department at Scotland Y"ard," the coverall said.

"That's right," I said. "I work for them, though. In my wallet, there's a card. International Affairs Department. There's a phone number."

"And?" the coverall said. I thought I had him sort of interested. He was talking in a lower tone and leaning closer toward the back of my neck. I could smell a whiff of kipper on his breath.

"I think you'll recognize the exchange—"

"I will?"

"—because it's the Scotland Yard exchange. You'll call this number—"

"Is that what I'll do?"

"—and tell them my name and where I am. Whoever answers, it doesn't matter—"

"Oh I will, will I?"

"Why not?" I said. "There'll still be time to break my back if it turns out to be a dodge."

He went quiet for a minute. I felt his breath stirring the small hairs on the back of my neck, and I almost thought I could hear the gears clicking back in the rear of his brain. Like the clockwork of that supposedly silent clock. A couple of my vertebrae went popping back into place when he took the truncheon away. His gum shoes went padding back off down the corridor. I closed my eyes and rested the side of my head against the bars, feeling rather cold and lonely. I'd called in the Dutchman, hadn't I just— done it of my own free will.

Toward the end of the hall, one of the skinheads began to raise an uproar. It was too far away for me to make out the circumstances clearly, but it seemed that the coveralls had chained this skinhead at a point of contiguity with a row of West Indians: a bad decision on their part. What I could see was a tumult like water going on the boil, with the skinned pate bobbing up above the others. He had a small swastika tattooed on his

**123**

forehead, jail-style it looked, done with a knife and ball-point ink, and he was missing two front teeth, which made his mouth look cavernous, and his diction indistinct.

"Wotcher, farking nignogs," he was crying. "Send the farking nignogs backter the farking jungle." And on in the same vein. I construed from various sounds I heard that he was in a kicking battle with the farking nignogs nearest him, but none of them could kick high enough to stop his mouth, apparently. After about half a minute a number of coveralls converged on the scrum. There followed some slapping noises and a couple of grunts, then a drop into relative stillness, flavored by the sound of labored breathing.

In the cell before me, the West Indian had drawn his legs onto the cot and curled up on his side. The redhead beside me still hung from his chains, his eyes half-lidded, tracking nothing. They both of them looked easier than I felt. I was getting a crick in my back from standing in that stoop so long. I squatted down, stood up again; the movement brought me little relief. But then two coveralls came and unlocked me from my bar. They rechained my hands behind my back and began marching me off down the hall. I wasn't sure if either of them might be the one I'd referred to the Dutchman—I hadn't got a good look at his face.

"I'm to be released then, am I?" I said. Couldn't seem to help myself.

"You're to be shifted," one coverall said.

"Shifted where?" I said. "What about my wallet and my papers? I had a laundry bag with me too."

"We've got our instructions," the coverall said. "Just keep quiet, you."

And they brought me out the rear of the building and loaded me into one of their vans. The barred window in the rear door had been covered over with pasteboard and tape, so I couldn't see out, and there was next to no light. I sat on one of the two opposite benches, heeling over helplessly whenever the van braked or took a turn, as I hadn't the use of my hands at all now. The drive took about fifteen minutes, or so I supposed, and I had no idea of its direction. I passed the time wondering whether I was going to be delivered to the Immigration authorities, or to an audience with the Dutchman.

When the van stopped for good the coveralls led me blinking out into a small enclosed court, where a few more official vehicles were parked. It was an anonymous cul-de-sac, walled completely away from the street, and I'd have had no idea where I was except for a dumpster stenciled WORM-

WOOD SCRUBS. That much I took for a good omen, as it was a place I'd been before. But I kept this surmise to myself.

A suit was waiting at the service door to meet me and the coveralls. He led the pack of us down a hall and up a flight of stairs and across another hall. I didn't recognize any of these locations, nor had I ever seen this particular suit before. When at length we arrived in a small white room, the suit instructed the coveralls to remove my handcuffs. Then he told me to empty out my pockets and take off my belt and my shoelaces. He put all that into a drawstring bag, then went out with the others, locking the door.

The room was much the same as the straight room except there was no mirror and no furniture. No table, no chair, no standpipes even. Not anything but four white walls and a gray steel door with a small observation port, which for the moment was shut. I stood in the middle of it for a moment, rubbing my wrists where the darbies had been. Not that they'd been screwed down all that tight, but still my skin felt funny there, as if the feel of the metal had clung. Then I remembered that I was finally free to roll up that sleeve. But it didn't relieve me quite so much as I'd expected.

I took a turn or two around the walls. The bumps in the paint were big enough to cast short shadows, some of them. My trousers dragged down at my heels, and my unlaced shoes were loose and awkward on my feet. All that was intentional of course—they'd hardly expect me to hang myself for brawling in the street, and anyway there wasn't a hook. I tried sitting down to rest for a bit, but I felt too abject there on the floor, so I had to get up again right away. Once more, they'd left me no way to get comfortable. It was a subtler version of the same head game, only I wondered who was playing it this time. The thought crossed my mind that I might have summoned the wrong demon, or even if the right one came I might not be able to control him. It had happened often enough to other necromancers in the past.

Uncheerful thought. I began to consider Stuart and his speech. Another export item from our fair country, another vision of perfected human being. . . . Out with the old personality, in with the new! But he hadn't had such a lot to say about what was wrong with the old one. Other than its vicious habit of shooting dope. Wouldn't you ever begin to wonder what made that bad old personality want to shoot dope in the first place?

Back on the verge: that was the other secret veiled by the spiderweb

**125**

tattoo. They gave up, those folk, out of an authentic understanding that their position was hopeless. Oh, they had been buying our dream for a long time, not knowing it was only a dream. A dream of luxuries and freedoms proffered to the many, available only to a few. Of man enthroned on the seat of God by the powers of will and reason alone, though most of them wouldn't have seen it in those terms. For most of them it was only a vision of leisure and chattels, still painful enough when proved false. We sold them a bill of goods—we'd been flogging it all around the world. We beat them at the confidence game, and beat the best of our own lot as well. No wonder that they hate us then. No wonder that we hate ourselves.

So that bad old unregenerate personality wants nothing better than to hang a needle in its arm, kick back, nod out, and dream forever. . . . What a splendid renunciation, to turn your back on illusion and reality all at once! I was sweating cold steel beads at the thought of being sent again to my own country. It would kill me, I knew it, to go back now.

But then the door popped open and more coveralls came in, puffing and grunting under the weight of a long honey-colored teak desk. They adjusted it at one end of the room, went out, and then successively returned with a leather-lined desk chair, two file cabinets, three potted plants and a rubber tree, a small throw rug, a monogrammed wastebasket, a desktop computer, a fax machine, a multiline telephone, a pen holder, a crystal paperweight, and a green blotting pad with brass-bound corners. I stood in the blank part of the room, watching them arrange everything. Just as well I'd lost track of the time, else it would only have been dragging.

When the coveralls had done and departed, there transpired a period in which nothing happened at all. The observation port slapped open and shut. Then the Dutchman came strolling in and took his seat behind the desk. He was a long cold colorless drink of water. I didn't know that he was really Dutch, it was only a way of referring to him. He didn't have any trace of an accent, no qualities whatsoever but the smooth burnished anonymity of an Interpol policeman, though I doubted he was really that either. He was on the cutting edge of Control, and that was just about all I knew for certain. When he'd first shown up at my door, masquerading as a client, I'd seen at a glance there was something absent from him, as though he'd fallen from a distant star and was only pretending to be human, for experimental purposes to be sure. Not that it did me any good, that recognition, because he knew my weakness. He knew one of them, anyway. I did work for him, as a matter of fact—I hadn't been lying about that. But nobody ever said I had to like it.

The Dutchman pulled a folder from a file cabinet, examined it briefly, set it down, struck a few keys on the computer, pursed his lips, and hesitated. A document came whispering out of the fax machine; the Dutchman took it and positioned it foursquare on the blotter. He took a black pen from the pen holder and clicked its end a few times against the blotter's brass corner. The whole situation was brilliantly staged, and I was impressed with the trouble he'd been to, but I didn't want to show it. I stood before him, clownish in my shapeless shoes, letting my face hang slack and dull, until he finally noticed me.

"Well then, *Doctor* Strother," he said. A nasty spin on the honorific.

"You know very well I'm not a doctor," I said.

"What does it really matter?" the Dutchman said, assuming a slightly bored expression.

"A thing should be called by its name, if it's known," I said.

"That's beside the point." The Dutchman frowned. "You've got yourself in an awkward place."

"I thought we had an understanding."

"It was *understood*," the Dutchman said, "that you were to maintain a low profile. Make yourself unremarkable, and certainly keep clear of Immigration, not to mention the regular police. You were explicitly *not* to become a visible embarrassment to my department or to me."

"If only you'd get me some good paper," I said cautiously, "there'd be no risk of embarrassments."

"If you'd stay out of street fights you wouldn't be having your papers examined."

He had a point there. I stood silently, shifting my feet.

"You look a ruin," the Dutchman said. "Clothes filthy and torn. Grubby face, dirty hands, you're scuffed up all over. Your eyes are bloodshot, why, you look like you haven't slept in weeks. You don't look healthy."

"Ah, but I do good work," I said.

"You're lucky," the Dutchman told me. "We've a use for you. We will have, soon." He looked at me narrowly. "An important subject, Doctor Strother. It won't be a dry run this time."

"I understand," I said. "When?"

"We'll find you." The Dutchman smiled thinly. "Just don't leave the country." He pressed a button on the phone, and there was a rasp and a buzz from the intercom.

"Doctor Strother is free to go," the Dutchman said. He took a small blue ticket from a desk drawer and held it across the blotter toward me. "Take this," he told me. "They'll give you back your things at the front gate."

# fourteen

So then I went home and took another shower. I stayed in the stall until the hot water ran out and the medallion Stuart had given me turned cold in the pit at the base of my neck, under the cold pelting of the water. But I still felt slightly soiled when I got out. That was down to the Dutchman, undoubtedly; all my contacts with him were at least a little queasy.

The sight of my nakedness in the mirror didn't move me in any direction this time. The stained styptic powder had rinsed away from my face, and the scab on my nostril had softened in the water. It looked bulbous, pregnant with blood, like a tick feeding there. The rest of my body was there too: my arms, my legs, my organs of generation. It seemed difficult to believe that it mirrored the universe.

I went into the bedroom and put on fresh clothes and tossed the dirty ones into the hamper. Then I took the tux out of the laundry bag and hung it in the closet. It had come through all the excitement and difficulty in surprisingly good condition, really. The bag had kept it from getting dirty or damp when I dropped it, and though it was slightly wrinkled I thought the creases would probably hang out by the next evening. Besides, the lighting at the Empress could cover for a lot worse than wrinkles. It had covered a multitude if the rumors were right. There was a tale that Walter Karnock had cut a bloke's ear off in one of the private dining rooms upstairs. Got the idea from swotting up on medieval punishments, that was the story— ear-lopping was a medieval punishment for thieving or some such. Karnock was that sort of a wrinkly chap. And no one in the ballroom below heard anything more than a bump and a grunt.

Funny sort of world I seemed to live in. At times it didn't bear thinking of. My pocket gear was lumped on the bureau, all intact. And yet it all felt queer, alienated from me, having so recently passed through the hands of the police. Who's to say that objects have no memory? Poor tawdry things that they were. . . . But they'd even saved me Nicole's gray cog. I put it into my pocket on top of my keys. Clara's note was there on the bureau too; I hadn't taken it out with me that morning, but I picked it up now and stuck it in another pocket. The cards and so forth in my wallet all seemed to be accounted for, though they'd been taken out and examined and put back wrong. I rearranged them in a more familiar order.

My green identification booklet had been left loose from the wallet, and I flipped it open to the page with my picture. Four years younger and fresh off the plane—my eyes were shriveled, and my skin had a greenish cast. Maybe I didn't look healthy now, but I had to look better than I did then. There was my first twelve months' visa stamp, provided that I did not engage in any business or profession, then the second visa and the police registration number beside it. It stopped there—nothing for last year or for this one. Because, suspecting that I would probably be denied resident alien status, I had opted to become an illegal alien instead, and it was in this condition that the Dutchman had discovered me, practicing my profession in covert defiance of the law.

That was the weakness with which he was acquainted. If Immigration had been looking for me they hadn't been trying very hard, but the Dutchman had his way of finding anyone. He had ways of knowing things too, and of influencing the course of various events. It was down to him they hadn't taken my green book right away this time, though the protocol called for it to be confiscated when it went out of date. Of course he could have got me a fresh visa too, but I supposed he wanted the thread from which he dangled me to remain as frail as possible.

He knew that I didn't want to go back to America, but I sometimes wondered if he knew *why*. I also sometimes wondered who was really winning the information war between us. . . . Because the business in which I engaged on his behalf was as well off the books as my own continued presence in the United Kingdom, if not even more so. It was a dodgy business that went forward in the straight room, there in the honeycombed heart of Wormwood Scrubs. The Dutchman, who cloudily appeared to represent a lot of other secret global policemen, had interested himself in testing the limits of the time-worn truism that no one can be hypnotized unwillingly. He was also interested in pushing this whole concept beyond the methodology of interrogation and into a methodology of actual mind control.

I put the ID book back in my pocket and went into the front room to answer the phone, which seemed to have been ringing for some time.

*"Finally."* A woman's voice. "You've become a hard man to . . . get in touch with."

"Well," I said, a bit uncertainly, for I hadn't quite made out who it was. "I'm in and out, you know how it is. There is an answering machine, you know."

"A machine won't do it. Not after four years. Though I did have to hang up on it quite a few times."

*"Nicole."* My free hand was scrambling through all my pockets like a panicked Daddy Long Legs, looking for a cigarette, I realized. I reminded the hand that I hadn't smoked for two or three years, and it calmed down.

"You're in town, I hear," I said to her.

"Yes," Nicole said. Her voice was the same—I might have heard it only yesterday. "And as you may have noticed, the ball is in your court. . . ."

"I found it," I said. That spidery hand had crept back into my pocket and closed around the little cog. "Well."

"Well. . . ." Nicole said.

"When can I see you? I suppose that would be my line," I said. "Tonight? Today?"

"I've got a show to do tonight," Nicole said. "And a late dinner after it."

"Tea, then," I said. "What time is it now, do you know?"

"It's a little after one," Nicole said.

"That's all, seriously?" I said. "You're not still on New York time or something?"

"No, why?" Nicole said, with a little jingling laugh.

"Nothing. Never mind. It's been a long day," I explained. "I suppose I was expecting it to be closer to over. Anyway. . . . How about three, three-thirty maybe? I'll meet you at the Harrods tearoom."

"How very English," Nicole said. "That sounds nice."

"Well. . . ." I said. Look how simple and easy it was! I might have started back smoking just as easily, just buy a pack and light one up. Simple. It was available at any time, along with a number of other things.

"See you at three," Nicole said archly. "I suppose we'll still recognize each other." And she hung up before I could reply.

I put the phone down and automatically staggered across the room to check out the snake situation. Nothing had changed on that front. The mouse hadn't even eaten its cereal. It looked like something was wrong with its hindquarters. I let the cover fall back over the tank. . . . I'd just made a date with Nicole, hadn't I? What was I, crazy? I had to get in touch with Clara, immediately, if not sooner.

I scrambled back to the telephone and dialed her work number. The phone must have rung for five whole minutes in that dim shuttered office across the city, before I recalled that it was Saturday, and a bank holiday to boot. I tried Val's number then—no answer, and nothing at the studio. Evidently some change of tactics was in order.

I crept down the stairs to the crooked room and put the copy of Attar in my jacket pocket, in case I might need it in my subsequent travels, and then went out. The weather had changed again; now the sun was shining. It was one of those very changeable days. To the north, the Carnival continued to roar. I went south as far as the Bayswater Road, then on down Kensington Church Street. It was vaguely in my mind to walk all the way over to Fulham, but I was too tired for it, I discovered. My legs were wobbly and my head felt light. Not to mention the date at three. . . . I got on the District Line at Kensington High Street and rode as far as Parsons Green.

Clara's studio was a railroad flat in a narrow brick tenement on Munster Road. The windows at either end of it gave her decent light, though not spectacular, and the rear windows overlooked the shabby greensward. But first I went to the front door and leaned against the third-floor bell. There was no response—I wasn't sure the bell was even working. The front of the building was all covered with one of those temporary pipework scaffoldings, so I couldn't see up to the windows.

I went round the corner of the block and crossed onto the green. Bits of shale were scattered in the patchy grass and I stooped to pick up a few of these. A little whiskered dog came up and sniffed my fingers, but a cross woman's voice called him from the narrow end of the green and he trotted obediently away. I stood below Clara's third-floor windows, rattling the loose shale in my hand. The panes reflected skylight, so I couldn't see in, and the angle was wrong anyway. I tossed a bit of shale up but it fell short. It splintered into three pieces when it struck a concrete sill. I threw another piece, spinning it with my forefinger. It clicked against the right-hand windowpane and rebounded, landing silently on the grass. I got one more hit in three more tries, then waited. Nothing. Because of the reflection, I couldn't tell if anyone had come to the window or not.

Discouraging. However, the lock on the front door did not appear to be too impressive when I went back to look at it again. It was really only a catch, and there was enough gap between the halves of the door that I could slip it quite easily with my library card. I went up the creaking sagging stairs, pausing at each landing, as my energy was at low ebb. The lower two floors were residential, and there was a stale smell of boiled cabbage wafting around the area. At the third floor I turned off from the stairs to pound on Clara's door. A hollow sound from the splintery panel. If she had seen me there on the green, she might not choose to answer. I waited awhile without knocking again. A crisp scent of primer and paint came over the transom, but it was dead quiet and the space beyond the door felt empty.

There was a slight crick in my neck from craning to see up to the windows from outside. I rolled my head around a few times to loosen it, which made me so dizzy I had to sag against the wall. Below, a door slapped open and shut, and the staircase groaned as someone went weightily down toward the street. I unfolded Clara's note and reread it quickly, but it gave me no notion of how to proceed, and I put it back in my pocket. Funny how I could live with someone and not know her. It was intimacy without . . . acquaintance? Strange. But now I needed very much to know.

If she *was* there in the silence on the far side of the door, what was she making, and what for? At the beginning and middle, not much was discussed. An attachment formed itself via tropism, like vines wrapping round each other. Vines don't talk it over, do they? On the other hand, they tend to stay wrapped. I couldn't recall we ever made any decision. Only a touch, an embrace, a reluctance to part at morning, the custom of creature comfort. Her sublease ended at the same time I was turned out of my squat, and suddenly we were talking about closets, kitchen counter space, the desirability of a back garden.

No, you'd better have the basement, the light's no good for painting there. We talked about that, but not each other. Like two vines braided, we burrowed through a wall and discovered an interior to pale in. That suited me well enough the way it happened; I never much cared for myself as a subject. I have a talent for forming habits—vicious ones more often than not, but this one seemed perfectly benign. It was Clara who had the tendency to come unraveled from the situation. Not three months in she did

*133*

her first bolt, and left me shivering and clutching at the air. Then a second time, a third. . . . I got accustomed to it happening on a more or less quarterly basis, but perhaps, by her, it was never meant to be part of the ordinary run of things.

"What made you go?" I did ask her that the first time. I was scared. There'd been no sign of a deliberate removal; she didn't take anything notable with her, and my first notion was that she must have had an accident, or got chewed up in someone else's plan.

"I got fed up," was all she'd tell me. Her face was puffy, from anger perhaps, and her voice was tight. I'd found her in a little sandwich shop not far from the architects, where she often went for lunch. It was easy, once I thought of it, though I was too ragged to be much rejoiced by my success, and besides the place was too crowded for a properly tactful negotiation of domestic difficulty.

"Fed up with what?"

"You figure it out." Her mouth was a sharp flat line, lips folded up under her teeth.

"Give us a clue, at least?"

But all she'd do was swing her head forward, so that her hair camouflaged her face, the ends of it brushing the crumbs on the table. I made my hand into a three-legged creature that walked awkwardly around a plate toward hers. Her shoulders began to shake, which worried me, but when she raised her head I saw that she was only laughing.

"My God you look a wreck," she said. Which was true, I saw, looking over her shoulder at a strip of mirror on the wall behind. My hair was lank, due to lack of maintenance, and the insomnia had painted a Zorro mask around my eyes.

"I haven't been getting by so well on my own."

Clara laughed again. Her mouth was bright, from the pressure released. "All right," she said. One of her hands just touched my fingers, while the other pulled her hair back over her shoulder. "All right," she said, and that was all till next time. I never got an answer to my question though, perhaps because I hadn't really wanted one.

I plucked the note from my hip pocket for another look. The paper had gone limp along its folded hinges. It was a talisman of sympathetic power; her hand and her intelligence had touched it. Her fingertips, if I could see them, were printed in electric whorls around the page. With this, if only I knew how, I could discover and recover her again.

*try if you like   see where it gets you*

Something was missing. I felt that something was actually gone from that note now, as if it had decayed or been erased since I had looked at it last. But that didn't sound very plausible. Then I remembered, it wasn't in the note at all, but something Val had said the night before.

*She says you don't have anything to say to her. . . .* Well now, suppose those pronouns weren't misplaced? I had a flash of comprehension, and also a notion of what I should do. I whipped out the note again. The bottom half of the sheet was blank and I tore it off carefully along the fold. Pressing the paper against the door, I took out a pen and began to write.

> *Dear Clara,*
> *You're wrong. No, you were right—but things have changed. Now there're some things I* do *want to tell you—*

The pen clogged up. I sucked on the end of it, considering, and then wrote on.

> *No trouble to find me at home, as you know. But I'll be taking a walk by the Putney Bridge tomorrow—let's say around midday. And if you happened by around that time, you might very well run into me. . . .*

I wrote my name at the foot of the paper and bent down to slip it under the door. That would save me sitting by the phone, at least for an hour or so. I went down the stairs feeling clever and quite well-pleased with myself, on the whole. And then I went over to the Putney Bridge, as if I expected her to have turned up there already. Of course she had not. But the sun was bright and the red flowers were nodding from their long stalks in the patchwork churchyard flower beds. A young mother had run her pram up against the rail and was sitting in a deck chair, her skirt hitched up slightly to bare her pale shins to the surprising warmth and light. At the pier on

**135**

the far side of the river, someone was putting a small sailboat in, though for the moment it was so still that the white triangle of canvas hung completely limp.

I walked down the Embankment a short way, trailing a finger along the green pipe of the guardrail, then stopped, unhooked the chain from my neck, and inspected the flip side of the medallion. The classical art of memory instructs the imagination's eye to turn within, in order to regard the mind's whole fund of knowledge stored in its abstract architectural order. Nowadays we suspect, or perhaps we know, that nothing can be truly lost from the mind. And possibly those old wizards of mnemonics were not so artificial after all in their construction of niche upon niche, room upon room, whole palaces and cathedrals of memory. Though for many minds the memory is more maze than classic temple, a labyrinth full of false trails, dead ends, sealed-off airless chambers. Enter it and risk being lost forever. . . .

The Roman rhetoricians took their own grand buildings and converted them into vast mental filing cabinets, and the Scholastics probably did something very similar with their Gothic architecture, but only Giordano Bruno was daring enough, or mad enough, to seize the whole universe for his scheme. That's the secret of the Brunian memory wheel—it's an entire cosmogony, embracing everything from the clot of dung to the wild and furious singing of the angels. He believed that he could remember everything, know everything and its exact relationship to everything else, and he must have believed that there would finally be no difference between omniscience and omnipotence. All-knowing, all-capable, he would have become as God . . . but unfortunately before he was able to complete these procedures the Inquisition caught up with him, convicted him as a heretic, imprisoned him for eight years, and then one day led him out into Campo dei Fiori, tied him to a stake, and burned him alive.

I have been there and seen his statue at the center of the irregular court: small, black, unremarkable; you might take it for an old iron pump if you don't look at it closely. The stones around it are littered with dead needles, for Campo dei Fiori is a needle park now, and the matte-black eyes of Giordano Bruno stare from their chiseled sockets at the low brown wall of a tenement opposite, though they are sightless. But the statue is not only a thing.

Well, but I had wandered into the wrong memory location now, or maybe not, considering the close and subtle interconnection of everything . . . still, the immediate point was that while I remembered all sorts of things about Clara, she had never had the chance of remembering anything parallel about me. I knew that she had been reincarnated from another life, just as I had been myself, which made it much easier for me to live with her, as I could now perceive. But I had never quite got around to making this knowledge reciprocal.

In her first avatar of identity, Clara was a hurdler, and she was the youngest member of the 1972 Olympic team, back when she was fifteen or something. Unlikely that I would have ever discovered this bit of information on my own, as hurdling is not my sport and I have never been terrifically interested in the rest of the Olympics either. But although Clara, or Carla Pedersen as she was then known, was only the third seed or whatever in the women's division, she was also the most youthful individual ever to make the team at all in the whole history of recorded time, which afforded her great celebrity for a season, and made her name and face intensely familiar to large numbers of people, including but not limited to that feckless preppy from Rice.

I have seen pictures of her from that time. There are all sorts of pictures and news items and film clips and videotapes. She looked different then, her body leaner and meaner, her gender less obvious, her hair cut short and shrunk tight to her head like a bathing cap. The images show her flying over the hurdles, legs stretched parallel to the ground, long tubes of muscle sprung tight from her hips to her ankles. They rather alarmed me, those pictures did, not representing the person I knew.

If you can believe her, which I do, she never cared much for the fame of it, really. What interested her was hurdling; it was the only thing that interested her much at all for a long time. It was her passion, but as the actual Olympics drew closer, it also became her cross. The trouble was that her muscles were stronger than her bones. All that taking off and especially all that landing began filling up her pelvis with deepening stress fractures, a skein of hairline cracks. Most athletes are used to living with a little pain, and Carla got used to living with a lot. With agony, in fact. And she was so good at taking the pain that by the time she got scared enough to turn herself in for the fatal X rays, it was already sort of too late.

The Olympics were only a week or so off, and the all-wise white-coats told her she could still run if she didn't mind a sixty or seventy percent chance of losing the use of her legs altogether and permanently after the race was over. Now Carla had been pointed in her single direction for such a long time that the deal seemed reasonable to her right up to the penultimate moment. She was ready and willing to live out her days as a cripple in exchange for that thirty seconds or so of qualified glory—she had next to no chance of actually winning, of course.

But then, as she eventually told me across the midnight pillow, something like a miracle happened in her thinking. Her sense of proportion was magically restored to her, at least partially. And the day before the race she dropped out, in what became a fog of bad publicity, because the real explanation was too prosaic for anyone to believe it. There were rumors of drugs, of infighting on the team, a rumor that Carla was born a boy and had a secret sex change. There was a lot of ugly talk. And she went back to anonymity wondering if she had made the right decision—after all, there'd been *some* chance that everything would have turned out okay.

She spent some time in the hospital, getting pins planted into her bones. When she came out she switched the letters in her name, grew her hair out, and began to become beautiful. She finished high school and went to architecture school and didn't finish, went to art school in Philadelphia, then to New York where she worked a few years as a draftsman. (I might have met her then, although I didn't. We weren't in the same circles, so to speak.) She came to London to go to the Slade and stayed on after she finished there. By the time I met her, she had been Clara for a solid ten years. For several years she'd been able to run again, a little, by her standards. She said she didn't take it very seriously. But every morning before work she'd set some fierce music howling in her headphones and go out and run about eight or ten miles . . . to keep trim. I never quite knew what it meant to her. But I would daydream about her sometimes while she was out, picturing her in my mind's eye running along the cool corridors of the Hyde Park chestnut trees that barred the damp dawn grass with their shades, so that she ran from shadow to light, to shadow.

So I'd come to know all that of her, leaving her knowing so little of me. That, if logic carried me in the right direction, was probably what she'd meant by that strange line relayed by Val last night. Of course, I'd always had my reasons. My past had nothing to do with our intended future. When I succeeded in becoming God, I meant to re-create the two of us wholly new, as I went about my business of making a whole rejuvenated world for us to live in. New Adam and New Eve, we'd rise up from the ashes of our former selves and blaze with a purifying, incandescent light.

. . . however, I had not yet been able to complete all the necessary procedures. Furthermore, this grand design left the problem of what to do about Nicole rather poorly defined. And I would be face-to-face with her again in only a few more minutes. . . . As I started back toward the tube stop, I realized what was wrong with that cunning note I'd left for Clara. The style of the appointment was inappropriate. Clara was a definite sort of person: definite place, definite time. Some unlikely wandering sort of thing—that was the way to meet Nicole.

# fifteen

Once I'd settled myself on the train again, my eyes began to blink uncontrollably, as if I'd suddenly developed some sort of a tic. They were quick to drop shut, and quite slow to roll open. Why, I was getting ready to nod out, wasn't I? What joy. . . . It occurred to me that I might be able to break the chain of insomnia altogether by just riding the Circle Line round and round and round all night. The only catch was that they shut down the whole London underground at one o'clock in the morning or so. . . .

For the moment, however, it seemed quite satisfactory to let myself go limp as a rag, only twining my arm around the armrest so I wouldn't tumble right over onto the floor of the car. My head lolled forward and back with every twist and lurch of the train, like a heavy boulder rolling around the inside of a barrel. There were two violet orbs of fuzzy light on the insides of my darkened eyelids, undoubtedly burned there by some electric fixture I'd recently and carelessly stared into. The hard square copy of Attar was wedged tight between my body and the armrest, imprinting the outline of its form onto my rib cage. By some occult process of osmosis a string of words from the volume seeped into my system and rose like smoke into the hollowing chamber of my brain.

*A man humbly asked permission to say a prayer on the carpet of the Prophet, who refused and said: The earth and the sand are burning. Put your face on the burning sand and on the earth of the road, since all those who are wounded by love must have the imprint on their face, and the scar must be seen. Let the scar of the heart be seen, for by their scars are known the men who are in the way of love.* And wouldn't the look of that bring her back? But it occurred to me I was no longer quite sure which her I was dreaming about. It would be a mistake to mix them up. They didn't go together.

The train, shuddering into the station, shook me three-quarters conscious again. I stumbled murkily up the steps and surrendered my ticket to the official at the booth. It was only when I got up to street level that I realized I ought to have changed trains at this station rather than disembarking

**140**

altogether. This wasn't Knightsbridge; it was South Ken. And a clock on a bracket overhanging was already reading three twenty-five.

It seemed to be making a slight ticking sound too. I scurried away from it, along Cromwell Road, at not quite a run but the next thing to it, a long-strided walk so hasty and desperate that it caused a number of the people I met to flinch away from me. Good thing too, since all the other pedestrians seemed to be headed in the opposite direction, by sheer perversity, as usual. The sidewalks of the Brompton Road were packed, mostly with foreign sightseers and shoppers. I was treating it as an obstacle course, twisting and dodging, zigging and zagging, but never slowing down for any impediment whatsoever. The tails of my jacket flew out behind me; the hard little book perpetually slapped against my hip. Ahead I could see the rose-colored fortress of Harrods rising out of the pale concrete; it occupied an entire city block. By the time I reached it I was soaking in sweat.

I entered by the men's department, which was almost as busy as the street outside. Still, a couple of clerks swarmed up to me, fawning and simpering; I shook them off, taking evasive action through the enormous food section, where I soon slowed down, bewildered. The smell and sight of so many complex comestibles made me a bit giddy, reminding me how little I'd been eating lately, but the tide of other shoppers carried me through without a pause. I trailed off on an eddy into a section of women's clothing—the area was mostly full of Arab women, robed and veiled. A tall woman had hoisted about a bale of clothing onto the cash desk; instead of a full veil she wore a leather harness apparatus that just covered her nose and cheekbones, like something you might use to hood a hawk. She must have been spending hundreds of pounds—on clothes she could never wear out of her own doors.

The procession of other shrouded women pushed up behind me and pressed me on. I floated out of the women's section and into an alcove full of ornate clocks, most of them chiming the quarter hour. It was already quarter to four. The time recalled me to my purpose. I found the elevator and rose to the sixth floor.

The main tearoom was broad, deep, and dim, with a fair number of people scattered among the tables. Knightsbridge matrons for the most part, graying and aging, coccooned in their mesh-veiled hats, their jewels and their furs. I hustled up to the velvet rope, craning my neck to search out Nicole, but then I recalled how sweaty and harried I would seem. So I turned tail and went to the gents'. I'd shaped up somewhat since the various events of the morning, but I was still rather a sorry sight, as the Dutchman had suggested. I ran cold water across my wrists until my whole body began to cool, then pressed my chilled fingers into my temples. *Beat, beat, beat.* . . . The scab on my nostril was hard and black, and after a moment's deliberation I wet a tissue and dampened it till it came loose. Pinpricks of blood came stippling over the faintly concave surface of the cut, pooled together, and turned brown. Well, well, it had been worth the gamble.

I returned then to the main tearoom and began to search among the small round tables. The ladies were taking their sweet teas, with a purling of hot water, a clinking of china and silver spoons. Their mandibles worked silently on their scones. I had to approach closely to this one or that to verify that she was not Nicole, or anything like her, only some squat middle-aged stranger, ribboned and bowed, upholstered in velvet, a hatpin stuck crazily through the top of her hair like some long-shot Indian arrow. I wandered between the lobed chair backs, feeling the eye of the headwaiter beginning to focus exclusively on me. Nicole was nowhere. Perhaps she had given up and gone away.

I felt a sort of relief at that notion, but just then the bone ring griped on my finger and I noticed another area opening off the main tearoom, flooded with green and yellow daylight. It was a sort of greenhouse affair, glass-walled and -roofed, full of hanging plants and rattan furniture, perched on a stretch of the Harrods south battlement. I stepped through the double doorway into the light, groping the little gray cog out of my pocket. Nicole was sitting in a huge fanback rattan chair, with her head turned down and away from me, cocked in an attentive posture as though she were listening to some small voice that emanated from the floor. I padded up to the small square table in front of her, stopped, and let the cog fall out of my turning hand. It dropped an inch or so to meet the pale pink tablecloth with a muffled tap, then flipped over and settled itself beside her small clutch purse.

Nicole had raised her head at the sound and was looking up at me. Her eyes were blue, and the slant of the afternoon sun among the leaves of the hanging ferns made them seem to brim with their own light. There was a frozen spot behind my belt buckle, sending cold trembling spasms along my arms and legs, and I had to hold myself quite rigid in order not to tremble visibly. Nicole smiled, tentatively, her mouth blood red against her pale, pale face. A fleck of her lipstick had got on one of her front teeth and

**142**

I did not know if this small imperfection was more a disturbance or a relief.

"Well?" Nicole said.

"Well . . ." I said. Nicole's mouth went open and shut and the point of lipstick disappeared.

"I look all right to you, do I?" she said. "Come *on*, Adrian, sit down." She patted the flowered cushion of the other huge fanback chair next to hers, and I fell into it.

"You'll always be beautiful," I said, as though marveling at some natural wonder. It was a lie, or a half-truth—Nicole was far and away the most beautiful woman I had ever been directly confronted with, but she had to be switched on for you to know it. Switched off, she looked like nothing at all, was practically invisible; certainly you wouldn't glance at her twice. At the moment, she was turned up to her most radiant intensity. The ice butterfly in my belly rustled its cold wings and I jerked my forearm involuntarily across the table, sweeping her purse off to the floor. Our heads knocked together as we bent to pick it up. Nicole winced, then settled back in her chair and started laughing. I picked up the purse, and then began to laugh myself. The frosted feeling thawed out of me quickly. There—it could be just that easy.

Another couple at a nearby table put down their tea implements and began to frown at us. Nicole subdued herself and spoke.

"Just tell me one thing, Adrian," she said. "What happened to your nose?"

"A shaving incident," I said. "When you go to shave your mustache, you just let the razor tilt forward toward it, like so. . . ." I demonstrated the subtle wrist motion. "And presto, it nicks off the edge of your nostril and there's blood all over the walls."

Nicole had barred her mouth with her long slim fingers and was tittering between them.

"All very well for you to laugh," I said. "You haven't got to shave every day, it's harder than you think."

Nicole took her hand away from her mouth and spread it on the table, near mine. I could look at her more easily now. She'd done herself simply, nicely too. Her hair was pulled back through a twist of silver wire at the nape of her neck and ran down between her shoulder blades, thick and black and warm as tar. I had an impulse to touch it, but didn't give in. Around her neck were three concentric silver chains from which depended

**143**

in a vertical file a small pale sand dollar, a tiny bleached conch shell, and one bright red droplet of polished coral. Her dress was a sort of long loose robe, nipped at the waist by a narrow belt and scooped low at the neckline to show her collarbone. The cloth was a thrilling shade of deep blue, and I realized with a slight jolt that here was the very image of the priestess I'd conjured for Miss Peavey's first induction, intoning Attar in that imaginary buried room.

"You look funny," Nicole said. "What's on your mind?"

"Oh, nothing," said I. "You haven't been by the British Museum this trip, have you?"

"Only to the gift shop, to pick up some trinkets. I haven't had time for a real tour. Why?"

"Yesterday morning, that would have been? You know, I think I walked right by you. Just barely saw you out of the corner of my eye."

"That's weird," she said. "And you didn't even stop?"

"Oh," I said. "Well, I was hardly expecting to run into you . . . I was just on my way in to the library."

A waiter appeared in the vicinity of our table and stood in a posture of expectancy. Nicole half-turned her head to him, then hesitated.

"It's a set menu here for afternoon tea," I said. "Inside they have the tea buffet."

"What's the difference?" She switched back to me.

"Cucumber sandwiches and things like that," I said. "You get that sort of thing with the afternoon tea."

"Oh, the afternoon tea, I think," Nicole said. "Yes, definitely."

"For two," I said.

The waiter nodded his head and went off. Nicole lowered her hand to the table and gave the cog a flick with her forefinger. It skidded a few inches across the stitching of the tablecloth toward me. The cloth was embroidered with a pattern of oak leaves and acorns, I observed. The balls of Nicole's fingers turned and touched the tracery of stitches. Her fingernails were cut in shallow white crescents, unpolished.

"You haven't been biting your nails," I said.

"No," Nicole said. "I gave that up."

"I'm impressed," I said, which was true enough, and pushed the cog back till it was just touching the edge of her hand. I looked up at her. She had leaned slightly forward so that our faces were near. Her skin was a translucent, alabaster pale, with the ghost of a bluish tint to it, like the faint blue tinge of new milk. Lovely stuff. It would bruise if you breathed on it, and she was sensitive about that. Stuart had almost always been careful not to hit her where it showed, though often she'd have fingerprint-size clamp marks on her wrists and forearms. There was a sort of sandbag I once stole from the Rare Book Room of the New York Public Library, I couldn't say any longer why I'd wanted it. It was supposed to be used to hold the books open—they called it a snake, though it looked more like a canvas sausage sack, stuffed with sand. Subsequently Stuart stole it from me and I think he kept it for quite some time. He used it to beat Nicole in her midsection. It had a very solid weight, and its softness made the marks it left ambiguous.

"I've missed you," Nicole said.

"Have you?" I said. "By your own choice. . . ."

"You left," Nicole said.

"I was dying," I said. "It was get out or else. . . . You were invited to come along, remember? A good many times, I think."

The waiter reappeared and began laying out a silver-plate teapot, a cream jug, a bowl of sugar cubes, two cups and two saucers, and two small plates. Nicole had stretched back into the wide brown fan of her chair. A thin screw of vapor came writhing out of the pot's silver spout.

"Would you be so kind?" I asked her.

"Oh?" said Nicole. "Oh, of course." When she picked up the teapot I noticed she was wearing her bone ring too. It had yellowed slightly. So had mine. Nicole picked up the sugar tongs. "One lump or two?"

"I don't take sugar," I said.

Nicole frowned. "You're interfering with my role."

"One lump, then," I said. I stirred the sugar into my tea and tasted it. Earl Grey. I couldn't remember if we'd asked for anything particular.

"All right?" Nicole said, toasting me with her own cup.

"*Parfait*," I said. "You do that very well indeed."

Nicole sipped, I sipped. A cloud passed over the sun outside, throwing a brief shadow over the area. Then it was sunny and bright again.

"Ah," I said. "So, I hear you're traveling for some gallery now?"

Nicole arched her eyebrows. "You hear, do you?"

"My spies are everywhere. . . ."

"Willet and Froyle," Nicole said. "You've probably never heard of

**145**

them. They're dealers, really, not a gallery. They don't do any contemporary stuff at all. They deal in etchings and some old master drawings. I've had to learn a lot in a hurry, but really it's all very interesting."

"Sounds it."

"Yes," Nicole said reflectively, cradling her cup in both hands. "And I like the trips. I've been to the West Coast a lot, but this is the first time they've sent me to England. I'll be coming more often if things go right."

"I see," I said. "Well, it certainly makes a change, doesn't it?"

Nicole clicked her cup back into its saucer. "Now, now," she said. "Let's not—"

Just then the waiter put down a plate of sandwiches. There were cucumber sandwiches as I had advertised, also salmon, egg, tomato, and ham, all on biscuit-size circlets of white bread with the crusts tidily trimmed away. Nicole arranged a pair of plates.

"And you?" she said. A cucumber sandwich disappeared inside her by a procedure of invisible nibbles. "What do you do to keep things going over here?"

"Hypnotherapy," I said. "I get paid for it a lot better now."

"You're a shrink?" Nicole tittered briefly. "Now that really is a change."

"Not a real one," I said, snapping a salmon sandwich into my jaws. "I do weight loss, mild phobias, smoking. . . . Little stuff. I'm just . . . a sort of psychological repairman. Actually, you'd be surprised how many applications there are."

"Sounds very respectable," Nicole said.

"Oh, impeccably." My hands were restless at the side of my empty plate. The wee sandwiches had all gone down like so many packets of empty air.

"But you don't really look the part," Nicole said. "In fact, you look sort of torn and frayed."

"So I keep hearing from almost everyone I meet," I said. "I'm clean, though. Honest . . . Just that I've been having a little run of insomnia these last few days."

"Lonely?" Nicole said.

"Not me."

"Adrian, are you seeing anyone? I mean, if I can ask . . ."

"You mean, this instant?" I said. "Only you."

The waiter reached between us and took away the sandwich plate, replacing it with a smaller one of buttered scones. There was a little bowl of cream and another of red jam. Nicole poured tea.

"What kind of jam is it?" she said.

I took a fraction of it with my teaspoon for a taste. "Raspberry," I said. "Not bad, either."

Nicole made herself a scone, a spoon of jam, spooning cream on top of that. A smidgen of the cream got stuck to her nose as she bit into it. That was an uncharacteristic bit of clumsiness on her part. I didn't say anything about it, though. The blot of cream was making her seem a little less frightening.

I ate a scone. Nicole pushed the tray over to my side of the table. "Finish them off," she said. "I don't want to be bloated."

"You won't be eating till late, though, eh?" I said aimlessly.

Nicole waved the question away. I watched her unsnap her purse, take out a packet of Players, and light one. The blue tang of tobacco sent a series of small hot pulses out along my neural network. So I made myself another scone and ate it. There was no ashtray on the table. Nicole smoked luxuriously and arranged her ashes in a neat half-circle along the rim of her saucer. The waiter seemed to frown at that when he came to take away the tray of scones.

"Neither am I," Nicole said with a faint smile. Neither are you *what?* I might have shouted, but I didn't. The whole thing could so easily just start up again, and that thought gave me vertigo. My fatigue was roaring back at me like a train from a tunnel, meaning I probably ought not to have eaten as much as I had. Only the point of cream aerating there on her nose kept me from caving in altogether. It proved, after all, that she didn't know everything.

Nicole balanced her cigarette filter on the saucer, centered inside the ring of ash. A twinned ribbon of smoke pulsed up from the hot head like an offering. She had picked up that habit from me originally, I seemed to recall. The cigarette burned briefly red at the edge of the brown filter paper and then the final spark went dead against the wadding.

"Adrian," Nicole said. "What are we going to do about . . . ?"

"About?"

"You know. Our arrangement. . . ."

I leaned forward to examine the sprinkling of crumbs that remained on my plate. My left hand was on my knee and my thumb had turned below my palm and was covertly stroking the roughened surface of that circle of bone, trying to make it turn round my ring finger. Funny: I hadn't been aware of that ring at all for at least a couple of years, and now it felt exactly like a shackle. Maybe it was my recent interim in stir suggesting the comparison.

"How long will you be around?" I said reluctantly. What I had been thinking of asking was, *When is your child's birthday?* But it didn't appear she intended to bring that up.

"I'm due to go back tomorrow, actually," Nicole said. "I'll be done with the business end of things tonight, all over but the shouting really. But it's a full-fare ticket, you know, so I could always change it."

"Oh," I said.

The waiter rolled up again, this time bearing a large and ornate silver tray of pastries. Nicole turned toward the ranks of cakes and tarts, pretending to consider. The cream on her nose gave all her gestures an air of burlesque, but if the waiter was amused he didn't show it.

"No thank you," Nicole said.

"No pudding?" I said. "No sweet?"

Nicole flipped her wrist and looked at her watch. "No, I really couldn't," she said. "In fact, I need to be going in just a minute or two."

I surveyed the selection myself for a moment, then pointed. The waiter set a strawberry tart before me and passed on to the next table. The little confection was so artfully achieved it seemed a shame to put the fork to it.

"Not even a taste?" I said.

"Ugh," Nicole said. "All that sugar, I think not. I think the scones were enough for me. With that heavy cream. . . ."

I chipped off a corner of the tart and set it on my tongue. Perhaps she was right, sugar shock seemed imminent. I put the fork down on my saucer. Nicole was burrowing in her purse. I looked at her watch where it flexed with her wrist. Four forty-five—it had been one of my briefer hours. She had the sort of watch with an additional sickle-shaped dial that told the phases of the moon.

"I've really got to run," Nicole said, plucking out a five-pound note. "Look, let me leave you something for the check."

"No no," I said, fluttering my hands. "My pleasure, altogether."

"I just wish we had more time . . ." Nicole said. "Look, I know what. . . ."

"Do you," I said.

"I'm staying at Fleming's Hotel. Room one-eighty-six. It's just near Green Park."

"I know the place," I said. "Half Moon Street."

"So maybe we could meet later," Nicole said. "You know, and really talk things over. That was the point of the arrangement, wasn't it? That eventually we'd have to think things through?"

"But you've got a late dinner," I said. "And probably an early flight."

"I *hear*," Nicole smiled slyly, "you can't sleep anyway. Don't worry about me."

I leaned across the table and put my two hands on her shoulders and kissed the point of cream off of her nose. Nicole blinked, but didn't withdraw.

"Cream on your nose," I explained.

"Oh," Nicole murmured. "Thanks." She made some slight movement and my hands slipped down and flattened onto the bare skin between her collar and her chains. Her chin was square, her wide mouth slightly open. I could hear my breath passing out of my body and into hers.

"I'll see you," Nicole breathed back to me. "Later on."

Then she was gone. Snap, just like that. I shook myself. Such a ghostly departure, as if I had only imagined her, after all. Perhaps it was just me. My hands still tingled with her warmth. For something to do, I finished the tart, though it felt like it was taking me to the edge of a diabetic coma.

The sun was failing rapidly and it was turning twilight in the greenhouse. Time to be off for the Tooth and Claw, I recollected, and I called the waiter to bring the bill. Higher than a cat's back too; it needed all my ready cash to pay it. I had to go through all my pockets for coins to make up a decent tip.

Then I got up and walked groggily off into the bowels of the store, all that sugar fouling my blood. There was a smacking sound behind me and I felt my jacket pocket suddenly lighten. When I turned, there was the copy of Attar lying on the floor behind me. I stooped woozily to pick it up and went on through the lower floors of the store clutching it in my hand.

Harrods was even more crowded than it had been when I came in, everyone packing in to capitalize on the short interval between the closing of their offices and the store. Everyone dragged forward by his scrabbling, snuffling dog of desire. . . . I struggled to the front of the store and spun through a revolving door out onto Brompton Road. The rapidly cooling air freshened my mind a little. Whatever else you might think of the Sufis, it was clever of them to understand how love is fundamentally terrifying. Because . . . *an ignorant person will ask, "What connection is there between belief or unbelief, and love?" But I say, "Do lovers regard their lives? The lover sets fire to all hope of harvest, he puts the blade to his neck, he pierces his body. With love comes sorrow and the heart's blood. Love loves the difficult things."*

# sixteen

Quite right too. Attar's image of things was a bit too otherworldly though—the drawback is that the Sufis just don't believe that the world is really there. *The throne and the world are only a talisman . . .* all that. Which is where I think they made their mistake—offending the *anima mundi.* There the wound of love should become love's power, which can carry the adept through the ether to the place of his heart's desire. Hers? I wasn't adept enough yet, obviously. It required much further study. The subject was power and who would have more of it, but no, no, it shouldn't be that. I walked back in the direction of South Ken, toward a branch of my bank where I seemed to remember there was an outdoor cash machine. And I was right, about that much at least. Someone was there ahead of me, so I had a minute to wait. Then I pushed in my card and tapped in my secret number. A lean sheaf of red and blue banknotes pushed out into my hand. I went down to the station, got onto the Circle Line, and rode ninety degrees back to Notting Hill Gate.

Stuart had already arrived at the Tooth and Claw and was sitting at the bar with a half-pint glass of seltzer next to his hand. It was perhaps a quarter hour past opening time but the place was relatively dead. The Carnival was roaring away outside, of course, so maybe that was keeping people on the street. Down at the far end of the bar, Terence was in close colloquy with some young woman whose face I couldn't quite make out in the shadows. When I caught his eye he came over and pulled me a pint of Guinness.

"Well met," I said to Stuart. "You get your business fixed all right?"

"Well enough," Stuart said. "We're set for the trip up to the country tomorrow, at any rate."

"How long will you be, up in Darlington?" I said. A *pro forma* question. A sip or two of the black-hearted stout had virtually stunned me, and I didn't really listen to the answer. I was looking down the bar, where Terence's

**151**

young lady had shifted herself into the light. A red satiny scarf was bound tight to her temples, covering her hair completely. She had skin the color of clotted cream, and a small silver ring through her nose. Terence was just touching one of her hands—I couldn't tell if the gesture was amorous or avuncular. It was the first time I'd ever seen her, I thought.

". . . and I'm only hoping it won't rain much," Stuart was saying.

"Oh, why's that?" I said, refocusing my attention.

"I was . . . *prevaricating* a little about those Nissen huts," Stuart said. "They're up there, all right, but they're still in little pieces in crates, I gather. What we've really got up there at the moment is a nice pup-tent city."

"Sneaky of you," I said. "Well, you've slept rough before."

"Yeah, but I'm getting past it now," Stuart said. "Tough on the rheumatism, all that. Well, and what have you been doing with yourself all day?" He winked. "Been remembering anything?"

*"What?"* My raised arm wigwagged, sloshing beer to the rim of the glass. It didn't quite spill over, though.

Stuart's eyes narrowed. "Easy," he said. "I only meant the medallion, you know."

"Oh," I said. "Right." Quite a turn he'd given me. Hardly twenty-four hours he'd been back in my area and I already had rather a lot to conceal from him. It was practically just like old times. . . .

"Maybe it takes awhile to take effect," I said. "But look, I'm wearing it."

I dipped my thumb under my collar and flipped out the golden disk. And all of a sudden I remembered I didn't know what had happened to that gray cog at the tearoom. Had Nicole taken it with her when she evanesced? Or had I just abandoned it there among the last of my coins on the tabletop?

"What you got there, man?" Terence said, drifting along the counter in our direction. "Jewelry?"

He reached to take the medal between his thumb and forefinger, and I leaned forward so as not to snap the chain. Terence turned the medal over, squinting at the inscriptions on the other side, then let it fall back into the hollow of my throat. "Magic, eh?" he said.

"That's it," I said. "It has some power. He gave it to me yesterday." I glanced at Stuart, who had lowered his head over his glass of seltzer. At this angle he looked younger than his years, unmarked, and I felt something powerful for him, about him, without quite knowing what it was.

"Ah, Mr. Boatwright," Terence said reflectively. "Wouldn't mind a word with you, no. I've been thinking of setting up one of your centers here."

"Here?" Stuart said, looking up suddenly.

"Yes, in Notting Hill," Terence said.

Stuart opened his mouth to say something, but just then the door swung open and several men came in to cluster at the middle of the bar. Terence slipped away to serve them. Stuart lifted a wedge of lime out of his seltzer, squeezed a drop or two from it, let it splash back.

"Don't play with your drink, son," I said to him.

Stuart chuckled softly and tapped his fingernail on the wall of his glass. Someone stuck a coin in the juke and the tinny music began to mix queasily with the jumbled beats of the various sound systems outside and down the street. I was beginning to feel a trifle restless.

"Want to shoot pool?" I said to Stuart.

He looked at me. "Is there a table?"

"Right this way," I said, sliding down from my stool. I led him around the bar, the opposite way from the saloon, into a small alcove at the rear. There was a telephone box here and past it a raised dais where a three-quarter-size snooker table stood in a trapezoidal formation of red velvet benches ranked against the walls. The ceiling was low and it was slightly cooler here than in the main room of the pub. I fed the table fifty p and the balls clacked down into the trough. Stuart had already found the triangle, balanced on the rectangular shade of the hanging light fixture above. I let him rack.

"Lag?" Stuart said.

"No, your honors."

Stuart picked up a stick, squinted at the tip, threw it up an inch or two and caught it lower on its length, testing the weight and balance. All terrifyingly familiar—I felt that same narcotized sensation of removal, as the old queer taste began to perk again at the back of my gullet. The wedge of balls went splintering apart; I hadn't actually seen him shoot.

My hand came automatically up to catch the stick Stuart had tossed me, just a few inches from my face. So, he hadn't hit anything. The striped eleven ball lay just touching the cushion, a foot away from the southwest corner pocket. The cue ball stood at something short of a right angle to the shot, still I thought a side spin might take it on down. I leaned over and stroked the inside edge of the cue ball and watched the blue chalk-mark the tip had left spinning counterclockwise. A click and the eleven went wobbling down the rail and dropped.

"Nice shot," Stuart said, as I straightened up. I could see only the buttons on his shirt—his head was lost in the shadows above the lamp, as though he'd been decapitated. On the table the cue was still palely rolling on the felt, which was black for some reason, instead of green. I waited for it to come to a halt. Most of the other balls still hung bunched in the lower end of the table. I took a shot at the fifteen, but it picked up a weird twirl from another ball I hadn't realized it was touching and went nowhere. Then the cue ball reversed and turned slowly backward, backing up across the dark felt. It went out of focus as I looked at it, a ghostly rent into . . . someplace else altogether. Somewhere I had never been. Was I remembering anything? I never actually saw any of the rooms where Nicole used to entertain her clients, but sometimes I would try to imagine them. I knew that she only worked the tippy-top of the best hotels and that most of her clients were out-of-towners, Europeans, Japanese.

Stuart took the cue out of my hand and stretched himself out over the table. The harsh light from the hanging fixture darkly hollowed his cheeks and his eyes. He was stretching to reach a long shot on the two. A hank of hair hung limp on his extended neck, which I could have broken quite easily in that position by hitting it with a hammer-fist. Most of her clients had been regulars too, generally everyone wanted her back. Stuart would boast about that sometimes, and she herself seemed proud of it. Was that odd? They brought her flowers, other gifts. Some even wrote to her after they went home. I believed she had more than one proposal of marriage. What kept her going back to Stuart? Of course she was already married herself for part of that time, but then she wouldn't come along with her husband, would she?

The cue flashed forward and the two ball thumped into the side pocket. Rebounding backward, the cue smashed into the pack and everything broke up. I watched Stuart watch the eight ball roll to the lip of a corner pocket and hang there by a thread.

"Damn," he said, but to himself. He didn't really have much of a shot. What he tried was an improbable bank on the four, but he didn't hit it. I took the stick, shot and missed. Something had distracted me. If memory was a piece of architecture then mine was a grand baroque hotel, where I'd lost myself in one of the more ostentatious suites, one with no exit, only halls and rooms of gilt-edged mirrors reflecting one another back and forth, infinitely receding. But when I finally found an authentic window it overlooked the block of Tenth Avenue where I used to live, back there in Hell's Kitchen. It was quiet, a calm spring dawn, and the air was fresh and cool beyond the sill. I heard a cab door squeak open, slap shut, then Nicole was coming down the block, passing the blobby colors of the Korean flower bins. She wore a cream linen suit with a white blouse and she looked perfectly bright and fresh, as if she were beginning her day instead of ending it. Her purse and a light cloth coat were clasped together under one elbow. She walked alone on the outside edge of the sidewalk, just beyond the shadows of the faded awnings, as though doing a balancing act on the curb. She didn't look up when she passed under my window, and for some reason I didn't call.

At the main entrance of my building she ducked in and during the few seconds she was out of view I knew as well as if I were still watching that she had taken the cog from her jacket pocket and was pushing it through the vent into my mailbox. Her signal she'd be waiting for me to search her out. . . . She was smoking a cigarette when she came back outdoors, and the smoke flagged back a few feet behind her, then invisibly diffused. Why didn't I just call down to her? It was as if the fact of our secret had become more important than its content.

Now she was going back to give Stuart her money. His money. I watched her back receding, the dark weight of her hair down the middle of it. Her jacket was padded to make her shoulders look a little wider than they actually were. Stuart could be very nice to her sometimes; if he were feeling cheerful this morning he might already have run her a bath, might sit on the edge of the tub and massage her feet while she lounged in it. If he was sick and angry he'd whip her with the cord to the coffeepot, very high up on the backs of her thighs where a garter belt, say, might partially camouflage the welts. She kept going back to him, either way.

The stick was in my hands again and I bent forward. There was an obvious bank shot on the ten, and I took it without paying attention to what the rest of the table looked like. *Crack!* There was the golden triangle. The ten ball slapped into the side pocket, but the cue kept traveling, till it kissed the eight into the corner pocket too.

"Hard luck," Stuart said, and shrugged. I looked at him, his hands empty and palm up, and felt the familiar titillating rush of rage. How often I used to pray for a chance to kill him . . . well, truth was I could have killed him plenty of times. When he was nodded out, for instance; often enough I'd seen Stuart tap with the needle still hanging in his arm. I could have cut off his head with a hatchet and he'd never have felt a thing—few enough people would have bothered to miss him either. Or just shot him up again with a stronger dose. But that wouldn't have done me, not satisfactory. I would have enjoyed killing him in a fair fight, so long as I was sure of winning, and getting away afterward. But that was the chance I never seemed to get.

It becoming difficult to control myself, I crouched down out of sight and fit another coin into the table's slide. All that was behind me, it should be said, though if life is really one big circle it was also all still ahead of me too. Like the notches on the dial of a clock that the hands must pass again and again, without stopping, without stopping. The slide moved crookedly when I shoved it, and got stuck. I crashed my fist into it a few times, but it wouldn't budge, though I rocked the whole table. All right, calm down, all right. I'm not angry. I'm not *angry.* . . . I'm not angry, anymore. . . .

"Terence," I called, hoisting myself up. "Looks like the table's jammed again." Stuart was looking a little concerned. I might have been pounding on the mechanism harder than I knew. Truth—a tithe of Nicole's earnings must have ended up in my own veins eventually, because Stuart was generous, for a junkie, and I was his best friend.

Terence came in twirling his keys on the long brass chain that fastened them to his belt. He squatted and unlocked the table. The remainder of the balls came rumbling down. I watched his big hands cozening the slide back into its normal position.

"You're so hard on it, Adrian," he muttered. "It only wants gentleness, after all."

"Stay and have a game," I said, as he stood up.

"What, three-handed?" Terence said. "Too complicated, your American games."

"Screw your buddy," Stuart said.

"Do what?" Terence turned to face him. That's the way, best keep him in sight.

"Simple," I said. "Chop the balls up high low middle and just try to keep your own five on the table."

"And get everybody else's off," Stuart said.

"A simulacrum of the state of nature," I said. "Just have a go, you'll get the hang of it."

Terence nodded and picked up a stick. I felt better knowing he would stay; it improved the situation's balance somehow. Only I couldn't help remembering how Nicole had always been so terrified of needles. She wouldn't even be in the room with one—she was morbidly afraid of blood as well. But what really seemed to bother her was the idea of the tracks, as if she'd be shut out of paradise if a scar was found on her body at the gate. She'd have left Stuart in an instant if he'd ever marked her permanently, but then he'd always seemed to be aware of that.

It was my turn suddenly. I stooped and sunk the four.

"What am I, by the way?" I said.

"Low," said Stuart.

"Oh, thanks for telling me," I said. "I'm sinking my own balls."

"The name of the game," Stuart said. "Hey. That was one of mine."

"Was it?" The fifteen was hanging on the rim of a corner pocket. I shuttled the stick and dropped it in.

"There's an empty church up above the A-forty," Terence said. "Two-floor building, an empty rectory built off the back. I could get charge of it probably, my local organization. We could have a center in the neighborhood right here."

There was a possible shot on the six. I lined it up and stopped to consider. Stuart was dragging a thumb along his jaw; the gesture pulled his mouth crooked.

"I don't know," he said. "Difficult to make that work. It's what I was telling that other fellow . . . what's his name? You know him. Begins with an S."

"Horace," Terence said. "That would be Horace Stamp."

I shot the six and got it. There was an almost straight shot on the eight. Okay to sink the eight, in Screw Your Buddy.

*157*

"That's it," Stuart said. "Well, he had the same idea—might even have been the same building, he said it was above the highway there."

"Did he?" Terence said, rather dryly. "I wonder."

I sank the eight and began to consider a distinctly more difficult shot on the twelve.

"Right," Stuart said. "Well, it's been tried in New York, and it *can* work. But it's harder that way. You've got to pull people out of context, that's the whole method. Leave them sitting right in the middle of everything they used to be into. . . ." He shrugged. "They fall."

I took my shot at the twelve and missed it.

"Fall?" Terence said. "Oh. You mean they go back on the game."

I passed the stick to Stuart, who turned to survey the table. "Hey," he said. "All of a sudden looks like we're in trouble here." But then he sank the five ball. He pushed himself up from the table and looked toward Terence. "Right, they go back," he said. "Then they come back into the program, and then they drop out again—you get a couple of people zigzagging like that and the whole center can crash."

"I see," Terence said. "But we've got a sort of village mentality here, you know, people don't like to go far off from the neighborhood."

"Sure, it's the same where I come from," Stuart said. "But the choice just got to be made, sometimes." He took a shot at the one ball.

"Wait a minute," I said. "This looks like persecution here."

But he hit it too hard so the ball rattled in the pocket and bounced back out. "Set you up at least," he said to Terence, passing him the stick.

"Thanks," I said. "Terrific."

"A halfway house *here*," Stuart said, "now that could be very useful."

Terence grunted and dropped the one. I took a look round the table. Someone must have taken the two ball off before I started paying attention. I had nothing left but the lonely three. However, Terence didn't have much of a shot at that.

"Because, you know," Stuart said. "There's always a fairly serious reentry problem too."

"I'll bet there is," I said.

Terence shot at the three and missed. Couldn't believe he'd tried it, there'd been plenty of easier shots. Sort of hurt my feelings, actually. He straightened up and gave me the stick.

"Why do you say that?" he said.

"Because," I said, "the real world is not a controlled environment."

"You think it won't hold up?" Terence said.

I turned and looked down at the table, where the layer of balls seemed to warp downward into the black surface. There was a wavy sensation in my head and for the moment I seemed to be having some difficulty recalling the rules of this game.

"Wouldn't surprise me if it didn't," I said briefly, and looked back at Terence again. Terence and Stuart exchanged a glance.

"It's held up for me all right," Stuart said.

"Ah, but you've got religion," I said. "Most of these people you're dealing with, they'll end up with nothing but technique. It's nothing but stimulus and response. It handles the person like a machine."

"But if it works. . . ." Terence said.

"Short-run gain and long-run loss," I said. "The world isn't a machine either, you know."

"Well, and what would you rather, then?" Terence said. "Magic?"

"Yes," I said. "Why not?"

"We'd welcome a little magic in the centers," Stuart said. "Just bring your wand by any time."

So I turned away from them to look at the table again. They were ganging up on me, my two friends, but that was the name of the game, after all. But I couldn't seem to see the shot I wanted.

"Adrian," Stuart said. "If everything in the world is alive . . ."

"Right," I said.

". . . and everything that lives is holy . . ."

"More or less."

". . . then where does evil come from?"

I swiveled back to him, but he wasn't smiling. The movement made my head swim, and I had to put the butt of the stick on the floor and use it for a prop. Maybe that stout had been a poor idea, even though I hadn't finished it. As a matter of fact I couldn't even seem to remember where I'd left it. The red-scarfed woman put her head in the door, saw Terence at the pool table, and pulled it back out.

"It's the world getting back at us," I said.

"For what?" Terence said.

"For trying to kill it," I said. "Hah," I said in Stuart's direction, "you thought I wouldn't have an answer, didn't you?"

**159**

"Well, but there does seem to be a slight odor of tautology in the room," Stuart said.

"Look," I said. "Have you been to Rome this trip? Been to Campo dei Fiori? Dead needles so thick on the ground in there you'd think it had been raining them, you'd think they were new articles of faith."

"I don't follow," Stuart said.

"That's because you've become a logic picker," I said, "in your old age. You're living in a Cartesian world, right? Descartes thought it would be simpler to live in a world of dead matter because dead things are easier to dissect. They don't flop around in that inconvenient way. . . ."

"What then?" Terence said.

"After a few centuries you can begin to actually believe that your own body is a machine," I said. "Or a corpse, more like. Then it needs some very special stimulation of one kind or another. To make it feel a bit more lively, do you see?"

"Ah," Stuart said, shifting restlessly against the wall. "Go ahead and shoot, why don't you?"

I turned around and looked at the table, but the table wasn't there anymore, only the balls turning and revolving around each other in a dark and vacuous depth of space. Bruno embraced Copernicanism because of the promise of infinite worlds, for the knowledge of their distant revolution around *those large animals, which are called stars. Let the earth move, that it may renew itself and be born again, for it cannot endure forever in the same form. . . .* Could a whole infinitude of worlds be cold and empty? For an instant my own faith was shaken and I believed that it could. While our own unfortunate world went limping toward an end of final stasis, where it would hang among the others, all smooth and blank as billiard balls, in that eternal silence.

I blinked the table back into focus: easy shot on the three in the side. I dropped it cold and started looking for another.

"Hold on," Stuart said. "That was your last ball."

"Was it?" I said. "Oh. Right. I just committed suicide, eh?" I handed the stick to Stuart and turned my back.

The balls clicked, a cushion thumped, and I heard him muttering surlily under his breath.

"So, what happens when you scratch in this game?" Terence said.

I sat down on one of the velvet benches, facing the others again. Stuart was still bent over with his full weight on his palms, inspecting the detritus of his bad shot.

"Technically, you pull up *two* balls," he said. "One for each of your buddies, so to speak. But since this is a coin table. . . ."

"Oh, that's no difficulty," Terence said, pulling out a loop of that brass chain. "After all, I've got the key."

And owing to that circumstance, this selfsame game went on for about another two hours. A classic comedy of errors, on all sides. So all three of us had to start laughing at it, in the end.

seventeen

There was more to it, though, than that; I really hadn't even come close to exhausting the topic with my bits and bobs of verbal machination. Somewhere, sometime, something had been mentally mislaid. The first man, when he fell to earth, forgot his origin, and in that oblivion began the world's great wrong . . . but there was also something else, some other thing I had forgotten—it nagged at me, and put me further off my game. I don't think we ever really finished it, but after another hour or so, business in the pub picked up and Terence had to go back behind the bar, taking his key chain with him. Stuart and I shoved the rest of the balls off the table somehow. Scratch or no scratch. So then it was over. Stuart propped the stick against the wall.

"Have another?" he said, with a yawn.

"No, I don't think." I didn't need it. And I never much liked drinking with teetotallers anyway. It always ends up seeming they've got an unfair advantage. Stuart yawned wider, so I could have seen his tonsils, if he had any tonsils. I didn't look close.

"Over your jet lag by this time?"

Stuart snorted. I followed him back into the public bar. Terence was just visible, head-high above a throng of people pushing empty glasses at him. The door was wedged open onto the street and the crowd within was becoming continuous with the crowd without. The jukebox was blinking and flashing, so it must have been turned on, but it was drowned out by the sound systems thundering in.

"Hello, Terence," I screamed. "What's the time?"

"Only half-ten," Terence shouted back. "Anything for you?"

I glanced back over my shoulder at Stuart, who was prying his lids apart with thumb and forefinger, so I could see the whole rondure of his reddened eyeball. I signaled back to Terence, thumbs down.

"Thanks for the evening," Stuart called out. "We'll talk again."

If Terence answered I didn't hear it. We shouldered over to the doorway and entered the roaring scrum outside. There was the thick smell of beer and sweat and meat burning somewhere nearby. All around us the steel whistles shrilled unbearably.

"Tour of the Carnival?" I cried into Stuart's ear.

"I think not," he mouthed at me. "Sorry, but I'm fading fast."

"Come on, then," I said. "Let's get out of it." And I led him around a corner or two, then south on Ledbury Road. We had been on the edge of the main activity, so it wasn't long before we were clear.

"They don't take it lightly, do they?" Stuart said, once we could hear ourselves again.

"Can't afford to, most of them," I said. "For most of the vendors and things, it's where they make their main money for the year."

Stuart nodded, stroking his chin. We went on quietly in the damp green dark, and I turned onto Chepstow Crescent.

"You live around here, right?" Stuart said. I felt a cold clutch in my gizzard, as if I'd accidentally swallowed a large chunk of dry ice.

"Not far," I said falteringly. "But I'll walk you to the tube stop."

"That's good," Stuart said. "Otherwise I'd have no idea at all where it is at this point."

"Oh, my pleasure," I said. It was very ungracious of me, I know, but I just didn't want Stuart to find out exactly where I lived, not that he didn't already know, but postcards were one thing and drop-ins another. However, my stomach began to unclench slightly as I realized that I could easily walk past the place without stopping to point it out. In fact we were already going by the front rails of my building. There was my nameplate screwed to the doorway, too dim and distant for him to do more than just make out the edges of it, supposing he were looking. Opposite the steps was parked a huge black Bentley, long as the block, with a pinprick of light in the front seat as if the driver were reading a map. I took a lingering look at it as we strolled along the endless stretch of its front fender. It was a lot of car for this neighborhood—must have taken a wrong turn to end up here. As we passed the front grille, the engine coughed discreetly and the car pulled out. It went past us and cruised along hesitantly a few yards ahead, as though the driver were still lost.

"What time's your train tomorrow?" I asked Stuart.

"There's one every hour or so from King's Cross, so I'm told," he said. "I'll leave from there around ten, most likely."

"Then you've got time to catch up on your sleep," I said.

Stuart yawned, contentedly I thought, and clicked his jaws shut neatly, like a cat. At the end of the block the Bentley made a half-turn and stopped, and someone got out of it to stand in our way. I thought he meant to ask me directions, but instead he only grunted and gestured at the car's open back door with some middle-sized dark object he held in both hands. At first it looked like a bottle of champagne; then I thought it was a lap dog or some kind of pet, from the nervous way he kept stroking the side of it. Then I saw it was one of those squatty little submachine guns of the sort that English criminals are not supposed to have.

"*Come* on," the fellow was saying. "*Get* in."

Stuart inclined his head suavely, as if it were all perfectly normal, and slid into the back of the car.

"Chop chop," the fellow said, in a parodic manner, giving me an unpleasant smile. I hadn't recognized him at first because his nose was all covered up with a big X of sticking plaster and his spikes had wilted, like the leaves of a dying houseplant. Looked silly enough to make me laugh, but that machine gun was describing tight figure eights not quite a full yard from my solar plexus. I wondered if he'd actually fire the thing if I made a dash. People aren't quite so casual about gunfire over here as they are in the States, but Stuart was already pinned down in the car and I didn't quite feel entitled to abandon him.

So I ducked down into the car myself. Stuart had scooted across the seat to make room for me. The upholstery was of a reddish leather, soft as a glove. There was a thick glass panel between the front and the back, but it had been lowered, so I got an unobstructed look at the Last Mohican's profile when he turned from the wheel to give me a squint. His hair was sticking up the way it was intended to, but there was a big blob of fresh stitching in the center of the web tattoo, as if some larger stronger spider had invaded and taken over.

"Nice car," Stuart said.

Mr. Liberty got into the front passenger seat and clapped the door shut. "Off," he said, and the Last Mohican faced forward and pulled out.

Mr. Liberty braced the gun barrel on the seat back, aimed at the base

*164*

of my left ear. The Last Mohican turned onto Pembridge Road. There was a rustle next to me, and when I rolled my eyes over I saw Stuart taking an ostentatious look at his watch.

"You can just take me to Piccadilly," he said. "The Regent Palace Hotel."

"Listen to this, would you, Sid?" Mr. Liberty said. "Another bloody clever farking Yank."

"Well, you don't have to drop me right at the door," said Stuart. "Anywhere near Piccadilly Circus would do nicely."

"We'll drop you in the river if you like," said Mr. Liberty. "Isn't *you* the boss wants to see."

I cut my eyes toward Stuart again and shook my head ever so slightly, because I thought I knew what he was thinking. That time when some strung-out junkie stuck up Uncle Bill's crib with a Saturday-night special when he and I'd been there waiting to score. The gunner had picked a bad moment because Uncle Bill himself was out, and it was only Stuart and me and a few other clients waiting for him to come back with our stuff. So while the lot of us were waiting, Stuart needled him until he got distracted and woggled the pistol and turned his head far enough from me that I had my chance to jump up and knock him winding across the room. Uncle Bill was so grateful for that one he gave us each five dime bags for free. . . . But I was younger then and had had more sleep and the other guy was sick and shaky and could barely hold the gun up anyway, and it would have been as likely to blow up in his hand as hit any of us if he did pull the trigger, and it wasn't a closed car and it wasn't a machine gun. Also I didn't much care if I got killed or not in those days. Maybe Stuart still didn't. Maybe *I* still didn't. There was a bit of a kick still, in that thought. But I shook my head again, very carefully. This gun barrel hadn't wavered a hair.

"You know these people?" Stuart said.

"We haven't really been introduced," I told him. "But they've been following me around all day. Maybe since yesterday evening, even."

"That's funny," Stuart said. "It can't be because they think you're beautiful."

"I doubt that," I said, beginning to get into the patter, better judgment or no.

"Put a cork in that, will you, Ted?" the Last Mohican said. Or not the Last Mohican—Sid, he was. Mr. Liberty made some expressive clicking sounds with levers on the side of the machine gun. But not Mr. Liberty—he was Ted.

"Better not," Stuart said. "Don't want to get blood and gristle all over this nice interior."

I didn't say anything. It appeared to be my blood and gristle in question, after all. My neck was feeling rather stiff from trying to hold my head perfectly still. I rolled my eyes to the near window to try and make out where we were headed. South. We must be getting near the river?

"Look at all this nifty stuff," Stuart was saying. "Intercom. Telephone. CD player. . . . Where's the television set? Oh, there. No Jacuzzi, though. . . . Now, what's this?"

I heard a click and shifted my eyeballs the other way, to see Stuart flipping down some sort of rosewood panel, or tray, from the back of the front seat. Behind it there was a miniature bar with a bottle of Bushmill's and another of gin hanging in silver clips, along with four short glasses. Stuart pulled the Bushmill's out.

"Leave that," Ted said. "That's for the boss."

Stuart poured out a sizable tot. I waited to see what he was planning to do with it.

"Pity I quit drinking," Stuart said, and held the glass toward me. "Here, you have it."

Oh, what the hell. I limbered up my neck, took the glass, and bolted it. There was a warm starburst in my belly, and that was all. Ted hadn't pulled his trigger. I supposed he wouldn't, not in the car. The Bentley made a left turn then, onto the Embankment. The Thames was just down there, low and brown on the far side of the retaining wall, though I couldn't actually see it at this angle. I passed the glass back to Stuart, who clipped it in place and shut up the bar.

"Good?" he said.

"Top notch," I said.

"The boss won't like it," Ted said.

"Who is he, this boss of yours?" said Stuart.

"Our Mister Kay?" Ted said. "Wait, you'll see."

"Must be doing fairly well," Stuart said musingly. "Plenty of jack to put into the car. . . . Not too much left over to hire the drivers, though."

**166**

I watched Sid's hands go tight on the wheel. "Clever barstard," he said. "Well, go on then. You'll get yours."

But Stuart didn't say anything more, in spite of this invitation. Maybe he had run out of cute ideas, and I hadn't been giving him much help, because I was occupied counting the bridges so I could figure out where we were. Wapping, was what I thought, the Docklands area, though it wasn't a place I knew my way around too well.

Sid stopped the car halfway down a long concrete pier. Ted got out, came round and yanked my door open, then stepped several yards back and gestured with the gun barrel. I got out. There was a line of pole lamps going down the dockside, illuminating an empty barge, a couple of defunct-looking tugs, and a sleek white yacht with maroon trim.

Stuart got out and stood beside me. Ted motioned in the direction of the yacht and slowly we began to walk that way. Sid must have been locking up the car, but he caught up with us soon enough. He drew a pace ahead of Stuart, then suddenly turned and hit him in the belly. I saw Stuart's eyes bulge white. When the second punch hit him he hung over double, gasping and bugging his eyes at the patches of oil on the asphalt. Sid waited a beat, then reached out and pushed him over with a flick of his hand and kicked him lightly in the ribs a few times with the steel toes of his boots.

"Get up, cocky," he said, pausing. "You're only mucking up your clothes."

When Stuart raised up to his knees, Sid kicked him again and knocked him back over. "Flash barstard," he said, and took a step back. "Go on, get up, why don't you?"

Stuart rolled over away from him and came tidily up on his feet. It was a neat, catlike movement, which showed he was less hurt than you might have supposed. But the first flush of the whiskey had worn away and I wasn't feeling very optimistic.

"Anything to say, cocky?" Sid inquired.

Stuart fidgeted with the zip of his jacket. "Not to the hired help, I don't think," he said. "Just run along and fetch the manager, hm?"

Sid sucked his breath and took a step forward.

"Leave it," Ted said. "*Come* on, let's get on the boat."

Sid lowered his hands and led the way up the gangplank, then down three narrow steps to the central cabin, where he rapped on the door. "Eh, Walt?" he called.

There was an indistinct murmur from within.

"We've got 'im," Sid said, and opened the door.

I stepped in after him. A largish cabin half below deck level, dim, with only one light, a desk lamp. A short, heavy-set man in a dark suit was sitting behind the desk, clipping something out of a newspaper. He had his head tipped far back to squint at his work through a pair of half-glasses at the end of his nose. But when we came in he put down the scissors and slipped the paper quickly into a file folder. Once he took the glasses off, I saw that he was Walter Karnock. He was smaller than he looked in pictures, but very solid. A careful wave had been carved in the grease of his thick black hair; he checked it with one finger as he looked up at us. His face was thick and beefy, his eyes two fishy protuberances. I wondered if he'd know me from the Empress. No, apparently not.

"I only asked for one, dint I?" Karnock said.

"It's him." Ted stuck a finger in the small of my back. "The other sod was trailing along so we thought we'd better bring him too."

"What happened to him, then?"

"Took a tumble," Sid said. "Appears to be a clumsy bugger."

Karnock didn't respond. His lips worked unconsciously as he inspected Stuart. A bit of a newsprint photo was peeping out of the folder at his elbow: two dark eyes that looked familiar to me even upside down, though I couldn't have said why. Karnock noticed I was noticing and brushed the photo all the way inside the folder. Then he began to stare at me. Well, I knew a trick worth two of that. I focused my eyes on the bridge of his nose. I couldn't be beaten at this game, he'd never break my gaze. But after about eighty seconds or something, the whole floor shuddered under my feet as the engines came on. Involuntarily I glanced to the starboard windows and saw the dock lights falling away.

"Orright, my son," Karnock said, in tones of satisfaction. "Let's go up on deck, shall we?"

So we went up those stairs again. In the stern were several swivel chairs grouped around a small white table. While we'd been below someone had come and laid out several bottles of Grolsch and, incongruously, an empty plastic jerry can. I looked out over the rail at the low horizon of the Wapping warehouses with the lights of the city rising behind.

"Good swimmer, are you?" Karnock was asking.

"So so," I said, and turned to face him. He picked up the jerry can and tossed it over the stern. It swirled backward about twenty yards in the engine's wake and then a sudden sharp rattle ripped it into pale shreds, which quickly sank. There was a bitter smell in the air. I turned my head and saw Ted changing clips.

"Orright," Karnock said, dropping into a chair. "Have a seat, have a drink, go on, it's orright."

We sat down then, except for Ted, who remained standing near the awning over the cabin steps, holding the machine gun at his hip and watching the rest of us. Two small lamps fixed to the awning's poles shed enough light for us to see each other's faces. But Karnock appeared to be looking over my shoulder instead, toward where the wake of the boat's motor had sucked down those shards of jerry can. The whole demonstration struck me as a touch too mannered, derivative even, you might say, and yet I wasn't in the right position to evaluate it from the purely aesthetic standpoint. No, not quite. The position to be in vis-à-vis Karnock was me in the chair and him on the couch—strapped down, preferably. I watched his eyes shorten their focus.

"Go on, have a swallow," Karnock said, lifting one of the Grolsch bottles to demonstrate. "It's not poisoned, d'you see?"

So I lifted a bottle and took a gulp. It tasted flat and slightly metallic. Maybe it was my state of mind.

"You've been poaching on my manor, my son," said Karnock. "You've been trespassing, you have. Can't have that, now can we?"

"What do you mean?"

"*You* know," Karnock said. "You've been interfering with my customers. You've been putting them off my product."

"I don't follow you," I said. "I'm not trying to be clever or anything, but I really don't know what you're talking about."

"Oh, Sid. . . ." Karnock whispered. Sid, who was sitting on my left, put down his beer and backhanded me across the mouth. The blow had a certain authority to it. It spun my chair three hundred degrees and left me staring out toward shore, a thick warm taste of blood on my tongue. We were in the middle of the river now, and the boat, I observed, was just rounding the Isle of Dogs.

Karnock had opened a discussion with Stuart. "You're not drinking your beer, my son."

"I don't drink," Stuart informed him.

*169*

I swung my chair back to face the group.

"Won't you just have a taste for me?" Karnock said. "Don't want to hurt my feelings, d'you?"

Stuart lifted the bottle in front of him and tossed it over his shoulder, not even turning his head to see the splash. Karnock's mouth worked, like a fish blowing bubbles. He had the lips of a bottom feeder.

"Aren't you going to have anyone shoot it?" Stuart said.

"Oh *shut up*, Stuart, for God's sake," I said. "I wouldn't mind coming out of this with a whole skin if it's possible. Go kill yourself on your own time."

"Here, half a minute," Karnock said to me. "None of your games. *You're* Stuart."

"Uh-oh," I said. "There's been a mix-up. . . ."

"No, you're Stuart Boatwright, eh?" Karnock said. "With Spiral Centers. The one's been tampering with my trade."

"I'm Adrian Strother," I said, reaching for my wallet.

Sid whacked me across the knuckles with a short steel bar he'd produced from somewhere. "Just let me, there's a good lad," he said.

"Sure, whatever pleases you," I said. I raised up so he could reach into my hip pocket. He flicked through my Immigration booklet and then tossed it on the table.

"Same name and photo, right enough," he said. "But I dunno, it's two years out of date."

But Stuart, meanwhile, had managed to take something out of his jacket without getting his fingers rapped at all.

"My passport," he said pleasantly, handing it over.

Karnock examined the document, looked at Stuart, looked again at the passport, then slapped it loudly down on the table. "Are you blind?" he shouted at Sid. "Or just bloody stupid? Did you go to that farking lecture or dint you? I want to know."

Sid hung his head. "We might have been a bit late getting there, Walt," he said. "But Colin was there right through the whole show. He pointed this one out to us as they were leaving the hall." Sid jerked his thumb at me.

"Bugger *Colin*," Karnock burbled. "Christ, you poxy idiots. You've been following the wrong bleeding bloke."

"Now then, Walt," Ted said from the rear. "Dint we bring you the right one too, after all?"

"Well, p'raps," Karnock said. "So you did, but. . . ." He appeared to lose his train of thought. I could practically see it retracting crabwise from behind his eyeballs, the self vanishing inward, who knew where? His eyes went flat and shiny, like mica in the funny light, and his head hung slightly forward, limp and still. You could see how it might unnerve a person, that sense of the abhorrent vacuum. It made me think. Then his eyes switched on again and he turned his head toward Stuart.

"Right, then," he said, pointing his stubby finger. "*You've* been poaching on my manor."

"Do what?" Stuart said.

"You've got a mouth on you, eh?" said Karnock. "Right, a lot of clever talk. Use my own networks, will you, my son? To put my customers off my product?"

"Oh," Stuart said. "I take it you're not in favor of drug rehabilitation?"

"That's it exactly, my son," said Karnock. "Not on my manor, it's no good for my business, is it?"

"I don't know about that," Stuart said. "Maybe there's no difficulty."

"No difficulty?" Karnock said. "You're touching me in my pocket, chum. It's been many a long day since anyone's got away with that."

Stuart didn't say anything for a bit. He swung around on his chair and looked off toward the south side of the river, where the shoreline was relatively dark. Next to me, Sid took out a cigarette and lit it and I caught the tang of the smoke as it blew back by me. If it looked like we were really going to get shot I decided I would ask him for one. I picked up my beer bottle and washed the mouthful of blood down my throat, then felt over the rough patch inside my lip with the tip of my tongue. Stuart was lost somewhere in his head; he might have been reciting poetry, or saying his prayers. Karnock seemed to have vacated his identity again. He sat without moving, his lips slack and his head slightly inclined. What were we here for? Then Stuart swiveled back toward the table.

"*You* think," he said, "that the Spiral Centers are going to take your customers away. You think you'll have less buyers than you did before? Have I got that straight? That's what you want to put us in the river for?"

*Us who?* I was thinking nervously.

**171**

Karnock cleared his throat. "I dint say *that*," he said. "P'raps we could come to an accommodation."

"Such as?" Stuart said.

"Just you clear off my manor, that's all," Karnock said. "Clear your whole lot back off to the States where you belong."

Stuart licked his fingertip and ran it along the edge of his lower lip. "No," he said eventually. "That won't do."

It annoyed me considerably to hear him say that. Because if ever there was a time that justified a touch of deception, downright dishonesty if need be, I thought this was really it. But then I had the nerve-racking thought that maybe Stuart *wanted* to become a martyr. He could fly away home to the arms of Jesus, after all, when I didn't have anything but the world. There's some serious question as to whether Giordano Bruno really enjoyed being burned alive. He didn't recant, though. They gave him eight days to change his mind, but he never did recant. Why didn't he just command the flames to stop?

"Well, my son," Karnock said. "You're for it, in that case."

"For what?" Stuart said innocently.

"For the long jump," Sid muttered. With a degree of gratification, so I thought.

"No no," Stuart said, spreading his hands and grinning. "You don't understand the situation. You won't be losing any business on account of the Spiral Centers."

"No?" Karnock said. "But you're putting people off my product, eh?"

"Sure," Stuart said, with the same easy smile, as though some omnipotent power had put him in charge of the entire predicament. "But it doesn't really matter, because you lose them anyway."

"Do what?" Karnock said, leaning forward.

Stuart spread his palms on the table. "They die," he said flatly. "That's how it goes. That's how it's always gone, with junkies. They quit or they die, one or the other. Either way, you don't have to worry. There'll always be some more."

"Eh," Karnock said. "I never thought of it like that."

His brow knitted up and he stared down at the tabletop for a long still time, at the spot where Stuart's fingertip tapped a slow patient rhythm. Again I felt his total absence, and wondered where he'd disappeared to, and what he might be doing there. It was a hell of a disappearing act, and who did I know who could match it? The question was a tiny prickling itch at the top of my cerebellum. It occurred to me that under other circumstances Karnock might make an excellent hypnotic. Something to remember for the Empress, supposing I ever got to the Empress again.

"Eh," Karnock said, without shifting his position. His head was still hanging dumb over the tabletop. "I'm tired. I've got a bit of a head, you know."

"Better have a powder, then," Ted said quietly. "There's a new box down in the cabin."

Karnock raised his head and waved at us. "Orright, Sid," he said shortly. "Clear off this lot."

"What, over the side, Walt?" Sid said.

"*No*, you berk," Karnock said. "Take them back into the city. Drive them wherever they want to go. *You* know, do the polite."

He pushed himself up onto his short legs and walked heavily down the stairs into the cabin. Ted let his machine gun drop to the length of its shoulder sling and followed. After a moment, the engines fell still and the boat began to swing in a quiet J curve, turning easily with the current. I craned my neck back. There was one bright star, but the rest of the sky was clouded over so I couldn't tell what constellation it belonged to.

"Never mind driving us," Stuart said. "We'll just take a cab, you know. We'll walk."

"Here, you don't have to worry," Sid said glumly. "No more punch-ups. He said we were to do the polite, you heard him."

"Wouldn't want to take you out of your way," Stuart muttered.

The engines cut in strong once more and the boat lunged forward against the slap of its own dying wake. Ted came up, without the machine gun, but with four more bottles of beer looped in his fingers.

"Who fancies a drink?" he said. "Come on, top up. No hard feelings, eh? It's only business."

"That's right," Sid said, more easily. "No one fancies being knocked about, but we don't bear malice, do we?"

"Sorry about that cut," I said dutifully. The beer was rising to my head, or something was, so that I felt light and distant.

"S'orright," Sid said, raising a finger to the lump of stitching. "Doctor says it won't scar, s'long's I get the stitches out in time."

"That's good, then," I said. "Wouldn't want to spoil your tattoo."

**173**

"Oh no," Sid said. "Well, it was just a mix-up. I'd likely have done the same in your place."

"You've had a bit of training, haven't you?" Ted said. "We'll be ready for you next time."

"I thought there wouldn't be any next time," I said, and feebly gathered my legs under me. The boat was still quite far from shore.

"Oh no," Sid said. "No more aggro. S'long's you don't offend Mister Kay."

"Odd duck, isn't he, your boss?" I said. Not very circumspect, but I was feeling too giddy to watch my tongue.

"I dunno about that," Sid said. He chucked his empty bottle over the side and reached to uncork another one. "Moody sometimes, you might say. He has his moods, he does."

"He's a deep 'un," Ted said proudly.

"He's a genius, in his way," Sid said. "That's the short of it. And geniuses are a little funny. But he's not a bad stick once you get to know him." He lifted his bottle and held it out toward me. After a second I got the idea, picked up my own bottle, and clicked it against his.

"Have a drink on it," Sid said. "It takes all kinds to make a world."

# eighteen

About forty-five minutes later Stuart and I were standing on the curb, watching the big Bentley spiral around the Piccadilly Circus monument and roll away back east where it had come from. Stuart yawned. I turned toward him when I heard his jaw click shut.

"Still crazy, hey?" I said.

"Am I the crazy one?" said Stuart. "So, want to come up for a minute, maybe?"

"I don't have any other engagements," I said, momentarily unable to remember exactly why this was not true. Stuart turned and began walking north around the curve of the Circus. I followed him into the mouth of Glasshouse Street to the door of the Regent Palace Hotel. Inside, Stuart cast about for a second, then moved toward the elevator bank.

On the upper floor where we disembarked, a worn carpet runner led down toward the point of the building's wedge. At an alcove along the way Stuart stopped at a drink machine and began patting his pockets for change.

"Care to partake?" he said, raising an eyebrow.

"No thanks," I said. "The caffeine, you know, this late. . . ."

Stuart bought a Coke, turned back, and opened the second door on the left. The room behind was dingy, but seemed clean enough; it was trapezoidal because of the building's funny pie-slice shape. Someone had thrown the covers forward on the bed, without actually making it up. Stuart sat down on the edge of the blanket and pointed me toward the chair at the little end of the room.

"Ah me," he said. There was a fizz as he opened his can. "The days are getting longer, seems."

"Always the unexpected extension." I scooted down on the chair's cold vinyl and let my head roll back against the faded paint on the wall. There was a smoky-looking ring on the ceiling around the light fixture. "That was a clever bit of argumentation back there," I said. "Saved our bacon, I would think."

"It was nothing but the truth," Stuart said. "And the truth shall set you free."

"I was wondering if you believed it, actually," I said. "Must tend to put you off your mission."

"Oh yes," Stuart said. He pried each shoe off with the opposite foot and swung his sock feet up onto the bed. "I don't think about it, that's the trick."

"The all-purpose trick," I said. "As long as it works for you. . . ."

"I'm kind of surprised they went for it, really." Stuart sipped at his Coke, and looked at me sharply over the top of the can. "Hey, who were those people, and what did they want? The whole proposition's ridiculous, did you happen to notice that?"

"Right," I said. "Well, it's different over here."

"Apparently so," Stuart said. He propped a pillow up against the headboard and sank down with his head against it, drawing up his knees. The weak overhead light cut deeper hollows under his eyes. "I mean," he said, "there was something sort of unbusinesslike about the whole encounter."

"I know, I know," I said, wagging my head. "Walter Karnock, that's our boy, is famous for being a whacko, really."

"Somehow I sensed this," Stuart said.

"He's got the idea he's Scarface, or Al Capone, or somebody from the movies," I said. "That appears to be the story. It's kid stuff, only with grown-up equipment."

"Real blood and all that," Stuart said. "So, but do I worry?"

He appeared to be directing this question to the ceiling, but after a moment I answered anyway. "No," I said. "No, I think not. I doubt you're really holding his attention."

"Not flattering," Stuart said, with a weak smile. He sipped from his can, gave it a shake, and stretched his arm down to set it on the floor. "But advantageous, you might say, under the circumstances."

"He does that sort of thing for amusement, so I hear," I said. "You know, hauling people off somewhere and giving them a fright. But now he's had his bit of fun, I doubt he'll bother us again. He doesn't have much cause to, really, like you said before."

"We're safe because he's a crazy sadist," Stuart said. "Am I understanding it right?"

"You'll be all right in Darlington, I think," I said. "Karnock is strictly a London phenomenon, if you believe what I read in the papers."

"That leaves you," Stuart said.

"Oh yes," I said. "I remain as always an interesting question to myself."

Stuart's arm flopped off the bed; his hand dangled down beside the Coke can. I watched him lower his knees and slide down further on the bed. There was a time I could remember when he'd been so thin you wouldn't know for sure if it was him in there or only wrinkles in the sheet. I couldn't tell now if his eyes were open. Bracing my hands on the spindly arms of the chair, I stood up.

Stuart's eyes popped open wide. "Ah," he said. "Sorry. I don't know what schedule I'm on."

"It's bedtime in England," I said. "You've got it straight."

"Ah," Stuart said, his eyelids pulling halfway down. "You better get some sleep yourself, Adrian, looks like you could use it."

Ugh, I wish he hadn't said that. The phrase hit my nervous system like a dose of amphetamine. Paradoxical suggestion.

"Maybe I'll see you tomorrow, then," I said. "I'll come up to the train station, buy you a cup of tea."

"All right," Stuart said. "Sounds reasonable." His head turned sideways on the pillow; I could see his breathing easing in his trachea. Two minutes later I was out and making my way west on Piccadilly. It was perfectly calm on the street, but I didn't feel at ease with myself at all; my bones felt like they were warping under some sort of an internal pressure, like the frame of a harp tuned up too tight. Very unpleasant sensation it was, and I did wish Stuart hadn't thought to mention sleep to me so directly. Or exemplify it, for that matter. The gaudy lights of the Ritz Hotel sign were scorching a hole in the darkness ahead of me. Then I was walking along the row of bright shop windows. The doorman, done up in his top hat and tails, sneered at me as I passed by. I had an impulse to hit him, but felt rather pleased with myself for resisting it.

Beyond the last hoop of the hotel's arcade the dark was spread out over Green Park as far as my eye could follow it. The park was theoretically shut at this hour, but the fence was little better than waist-high and I cleared it easily with a vault, landing with a spongy thump on the rain-soaked grassy earth inside. For a minute or more I remained in my crouch, until my eyes

**177**

adjusted and I could see the whole sweep of the meadow expanding palely before me. Just what the doctor ordered. . . . There once was a queen who upon discovering that her king was gathering flowers for his mistress from that park decreed that no more flowers should ever be grown there, which is why it is now called Green Park, so I'm told. The king was one of the Henrys, I think, and I have no idea what queen it was, but certainly there are no flowers here, only the grass with its wet, verdant smell. After a time I got up and began to walk across the meadow.

Somewhere around the middle I paused to look back. At this distance no sound came to me from the broad street, only the flicker or movement of the various lights, which might have been an optical illusion. I revolved on my heels and leaned my head back. The sky had cleared and was very deep and the constellations had combined themselves to tower to the height of the universe. If I had only been a little quieter in myself I believed I could have heard the ringing music of the spheres as they turned, each inside the next above it, something like a wet thumb run round the edge of a wineglass, something like the voice of angelic hosts. The sound came flooding down over me out of the celestial silence, but inaudibly, obscured by the sodden thump of my own heart.

I went on to the western edge of the meadow, where the first trees began, set sparsely at first, then growing closer together. A low breeze sprang up and the branches whispered, stroking each other's feathered lengths. I stopped to listen; the sound of it died and then came again. The shadowed tree trunks leaned toward me in a brotherly fashion, and somewhere behind the rustle of their movement was another sound of water purling. It seemed an age since I had known such happiness, flowing through me like a warm bright fluid. I had no reason and needed none for it; I was snug, barely conscious, on the breast of the living earth. A green thought in a green shade . . . but what was that thought thinking? The wind came higher, then fell to nothing, and in the stillness I remembered that Nicole was somewhere near and that she was expecting me.

I went back up a gentle slope through the trees until I reached the fence again, and hopped over it back onto the sidewalk. A double-decker bus went lurching and groaning by, and then for a moment it was quiet and the several lanes of the street were empty. Once I had crossed to the north side I perceived that I had gone past the opening of Half Moon Street in my wandering through the park. What time was it? Somewhere back in the city a large bell was giving tongue, but I couldn't manage to keep count of the strokes. I walked back to Half Moon Street, then up the block to Fleming's Hotel.

There was a small cozy bar to the left of the entrance and for an instant I was tempted to go in, but I did not. The desk clerks were dressed in black and looked rather disapproving, but I realized I didn't have to bother with them, since Nicole had given me her room number beforehand. 186. I turned quickly down the nearest corridor to get out from under the eyes of the management.

There was a short set of steps that went down and then up across a sort of T-square junction of more hallways. I went to the left—this turn took me completely out of view of the lobby. A pair of glass swing doors appeared in front of me and I pushed through and turned left again at another T-square intersection. The hall was low-ceilinged and quite narrow, and the room doors on the right-hand side appeared to tilt toward me, proffering their number plates. 176, 177. . . . Good. 180, 181. . . . 190.

Wait a minute. But there were no doors on the other side of the hall. I hesitated, then returned to the previous set of steps, went down, and turned to the left again. 169, 168. No. My feet were silent on the thick green carpet runner, and ahead of me the passage seemed to narrow to a point. I went back to the steps and the T square, or perhaps it was a different junction now. I turned left. 200, 202, 203, 205. But I hadn't gone up a floor, or had I? Then I realized I no longer had a clear notion of how to get back to the lobby either, and this thought made me inordinately nervous. An itchy sweat broke out on my forehead, and I began to have trouble getting my breath, as though the tightening of the hall were throttling me.

After a moment I got some kind of hold on myself and went through a pair of swing doors and down more steps into another T square. Breathing heavily, I closed my eyes, selected a corridor by touch, and went down it blind, dragging my fingers from doorframe to doorframe. When it felt right I stopped and looked. 188. On. 187. Looked promising. 186. I waited outside the door until my breathing slowed to normal, and then knocked. No answer, and none when I knocked again, considerably louder. Perhaps she hadn't yet returned. But when I pressed my palm against the door, the latch clicked open and the door went softly floating inward.

From where I stood I could see the bed, with the nightstand lamp illuminating the white triangle of sheet that had already been turned down.

*179*

There was the sound of running water. I crept in and gingerly closed the door behind me. The room was small (though definitely upmarket from the one Stuart was using), with barely enough space to allow a path around the bed, the desk, and the bureau. Up a pair of steps at the other end of it, a thread of steam was curling around the cracked bathroom door. Nicole could stay in her bath for hours at a stretch, which meant that I probably still had a little time.

On the far side of the bed was a single window, but when I thumbed the shade back I saw that it only overlooked some air shaft central to the building. I let the shade fall back in place. The room was being kept strikingly neat, which surprised me slightly, since in former times Nicole had inhabited her space like a tornado. Now everything was perfectly in order. A paperback book and a crisp fan of magazines lay on the nightstand next to a small travel alarm, somewhat reminiscent of the one I'd smashed the previous night. A briefcase and a few papers were foursquare on the desk, and on the bureau her watch and chains were laid out in a tidy row beside her purse. A few inches of a fabric belt or sash were pinched in the closure of her suitcase on its stand, and that was the only trace of incongruity.

I went to the bureau. The minuscule tick of her watch caught my attention and I saw that it was about a quarter past eleven. She had taken off her bone ring too and placed it within the neat concentric loops of her three silver chains. Next to it lay the little cog—so she had picked it up, after all. I opened the purse and thumbed through the contents but there was nothing in it especially revealing. Lipstick, compact, change purse, money clip, ball-point pen, packet of Players, pack of U.S. traveler's checks and another in sterling, a brass bullet lighter, a vial of aspirin, some business cards, some crumpled receipts. A key ring, with five keys on it, and her brass initial on a leather tag. I looked through her passport to see if she'd been making any interesting movements, but it appeared she had not left the States for several years prior to this trip.

The water shut off in the bathroom, and I hesitated, listening to the screech and shudder of the plumbing. Then came a splash, a slosh, the sound of a long luxurious lowering. I began putting the various articles back inside the purse. Let me say that I felt no compunction about all this poking and prying, though it was more characteristic of what I'd been in the old days than what I thought I was becoming now. The old days, well. For instance, Nicole and I had decided to exchange *bone* rings because they had no monetary value and therefore couldn't be converted into scag. And it wasn't only that Stuart might have taken her ring away and sold it, but that I would have been quite capable of doing the same with my own.

When I tucked the passport back into the purse, my fingers found the edge of a small stiff envelope. I hadn't noticed it before because it was the same color as the purse's lining, black. It had a pattern of fine white checks, I saw when I took it out into the light. Italian stationery. Inside were several snapshots of a three- or four-year-old Oriental boy. A handsome little thing he was too. He looked likely to grow into the type whose good looks would prove a kind of curse. Two of the pictures showed him sitting on a pair of skirted knees, and in one of these, the woman had leaned forward, partly into the frame, so that I could see the wide mouth and the square turn of the chin, with the black hair hanging loose and long on either side of it. When I realized the boy was probably only *half*-Chinese, or whatever, I got such a warm watery feeling in my knees that I had to use the bureau to hold myself up. All day, all night, ever since I'd first talked to Stuart probably, some secret chamber of my mind had been remembering and remembering that four years ago Nicole and I had still been seizing every opportunity to make our separate fleshes one. And everything would have suddenly turned different if. . . . If. But now it looked very much as if it wasn't so.

I straightened up then, and began turning the ring on my finger. It was loose and turned unevenly, but somehow it wouldn't go over the joint, so that in a minute I was scratching and clawing at it, like an animal with its leg in a trap. Then something gave way, with a slight sharp pain in my knuckle, and I saw the ring lying in the palm of my other hand. I took it and stacked it on the other one; the two were still a perfect, seamless fit. The rings had been cut from the same length of bone, and your finger passed through the channel where the marrow had once flowed, which accounted for their flattened, elliptical shape. The water surged on again in the bathroom; Nicole was rewarming her tub. Automatically I picked up the cog and dropped it into my pocket. Then I tiptoed over to the bathroom door.

A small mirror was fixed above the sink, and the far wall, above the tub, was simply one large mirror. The two together made a sort of periscope through which I saw the tub, with Nicole in it. Quite a fancy tub, for a modest room. It was raised, itself, on a sort of dais, and the green enamel of its rim was fluted. Nicole was lying at length with the back of her head

*181*

cupped in one of these flutes. In the doubled reflection of the mirrored wall, I could see that her eyes were closed, the long lashes lying on her cheeks. They were generous with their hot water here, for the splashing faucet was wreathed in steam. When the water reached the rim of the tub, her foot came questing up out of the suds to fumble at the tap. She had long toes, but they couldn't turn the faucet all the way off, and finally she had to sit up and do it with her hand.

The water roiled, lipping to the tub's edges, then subsided. Nicole remained in her sitting position. In the near mirror I could admire the long, long curving line of her back. She twisted her hair back over her shoulder so that the tangle of it lay halfway down the chain of vertebrae. She leaned closer to the mirrored wall of the tub and for a second I thought that she had seen me, through the reversed angles of the periscope, but then I saw that she was only looking at herself. Her eyes searched her reflection in the glass, and her hands came up and touched the different parts of her, a breast, a shoulder, as if to ascertain by touch that she was really still all there. Then with a sigh she let herself recline.

Probably it was too dark for her to have noticed me anyway; it was comparatively dim in the bedroom. And maybe Actaeon didn't really fare so terribly when he was caught spying on Artemis in her moonlit pool. True that she turned him into a beast by splashing the bright water in his face, true that his own hunting dogs no longer knew him, so they ran him to earth and tore him to pieces. But it was Actaeon himself who trained his dogs to seek the traces of the divine in nature, as he himself sought the sun's light reflected in the nakedness of the goddess of the moon. The dogs only did as they were taught, and Actaeon, ripped limb from limb, achieved the union he was seeking. *This is not death, but the dissolution of a mixture. . . .* Love is the fourth *furor*, and the most powerful, undoubtedly the most dangerous also, but surely Actaeon, through suffering the fury, won his empowerment as well and returned to his original home with the divine, passing into the nature of God.

I retreated a little then from the crack in the bathroom door, until I couldn't see Nicole any longer, only a semaphoric winking of the mirror's light. Was I fool or madman enough to believe she really was a goddess? Our present politics of personal relations holds it almost wicked to believe such things, but people do it anyway, and for a long time I really had believed that it was Nicole, only Nicole, who held the two chains in her hands and linked heaven and earth together through the magically mediated union of her body and her soul. But of course she was a person too, and I had done this person a disservice by making her my goddess. . . . Now the time had come to stop.

I was wandering in my thoughts and I didn't notice the noise of ingurgitation when the bathtub plug was pulled. By the time I thought to look up, she was already standing there on the top step, trailing a towel from her left hand, revealed. I saw that it was wholly true, what I had said that afternoon; she always *would* be beautiful. Not a mark on her, she was untouched, from her ten toes to the crown of her head; she looked as if that instant she'd created herself from nothing.

"So," she said to me. "You came." But when she saw I wasn't coming any further, she turned her head toward her suitcase. "There's a robe in there," she said. "Could you hand it to me?"

I went and lifted the suitcase's lid. That belt that had been hanging out turned out to be the sash of a blue and gold kimono. I carried it to her and she shrugged into it and cinched the sash around her waist. With that same slightly impatient movement she wrenched the wet rope of her hair out of her collar and let it drop onto her back. Then she came down the second step and drifted toward the bureau.

"I didn't know if you'd come or not," she said. "Oh. I see you found the pictures."

"Yes," I said. "Good-looking boy."

Nicole nodded, but not as though she'd really heard me. She gathered the snapshots into a pack and went with them to sit down in the desk chair.

"He's yours, I take it," I said to her.

"Yes," Nicole said. She put the pictures down on top of her shut briefcase and began to push them apart from each other with the point of her fingernail. "That's right."

"Who was the father?" I said. "If you don't mind my asking. . . ."

"Some Chinese gangster," Nicole said. There was another mirror hung above the desk and in it I saw her mouth turn sour for a second. Then she turned in the chair to look at me. "You don't mind, do you?"

"Of course not," I said. "No, it doesn't make any difference to me."

"He's dead anyway," Nicole said. "Somebody shot him, about three years ago. He was a drug dealer down in Chinatown. Do you see my cigarettes?"

*183*

I got the pack and the lighter from her purse and carried them across to her.

"I'm sorry," I said. "I mean, that the guy got killed."

"I'm not," Nicole said, lighting up. "I never missed him. It was an accident in the first place, the baby was."

"But you kept him."

"He was *mine*." Nicole took a long draw at the cigarette and shifted back to face the mirror, but she wasn't looking at herself this time. She appeared to be using the glass as a means of divination. "He was mine," she said at length, more easily. "You don't know what it was like, Adrian. You disappeared, Stuart went upstate, forever, what it seemed like. People were leaving town, or dying. . . . Then there was just me."

"I asked you to go with me," I said. "I begged you, as a matter of fact."

Nicole snapped her ash impatiently into the hotel ashtray. "Does it really matter who was in the right?"

"No," I said. "Well, look at you. You turned it all around, didn't you?"

"I did that," Nicole said, locking eyes with herself in the mirror now.

"He's a beautiful child," I said, and put my fingers on her shoulders, so lightly I felt the embossing of the fabric and nothing at all of the body beneath. "Has he got a name?"

"William," Nicole said, and stubbed out her cigarette. The tube of it broke in the ashtray because it was only half-smoked. "Will. I wanted something ordinary, he won't have a Chinese life. He's going to start school next year."

"Time flies," I said, noting how her wet coil of hair was darkening the cloth of the kimono. I went and picked up the towel she'd dropped on the bathroom step and brought it back. A tearing arid sadness started up in me when I began to dry her hair. I never even *liked* Nicole, in the beginning. At first I didn't understand what Stuart saw in her, and later when I had understood too well and also learned what he was doing to her, I ended up being angrier at her, for letting him. During that first long period she used me as her confidant; it was that sort of triangle, with the last vertex only done in dots. But even the most faithful confidant eventually gets tired of the position and I remember when I got fed up for good. It was one of those Ninth Avenue railroad bars, with a lot of old drunks and a few hookers and junkies; they even had food there, a long steam table. I was drinking vodka neat from short glasses and listening, half-listening, to Nicole. We sat in a booth by the plate-glass window; the bar was on a corner and outside one of those torrential spring thunderstorms was going on, so whenever a car passed a little too quickly it threw up a great slosh of dirty water on the glass, as though we were on some kind of ship.

I had done up in the bathroom, crouched on the toilet seat for greater privacy, about an hour before, so I wasn't hungry. I didn't think I'd ever be hungry again, but I'd bought Nicole a sandwich. She sat there picking at the beef and filling me in on the most recent chapters of her personal horror story. It had been a shaky, messy jab, still seeping a little blood, which stuck in wet red patches to the inside of my white shirtsleeve. I kept nervously plucking the fabric away, though it only freshened the bleeding to do it. I wasn't really listening to her, since I'd heard it all before; I knew she was somehow drawn to the pain, but deathly afraid of being scarred, and what more was there to know than that? She had fidgeted the top slice of the sandwich into a heap of crumbs and went *pickpickpick* at the meat inside while she was speaking.

So I knocked the plate and glasses to the floor, all in one clean splintering sweep, which got me barred from the place for the next six weeks. Very useful. Her eyes got big and dark and she looked at me—she had no idea, you understand; I'd been perfectly avuncular and consoling all along until that time. *I don't want to hear it*, I said, *I don't want to hear any more of it*. And I got up and stalked out of the place. I'd had an umbrella and a few other things in a bag but I forgot them, and it was six weeks before I could get them back.

Outside the rain had stopped and the air was a nacreous green, like the light was filtered through thick green glass and the whole atmosphere was pregnant with something misbegotten. It occurred to me that maybe the bomb had fallen somewhere in the vicinity and that was the explanation for it. I dithered on the corner for a second, still irrationally fuming, then started in the direction of my place. As soon as I had taken my first long step there was a crack, a grumble, and the rain fell in waves, even harder than before. After half a block or so I noticed that Nicole was walking a pace back from my side. She had on cotton pants and some crepey kind of blouse, and she was so wet it all stuck to her like sealskin. The sight of her only made me angrier. *Don't follow me*, I raved at her, *you better not follow me anywhere*. Maybe she couldn't hear me through the rain, which was noisy; it was raining so hard and fast I could scarcely see. She kept coming along, neither near nor far, as if she couldn't help herself. It was the only time, I think, I ever saw her completely bared of her essential self-possession.

She followed me up the stairs to my apartment, and halfway there my mood turned upside down. A perfect calm came over me while I was unlocking the door, a new kind of certainty, as though the world, knocked off one balance point, had found a new and superior one. She came in hugging herself, her teeth chattering loudly, and I slapped the door shut behind her and went to get a towel. Her hair was in a snaky snarl and I began chafing it with the towel, while my consolidated anger dried me from within, radiating like a furnace. After a while the towel was sopped and I dried and warmed the rest of her with the heat of my bare hands. That was only the first time, but she wouldn't leave Stuart, no matter what, not then and not any time later.

Such was the foundation of our very special arrangement. It wasn't much of a towel I'd used then, threadbare and probably dirty to boot, nothing so nice as this sample of hotel linen I was plying now. I finished, and tossed the towel back in the direction of the bathroom. By luck it caught on the doorknob and hung there. I picked up a brush from the desk and began to brush her hair out over the crook of my arm. It was wonderful hair, long and thick and a perfect black, like night itself, and it had a good clean smell. I brushed it somewhat longer than necessary. Nicole let her head rock back under the slow strokes, and in the mirror I saw the articulation of her long neck, with the arteries warmly throbbing somewhere in concealment. She left her head lying in my palm for a moment after I'd put down the brush, then straightened herself lethargically as though waking from a dream.

"That's been a long time," she said.

"So it has," I said, and moved a little distance from the back of her chair.

"Well, Adrian," she said, looking for me in the mirror. "What will we ever do?"

"We'll get a divorce," I said, with a slight effort.

"Ah," said Nicole. She took a cigarette out of the pack, but didn't light it. "I wondered if that's what you'd say, I wasn't sure. . . ."

"It wasn't your imagination."

Nicole swung round in the chair toward me. "There is someone in New York," she said. "But that wouldn't make any difference if—"

"It's all right," I said. "Will you marry again?"

Nicole shifted back to the mirror and frowned. "I don't know. I've been putting him off."

"So he doesn't know."

"Nobody knows."

"Better do it quietly, then," I said. "You think you can take care of the paperwork?"

"I can try," Nicole said. "I don't know if you'll have to appear or something."

"Oh God," I said, and sat heavily on the corner of the bed without knowing I was going to. "I don't know if I'm ready for that. Can't you just sue me for desertion or whatever?"

Nicole faced around and pointed with the unlit cigarette. "I can try," she said. "But really, I don't know much about it, do I? I'll let you know."

"Right," I said. "Well, I suppose I'd better go." But I didn't have the energy, just then, to push myself up from the bed.

Nicole put the cigarette down in the ashtray, stood up and threw off her robe. "I need to go to bed myself," she said. "Tomorrow will be quite a day."

She dropped the kimono over the chair back and walked around to the opened corner of the bed. I remained sitting just where I was, my dull eye tracing a pattern of the carpet, until her feet came pushing at me underneath the coverlet. Then I stood up.

"Tuck me in, Adrian?" Nicole said in a small voice. "Just this once?"

"All right."

I came to the head of the bed and stooped over her, drawing the covers up to her armpits, and smoothed the fold of the sheet back down. Her arms were slender on the quilting. They levitated, and her hands wrapped round my wrists.

"I don't know if I can sleep now," she said. *Hah!* Very likely this was one of her enchantments she was practicing, and perhaps I had just as well let it work on me. I could so easily have stayed, to worship her with my body all night long. Almost certain I wouldn't be doing anything better with my time, and at the worst it would make a change, eh? I turned my hands so that my fingers touched her pulse.

"Of course you'll sleep," I said. "Just . . . look at me. Your hands are getting very warm. Your heart is slowing, you can feel it slowing down. Now look at me . . . now, *close your eyes*. You're sleeping now. . . ." But it was no longer necessary; she was gone, lips slightly parted and the air passing through them in long deep breaths. I saw her eyes roll under the lids, looking at something in a dream. I could do that so easily sometimes . . . to someone else. When I released them, her hands dropped to the quilt like two feathers falling from a bird.

I bent down and switched out the light. I found my way to the door by the bright crack under it and flipped the lever by the knob so that it locked itself behind me when I went out. The corridor had corrected itself to a straight line of glass doors and shrinking doorframes, receding toward the lobby in the front. The lobster trap turned inside out. I passed the gloomy clerks and went into the cool air of the street. A little light-headed, and at first that was all. I had gone as far as Hyde Park Corner before the cog clicked into something in my pocket and I took it out and looked at it. It was never too late, at any time, to just *go back, go back, go back*. I set the cog underneath my tongue and felt the metallic taste spread upward, communicating the object's sympathetic power over the whole sector of the universe to which it belonged. It connected with the other old taste that had been in the back of my throat for two days. A whiff of blue smoke, burn of vodka from the neck of a bottle Stuart passed me, a salt tang on Nicole's hot skin, the smell of the dirty New York rain, and behind it the white acrid clarity of heroin. I took the cog back out of my mouth and dropped it between two bars of the grating I seemed to be standing on.

Though the trains were still running, I walked home just the same. After all I was in no hurry; I knew I didn't have a hope in hell of sleeping. The last soporific power I possessed had all been spent upon Nicole. And when I arrived at my own door, footsore but hideously alert, I realized I didn't even want to go in. The walls of the place would be too confining; even the thought of them put me off. I sat down on the top step and hooked an arm around one of the stair rails to hold me up in case by some freak I did nod out. Faint music came drifting down from the Carnival for the first hour or two, then it ceased. To occupy the silence, I began to tell myself the familiar stories. There once was a shaikh . . . and so on and so forth. After a long time I began to hear the birds.

*188*

# PART 3

## A Love Supreme

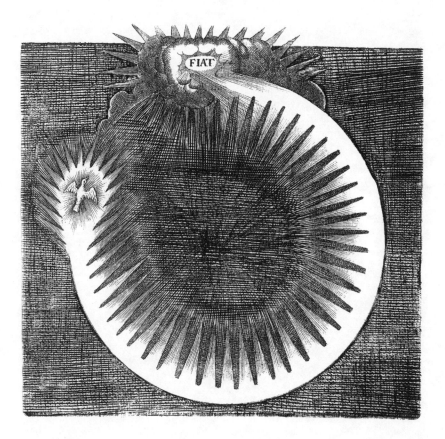

## nineteen

Hermes Trismegistus slept, his corporeal sense bound as by some heavy ligature, but his soul went gliding to the heights, and in the inspiration of his sleep a being called Pimander appeared to him. Pimander showed him a vision of a serene and joyful light; nothing was there but the limitless light, and the dreamer could not help but love it, but a vision of darkness followed it. The darkness of the infinite void became the very medium of Hermes Trismegistus's sleep, and the darkness turned in tortured spirals, like the body of a serpent. Then the darkness produced a vapor, like a fire, and it made an indescribable groan, like a cry of help from out of the fire. There was light again, and a holy Word written in the fire and leaping upward, and the air leapt upward after the fiery breath. Then the water and the earth appeared, intermingled so that one could not be told from the other, mixed in the moving breath of the Word.

That light, Pimander said, is I myself, Nous, thy God, and the luminous word issuing from the Nous is the Son of God. And that within you which watches and hears is the Word of the Lord, and your own spirit is God the Father; they may not be separated one from the other, because their union is life. Then fix your spirit on the light, and learn to know it well.

From the illuminated Word, Pimander said, next sprang the Demiurge, god of fire and of breath, to make the seven planets, Seven Governors each with its own powers, encircling one another in seven spheres, and the name of their government is destiny. The Word and the Demiurge combined themselves to cause the seven spheres to shudder and begin to move, and by reason of this movement the elements of the earth produced the animals who walk, and the air, the animals who fly, and the water, the animals who swim. And the elements sprang from the will of God, which was the maker of souls.

Then Nous, who was life and light, produced a Man like to himself, and loved him as a child. The Man was brother to the creative Demiurge and when he saw what his brother had made, he wished to make a work

*191*

of his own. The Seven Governors became enamored of him also, and they shared their powers with the Man, and taught him to know their essence and to participate in their being. Then the Man leaned down across the seven spheres, breaking through the envelopes that separated them one from another, and revealed the beautiful form of God to Nature. Seeing the inexhaustible beauty and energy of the Seven Governors joined to the form of God in Man, Nature smiled with love, for she had seen Man's marvelous beauty reflected brightly in the water of the oceans, and in Man's shadow covering the earth. Perceiving how it was like to himself, the Man fell in love with the beautiful body of Nature, and desiring to live with her, he entered the earth, so that he and the world were forged together in the heat of their love for one another.

Because of this movement, Pimander said, the nature of Man is always double. What had been Man's life became his soul, and his light became the intellect, and his body was like to the body of Nature, reflecting it, but it was bound by mortality. And the Man, who was above the armature of the seven spheres, submitted himself to live beneath it, and submitted himself to the rule of destiny.

Turning in the darkness of his trance, Hermes Trismegistus longed to discover the path of liberation from this confinement, the way to reascend the seven spheres and return to his first home in the Divine. You are light and life, Pimander told him, like God the Father of whom Man was born. If therefore you learn to know yourself as made of light and life. . . .

But for the present everything was dark, corporeal darkness, like a pane of glass painted solid black and presented very near to the eye. Dark and growing very cold, a morbid cold of old iron and old stone pressed close to the chilled skin. Still somewhere off behind the black pane a bird was crying *chkshkshk*, and another, *swoo-ee, ee-ee*, and another, *ark-ark, ark-ark*. So time, somewhere, was still secretly passing. Then slowly the dark pane was interrupted with a blue dilution, faint blue threads of light running all down through it, like mineral veins in a face of rock. The light was rising, more and more light, and out of it emerged the *things*. Here was the iron stair rail with the dulled brass knob at the end of it, and here were the bolts where the railing joined the stone steps, and here was my foot, my knee, my crooked elbow, linked to the railing. Here were the cracked paving stones of the walk and here were the weeds sprouting through the cracks, and here were the brown sparrows, chittering, clustering, starting away or darting back down, as though they were searching for something. What?

Morning, Sunday morning, it looked as if the day would be fair. I had a crick in my neck, though, from sitting there awkwardly the whole night through, and a cramp in my arm where it was wrapped round the iron bar. The old cold chill of the metal and stone cut through my clothes and my flesh to my bones. So I shifted myself around on the step, untangled my one arm from the railing, and pounded on my numbest places till they tingled and burned with fresh circulation. Of course I could've got up and gone indoors, taken a hot shower, whatever I felt like. But I didn't really seem to be feeling that decisive.

I set my back against the railing and stuck my legs straight out, bracing my shoe soles against the opposite rail. Ah, now, that was better. Suddenly a pool of warm sunshine was lying in my lap, and I let my eyes half-close, so that its edges shimmered. *Ark-ark, ark-ark.* That one was a crow. He flopped down onto the walk at the foot of the steps and stalked around in a figure eight, scruffing up the feathers on his shoulders. The sparrows chittered furiously at him from the place where they'd retreated on the far side of the street. Then a bike came into the head of the road and the crow dragged himself into the air and flew weightily off. It was some long and lean gray-bearded gent riding the bike, an old brown one-speed, with a heavy frame. He was old enough to know better than to swoop all around the road like he was doing, leaving a sine-wave track on the dew-dampened blacktop. I watched him swish round the corner, and then a clapping of heels made me turn my head the other way.

She looked like she'd had quite the night of it herself, wherever she'd been, whoever she was. One red spandex strap of her minidress had slipped down off her shoulder and a part of her black lipstick had smeared sidewise onto her cheek. The fake boa she carried trailed in the dirt, and the canvas bag slung to her other shoulder looked heavy enough to haul her off balance. But she was stepping out smartly with the white go-go boots—*clap-clap, clap-clap*, and her eyes fixed a thousand yards off in the distance. . . . When she got near the steps I saw it was Miss Peavey?? Well, no, not really, Nell would be more like it.

"Hello," I said. Never mind the name for now. She threw on the brakes and looked at me strangely. Her eyes narrowed and then cleared.

"Oh," she said. "You're that trick cyclist. Look a proper fright, you do."

"Undoubtedly," I said, hauling myself up by the railing. "Well, right, come on in."

"What, d'you think *I've* come to see *you*?" Nell said, with various sweeping gestures of incredulity. "*I'm* not after having my head examined."

"No?" I said. "Then what do you think you're doing here, this hour of the morning? You live in Marylebone, remember?"

Her face went slack, the blackened lips slightly parting. I snapped my fingers, very loud, to take advantage of her moment of confusion.

"Come on, then. In we go." And I went up and unlocked the door and held it for her. She went in and I followed. It seemed a trifle stale in the flat, so I opened a window in the front room.

"Tea?" I said, turning to Nell.

"Coffee, if you don't mind." She dropped the big canvas bag in the middle of the carpet.

"Have a seat, then," I said, and I went in the kitchen and started a pot.

When I came back Nell had seated herself on the sofa, one go-go boot crossed broadly over the other. A swath of pasty flesh showed between the red hem of her dress and the cracked and yellowing vinyl boot top. It wasn't the sort of getup meant to be seen in such good light.

"Here, what are *you* looking at?" Nell said, giving me an equally inquisitorial stare. "You're not such a picture yourself, you know. I think you might at least have a shave. Funny way to run a business."

I backed out of her presence and went to the bathroom. Okay, she had a point. I loosened my shirt, washed up with cold water, and shaved, with exquisite care to avoid any further lacerations. With a damp cloth I loosened the scab from my nose; it came free without any fresh bleeding. Very good. The bruise at my temple had turned livid green, but there wasn't a lot I could do about that.

When I went back, Nell was smoking a cigarette and tipping the ashes into her cupped palm. I reached to a shelf and got her an ashtray.

"You're welcome to the bath yourself, of course," I said. "Take a shower, if you like. I'll put out a towel for you. . . ."

"That's a good one," Nell said slyly. "I've heard that one a time or two."

"What do you mean?" I said. From the kitchen, the coffeepot uttered a few strangling sounds.

"I don't do business on tick, you know," Nell said. "Wouldn't really pay me, would it?"

"No, I don't suppose it would," I said. And I went into the kitchen and poured out the coffee.

"Take anything in it?" I called back.

"No. Black, thanks." She took a big draw on the mug I handed her, sighed and stubbed out her cigarette.

"Look, it's nothing to me, but you might just want to do your makeup," I said. "Go have a look, it's got all smudged."

She shot me another mistrustful glance, over the steaming rim of her mug. It was a crafty child's expression . . . reminded me of that small Scots voice. Then she went and knelt beside the canvas tote and rooted out a small jar of cold cream. With one glance over her shoulder she was off to the loo. When I heard the water running I went to the tote and had a quick look. There was the Sloane Ranger outfit, Miss P's more conventional garb, shoes as well and a purse to match. Also several cheap plastic zip bags, a big packet of tissues, and a large economy box of condoms. The plumbing shuddered as the water shut off, and I sprang back into the kitchen and bolted a second mug of coffee, feeling the various acids roiling in my belly.

Nell had taken all her makeup off and scrubbed her face to a faint raw flush. The change made a curious effect, as though one of your more perverse mad scientists had grafted Miss Peavey's head onto Nell's body, thinking it a jolly good joke. I opened the door to the crooked room and snapped my fingers very loud.

"Let's go down, shall we?"

She lowered her head and walked up to the threshold, then stopped cold. "Down where?"

"It's what you came for," I said, beckoning.

And she passed ahead of me into the corkscrew of the lowering stair. There was the measure of stubbornness, yes. But her first impulse was still to obey.

She stood in front of the brown chair and looked down at it. I flipped on my desk light and switched on the tape.

"I can't *be* hypnotized, you know," Nell said crossly.

"No, no, of course you can't," I said. "I wouldn't try to hypnotize you—we'll just do a couple of simple tests. Just stick your right arm out, *very* stiff—no no, the left arm, now the left. And *don't* close your eyes, keep your eyes open, now put your arms down. Take a deep breath, ah, eyes *open!* Sit down now, sit down in the chair and watch my fingertip, up, up, up. . . . *Now* close your eyes. Now. Good. Who are you? Who are you? *Who are you?*"

But it was obvious enough she no longer had much of any idea. She was slack in the chair as a hamstrung puppet. Induction by confusion, I've always been fairly good at that. In fact, I'm a freaking genius at it. It's why the Dutchman is so proud of me. I went to my desk chair and sat heavily down. She rolled in the chair and let out a moan from the depth of some nightmare.

"It's all right," I said. "Nothing's going to hurt you."

"*Liar!*" she cried, jerking up in the chair. I thought her eyes would pop right open, but they only bulged beneath the lids. "Liar, it *does* hurt, it hurt me every time."

I wasn't even sure I recognized the voice. Hard to tell which one it was when she was shouting so.

"All right," I said automatically. "All right, relax, it's over now."

"No?" she said. "No?" The small voice, weak and petulant, there it was back again. Her lips were pursed and she'd puffed her cheeks slightly— a big baby face screwed on to the tart's working costume.

"What happened?" I said. "Listen. You need to tell me what happened."

She began to wag her head mechanically from side to side, speaking in a singsong. "I mustn't tell. I mustn't tell. I *mustn't tell.*"

"It's all right now," I said. "You can tell, now. It doesn't matter anymore."

Her face puckered up, around her eyes. "No, I *mustn't.* Because Cuz says—" She stopped.

"Who's Cuz?"

"'E isn't *really* my cousin, you know. Only an old friend of Mum's. I'm to go to London and stay with him."

"I see. And will your mum be along with you, then?"

"Nay-o, silly. She's got to stay by the hospital. With me dad."

"I see," I said. "I wonder, what will you do in London? With Mum's friend Cuz."

"Oh, he'll take me to the zoo. . . . He'll take me on a riverboat. To Greenwich, you know." She frowned. "He'll take me to the Queen's Tower." The frown creased deeper into her forehead.

"The Queen's Tower?" I said. Oh, indeed. "Will you go right to the top, do you think?"

She began switching her head from side to side again, but more a jerk than a wag this time.

"Quite the view from up there," I said. "You'll see the whole city, you can see for miles. Why, if the day's clear enough, you probably can look out as far as the sea."

She made her hands into weak loose fists and began to beat them on the cushioned arms of the chair. In another moment she was crying, round clear tears running carelessly down her face.

"All right now," I said. "It's all right. Stop crying now. . . . It's all over. There's nothing to cry about now. . . ." And so on. Maybe if I offered her an ice cream?

When she did stop, she sat up straighter in the chair and her movements became more angular and definite. She swiped the back of her wrist across her nose and cleared her throat.

"Christ," she said, in Nell's voice now. "Haven't I just got a headache."

"Not you," I said. "It's the little one I want to talk to now."

"Hard luck," Nell said. "She hasn't got 'owt to tell you."

"Yes she does."

"Well, but she won't."

"Why won't she?"

"She's frightened," Nell said, and hesitated. "You think it's over, do you? *It's not over!* Time doesn't pass, not where she is."

It doesn't, hey? "Where is she?" I said.

"Where d'you think, clever clock," Nell said. "She's in the Queen's Tower."

Oh.

"Well, yes," I said. "That was where Cuz took her, wasn't it? Showing her the sights of London, eh?"

"Oh yes," Nell said, with a bitter laugh. "And that's not all he showed her."

"What else, then? You're the one that knows that, aren't you, Nell?"

"I'm the *only* one that knows," Nell said. "Yeh, that's right. He showed her his billy stick. Jolly springy thing it was, like rubber. Then it split her right in two."

"What, in the *Queen's Tower?*"

"No, stupid, at his flat. He took her to the Queen's Tower after. Swung her out over the railing by her heels. *Wheee! Wheee!* Till she was screaming. . . ."

"And nobody noticed any of that?"

"If anyone did they must have thought they were only having a little game," Nell said. "Then he said, if she ever told, if she ever told anyone, why, he'd drop her right over, that's what he'd do. And *hahahahahah!*"

"So that's it," I said. "And just the one time?"

"The tower, that was only the once," Nell said. "No, she never needed another dose of that. But we had the billy stick every night. Cops and robbers the whole six weeks. Round and round the mulberry bush and the monkey wrapped his tail round the flagpole."

"And she never told," I said.

"She never dared to."

"But now you've told."

"Yes, but what's the use of making a fuss?" Nell said. "It's only the way of men and women. Everyone comes to it sooner or later, don't they?"

"Do they," I said, abstractedly. "Well, well."

"So now you know, clever clock," Nell said. "What d'you think you'll do about it?"

Good question. My finger, more or less of its own accord, began tap-tapping on the case of the recorder.

"Stop that bloody noise, would you?" Nell said.

I stopped the tapping, with a deliberate effort. Nell rolled away from me, into the shadow. I sat there a little longer, with my mouth hanging slack, but I couldn't think of a word to say, so I pushed myself up from the chair and went out of the room. Upstairs, I swallowed a small handful of aspirin and chased it with another cup of coffee. Now it was bright and sunny in the flat, and the sharpness of the light made my eyes painfully contract.

Right, what *was* I going to do about it? The temptation was there to simply admit I was out of my depth and pass the problem along somewhere else. I never asked for this sort of thing, did I? No, let her do a few years with a regular analyst—learn to believe she'd imagined the whole episode. Or else, out with the Thorazine, clean the unpleasantness right off of those brain cells with some powerful chemical corrosion. Oh yes. . . .

I made a cup of tea and went back down to the crooked room. Whoever-she-was was sleeping with her cheek pressed damply to the brown cushion, breathing with an audible rasp. Hypnosis, left unattended, will drift into ordinary sleep, and I'm sure she needed it in this case, seeing that she'd been up all night. I turned up the lights around the room.

"Miss Peavey?" I called. "Eleanor? Time to wake up, now. Here's a nice cup of tea for you. Do wake up, Miss Peavey."

And she opened her eyes and straightened herself, blinking at the room and uneasily smiling. "O," she said. "O. I must really have gone deep that time, I hardly knew where I was at all."

"That's right," I said. "Now, have your tea."

She closed her elegant fingers round the cup, and I went back to the desk, took out her slim file, and sat there tapping it with a pencil, exhibiting the most professorial manner I could muster. There she sat, demurely sipping, knees and ankles primly pressed together—strange picture she made, given the boots and the super-short skirt.

"A little update on your history, if you don't mind," I said. "Let's see, when was it you first came to London?"

"After university," she said. "To live here, I mean. Not including an excursion or two when I was at school."

"Right," I said. "And you grew up . . . where was it?"

"In Birmingham."

"Only Birmingham?" I said. "Family never moved around?"

"Well, yes," she said. "We lived in Glasgow, for about three years, but I hardly remember anything of that time. I was too small—I was only two when we went there, I think. My father had a job with the railway."

"But you didn't stay?"

"My father took ill," Miss Peavey said. "Cancer. He had to stop work, you see, and then we moved back to Birmingham. He died, oh, a couple of years later."

"I'm sorry," I said. "And while he was in hospital, you were sent down to London for a spell?"

"O . . . yes! Why yes, I believe I was," Miss Peavey said. "They had to send me away for a little. I came down here to some friend of the family, I couldn't so much as tell you his name, not now. I don't remember anything of that trip, only what I was told about it. Pity, my mother always said, it never made more impression on me. . . ." She smiled thinly, inwardly. "Of course, I was only five at the time."

Five. Ah well, we all come to it sooner or later, eh? No use making a fuss about it. "You're not still in touch with him, are you now? Haven't seen Cuz since you moved down to London?"

"O no, he might be dead for all I know," Miss Peavey said. "I don't even remember his face."

Pity, that. Because it would have been an idea to take a hammer and nails and a good kitchen knife and . . . very therapeutic. The Dutchman wouldn't care for it, though. I'd been cutting up enough as it stood.

"And did you make any friends in London?" I said. "On that one first visit, I mean."

"I told you," she said. "I was too small to remember. . . ."

"A bold little girl?" I said. "By the name of Nell? Tough creature— a bit hard, possibly."

"No . . ." she said. "No, but . . . maybe later on, in Birmingham? I'm not sure. But how would you—"

"Never mind," I said, rather quickly. "I'm wondering, have you been having any sort of symptoms you haven't ever mentioned to me? Other than what we discussed before."

"No," she said, with confidence. "No, nothing."

"Mysterious fatigue, for instance."

"No more than what my work would explain."

"Memory lapses?"

"I don't know what you mean."

"Well, let's say you might not always recall just how you'd spent your evening. Or on the other hand, some chap might seem to recognize you, but you wouldn't think you knew him at all."

"No," she said, stiffening along her back and around her mouth. "No, nothing at all of that kind."

"And your personal life," I said. "That's all right? All clear with the boyfriend and that?"

"Doctor Strother," she said frostily, her hands going rigid on the cooling cup. "I really don't see what that has to do—"

But I snapped my fingers, very loud, and startled her into silence. I put down my clipboard and rolled my chair considerably closer to her.

"My dear Miss Peavey," I said intently. "You are a *very* talented hypnotic subject, much more so than I ever would have suspected when you first came here. I think I may have explained to you that all hypnosis is self-hypnosis. What that means, one of the things, is that you may actually have been hypnotizing yourself for years perhaps, perhaps since you were very small."

"But I've never been hypnotized before I came here."

"Not to your knowledge," I said. "You wouldn't have used that word, anyway. And you wouldn't have remembered it either, because one of the uses of self-hypnosis, Miss Peavey, is to hide certain memories away. Bad memories, especially, the most unpleasant sorts. And if the memory is really very bad, hypnosis may create . . . a sort of separate identity, a personality if you will, to try and protect you from it. . . ."

"O yes," Miss Peavey said, miming a look of intelligent interest. "I think I once read a book about it. But isn't that extremely rare?"

"Not necessarily," I said. "Not nearly so much as most people think. Are you sure you don't remember your little friend Nell? From London, or Birmingham, or maybe *both* places?"

"No— I'm not sure . . . I told you, I don't recall."

"A pity, because she certainly remembers you. . . . Well, you may find this difficult to credit, Miss Peavey." I had to stop and clear my throat. "And it isn't very pleasant either. When your father was ill, Miss Peavey, you were sent down to London to stay with that family friend, called Cuz, and he raped you repeatedly, I'm sorry to say it, and said he'd kill you if you ever told."

"*No*," Miss Peavey said. "Why—I never could have forgotten anything like that. And who would do such a thing, to a child? It *never happened*."

"Well, perhaps you're right, in a way," I said soothingly. "It didn't precisely happen to . . . who you are now, but it did happen just the same. You don't remember it, but Nell does remember it, but it didn't happen to Nell either. It happened to whoever it was you used to be when you were small, and Nell had to come out then, to protect you from it. As best she could. She stopped you having to remember it, at least. . . ."

"Well, it's as good as a play, isn't it?" she said. "Well, but of course you're making it all up."

"Yes, that's possible, though not likely," I said. "You'll have to ask Nell about that part. Only I'm afraid you may not like the answer."

"Ask her what?" Miss Peavey said. "This . . . imaginary person."

"Why you're always so tired in the mornings, as if you've been walking the street all night. And that funny feeling in your head, that's a hangover,

*201*

Miss Peavey, though I don't think you even drink, do you? And a taste of tobacco in your mouth, but you don't smoke, do you? Ask Nell why you don't always remember where you've been, why men keep giving you funny looks, when you never did anything to invite it. Nell's got your body about half the time, Miss Peavey, and you won't want to hear it, but it looks very much as if she's a prostitute."

Miss Peavey looked frantically around for some place to set down her cup, but there was no table handy.

"I did *not* come here to be insulted," she said. "I came about the ag- ag—"

"Agoraphobia," I said. "And the reason you *have* agoraphobia, Miss Peavey, is that Cuz took you to the top of the Queen's Tower when you were five and told you he'd throw you right off if you ever told anyone about the rapes. And—what did they used to call you when you were small, Miss Peavey, did you ever have a nickname?"

"My mum used to call me S-S-Sissy," Miss Peavey faltered. "For S-sister, it was sort of her joke. I never had any s-s-sister."

"Well, Sissy never *did* tell anyone," I said, raising my voice more than I should. "Not her fault, she was just too frightened. Who would have listened, anyway? Da was dying and Mum was too worried and nobody would have believed her and Nell couldn't do anything to help her, though Nell did know about it all along. So she never told, and she's *still* not telling. She just lies there and takes the pain, because time doesn't go forward in the place where she is. And someone needs to listen to her, Miss Peavey—"

"*No!*" she cried, and leapt out of the chair, her cup still shaking between her two hands. "I won't hear it. It's wicked, wicked nonsense, *I won't hear a word of it.* You're no doctor, you're a madman, and you're only making it all up."

"Right," I said. "You're quite right about me, I wouldn't wonder, but tell me, where did you get those clothes?"

She looked down at herself, and went still for an instant, a frightening frozen immobility. Then she hurled the cup at the floor. There was a considerable splash of cold tea, but the cup didn't break, because of the carpet.

"You— you—" she said. "I *hate* you!" Then she was thumping up the stairs.

I went after her, but not in any special rush, and by the time I came out of the stairwell she was gone, and her tote bag with her, I took in. More distasteful discoveries waiting for her there, if she was cogent enough to make them. Time would tell—only it wouldn't tell me, because I had my doubts she'd be coming back. The hall door was swinging open, and I went through it and out onto the steps, where I stood shading my eyes from the sudden glare. She was halfway up the block and stepping high, still vibrating, the best I could tell at such range, with rage and disbelief. Not the shadow of an agoraphobic symptom though—an optimist might have called that progress, of a kind.

# twenty

This putative optimist, however, was not I. I wasn't remotely pleased with my morning's work, no. Indeed, it was beginning to look very much like wicked, wicked nonsense, at its bottom. Poor Miss Peavey—she hadn't been delivered a very therapeutic experience, I didn't think. Couldn't blame her if she went right round the bend after this one, taking her whole congregation of alternate identities along with her.

If so, it would be my fault, helpful fellow that I was. What a clever plan I'd had, to set up as a benefactor of humanity. . . . Without knowing it I had made a circuit of the flat's interior and fetched up in the bedroom in front of the one drawing Clara had left among the empty picture nails. The walls of the room were barred with streaks of gray shadow and blue light. . . . In the drawing my eyes were open, but now I saw they still looked blind, and it occurred to me that the queer lurid colors of my pictured flesh suggested death as much as sleep.

If so, that shadow floating upward in the background—well, who knew for certain it was Clara anyway? It might be only some sexless spirit rising from the carcass. I shook my head, to make it ache, but nevertheless the thought of death continued to exert its familiar tug at my mind. Even a pig would love death, given the right circumstances. I searched through the shipwreck of my cogitative power to salvage the remembrance that this was a senseless train of thought. The insomnia *would pass*, in time. Somehow it would end, something would have to give . . . snap . . . ? However, at this stage of the game I always found myself believing it really would go on forever. My widened eyes would never close again, only go on hopelessly prying into darkness and light, indifferently, parched and bald and naked as the eyes of G- G- G-

Stop it.

I went into the front room and fell down on the floor. It happened easily, painlessly, reflexive as a blink. I lay on the carpet, quite comfortably, and presently I reached out my hand and pulled the cover off the snake tank.

But all was not well in the denatured microcosmos there. Things had not taken their natural course. As for the snake himself, I couldn't see much of him. He had tied himself in a Gordian knot and pushed himself up under his rock as far as he would fit. The couple of loops of him that were visible looked even more scrofulous than on the previous day.

In the foreground of this tableau, the mouse was lying on his side in such a manner as to occupy the greater part of my attention. His little red eyes were sealed with pus. His lungs worked slowly, heavily, puffing the belly skin up to near transparency, pink under the sparse white hairs, then went into a rheumy collapse. Now and then he twitched a leg. He'd never touched his cereal.

Once again, it appeared that I had done a bad thing.

Though of course, I never deliberately intended to. I sat up, lifted the lid from the tank, reached in, and gave the mouse a poke with my forefinger. It worked! The mouse began to move, that's to say he dragged himself with his front paws tortuously across the tank floor, the best he could manage since it seemed that his hindquarters were completely paralyzed. In an interminable time he traversed a fan-shaped patch of sunlight that was spread on the fine gravel and entered the area of shadow which my own body cast. There he lay, inflating and deflating himself with the hideous repetitions of his breath.

What was my obligation here? Evidently it was time for me to put him out of his damned eternal misery. I reached into the tank again to scoop him up. He shuddered in my palm and that was all. The small ballooning of his lungs pressed lightly against my skin. I replaced the lid on the tank and stood up. Now, the problem of method. Smash him with the hammer, like I had the clock? Cut off his head with pinking shears? Maybe I could persuade him to take an overdose of sleeping pills, oh *hahahahahah!*

I went to the bathroom, laid the mouse temporarily on the edge of the sink, shut the drain, and turned the water on. Cold— I put my hands in and a bitter frigid pain shot straight up to my shoulders. I waited until the water reached almost to the lip, then shut it off. The mouse lay torpid on the sink's rim. He had scarcely moved a muscle, was scarcely even breathing anymore. He was in a coma, definitely.

But when I held him underneath, he had such a miraculous return to health and vigor as you would not believe. I was holding the ratty base of his tail, and it was the best I could do to keep my grip. The back of my wrist pressed hard against the drain's closure; still the sink was shallow and by striving furiously upward he could almost reach the surface. All four of his legs were wildly cycling, the bunched claws slashing through the water. His jaws strained apart so that I saw his two buck teeth and the pale, tiny tongue behind them. His eyes were wide and a hot boiling red, magnified by the water's lens. There was the whole of him thrown behind this one last effort to live and be well.

It took forever. The little bubbles kept rising and rising . . . how could there be so much air inside a mouse? But even forever has its term and at last he stopped struggling and only swayed lightly, to and fro, like some brand-new variety of underwater plant. I held him down perhaps a minute more, just in case. When I let go, he floated to the top as readily as a cork, and lay against the surface, drowned.

I pulled the plug and turned to the wall. My teeth had begun to chatter, loudly. There were people, to be sure, who took great pleasure from the exercise of absolute power over some small and helpless thing. And somewhere a door was banging, *clap*, then *clap*, and against that steady rhythm my teeth kept rattling on.

When I had got the shaking under control and lifted the soggy carcass from the bottom of the sink, I realized I wanted it out. Out of my house, though it was nothing but an object. . . . I'd neglected to close the front door and it was banging with the breeze, into the frame, and out and in—that was the sound I'd heard before. So I went out and locked up behind me. A bit of a fumble, managing the key one-handed. Partway up the street I tossed the dead mouse into a flower bed and went on, holding my corrupted hand at a safe and sanitary distance from my body.

Although I didn't know where I meant to go, soon enough I had arrived at the door of Waltham's shop. It looked dark behind the windows, but he was open. The bell on the door released its jingle as I pushed in. There was the rank smell of cages, slow strangulated expiration of the immured animal life. I stopped a pace or two inside the door and waited for my eyes to adjust to the dim. A long cold triangle of daylight reached along the floor from the doorway, pointing like an icicle to the place where Waltham sat on his high stool, peeping down at a page of his newspaper as though it were something delectable he meant to postpone consuming for as long as he could stand it, until he absolutely couldn't help himself. After an extended moment, he slowly raised his head and pushed his glasses up his nose. The lenses bounced a little daylight back at me.

"You sold me my snake," I said. I could hear that I was saying it in an ordinary, reasonable tone. "You sold it to me, yourself—you knew what it ate. Didn't you? Didn't you? Of course you did."

Mr. Waltham was silent, only looking at me as though I were mad. By any ordinary standard, I suppose I was.

"Push off, you berk," the parrot said. I couldn't see where the parrot was, but I knew that voice well enough. The bell rang once more as I went out to the street.

What? What? What now? Well, sharing the blame, yes, let's share as much of the blame as possible. Could I really put any part of it off onto someone else? If everyone was implicated I might as well have waylaid a stranger on the street. And if I started doing that, I would soon be out of my present predicament. Though into another one, of course. Hospital, jail, deportation. . . . Stop. I wasn't making sense, not even to myself anymore; my mind only turned useless as a big ball of lint, attracting more and more detritus. It was only the sleeplessness, however; if I got sleep, my reason would return. Morphia. No, not that.

And so, continuing to walk without purpose, I came into Ledbury Road. It was quiet there, distinctly still; it was early yet, and Sunday morning. The big amps and speakers stood on the sidewalks like monuments to expired sounds; their silence thrummed between my ears. Well, but it would all start over soon enough. The sunshine ran warmly down the dip of the pavement, and already there began to be birdlike movements in and out of the rows of shops. There was a smell of coffee, and fresh bread. Ahead of me a woman emerged from a pastry shop, carrying a white paper sack and a lidded cup. She turned and walked a door or two away, then stopped and propped her back against the plywood wall of a giant speaker, closed her eyes, and turned her face up to the sun.

I came a little nearer, only a pace or two away, and stopped myself. Her hair was bound in a tight red scarf—she was familiar, that was it. The same young woman Terence had been talking to the night before. I felt a strange and powerful welling of delight at this recognition. She had a long neck and a cat-shaped face and her skin was a fine gold color, under the sun. I saw the pulse of a long blue vein in her throat. The ornament in her nose was a silver star—last night it had been a hoop, so I even remembered that. The pastry bag had dropped between her feet, or she had set it there. Her shoes were red too, the leather cracked. She held the cup between her two hands, near her belt buckle, steam rising from the crescent cut out of the plastic lid.

I spread my hands to the sun myself and felt the light and heat center on my palms. The euphoria was still rising, climbing, I had no idea where it came from or what to do with it. Yet even the plywood either side of her still head seemed in itself miraculous, how the pale splinters showed through the messy black paint, so and only precisely so. But then she must have felt someone was watching—she snatched her head forward and opened her eyes.

"Hello," I said, and watched her frown.

"I don't think I know you," she said, her tone perfectly neutral.

"No, no you don't, er, well, I—I just noticed that you dropped something." And I pointed to the bag between her feet.

"Oh, thanks then."

She stooped for the bag, keeping her eyes cautiously on me the while, a polite masking smile on her long thin lips. So I pushed off. There was no cloud, the sunshine was as bright as ever, but now it seemed a chilly tinsel glitter, and the blue sky surrounding it was only a veil—rip it away and there would be the cold devouring darkness of dead space. Oh, and it was only the insomnia that accounted for these savage mood swings, but still— Still, there was something catching at the corner of my eye, from the rack outside a news agent I was passing, at the corner. Something like a wink, or a leer, but I ignored it and went on.

*What talent you have for deceiving yourself,* Clara said. I could look up out of my two dimensions and see her there, so much larger and more real than the thin life I was living, as though I were a figure she was sketching on the fresh primed canvas. I felt her redefine a line with the soft lead of the pencil.

"Eh," I said. "I didn't quite catch that."

*Oh, you heard me,* Clara said. *You just didn't want to hear.* She twisted up an end of her hair and chewed it at the corner of her mouth.

"I'm listening," I said, with all the humility I could summon.

*Yes, but how well are you following?* Clara said. And she was gone without so much as a pop or a puff of smoke. Something had been turned around; I was out in her studio now, pinching my arm to reassure myself of my solidity, and the canvas was still there with a few blurred lines on it, but she was nowhere.

"What are you always disappearing for?" I muttered.

*Better ask why you have such trouble seeing me*—and all of a sudden I did again. She was at the far end of the long flat, crouching under the bluish light from the pair of windows there, painting greeny golden scales on a roller of wood that seemed to dovetail smoothly with the floor.

"I see you now," I said, and pointed, as in hide-and-seek. She shifted along the floor, still in her hunker, to another one of those wooden U bends. There seemed to be a lot of them, scattered along the length of the floor. The one she stopped at was ornamented with a sort of jigsaw dorsal fin.

*And now you don't . . .* she said, tipping the fin with dots of red. *It's a question of attention, what you pay attention to. Did I ask to be a figment of your imagination? How would it feel to you to be stuck in someone else's dream?*

"If that's how it is," I said uneasily, "then I don't understand why you ever do come back."

Clara got up quickly and crossed the floor to me. It's a rare thing to be looked at so that you're really seen—I don't think many people know how to do it. Flattering and also disconcerting to be the subject of such a regard. I thought she was seeing through my skin and flesh to study how my bones were arranged. But maybe this was the nature of love, such transparent vision.

*Maybe,* Clara said, and broke her gaze, and strolled away, back among those humps and curves of wood. They were all of them scaly and sinuous, glistening with the damp of paint. I'd always liked to watch her work—the idea of someone good with her hands, like that. She dipped a new color onto a brush and rolled up on the balls of her feet. I noticed the beginning of a hole in the heel of her left sneaker.

"What are you making," I said then, "what are all those things?"

*They go together.* She wiped her painty fingers on her sweat shirt, and twisted round for a brief glance at me.

"A creature?"

**209**

*A sea monster, maybe. I don't know, it's hard to tell . . . when most of it's always underwater.*

She turned back to her mysterious design, as my eyes rolled open help-lessly on a long despairing stretch of street. A little exercise in sleep-walking there? At first I didn't know just where I'd got to, but where I'd been . . . it wasn't a memory. That was some authentic traveling, into present or future I couldn't have said. Would it seem to Clara, wherever she was, that I had disappeared from her? A horrid thought, and still I didn't have the power to get back.

Now I could recognize that I had circled back near my home block, but I had no reason to go home, did I? No, no clients coming today, it being Sunday. I wouldn't even have engaged with Miss Peavey had I not forgotten what day it would be, and besides, she was so *interesting*. But to go there now and close the door behind me, that was a truly loathsome thought. I walked south, for a long way, crossing the Bayswater Road into Kensington Gardens. I went down the length of the Broad Walk, among the mothers or nannies pushing the big black prams, and exited from the lower side. My legs were tiring, numbing nearly, and yet I couldn't seem to stop. I was waiting for something to happen that would turn my mood the other way—a touch of a feather might be enough to do it for me, in my present delicate state. But nothing came, only the same dreadful apprehen-sion, which made the jolly sunlight seem deception.

Finally I went into a little caff and ordered a plate of egg-and-chips. But when it was served I couldn't persuade myself to eat it. The food congealed on the plate before me, while I sat with it long enough to rest a little, to drink about half my cup of dishwater coffee. Time to turn back. I went out to the street and walked back north, but a few doors up was another newsstand, and something stopped me, something. . . . On the cover of a tabloid, behind the plate glass, was a large picture of a bundle of rags, and big strident print beneath it made mention of Wapping, I saw at a random glance, and of certain witnesses who had seen a large black car. . . . Then the words began to crawl round like insects on the walls of a jar and they wouldn't allow me to read any more of them.

However, I went on looking at that big grainy photograph, and presently I saw that somewhere in the heap of tatters, there was a shoe, a small black shoe with a little strap, and above was a hand, on an arm flung back, a wrenched neck and a twist of hair, and so the whole image resolved itself. There. It was the body of a little girl, the third these last three days. She was dead, yes. Someone had used her, used her right up. I could not take my eyes away. Here it was, the very universal truth of things, and the knowledge had been searching me out for all this time, intent as though it had, itself, a heart and soul. It had come a long, long way, perhaps even from beyond the stars, to reach me here.

My shadow was flattened on the glass, and within the border of my shade I still saw the photograph, and I saw how the one thing was mingled with the other thing. It belonged to me now, this information, and nothing could come between us anymore. But when I reached out to take the paper, there was a tremendous hue and cry. The glass fell down in a thousand singing pieces and a great flurry and shouting started up inside the shop. It was me they were shouting at, I perceived, so I began laboredly to run away, clutching the paper, feeling the hot sticky blood pour out of the gashes on my inner arm and blot itself on the soft newsprint.

Ugh, I was too tired to run very fast, and another one of those damned whistles was squealing in my ear. Only it wasn't the Carnival this time, it was a bobby's whistle, standing brightly out ahead of the terrific quantity of other noises made by the several people who were overtaking me. And already I had a stitch in my side, bending me over to the left. I wouldn't make it, not this time. But there seemed something familiar about the little brown church just ahead. I ran around the rear of it and saw the small stair I thought I was remembering. The brick steps let down into a close alley, and thence into a mews, then back to the join of some completely different street.

Very well. I jogged around one more corner and slowed to a walk. No one on this block was taking any particular notice of me. I brushed myself off a bit and walked rapidly, though in no unseemly haste, to the Earl's Court tube station. Because I had just recollected that I did have somewhere to be. I'd told Stuart I'd catch up with him this morning at King's Cross. Buy him a coffee, and all that. Right, there was my destination.

I bought my ticket and went down to the platform, and waiting there I unfolded the newspaper, only to see if any part of it was sufficiently unblood-soaked to be legible. But, funny thing, the paper was completely clean and dry. When I inspected the inside of my forearm, it looked as if my sleeve was whole as well. I unbuttoned it and pushed it back, but there was no mark on the flesh of my arm, other than the pale old pocked scars. The glass cuts had closed themselves, invisibly, by magic, or perhaps I had only imagined them in the first place.

?

Curious, that. The train slithered up to the platform and stopped. I slapped the paper into a dustbin as I boarded; nothing in it I didn't already know, after all. The car was half-empty so there was no difficulty finding a seat. The first forward lurch rocked me back against the padding, and suddenly I was drenched in another breaking wave of sadness. O poor little mousie, O poor Miss Peavey, O, poor this, poor that. . . . Funny how easily those secrets surfaced sometimes. Back in the beginning when I did hypnosis only as a sort of parlor trick, I had once hypnotized Nicole. She was a dream subject too, sank like a stone at the slightest prompt, and in her trance she chattered eagerly about all sorts of topics I never would have dreamed of raising. Her given name wasn't Nicole, I learned—it was Mabel or Betsy or something like that; she'd changed it when she first came east. She was the oldest of her family and she couldn't wait to get away. Her parents had never really wanted her, it developed, though apparently they liked her siblings well enough. She was an accident, came too soon to suit them. So I suppose she'd learned to expect a kick with every shred of comfort . . . and naturally that explained everything, didn't it? No, it didn't explain anything at all.

Ah, if I'd known then what I know now, I could have wormed out her every other secret. But I was in love at the time, of course, so I didn't want to hear about it. Ahhh. . . . I leaned back and yawned again, wide enough to swallow myself—oh me I was tired, tired to destruction. But another thing Pimander told Hermes Trismegistus is that before his descent into Nature, the Man was immune to sleep, like God, and the Man was male and female at once, as the male and the female are combined in the nature of God. It was later, later, during the fall, that God divided humanity into sexes, and so you will easily see, Pimander said, how love is the cause of death.

# twenty-one

I came up from the tube and began wandering somewhat aimlessly around the station. A pale ghost of daylight came filtering down from the arc of the glass roof, flung so high on its crisscross webbings of steel. The electric signs of the various stalls stood sharply out against the dullness of the dirty light. There were the usual lengthy lines at the ticket booths, the usual hustle and bustle across the expanses of the floor. I didn't see Stuart anywhere, not at any ticket window, not at the platform for the next train to Darlington, when I finally realized that that was where I'd best be looking.

The station pub was just then opening, I saw as I turned away from the barrier, which probably meant that I had missed him. Came too late. However, I stayed on, still floating idly along over the gritty concrete surfaces, as though I wasn't capable of finding my way out. There were several flocks of pigeons scavenging among the hurried feet or, every now and then, bursting into short inconclusive flights. I began to follow them. More than possible, I thought, that they were really trapped; having got in, they couldn't get out. The whole station became something like a penitentiary for pigeons. Or maybe, on the other hand, they really preferred it here, and the heights and depths of the real sky outside would only have baffled and terrified them. . . .

Litter aplenty went blowing along the concrete floors, but not much of the sort of crumb to feed a bird, I didn't think. The pigeons were indiscriminate in their foraging, pecking up some scrap of paper or shred of plastic, then discarding it in favor of another much the same. A kind of endless, futile hopefulness. I watched a big pompous one, gray with white speckles, try to crop down a fag end—the thing was still lit, and visibly smoking, but I suppose his beak didn't detect the heat immediately. The pigeon rattled his head and shook the butt away, then let out a sort of avian sneeze. It's true what they say: pigeons are stupid, and I've never thought they have any compensatory virtues to make up for this lack of intelligence.

I don't like pigeons much at all, to tell the truth. Nevertheless I went

**213**

to a snack stall, stumbling a little with fatigue, bought a packet of crisps and began to crumble and scatter them. It was not long before a few dozens of pigeons were gathered at my feet, bowing down in deep obeisance, then raising up again once more to contemplate the marvel. Peck-peck, and coo-coo, and the good news was definitely spreading, as more and more pigeons came fluttering down from the high metal rafters to join the fringes of my circle. How simple it was to appeal to them. But passersby were beginning to give me very strange glances, even hostile looks, I began to feel. And by the time I had bought a second bag of crisps and opened it, I'd attracted a policeman too.

Really, drawing officers my way was beginning to look like my most prominent talent. I took a long look at this one to see if I might recognize him from any of my other recent encounters, but he appeared to be a stranger. His helmet was tipped forward all the way to the line of his eyebrows, which made it difficult to form a clear impression of his face. He had dark eyes, and muscular knots working at the join of his jaws. A young chap, thin as a rail; the weight of his two-way radio dragged his belt down off his hip. Definitely no one I'd ever seen anywhere before.

"Look here, now," he said to me evenly. "You mustn't feed the pigeons in the station."

"Well, and why not?" I said, and crunched up another handful of crisps.

"Why, it isn't allowed," the policeman said. He linked his hands behind him and rocked back from his ankles, his well-shined shoes still sticking flat to the floor. The movement reminded me of one of those inflatable clowns that bob back up at you after you've punched them down. "Haven't you read the notice boards?"

"I'm sorry, no, I can't say I have," I told him, letting the crumbled crisps leak out between my parted fingers. A wave of pigeons swelled over both my shoes and his. A piebald one with a shiny green neck hopped up onto his toe and he kicked it away with an irritable jerk, then rocked forward, clownlike, so that his nose came close to mine.

"Look there," he said, rocking back again. "And there and there. What do you see?"

I swung my head in a half-circle. I saw, well . . . all sorts of things. There were a great number of placards of different sizes and shapes affixed to the nearby walls, and undoubtedly some of these may have borne on the subject of pigeons, but they were too far away to read, and besides my eyes were swimming.

"Sorry," I said. "Can't make them out. Something about the pigeons, you say?"

"Pigeons are a filthy nuisance," the policeman said, in slow and measured tones. "Why, they're no better than rats or mice. They bring in filth, they carry disease. We haven't any use for them here, d'you follow?"

"Yes, but . . ." I let the bag turn over in my hand so that the few whole crisps remaining went wafting down to the floor. The flock of pigeons began to quarrel over them, pecking them into smaller pieces. "They're here anyway, aren't they?" This felt like a very radical insight to me, somehow. "I mean, whether they're wanted or not."

The policeman kicked out at a fluttering cooing mass of pigeons, which re-formed itself instantly as soon as he'd withdrawn his foot. Then he rocked forward, his nose approaching mine.

"You listen, chum," he said, fogging me into a cloud of his toothpaste breath. "I'm making an effort to be reasonable, you know, but I shouldn't try my patience if I were you. Why, I've a good mind—"

At this point I felt a hand clamp down very hard on my upper arm, and I began to think *hey-ho, looks like I did it again.* . . . But when I turned my head I saw that it was Stuart there, standing in close and smiling tightly at the policeman over my shoulder.

"It's all right," he said soothingly. Then to me. "Been feeding those pigeons again, haven't you? I thought I told you to let those pigeons alone." He gave me a vigorous shake. "Don't worry about him, officer, he's just simpleminded. I'll make sure he doesn't cause any more trouble."

"In charge of him, are you?" The policeman rocked back on his heels, frowning. The box on his belt said *quackquackquack* and he touched a button to silence it.

"Yes, I'll be responsible," Stuart said.

"Best have a care then," the policeman said.

"Thanks, we'll both be careful," Stuart said. "Come on, Adrian, let's look lively." He swung me away, keeping that same close seizure on my arm, so that we went walking lockstep and shoulder pressed to shoulder.

"Now try to look sane for just a few minutes," he hissed into my ear. "Cop's still watching us, I can feel it, is there anywhere to get out of sight?"

"There," I said, pointing at the pub, which was just ahead, and Stuart steered me into it. It was a shallow place, but it had a tinted glass door, and there was an alcove around the turn of the bar big enough for the two of us to stand in. Stuart let go of me and I rubbed at my arm. He'd been carrying a fabric shoulder bag in his free hand, and now he balanced it on the foot rail and wedged it into position with his shin.

"Quite a grip you've developed," I said. "Did they have you milking cows up there in the country?"

Stuart smiled briefly, the gold tooth winking, and set his elbow on the bar. "Wising off at the cops again, weren't you?"

"I suppose," I said. "How'd you know?"

"Body language," Stuart said. "Couldn't miss it at a hundred yards. There's that certain pose they all fall into when they're deciding to take you in."

"Some things you never forget, I suppose," I said.

"Like riding a bicycle. . . ." Stuart shrugged.

"Well . . . where did you materialize from, anyway?" I said. "I thought you must have already gone."

"Overslept."

"You're entitled to it."

"And it did me good," Stuart said. "I feel a whole lot fresher now."

"Looks like you're always getting me out of some pickle or other," I said. "Here, let me buy you a lemonade." I turned to the barmaid, who'd appeared at our end of the counter.

"Just the local wimp water, whatever it is," Stuart said.

The barmaid gaped at him. She was a plump damp thing with pale hair and reddened cheeks; a small pimple stood in the center of her forehead just where a beauty spot might have gone.

"A Perrier for the gentleman," I said. "I'll have a half of Guinness, please."

The barmaid withdrew and then returned. I paid, then clinked my glass to Stuart's. "My savior."

Stuart gave me a skeptical look. "I could have always left you to your own devices."

"But your missionary zeal overwhelmed you. . . ."

Stuart wiped his hair back from his forehead and frowned. He looked cornered somehow, though in the literal situation it was I who had my back to the wall. Over his shoulder I saw a gaggle of brightly dressed girls come jingling in and arrange themselves around one of the three small tables.

"Is this an ambush?" Stuart said.

"Sorry," I said. I licked a little foam from the rim of my glass; it tasted black and bitter. "No harm intended."

"None taken, then," Stuart said, sipping from his soda water.

"Will you be late, going up to the country?"

"I suppose they'll meet the next few trains," Stuart said, and glanced at his watch. "There's one that goes in half an hour, so they tell me. I'm willing to miss an hour of it anyway, it'll only be a week of rolling around in the mud."

"The missionary impulse strikes again," I said.

Stuart gave me a lengthy look at all his teeth—I saw that heart shape cut white from the gold. "Come on, Adrian, what's on your mind?"

"Clouds of confusion, maybe," I said. "A logical inconsistency, I think."

"All right," Stuart said. "We've got a few minutes for the debate."

He rested the small of his back against the bar and braced his other elbow there. Beyond him, at the one small table, those three girls were all talking at once and waving their arms; I saw bracelets go oscillating around one long slim wrist. Some song was playing faintly from a speaker in the ceiling, but I couldn't make out the melody. In former times, Stuart and I would always argue about abstractions, talking round and round some perfect purified figure for whatever it really was between us.

"Well, then," I said. "I don't suppose you really think the soul is hiding in the pineal gland, do you?"

"No," Stuart said. "Not really."

"Where is it, then?" I said. "I mean, you're obliged to think there is one, what with Jesus and all that. Do you suppose it only haunts the body, like a ghost?"

"I don't suppose it's my business to know."

"And I bet you don't talk to them about Jesus, there at the Spiral Center," I said.

"They mostly don't want to hear about it," Stuart said.

"Mechanical problem, mechanical solution," I said. "But where do you accommodate a soul in a machine?" I had raised my voice without knowing it, so that one of the girls at the table dropped her part in the conversation and turned half-curiously our way.

"Maybe it is mechanical," Stuart said. "But it works."

"It's symptomatic," I said, more quietly. "What do you think made us start shooting dope in the first place?"

"I'll speak for myself," Stuart said. "I didn't see anything better to do, at the time, but that was then."

"I think I wanted an anesthetic," I said. "I had such a big pain it took something strong to numb it out. . . . But you tell me, if Christ does come again, do you think he'll be preaching operant conditioning?"

"Sure, all right," Stuart said. "Maybe there is a missing link. But I can't afford to worry about that. Here we have a method that works and it's a way of helping people—maybe only materially, I don't know. An meanwhile, myself, I need to believe in something. What about you? Can you solve that kind of a problem just by magic?"

"I'm still practicing," I said.

"Sure," Stuart said. "Let me know when you get it worked out."

"Stuck again," I said, and lifted my glass, as if to toast the sticking place. Because those arguments always did end up at some such choke point. There was a kind of enduring quality to that.

"You're trying to do it all by yourself," Stuart said. "I'm impressed, I really am, but I don't see how you can do it all alone, no matter *what* you think you are."

"I think I'm the mirror of the universe," I said. "So, by the way, are you."

"I've heard you say that," Stuart said. "What then?"

"Then nothing can be separated," I said. "You can't take one thing apart from another one, see? And what that means is. . . ." But I had to falter off into mumbling, then stop. The idea was still there, certainly, but somehow I couldn't seem to wrap my tongue around the word. Or maybe I didn't really want to, not just then. The old magi were cagey, all of them, very secretive and elliptical when it came down to the wire. After a period of silence I hooked the medallion out of my collar and pulled it forward with my thumb.

"It did the trick," I said. "I remembered. I remembered quite a bit. . . ."

"Only good things, I trust," Stuart said, with a twist of his lips that didn't quite make a smile.

I let the medallion drop back against my skin. It seemed to have cooled slightly out in the air, so that now I felt the difference more distinctly: me, it; me, it.

"I'm wondering, when you're born again, do you lose all your memories?" I said.

"No," Stuart said. "No, you don't do that, at least I didn't."

"What about at the Spiral Center? When the new personality drives out the old one?"

Stuart shifted restlessly, and his bag came unbalanced from the rail and toppled out onto the floor. "Come on, Adrian, that's a metaphor," he said. "You should know, you use enough of them yourself."

"You never know what's literal and what's not, these days."

"I'm still an addict, that's the short of it," Stuart said, with the same grimace as before. "So are you. We're just not *practicing*, that's all."

"Ah," I said. "But if memory really was a house, you could just go out and close the door. Lock it up and throw away the key. . . ."

"But it isn't like that," Stuart said. "We'll always keep knowing what we know."

"Who says it can't be both ways?" I muttered.

Stuart laughed. "*You* do," he said. "That would be a logical inconsistency, right?" He stooped over and hoisted his bag. "Good to see you, Adrian. So, anyway, what do you think, you still want to be my friend?"

That was the new Stuart talking, definitely—the old version was never quite so confrontational. Took me rather by surprise.

"I don't know," I said, fingering the chain round my neck. "I don't know, I love you, man, but I'm not sure we're good for each other."

"I've had that feeling from time to time," Stuart said. "How soon do you think they'll let me on the train?"

"Now, probably," I said. "I'll walk you down."

As we circled back around the bar one of those three girls looked up, tracking Stuart with her almond eyes. . . . In the wide cavernous spaces of the station, people went on shuffling and rushing, their movements echoing slightly from the glass and metal vault. The pigeons had broken up into small separate flocks that went on behaving much as before, and indeed it was all entirely the same as it had been earlier. Everything was exactly so and could not have been otherwise. A medium queue had formed for the Lancashire train. As we approached a railway guard in a flat cap drew back the metal barrier and the queue began to lurch forward.

"That's me, I think," Stuart said, quickening his step.

"Wait," I said. "You've got a minute yet." I pulled him back around to face me.

"Sure," Stuart said. "So, what is it?"

"I don't care anything about pigeons, understand? I wasn't feeding them because I like them. I think they're kind of disgusting actually."

"It's okay, Adrian," Stuart said. "A lot of people feel that way."

"Yes but. . . ." It seemed important to complete the thought. What thought? Stuart was swinging his bag in a pendulum sweep at his knee level, and beginning to look just faintly impatient. "It's only love gone wrong," I said hastily.

"What is?" Stuart said. I'd bewildered him now, it was easy to see. Confusion—amazing what you could do with it. If there was a little more time.

"Everything," I said. "It's the explanation for everything." I put my hand on his shoulder and pushed him away. "Go on, hop it, catch that train."

And I went staggering off as quickly as I could, toward the stairway for the tube—I wanted to get off the station floor as soon as possible, before that policeman noticed I was once again without a keeper. I dove deep down the creaking escalator to the Piccadilly Line, where the platform was completely empty. A train must have just passed through. I walked all the way down the farthest end and stared into the turning darkness of the long low tunnel, which gave back to me the sound of my own groans. Maybe Stuart and I had each managed to utter a half-truth. We weren't good for each other, I didn't think. The divided halves of our old addiction still lurked in each of us, waiting their chance to rejoin in a demonic whole and take possession of us both once more. No good could come of such a union, but still the separation was grindingly sad. I hadn't finished all I had to say to him! And I couldn't find a handkerchief either, or any paper or anything, so there was nothing to do but use my sleeves, while that awful moaning choking sound kept coming back to me out of the tunnel. Stupid, stupid crying jags— I'd lost the last of my self-control.

But then it suddenly occurred to me that this time I was crying for a reason. The reason was obvious: I had lost my friend. It wasn't pointless this time, it all made perfect sense. For once I had managed to connect the right event to the right emotion, and if I could do that, there might be some hope for me after all.

That thought impressed me so much that I stopped sniveling altogether. People had begun to gather at the far end of the platform, where the stairway came down. Every so often one of them would crane out and look over the tracks, in my direction. I turned and stared down the tunnel myself, but there was nothing, only the dark. Still I felt that something was coming. A shudder came to me, right through the fabric of the earth, when I laid my palm against the tile. The wall was curved, slightly damp, slightly palpitating. It was rising, dancing, this excitement, and it was alive, *alive*. I believed that, I could have told Stuart or anyone now—it's so difficult to believe anything nowadays, why not believe the impossible?

I was the world and the world was I and I felt the unity trembling in my hand. Light was opening at the bottom of the shaft, though only a pinpoint as yet. Was I thinking, or speaking aloud? It didn't matter, it was coming now, I knew I couldn't stop it if I tried. I was the mirror of the universe, so anything that happened to any other person or thing also happened to me personally, and whatever I might do to myself was done to the world and everything in it, which was the meaning of each small act of my self-destruction. A howling began at the bottom of the tunnel, roaring at me again and again that the world itself is the body of God. And so, so long as that holds true, then God Himself can be destroyed—I and my brother humans have gone a long way toward proving that, but not yet all the way, and truly it remains a fearful thing to fall into the hands of the living God. The tunnel contorted, like a snake, and I felt its tremble run the whole length of my body, and the light had dilated now so there was nothing left but it, surrounding me, searing my eyes, drawing me inexorably down toward its brilliant core. I knew—I knew—I understood for instance why the rabbit won't *get out of the road*, because there's nowhere left to go, no place, no thing, only *more light, more light, more light—*

**221**

# twenty-two

In the event, however, I did not throw myself onto the tracks. Instead, I waited meekly for the train to come to a complete stop, then got aboard with all the other sheep. I sat down on a narrow padded seat, staring back out through the grimy window at the frigid white reflections on the platform tile. "Mind . . . the gap," a robot voice pronounced a time or two, and then the doors slipped shut and the train gave a bump and a grind and started rolling. Someone was flurrying down the stairs as though he thought he still might make it—then the glass of the window turned black and there was only the shadow of my own face lying as a thin veneer on its surface.

Something I didn't like about the look of it, something that reminded me . . . I shut my eyes, feeling them sizzle in their acid pools, and when I opened them again I seemed to be looking out over one of those strangely marvelous cloudscapes, such as one sees from the portholes of planes. Sunset over Antarctica, or so it appeared, and the clouds looked solid as snowdrifts; I felt confident that I could just step through the window and go walking around out there. Slipping back on my left side was a sort of bay or estuary, bound by enormous cliffs of ice, frozen into fantastic forms. On either side the snow rolled back in woolly humps and hollows, all the way to the horizon, where the sun's red disk was bearing down and cutting through.

And nothing of it was real, only the sun. The freezing lake with the ice drifting in it was nothing but a vapor. If I looked down on it hard enough I could see through to the shapes of the material world, turning down below in the darkness and shadow. Unbelievably bright, red as a rabid eye, the sun was spinning like a saw blade, lowering, tearing through the cloudy veil. Well, perhaps I *should* have jumped under the train. . . . This was a bit more impressive a hallucination than I was quite prepared to cope with, and yet I was afraid what I might see if I shut my eyes against it. If the situation developed very much further, I'd be mad as Miss Peavey, at least, perhaps madder. Then I did shut my eyes, in a sort of panic, but nothing was there,

**222**

nothing but the spectral rounds of radiance that the sun had burned onto my rods and cones.

These, at least, made some sort of physiological sense, except of course there couldn't have been any actual sun out there, given that I was traveling along the deepest darkest tunnel of the whole London underground. Well, it was only sleep deprivation, that accounted for it. That was the answer to everything, except . . . my rationalizations didn't seem to be rationalizing adequately at the moment. I felt clammy, and nervous tendrils of sweat were beginning to move around under my clothes, as if they had a life of their own, like bugs or little glassine worms. The sound of the train rushed and roared at my ear and I was dreaming a newspaper behind a darkened pane of glass, whose front page was trying to communicate some woeful intelligence to me, something I didn't want to learn. Anyway I couldn't make out the message because the letters were all in a foreign alphabet. Good—then there was a tinkling jingling sound and I felt a pain of something carving up my forearm, like a hundred tiny knives.

My eyes popped open and bugged out at my inner arm. What happened? Had I somehow healed those cuts, by magic? Or had all that been a hallucination too, breaking the show window, and my escape? Neither alternative seemed especially reassuring. Another tide of dreadful sweat came pulsing out of my gaping pores. Fearfully, I turned my eye to the window, but, let every god be praised, all I saw there was the greasy dark pane. Then it clarified and out beyond it the image of another platform appeared, with the writing on its wall: SOUTH KEN. South Ken?

My, I'd missed rather a lot of stations, in my peculiar reverie. I hopped off the train and dragged myself over to the rickety wooden escalator, and let it drag me toward the higher level. The escalator was very brown and narrow, and so steep it made me giddy to look either up or down the length of it. I let my eyes sink shut—no, bad idea. I looked again at my forearm, at the pattern of faded needle scars. That was the trick, intermediate range. My arm kept on being itself and didn't even try to become anything else, which relieved me; I'd had enough of metamorphosis, for the moment, anyway. The big risk of trying to summon powers is not being able to control them if they come.

Or maybe it was the powers summoning me. Love is a form of natural magic; no, better said that magic is a focused form of love. A cord of sympathy whereby I could represent myself to Clara, or knit a net to catch

**223**

her, draw her back. A higher comprehension of seduction, only I wasn't quite sure which of us was being seduced. What if Clara's fantastic emanation was more powerful than mine? —*and what would be the difference?* I seemed to hear her saying. *If both are trying to bring about one thing. It's not about power anyway, it's*

Abdication. The wooden plates of the escalator shifted under my feet, like scales on the back of that great sea serpent. In my rapture, I failed to notice my arrival at the top, and the grooves of the belt caught the edge of my shoe and flung me sprawling on the floor.

"Bloody idiot," someone grumbled, lifting his leg high to step over me. I pushed myself up to a sitting position and brushed loose the various debris that had embedded itself in the skin of my palms. Well, what if I *had* healed myself, by magic? Why couldn't I heal the two of us as well? Pity I couldn't remember just how it was supposed to work. . . . Ever since we'd met two days before, Stuart had been menacing me with the skewer of the literal, that critical sticking point. No matter what I knew or believed, I never had worked any significant miracles. Had I? Why didn't Giordano Bruno forbid the fire to burn him?

Maybe he did, but it burned him anyway. His scorched bones fell down, as the smoke and sparks went flying up, and ever after the ways of science and religion were divorced. A terrible mistake, that was, because the proper end of science is to know *all*— Behind me, the escalator rattled and clacked, and a stream of recently disgorged passengers began to part itself around the obstacle I presented in their path. They all seemed to be grumbling as they veered to avoid me. And here came another bobby toward the outer barrier. . . . Hastily I pushed myself up and scurried across to the Circle Line platform, which, at this station, was open to the sky. The surprise of the sunlight made my eyes begin to water. For no reason I was thinking of the monument to that dog in Battersea Park, the mangy little brown terrier whirling in a circle, snapping at the parasites on his flank. Worthless and scurvy, yes he was, but still a *creature*, and didn't the fools of scientists even suspect, when they cut out his living heart, that his terrier's soul would ever after worry at their heels?

Well, but the desire to operate is strong and serious, I thought, as the train pulled in and I embarked. The car was too crowded for me to find a seat; I wrapped one arm around a pole and hung there, as the sunlight strobed between the concrete columns and then the dark of the tunnel swallowed up the train again. I felt it myself, the urge to operate, to do something, but not with a knife or a needle. The gold medallion throbbed at my throat, lifting and lowering on the currents of my jugular. I didn't want to murder the world in order to dissect it, but coax its innate powers out to join me in some collaboration. To use this circle of auriferous metal to bring down an angel (or I'd settle for a demon), to do my will. So then it was about power after all. The secret of the thing is to be able to entertain paradoxical ideas—keep them happy and amused.

The train stopped curtly at Kensington High Street, and my momentum threw me forward roughly. My elbow, linked to the chrome pole, caught me somewhat painfully up. Should have asked Stuart what he thought of the theory that Christ, during his mysteriously unrecorded twenty-year disappearance, had actually been among the Essenes, learning to work miracles by techniques of practical magic. A rather major heresy, yes, but many of the Renaissance magi had secretly believed it. Which put rather a different spin on the ideal of the *imitatio Christi*. . . .

However, I still couldn't seem to climb over the hair that Stuart's shade kept placing across my path: theory and faith aside, I'd proven no power to make or unmake, to bind or to loose, and had worked no serious miracles so far. Well, but I did stop people smoking, cured phobias and insomnia, changed personalities from Type A to Type B. . . . Not miracles, though, not precisely that. Yes, but I came off dope, myself, didn't I, and through my own agency too. Would that pass for a miracle? Jesus still sometimes got miraculous credit for cures of that kind, didn't he?

The catch continued to be, as Stuart would have reminded me had he been present, that it was difficult to sustain that miracle, if it really was one, all on my own. Yesterday I'd been clean, all right, but there still was tomorrow, and the day after that, or even, God forbid, today. And with every successive hour I kept going without sleep, the memory of the narcoleptic trance grew more and more seductive.

*Stop it!* Luckily the train shuddered to another halt at Notting Hill Gate, and broke this lethal sequence of thought. I left the station and began to walk leadenly in a homeward direction. Go back to the flat and have a nap, that's what I'd do. A perfectly simple procedure—people did it all the time. And even just an hour of sleep would do a lot to clear my head of these snares and delusions.

But when I turned into my own street, I experienced a strange and

powerful sense of *déjà vu*. Opposite my front steps was parked a huge black
Bentley, long as the block, and as I drew near someone got out of the
driver's side to stand in my way. It was last night's abduction as seen in a
mirror, with night exchanged for day and the car facing the opposite way
on the street. The prospect of a reprise of the whole Karnock episode
depressed me severely; I didn't think I had the resources to withstand that
just now. But when I got closer I saw that it wasn't Sid or Ted this time.
It was one of the suits from Wormwood Scrubs, a suit I was slightly
acquainted with from my previous visits there. His name was George or
Sam or something, I couldn't quite remember which.

"Hallo, Doctor Strother," George or Sam said, stooping to open the
car's rear door. "Jump in, would you? There's a good fellow."

I complied. The Dutchman was reclining on the soft red leather of the
far seat, smoking a thin cheroot and staring at me with his colorless eyes.
George or Sam slapped the door shut behind me and got in the front, behind
the wheel. There was a heavy chunking sound as some magic button on the
dash closed all four locks at once.

"I wasn't expecting you," I said to the Dutchman, regretting each word
as it left my lips. With him it was almost always a mistake to be the first
to speak. The Dutchman stared at me about a minute more, lingering on
my ragged sleeve. Then, as the car pulled out, he took a puff on his cheroot
and averted his eye, with some distaste, turning toward the smoked-glass
window.

"I shouldn't suppose you were expecting anyone, from the look of you,"
he said. "Your appearance hardly does much credit to your . . . practice."

"Posh car, eh?" I said, wishing to distract him, and perhaps annoy him
also. "New, isn't it?" New to the Dutchman, anyway. But the *déjà vu*
sensation was intensifying. This interior had the same upholstery as the car
of the night before, the same electronic gadgetry, the same rosewood panel
hiding the bar. . . . All these resemblances struck me as altogether strange.
Maybe it was all in my mind. . . .

"It's impounded," the Dutchman said, with his lipless smile.

"Impounded?"

"This automobile has been used for criminal activity," the Dutchman
recited. "It belongs, or rather did belong, to a quite notorious criminal.
Walter Karnock. As a matter of fact, I'm taking you to interview him now."

"You want me to work on Walter Karnock?" Despite the plethora of clues, I was genuinely startled. "But he's really bent, that one. He's bent so far his heels are practically in his mouth."

The Dutchman turned and released a puff of smoke, approximately in my direction, though not quite in my face.

"How would you know that?"

*Fool!* I said to myself sharply. I'd given the Dutchman a bit of free information, or come uncomfortably close to doing that.

"I read the papers," I muttered underconfidently. "Doesn't everyone?"

The Dutchman took a long suck at the cheroot and sighted at me down the length of its tottering ash. "And?" he said.

"Well," I mumbled. "I've seen him at the Empress sometimes. There's even a rumor he owns the place. I suppose you might know better than I."

"The Empress?"

"A nightclub. I work there a couple of nights a week. As you've probably made it your business to know."

"Yes, quite."

I felt a little easier now. "How did you get your hook in him again so quickly?" I inquired. "Didn't he just come out from under those gambling charges down at the Old Bailey?"

"A detail," the Dutchman said, and extinguished his cheroot in the brass-fitted ashtray. "We haven't precisely arrested him, in any case. We've merely detained him. For an interview. Perhaps a few little tests, as well."

"You want me to nobble him, then, do you?" I said. "Find out what will stick to him in court?"

"Far from it," the Dutchman said. He withdrew a box of cheroots from the interior of his pin-striped suit and held it out to me. AMBASSADOR was lettered on the lid. I shook my head. The Dutchman replaced the box in his clothing, flipped open the rosewood bar tray, and raised an eyebrow. I contemplated the bottles and glasses just for a bit.

"No thanks," I said, at length. "Best keep a clear head."

"Admirable," the Dutchman said, and shut the bar. "Well, let us proceed. I suggest that you think of Walter Karnock simply as an international businessman. You needn't concern yourself at all with the nature of the business."

"You're going into a partnership, then."

The Dutchman revealed a row of his teeth. "Not precisely. My intention is to . . . subordinate him to the goals and policies of the organization that I represent."

"I see."

"My vision of life is utilitarian," the Dutchman said, adjusting the knot of his club tie. "The end of each man is to realize a purpose. In this sense every man may be considered as a tool."

"No surprise there," I said, under my breath.

The Dutchman didn't appear to have heard me. "Walter Karnock is sitting at the center of a network, or a web, if you will," he said. "The threads of this web go all over Western Europe now, and into Turkey, into Iran. . . . Why, it's a mirror image, in its way, of the organization that I represent."

"An interesting way of looking at it," I said. "Didn't you just call him a criminal though?"

"He's a tool without a handle." The Dutchman turned to look at me very sharply indeed. "I want you to fit a handle to him. By any means possible. I'm not concerned with his private habits, or the state of his psychological health. I only want him under control. Do you understand me clearly?"

"Yes, of course," I said. I had ceased to take note of our progress, but we must have passed through a couple of gates, for I now took in that the car had stopped in that same cul-de-sac, beside the same dumpster even, as on the day before. Rather a hole-in-corner business, this appeared to be.

"Then see that you follow through," the Dutchman said.

All four locks thunked open then, and George or Sam came round and opened the Dutchman's door for him. The Dutchman gave me one more distasteful scan before he got out. "Fetch Doctor Strother a fresh shirt," he said to George or Sam. "Then you can take him straight along to his interview." And by the time I'd levered myself out of my seat, the Dutchman had disappeared from view. As if he'd been a figment of my imagination . . . but that was only wishful thinking, wasn't it?

"Well then, just step this way?" George or Sam said, giving his palms a nervous rub together. I followed him through the service door and down a hall in and out of an elevator and up a flight of stairs and across another hall. . . . Eventually we fetched up in a cluttered office, about the size of a charwoman's closet and as sloppily choked with this and that.

"Er, well," George or Sam said nasally. "Just wait here for a moment, would you? Just have a seat? Back in a tick. . . ."

He went out. I turned about a time or two, there was just room enough for that. The couple of chairs in the cubicle were stacked so high with discs and documents that the offer of a seat seemed altogether hollow. On the buried desk blotter stood a photo of George or Sam's wife and kiddies, so I took it, all looking rather like uncooked sausages. A yellowed blind was pulled down to the sill of the single small window. I stepped over some stacked files to thumb it back. Perhaps we'd mounted to one of the prison's stale gingerbread towers; at any rate I overlooked the withered common from what seemed a significant height. Through the wire checks sunk in the heavy glass, I observed a number of large crows standing at a considerable remove from one another on the pale grass, motionless as if frozen or glued, all facing back toward the brown brick prison wall. The slate-colored sky that stooped to meet the common behind them looked most unsuitable for flight. I let the blind drop back. It was difficult to estimate the passage of time. But presently George or Sam returned, bearing a faded blue shirt with white buttons and a number stenciled in black across the pocket.

"Gaol issue, I'm afraid," he said. "Not quite the thing, perhaps you don't want it? But then, the Head gave explicit instructions. . . ."

"Oh, I wouldn't want to get you in Dutch with the Head," I said, pleased with the secret pun. "I'll wear it, never fear. Just so you make sure I don't get mixed in with the regular lags."

"Heh heh," George or Sam said. "Perish the thought. Well, you might just change in the loo?"

In the lav, I dropped my torn shirt in the dustbin, and washed my face with soap and a towel. The water was very, very cold, and I held my wrists under the tap till they went numb, then pressed them to the sides of my head. The chill at my temples made me feel very much fresher and sharper. I put on the shirt I'd been given, which was papery with starch, and read the number backwards in the mirror: 6655321. Not a bad fit, actually. Wonder who'd had it before me?

George or Sam was waiting for me in the hall. He conducted me along to another door and unlocked it with his key. A gray steel door with an observation port, and hinges so well greased it opened without a shadow of a sound.

"I'll bring the subject right along then, shall I?" George or Sam said.

"Right," said I, stepping through the doorway. The lock did make a noticeable clicking sound as it turned behind me. Otherwise it was perfectly still in the straight room. I sat down in a chair with my back to the mirror, folded my arms on the Formica tabletop, and gazed across at the blank white wall. No windows in here either, of course, so I didn't know how long I was waiting, but I did not become impatient. I was alert and perfectly calm and I felt I knew exactly what was happening now. I could see the coveralls bringing Karnock through all the mazy corridors, as obviously as if their images were projected on the wall. And when I heard the key turn in the lock, I began to believe that I already knew everything I was about to make him tell me.

# twenty-three

*Did you remember anything?*

Oh yes. You may be very sure I did. But what mind could know and remember all the infinite world and the things it contains? From the dancing dust mote to the smallest burning atom of the distant star which makes that dust mote gleam. . . . The key was still turning in the door of the straight room; I could hear the lock tumbling over and over, and still the door did not open. A cog had come loose in time's clockwork to turn interminably without engaging anything, and for this reason time had stopped.

I was looking at the blank bare wall of the straight room. Some of the bumps in the paint were big enough to cast short shadows, and it rather alarmed me to notice how the shadows fell in all different directions, as though the source of light were indiscriminate, insane. Either the light was really getting louder or some filament was flaring up behind my eyes, burning brighter than magnesium. Tiny pinpoints of a golden light went floating before me like a veil. I cupped the metal disk at my throat and of a sudden saw the image of the celestial Venus as though graven on the wall, linked to the ape of nature by a rope woven of her own soft hair, and to the shining cloud of the divine by that same golden chain. At her back the astral and planetary spheres were revolving each within another, turning and tumbling, all unlocked by the Great Key.

My eye rolled backward toward the core of my mind, searched every corner of my memory, and saw the whole cosmogony etched in the Brunian memory scheme that Clara had drawn out for me with her draftsman's pen and ink, with all the universe contained therein, arranged in its infinitude of combinations. It was there; it comprehended everything that is. I could see through the transparent plurality of things to the world revealed as a single organism, the most marvelously beautiful creature ever made. The naked Venus smiled at me, out of Clara's lips and eyes, and I saw how the *clavis magna* depended on each of her two hands. I reached for her and the key she held . . . she *was* the key, she embodied it. O only come back, come

**231**

back to me now, and I promise I will serve you forever. Clara's voice was oddly matched to the Venusian smile. *I never asked for worship*, she ventriloquized. *I'd settle for a little warmth and sunlight, rational conversation, concrete things. Something to be sure of. I'm made of flesh and blood, you know.* Which of course she was. But body and soul at the same time, not one shackled to the other. Right, and that's what makes the world go round. I could see it clear as day. Now, now, and only now, I knew it. The whole of the universe was reflected on the concave curve of my mind's dome, and I knew I was finally on the point of recovering the divine powers I had surrendered to join the body of Earth; I knew, I knew, I knew—

But when I began to reinhabit my body, Walter Karnock had already come into the room somehow and was sitting across the table from me. Perhaps I had even had some sort of exchange with whoever had brought him along, though I didn't remember a bit of it. Oh, what George or Sam must think of me . . . though the truth was I didn't really care.

Time had started up again. While I hadn't been paying attention.

Karnock was looking at me, or at least in my direction, though he didn't seem to know me. His eyes weren't focused properly, and he had an abstracted expression, as though he were paying most of his attention to some unscratchable itch way up in the inside of his head. His fishy lips were slightly parted, and he breathed through them with a faintly audible sighing sound. They hadn't made him change *his* shirt, I noticed. He was all rigged out in what I supposed were his usual street clothes: a banker's pinstripe, but with a gangster's cut, and a cream silk shirt with a monogrammed *K.* And a matching handkerchief too, blooming out of his breast pocket.

How to begin? There was a weight on my jaws—I couldn't seem to part them. Karnock's oily eyes flicked over my shoulder to the mirror. He raised one hand and touched the polished surfaces of his hair, then patted his tie and his hanky too.

"Let's get on with it, shall we?" he said. He lifted his forearm and looked at his fat gold wristwatch. "I can't stop here all day, you know. I'm a busy man."

*Think of him as a businessman.* All right, then.

"What exactly are you here for, Mister Karnock?"

Karnock smiled, checking the sheen of his teeth in the mirror over my shoulder. "Why, they'd like to give me a lagging, wouldn't they? Only they can't manage it. But they won't give over trying, will they? No, I'm only here on my own sufferance—you make very sure of that, my son. Got my barrister on the blower now, I should think, onto that long smooth Johnny who brought me up here. . . . You know me, my son, I'll be home by evening."

"I see," I said.

Karnock snorted. "That's all your lot'll ever say, innit? All you trick cyclists. 'I see. Tell me more.' You could get a doll to do it. You know, one of that sort where you pull a string. Had my dose of that in the army, I did. No, you won't come it over me."

"Tell me more," I dutifully said. He hadn't been half so chatty on the boat, and I didn't quite know what to make of this queer loquacity now. Perhaps it was somehow a sign of weakness. Let him run on. Psychopaths are often very hard to hypnotize, like infants are. Let him show me his own way.

"Go on, then, ask me a question." Karnock slouched back in his chair and smoothed down the tabletop with his big blunt hands. Something in that gesture rang a bell. "Care to hear about my mum?" he said.

"Tell me anything you like," I told him.

"Hah! Hah!" Karnock cried out, opening his mouth so wide I could see the gold plugs in his back molars. "I haven't *got* a mum, you see. Because I'm an orphing! Isn't it sad? Care to hear about my bum?"

"I suppose you must have one of those," I said.

"Haw," said Karnock, winding down. "You know me. I like my joke." He made that same movement with his two hands on the table, as though he were gathering something toward him, hogging his plate, something like that. Then he stared at the mirror, very hard. It was almost enough to make me turn round to check if the one-way glass had gone wrong somehow and exposed the Dutchman and the other observers hunched over their recorders and notepads in the recess behind it. But that couldn't be—it was only his own physiognomy Karnock was so interested in, or maybe it was the look of the back of my head. And he wasn't anyone to turn your back on, I didn't much think, not even under the present circumstances.

"You're a witty fellow and no mistake," I said idly, and still with no clear idea how to get started. Confusion? But Karnock was pretty well used to confusion; I suspected it was his customary state. I hadn't been lying to the Dutchman; I thought Karnock was about as twisted as they come.

"Like practical jokes too, I shouldn't wonder," I muttered. Karnock frowned and narrowed his eyes. "Here," he said. "I think I *know* you. Something awfully familiar about the face of you." He leaned nearer to me, so near I could almost feel the heat coming off his face. "Here, just let me get a better butcher's."

"Of course," I said. Foolishly, perhaps. Might be better to let him think he was imagining that resemblance—out of context as we were, he probably couldn't be quite certain. "Don't you remember, last night, on your boat?"

This ploy elicited a more powerful reaction than I had prepared myself to handle.

"You!" Karnock cried, starting up from his chair with spittle ringing out of his mouth. "It's down to you, innit? You shopped me to this lot here, dint you?"

I scooted my chair back, automatically, which was a good thing, because Karnock instantly seized the table in both hands and flung it out from in between us. It was only a light aluminum tubing thing, but it made an awful clatter. The wire to the donkey's-ear microphone attached to its underside kept it from flying very far. I got up and began circling lazily around with my back to the walls of the straight room. Karnock was fearfully excited, but I wasn't taking it too seriously because I knew a gang of coveralls would burst in and pounce on him directly.

I even had my hands in my pockets still, and an ingratiating smile all over my face, and was letting out quantities of the typical pull-string doll's patter, such as *Now then, now then* and *Do let's be calm.* Then Karnock stepped in very suddenly and took a neat front-hand jab at my nose. I snatched my hands free of my trousers and pushed the punch aside with my palm—barely. The arm felt thick and hard as pig iron through the pin-striped cloth. And as I was swiveling out of the corner I seemed to have let myself get backed into, the other arm caught me grazingly on the floating ribs. It was almost only a brush, but it hurt quite some. Enough for me to begin taking the whole predicament much more gravely. And move to the middle of the room, where there was more mobility, or would have been, if not for the overturned table.

The straight room was more cramped than I remembered it. Also all the angles were right angles; I'd always disliked that. Karnock was moving in on me quite efficiently again. He hadn't added much to his height by standing up, I noticed. I had a slight advantage of reach. He was a bandy-legged man and the length of him was all in his torso. In the enthusiasm of that second punch, he'd ripped his coat sleeve loose at the shoulder seam. His mouth was hanging open and his face was throbbing sunset colors, and one eye was reddened by a small exploded vein. Funny how much more frightening he was than his own frighteners. Sid and Ted were only good and dutiful journeymen, while Mr. Kay himself was dead mad, yes.

I swung my leg high over the toppled table and skipped back to avoid him. He'd done his own enforcing when he first got into his business, so I seemed to recall, and I supposed he must have enjoyed the work. I had the leisure to think such thoughts because of the dragging quality of time; all of his movements were exceedingly slow and syrupy. The trouble was, so were mine, and I couldn't get myself to go faster. I bowed my waist and twisted to barely avoid a body punch, and Karnock, with a tidy twist of his hips, slugged the steel door with his whole weight. The entire room boomed like a drum, but it didn't seem to faze him. He came around roaring, two of his knuckles split and swelling. I shouldn't have stopped to look at that. I moved back with the same inevitable lassitude and got hung up on the legs of the table.

Karnock stepped in with another short forehand punch that hit me smartly on my sternum. I tripped backwards over the microphone wire and fell, bashing my head into the mirror with such a terrific crash that I thought I had broken either it or my skull. The coveralls ought to have showed up long since, with long needles slavering sodium pentothal, and that's when I finally figured out that there was *nobody back there*, behind the silvered glass. Nobody was watching this sparrow fall, just me.

Karnock's foot was hanging in the air above me, waiting to stamp down and crush my rib cage. I rolled up to my feet, really quite gracefully for me, and as he moved in I clipped him in the side of the neck with the inside edge of my stiffened palm. For almost a whole second, nothing happened. Then the whites of his eyes flashed up. I put my hands on his collarbone and, watching the action doubled in the mirror, pedaled him backwards and down into the one chair that had somehow remained standing throughout this whole affair.

My hands brushed over his shark-fin lapels; my thumbs dug into the muscles of his neck. A balloon of sour breath puffed out of him. He didn't breathe back in immediately. Inducing hypnosis by pressure on the carotid artery is unethical, dangerous, and usually doesn't work very well—however, this was a special case.

**235**

"*Close your eyes*," I said. "Close your eyes *now*. Your arms are rising straight up to shoulder height—lift your arms. They are straight out at shoulder height, you *cannot* move your arms. Your arms are stiff like they were nailed to the cross. As a matter of fact, your arms *are* the cross."

I took my hands off the pressure point and stepped back. Karnock sat upright with his eyes squinched shut and his arms stuck out like the wings of an airplane.

"Very good," I panted at him. "Very nice. Oh yes, you can breathe now, go ahead and take a breath." And I heard a long expiration come out of him as I bent to pick up the other chair.

Then I set the table onto its legs again. Back in between us, where it belonged. The wire to the donkey's-ear mike still looked intact, though I had formed doubts as to whether anyone was actually listening in. Maybe later someone would listen to the tape. Or maybe that wire just ran down an empty hole, I didn't know. I sat down with my back to the mirror (which hadn't been fractured after all) and contemplated Karnock. There he was, and what a marvel! How to get a handle on him?

I turned halfway in my chair, so I could see the mirror. There was the other Karnock, and the other me, sitting at opposite ends of the other table. Karnock looked even sillier in the reflection, in his pose of imaginary crucifixion. The one sleeve had already ripped completely free with his exertions, and now was wrinkled down around his wrist. When I turned back to look at him head on, he hardly seemed more palpable. It was as though his image and mine as well had simply been printed on the air of the straight room, dimensionless as they were printed on the mirrored glass.

That was what I really hated about the straight room—it took the reality right out of you, with its rectilinear rigidity. I was so tired I had to close my eyes a little, but in my head an annoying ticking sound kept on. *Put another sock on it.* . . . When I looked again I saw that it must be Karnock's heavy wristwatch I was hearing. Tendons were beginning to pull tight on his neck, and his face was all wrinkled up with the effort of holding his arms outstretched.

"All right then," I said. "Your arms are lowering, all by themselves, your arms are coming down. You can't hold them up any longer. They've got too heavy. . . . Your hands are coming down, palm down on the table. There's a ten-ton magnetic attraction between that tabletop and the palms of your hands. All right. Good. Your hands are stuck to the tabletop. Good. Just . . . try to lift your hand now. One or the other, or both together. Go on, try it."

Karnock's face was turning colors again, as he strained to lift his arms back up, but the more he struggled the more tightly his fingers splayed out against the table's polished surface. A better restraint than a straitjacket, really. Who'd have thought he'd be so suggestible? But I mustn't let him try too long.

Time for me to do my work and earn my—my what? What was it I was earning, with this chore?

"Very well," I said. "Relax now, Mister Karnock, you can just . . . relax. You can stop straining now. Let your body become soft. You're relaxing very deeply now, Mister Kay. You've never felt so much at ease. . . . Under your hand there are two buttons, a red button and a black button. These buttons control the elevator. The *red* button brings the elevator up, and the *black* button sends it down. Down. . . . Press the black button, now, Mister Kay, and feel the elevator dropping like a stone . . . down . . . down . . . down . . . straight to the very bottom of the shaft."

Karnock's left forefinger tapped the table, and gradually his face began to clear. His eyeballs, bulging against their lids, were darting as in dream. Something on his left wrist caught my eye, the flicker of his watch's second hand. It was a crisp periodic movement: flick-stop . . . flick-stop. . . . Thus it made its way round the dial. I couldn't take my eyes off of it, though it was time I said something more. What?

"You're down in the very deepest place now, Mister Kay, where it's perfectly warm and dark and safe . . . and comfortable. Except. . . ."

Well, now what? Let him tell me.

"There's something sticking in you, Mister Kay. Like a thorn, or a sharp stone in your shoe. It's jabbing at you and it won't let you rest. And what it is, this little sticker, is a piece of . . . information. Something you know, that you haven't told anyone. . . . And you have to just . . . pull it out. If you tell me now, that jabbing pricking feeling will just go away. You can rest then, Mister Kay, you can simply rest and relax. . . ."

I yawned—falling for my own induction again, wasn't I? It hurt my bruised ribs rather considerably to breathe in deep. Blearily I moved my glance to his face to check for any clue I might be getting somewhere. His lips had begun to work in a sort of writhing way as if he'd bitten into something tart and sour. So, there was something. Naturally, there would be.

"Go on," I said. "Relieve yourself, take off that weight. Go on and tell. You'll feel much better afterwards."

"You're a grass, you are," Karnock said. "Anyway. . . ."

"Anyway?" I leaned forward and lowered my head, and my eye got hung on that second hand again. The watch face seemed to be expanding, somehow.

"It's . . . not . . . my fault," Karnock whispered.

"What?"

"It's not . . . my fault," said Karnock. "They're a lot of . . . little teases . . . all of them. . . ."

"All of who?" The watch face had swollen to fill the room and inside it I saw the movement of the spheres, the endless cycling that revealed to me the whole spectacular scheme of things and within it every most minute detail, including the cupping movement Karnock now made with his left hand, drawing it in toward himself. I'd seen him do that once before and now I saw him on the boat, behind his desk, gathering a paper to him. Newsprint, a newsprint photo. Two black eyes looking at me, upside down, before Karnock tucked the clipping in the folder.

Pini Mukhtar. I shook my head, to make it ache, and straightened in my chair.

"Pini Mukhtar," I said. "Heather Jolley. Are they little teases? Were they?"

Karnock's eyes rolled under the sealed lids. "I never know their names till . . . after."

"No," I said. "I suppose you wouldn't." And what was the name of the one last night, I wondered. Whose picture I had darkly seen through the news agent's show window this morning.

"I find out . . . after," Karnock explained dreamily. "From the papers."

Wapping, that newspaper had said. There would have been several hours of darkness left when Sid and Ted brought the big black car back to him.

"They . . . they all ask for it," Karnock said. "They lead me on, you know. They do."

"Quite right," I said.

"You'd do the same if you were in my place. Wouldn't you?"

"No doubt," I said, with only mild revulsion. I was losing interest now. After all, my work was done. Here was a handle on Karnock and then some. To what use would he be put? I wondered. If, in the Dutchman's version of utilitarianism, Karnock was a machine, then the little girls would have to be regarded as . . . fuel. Which suggested that the Dutchman would continue to throw a little girl into Karnock now and again, to keep him running smoothly. That was a merry process for me to be participating in. But I was powerless to do otherwise, wasn't I?

In the beginning of things, Nature looked on the Man and smiled with love, and the Man looked on Nature and. . . . And we all come to it, don't we? Love gone wrong. Love gone wrong, and with a vengeance.

I was tired, so tired of it all that when I shut my eyes I thought I would just disappear, but instead I saw again the universal map reflected in me. Here was the ultimate end of the Hermetic gnosis, to make this microcosmos the perfect replication of the world without, just so. Because, as Hermes Trismegistus was told by the Nous within him, *God made eternity. Eternity made the world, the world made time, and time made becoming. And eternity is the image of God, as the world is the image of eternity, the sun the image of the world, and man the image of the sun.*

*Therefore, unless you make yourself equal to God, you cannot understand God: for the like is not intelligible, save to the like. Make yourself grow to a greatness beyond measure, by a bound free yourself from the body, raise yourself above all time, become Eternity; then you will understand God. Mount higher than the highest height; descend lower than the deepest depth. Draw into yourself all sensations of everything created, fire and water, dry and moist, imagining that you are everywhere, on earth, in the sea, in the sky, that you are not yet born, in the maternal womb, adolescent, old, dead, beyond death. If you embrace in your thought all things at once, times, places, substances, qualities, quantities, then you may understand God.*

I had been seeking this understanding for a long time, and also the power that came with it, to make water burn, drink fire to quench my thirst, bring forth the living from the dead and the dead also from the living. But the straight room was where I had come instead.

Karnock had been babbling all this time, in a sort of childish whine. I opened my eyes and watched his muttering: "It's a miserable life . . . no life for a man . . . I can't help myself . . . when they taunt me so . . . it's

**239**

not my fault . . . you'd do much the same as me I shouldn't wonder . . ."
and on and on in that same direction.

"There now," I said. "There now, just you relax. Just sleep a little
more deeply now."

Karnock was in deep trance already, but very, very agitated. "They've
been getting worse, they have. All the time, they try me more," he said.
"And now . . . now it's almost every day."

"Now then," I said. "Never mind. Perhaps we'll cure you."

Karnock's head shook itself. "There's no cure. . . . And it's not my
fault. . . . They're little teases . . . all the lot of them. . . ."

"Of course they are," I said. "Well then. Just let me think a bit." I
rolled my eyes back for one more look—there was my universe with everything
in it, including Karnock. Did I want Karnock in my universe? No. What
would be lost if he were removed? Not much.

I ran my fingers down the table leg, took hold of the little braid of bell
wire, and tugged till I felt it come altogether loose. I set my back more
firmly to the mirror, against the outside chance that someone might be reading
my lips. Karnock had stopped burbling and was waiting attentively for me
to speak.

"Kill yourself," I said.

For a moment he didn't reply.

"That's the cure for you," I said. "Just do yourself right away."

"I can't do that," Karnock said.

"Why not?" I said. "It's the only answer."

"No way to do it, in these cells."

"Why not," I said. "They've let you keep your belt and shoelaces."

"No pipes," Karnock said. "No hook."

"What about the window bars?"

"No window."

Evidently his confinement wasn't so plush as he'd have liked me to believe.
Here on his own sufferance, my eye.

"There's a way round that," I said. "Do you want to hear it?"

"Yes," Karnock said.

"You want to die," I said to him. "Don't you? It'll get you away from
those little teases once for all. Dying is your very deepest desire, isn't it?
Isn't it, though?"

"Yes," Karnock said.

"Here's how," I said. "Stand on your chair. Perfectly straight. Lock your neck and your back and your knees, till you're as rigid as a post. Then jump straight down and land on your heels. Don't bend anything. Your back will break and you'll die instantly."

"Yes," Karnock said.

"Best do it soon," I said. "The soonest you're alone again."

"Yes," Karnock said.

"You'll feel much better afterwards," I said.

# twenty-four

"You must have done a miracle," George or Sam said afterward. "I don't know when I've ever seen the Head so pleased."

"My pleasure to serve," I said. "That goes without saying, doesn't it?"

"What did you do then, eh?" George or Sam said, pulling open the passenger door of his khaki-colored Austin Mini. He was giving me a lift home, not that I much wanted that, but of course in this sort of situation my own overmastering desire was to make myself as invisibly agreeable as possible. Joint by joint, I folded myself down into the little car. It was the sort of car you expect to see large numbers of clowns emerging from, in the second ring of the circus.

"What did you do then, eh?" George or Sam repeated, twisting the key and pumping the petrol. The starter made a noise like a lot of thumbtacks being shaken in a can. Then the motor caught with a lawnmower grumble, and the car plunged forward, throwing me back against the dead springs of the seat.

"That's confidential," I said snottily. "Doctor-client privilege, you understand."

"Yes, of course," said George or Sam. "Still, we're among family here, in a manner of speaking. . . ." He skated the car around the dumpster and up toward the prison's main gate. Well, perhaps we had come up in the world—in by the servants' door, out by the front . . . but *We're among family?* That was a different manner of speaking than I was accustomed to in these quarters, and no mistake about it. Still, everyone had been acting slightly delirious since I'd emerged with my valuable intelligence from the straight room. I couldn't resist screwing my head around to watch the huge wooden doors closing up behind the car, joining their halves so smoothly into the great brick arch. At the outer barrier, a guard touched his cap and waved us through.

"Loose talk doesn't please our master," I said. "You do know what I mean."

**242**

"Yes, quite," George or Sam said, shifting gears with a threatening clank and surging up onto the motorway. "Of course, and I didn't intend to pry."

I leaned my head back and shut my eyes. George or Sam drove like a New York cabbie, though you'd never think it to look at him outside of his comical car. I peeked out briefly through my eyelashes to see the landscape go smearing hazily by. Ugh, made me a little nauseous, that did. Maybe it was the exhaustion, or just how low the car sat on the road—I could have hung my arm out the window and filed my fingernails on the pavement.

Maybe it was something else. George or Sam was probably right. I'd never seen the Dutchman half so pleased myself. He'd been so overjoyed that he actually had the ghost of an expression on his face: the look of a man who's struggling not to reveal how scrumptious it truly is, the thing he's eating, lest he be asked to share it with somebody else. The very look of love, that was, though only for an instant. And chalk up a lost opportunity for me, I realized, with powerful inner twinge of regret. Ought to have asked him to do something about my papers while he was in such a sunny mood, because I didn't expect the Dutchman's memory of gratification to endure for very long. Next time I saw him he would undoubtedly have turned into a popsicle again.

"Here we are, then," George or Sam chirped, jabbing at the brakes with a loud squeak. "Home again, home again, jiggety-jog."

"That was quick," I said, opening my eyes with a start. "Where did the time go?" Here I was at my own doorstep once again. I craned my neck out the Austin's window. No sinister black limousines seemed to be lingering at either end of the street.

"Having a little snooze there, were you?" George or Sam said.

I smiled weakly. No, but I'd certainly drifted off somewhere.

"You've earned it after this day's work," George or Sam said, grinning at me with his rodenty teeth. He reached his hand across the seat. "Soon again, I should think. I believe you've a fine future with the firm now, what do you suppose?"

His hand was distinctly clammy when I took it. "Thanks for the ride," I said, and hauled myself up out of the car.

George or Sam crunched his transmission and drove off whistling. I went up the steps, wiping my dampened palm reflexively on my pants leg, unlocked and went directly to the bathroom, where I knelt over the toilet bowl in a lengthy seizure of dry heaves. There was nothing in me, though; I was empty as a jar. Eventually I regained control of my insides and pulled myself upright by the edge of the sink, my eyes wet and blurry from the effort of so much hollow retching. Possibly that beer I'd had for breakfast at the station hadn't been an altogether bright idea.

I went and kicked the front door shut where I'd left it dangling open, and then turned back to the interior of the flat. The light had tilted away from all the windows so it was dreary in every room. In the dim, the wee red dot of the answering machine throbbed painfully: one, two, three. Calls from clients, or potential clients, it developed, with no respect for the Sabbath, no. I jotted down their names and numbers on a pad to call them later, and floated helplessly away into the bedroom.

I couldn't stay here, that much was obvious; it was too gloomy and miserable a place to remain. But where to go? And what to do when I arrived there? There was something pressing on the edge of my brain, but I couldn't quite make out the shape of it. I was cold, or else the flat was, cold as an abandoned tomb. So I went into Clara's closet and sat down on the floor. The belt with the buckle broken loose was still there, and I picked it up and ran it through my fingers, but it wasn't enough for me to transport myself again. I couldn't heave myself back into the fantastic gyre, not now. I hooked the closet door with my toe and pulled it almost shut.

Enclosed in the near dark, I thought I felt a little warmer. A line of light from the door's crack broke over my shoulder and fell in pieces on the wall behind. An essence or aura of Clara swam through the vacated space. There was a slight pungency of paint, and a hint of an orangy perfume she'd sometimes dot on the inside of her wrist, so that it hovered under the natural odor of her body, and was that all I knew? It couldn't be. The first time she left, once she came back, I was so delirious with relief I might have told her everything. But didn't. What if it scared her off again? Better to simply go on living intertwined. I only wanted us to curl like cubs in a burrow, and I left my arm through hers the whole night through, but in the morning I let go. She was back that evening after all, and then the next. . . .

The next time she was gone I thought I knew a little better what to do. After the first frozen lurch and tumble of the discovery, I understood there was a pattern there and I could follow it. A pub she liked to go in the evening, say, where I could happen to walk in. "Well, miss, what were you having? It would be an honor to buy you a libation. . . ."

Or somewhere else. The third time she left it was Val's, I think, and the time after, at her studio. Never mind the venue, there'd always been some ordinary ground where I could court her back again. It needed a lot of care, but not much urgency. She seemed to like it taken lightly. I asked no questions beginning with *Why*.

And never had to answer any. How did I know it wouldn't work this time? Somehow I did. I only wanted to get along, was that so terrible? Just keep interlacing in the pattern of our braid. I'd make her a fish soup, say, and eat it with her. A walk around a corner or two, summer nights when the light would linger, two drinks before closing time, and home to bed. I liked to scrub her back when she was in the bath, till it got red, and she would start to giggle. It could be that simple, then. On a Saturday afternoon I'd follow her to the studio, sit in a corner with my feet folded under me, watch her over the top of my book to try to see the way she saw. That was it, natural as breathing.

Until she did another bolt. Did it start with my not sleeping all the other times? I'd get awake, my eyeballs peeled, scraped rawly aware of her least movement, until the next thing I knew was she moved out. The last time she left me, I never found her anywhere. That's what happened when she stopped trying to find me.

*And who disappeared on whom, had you thought of that?* She spoke around the barrel of a brush clamped in her teeth, about the bore of a cigarette, though longer. With another bigger brush, she touched up a length of sea serpent there on the studio floor. Big lumps of snake was what those were, and I always thought she didn't care for them.

"Is that the creature you wanted to make?" I said.

Clara pulled the brush from her teeth and set it on a bit of cardboard on the windowsill. *I'm not making it. I'm trying to describe it. It's a portrait, of a sort.*

"Of who?"

*Of you. A lot of parts I don't see where they come together.*

"You don't."

*How could I? It's all hidden.* She shook her hair out and then stroked it back, unconsciously streaking it with ocher. I wanted to smile, but held it back. Later I'd cut out the clot with nail scissors. That's if all went well.

*It's you who goes off first, if you'd admit it. It looks like you're there when you're really not. You get somewhere nobody can follow, when you*

stop sleeping and start seeing ghosts. *I don't like being taken for a ghost—
makes me feel invisible. I'm either here or else I'm not.*

"It's the 'not' part that upsets me."

*You're outwitting yourself again,* she said. *Didn't I tell you you've got a
knack for that?* She walked up to me and brushed a dot of yellow onto the
center of my forehead, then stepped back to inspect it. *Now that I can see,*
she said, *but you, looks like you're still hiding.*

"Hiding where? You're talking in circles."

*In the closet, birdbrain. Don't you know where you're supposed to be?*

Oh no. I kicked the closet door open and bounced out, snapping the
broken belt between my hands. Then I dropped it. That was it: Clara,
*claraclaraclara*—I said I'd wait for her at Putney Bridge, and look already,
look at the time. I shoveled a few necessities into my shoulder bag and ran.

I couldn't remember now exactly when my note had implied to her I
would be there, though I thought it was noon or something like that. The
angle of the sun suggested that I was at least two hours late, when I came
up onto the long esplanade. There was a dying slant to the light, but at
least the light was there. I walked the length of the green railing, leaning
on the middle pipe to support my dizzy self, to a point opposite Bishop's
Palace, without meeting anyone I could even momentarily mistake for Clara.

Too late, too late, too late. Perhaps she never came at all. I stopped
and pressed my belly against the railing and looked down. The river was
low and brown and sluggish. At the landing on the other side, they were
trying to put in the same small sailboat as on the day before, or one just
like it. It was dead calm, so the sail was slack, and the boom kept swinging
around the wrong way to the boat. That was the only motion on the river;
the pleasure boats at anchor were dead still. On the sidewalk at street level
above the landing, a man with a leashed dog moved past the doors of the
Star & Garter.

A crash behind me made me turn, but it was only two schoolboys,
jackets and ties askew, scrambling through the hedgerow that bordered the
allotments, up in the cool green cavern under the tall trees. I began to walk
back, with my opposite hand now depending on the rail. The curve of the
overhanging branches made a long recession eastward—it reminded me of
the shrinking boxes Clara had drawn on that lethal envelope she'd left me.
Oh well. There at the vanishing point, someone all in white was standing
at the railing, with one foot cocked up on the toe, looking down at the river

**246**

just as I'd been a few minutes before. Two black and tan dogs came dashing toward me from that direction, as if they were expecting to meet me, but when they came close they passed me by to tumble each other over on the grass. Puppies. Someone whistled for them; they both pricked up their ears, trembled for an instant, then ran off.

That woman just ahead did look a lot like Clara from the back, about the same height and with the same length of that honey-colored hair, only Clara seldom looked so put together. This stranger was cool and chic in a coarse-woven white cotton blouse and linen trousers with ironed pleats that dropped faultlessly to the nip at the ankles—very un-Claraish, that detail. However, the railing pipe was beginning to hum just slightly under my hand, and maybe the woman felt it too, because something made her turn toward me.

"Good Lord," I said. "You're all dressed up."

"I have a date," Clara said, with a half-smile.

I stopped, about three feet short of her, and looked down at the ground. The loose brown bits of gravel there were vividly present to my eye. Clara had on her old down-at-heel running shoes, I noticed—that might have been a giveaway, before.

"Ah well," I said. "I'll try not to keep you long."

"With *you*, stupid," Clara said, shaking her hair back over her shoulder with an impatient jerk of her head.

"You dressed for me?" I said, stupidly as I'd been described. "New outfit too. New belt?" The belt was blue, and thin as a string.

"I went shopping," Clara said. "You're looking sort of unusual yourself. Have you been in jail or something? What's that number doing on your shirt?"

"Oh, ah, well . . ." I said. "In a manner of speaking. You might say."

Clara shook her head. "Same old story," she said. "Same old won't-tell-me-the-story. I thought you wanted to tell me something. Or is that going to be a bait-and-switch?"

"Oh no," I said. "I—I promise you a full confession. Or as much as we can fit in at one session."

"You might try that," Clara said. "Should I believe whatever I hear?"

"I won't deceive you," I said. "Also, I had an idea that needed mentioning. A proposition, you would call it. We could get married, you and I."

Clara blushed, to my surprise, bit her lip lightly, then forced a laugh out over it, covering up. "*That's* different," she said. "Is that supposed to be confessional?"

"I'll get to that part," I said. "In just a minute. Let's walk a little, shall we?" I stepped nearer to touch her arm, lightly but enough to bring her along; we began strolling back in the direction of the bridge. She had tucked her fingers in her pockets, behind the seam where the pleats began. As casually as I could manage, I linked my arm through the crook of hers.

"So how are things?" I said, to disguise this action.

"Another question?" Clara said. "Well. I'm getting outdone staying with Val. It isn't her, of course, it's Richard."

"Pinhead Richard," I said reflexively.

"I'm beginning to think you're right about him," Clara said. "I may move into the studio, just till I can find my own place."

"Don't," I said. "You ought not to sleep in all those paint fumes."

"Touched by your concern. . . ." Clara said.

"Plenty of room back at our flat as well," I said.

She didn't answer right away, and I could hear our paired footsteps hushing against the pavement as we walked on. Here, the long knotted branches of the trees stretched completely over us and the balustrade, reaching down almost far enough to brush the surface of the water. Because of the gentle curve of the walkway, I couldn't see very far ahead, which made it possible to continue to hope.

"Ah," Clara said. "How are things there?"

"Not what they used to be," I said. "Dismal, really. Everyone misses you."

"Everyone who?"

"Well, me, obviously . . . and the snake misses you."

Clara snorted. "How can you tell?"

"He won't eat." I kept walking her along, still hopeful. Never know what might appear around that bend.

"Too bad for him," Clara said, disengaging her arm from mine so smoothly it took me a couple of seconds to notice it. "He'll die if he keeps that up. Good riddance too."

"I miss you," I said. "I really miss you . . . a lot."

"How can you tell?"

"I haven't been sleeping. . . ."

*248*

"You weren't sleeping before I left." She halted, repositioned my head by the chin, and looked me hard in the eye. "God, you do look terrible, though. You still haven't slept at all?"

"No, it's a bad one, this time. I'm thinking I might go right round the bend this t— actually, no, it's sure to stop soon. Tomorrow, or the next day. You know how it is, it always stops."

"Yes," Clara said. "Then it starts up again. No, you can't work me for sympathy, not about that. You won't let anyone help you with it. Not me, not anyone."

I looked out across the river. Someone in the sailboat was leaning way out to reach for the end of that wayward boom, and the boat heeled down in the water under his weight. The clinking of a pulley against the aluminum mast came to us clearly through the dead air.

"You don't suffer in silence, exactly," Clara said. "But you certainly do it in solitude. So. What was it you were about to tell me?"

"Come back," I said.

"That's *it?*" Clara bowed her neck like a rearing horse. "Did you think I came out to hear that? Goddamn it, *I am not a snake*. I need a little more than body heat, you know."

"There's a bit of the snake in everyone," I said.

"You've told me that before," Clara said, "though I can't say it ever really sent me."

I looked back out over the river. The fellow had got the sail lashed to a cleat or something, and the boat had come upright again. Someone on the landing gave him a push and the boat slid out a little way into the water.

"Enough," Clara said. "You're not getting anywhere, again. I'm going to have to go."

"Wait," I said. "Wait, and I'll tell you."

Clara looked at me, through me, her eyes bright, but hard. "Then no more stalling."

I cleared my throat. "I'm married," I said. "It's a bit late in the game, I know, that I never got round to telling you, but at the moment I happen to be married."

"Just a minute," Clara said. "I thought you said just now—"

"Yes, and I meant it too, but at the moment I'm technically married already. To the wrong person, though. Not you."

**249**

Clara's eyes widened, then relaxed. "This is becoming extremely confusing," she said.

"Can't be helped," I said. "You know, it's confusing to me too."

"I suppose it must be. . . ." She set her hip against the rail and tapped the metal with her fingernail. "Tell me more?"

"It's sort of complicated," I said.

"That figures," Clara said. "Just pick a place and start."

There were two people in that sailboat now, I noticed. One of them was diddling with the sail, and the other rowing, putting his back well into it. The oar blades made little whirlpools that widened as they diverged away from the stern.

"You're not telling me," Clara said. She swung and began to walk away, but not so fast as if she definitely meant to lose me. I followed a pace or two behind. There was a kink and the walkway straightened; now there was a clear view all the way over to the bridge. Clara paused at a break in the balustrade where a set of concrete steps let down into the water. Beside the steps was a hook for a life ring, which was missing. Clara fingered the empty place and then skipped up onto the cement base of the balustrade, and rested her elbows on the top green rail. I came up below her and looked in the direction of her gaze. The sailboat was momentarily obscured by a tour boat churning along the river. The amplified mutter of the guide came bouncing off the water.

"I used to be a heroin addict," I said. "Still am, by some accounts, but I don't take it anymore. I was a junkie for about five years or so."

"I know that," Clara said. "But about this marriage—"

"You *what?*" I said. "I never told you that."

Clara reversed her position and looked down on me. "You never tell me anything," she said. "But I'm not stupid, generally. I know what needle tracks look like, going up and down your arms. I used to live with you, remember? I saw you with your clothes off all the time."

"Right," I said. "Well, that makes sense."

"I put those scars on you in that drawing you claim to like so much," she said. "Haven't you ever noticed that yet?"

"I suppose you might say I never made the connection," I said.

Clara ducked her head and laughed. Taking this for an encouraging sign, I reached up and touched her with my finger. But she bounced my whole hand away by stiffening her arm.

"The trouble is, you're too wrapped up in your esoterica to ever see what's in front of your nose," she said.

"Yes, that's true too," I admitted.

"I could draw you blindfold," Clara said, more softly as she hopped down to the walk. "I could draw you in the dark. But please, don't let me interrupt."

"Let's walk," I said, and began shifting along the straight path to the bridge. Clara came along with me, about half a step behind.

"So," I said. "My best junkie pal was a man named Stuart Boatwright. You might have noticed his name on an envelope, as a matter of fact, I've had a couple of letters from him recently."

"Those are the letters that when they come you take them down in the cellar and hide?" Clara said.

"Those ones, yes," I said. "That's right."

"But I don't suppose you were married to *him*, were you?"

"I was married to his girl friend," I said. "The woman he lived with, whatever you call it. Her name was Nicole, Nicole Hannon."

"Stop a minute," Clara said, holding onto the rail and arresting me with a pluck at the strap of my shoulder bag. "I'm not sure I understand exactly how this worked."

There was another hook for a life ring here, with a placard giving instructions for its use. I peered out into the water and saw some clots of debris floating below, some soggy papers and bits of wood that the river's motion lapped against the wall and then drew back away.

"Strangely," I said. "She never would live with me. I tried to get her to, but she wouldn't—I mean we were lovers, all of that, but she just wouldn't move out from Stuart. So we just got married instead."

"That simple, was it?" Clara said. I could see circles of white around her eyes. "So, all this without him knowing?"

"I doubt he ever knew about the marriage. No one ever knew about that other than the two of us. I'm sure he knew about the rest in time . . . don't quite know what it meant to him, though. He had her turned out as a prostitute before I ever got to know her."

"I see," Clara said, turning and bracing both hands on the railing. The oarsman had pulled the oars back into the boat, which sat becalmed, its sail still flaccid. All around it were patches of blue-black on the brownish water, shadows from the clouds beginning to thicken over the sun.

"That *is* strange," Clara said. "Strange as it gets, I'd think. But . . . I suppose it sounds like something you'd do. Something completely metaphysical."

"Maybe," I said. "Of course, it did have its physical aspects. He used to beat her too, that was a big part of it. He beat her up but she still wouldn't leave him. It wasn't a healthy situation, I see now."

"No," Clara said, remotely. In profile, her face looked calm as a carving. "Why didn't you just . . . get out of it?"

"I did, eventually," I said. "But . . . have you ever been so powerfully attracted to something you *knew* was killing you and still just couldn't give it up?"

Clara turned and looked at me narrowly. "That's called addiction," she said.

"So it is," I said. "Although not everyone always knows to call it that."

"How did you quit heroin?" Clara said.

"I put it down and walked away," I said. "It's not so hard, once you come down to it. I was sick for a week and then it wasn't so bad. The catch is, it doesn't get much better."

"And then?"

"Then I came here."

Clara shook her head and moved out along the rail, briskly, beginning to overtake the sailboat, which sat stock-still in its pattern of fading ripples, rocking gently whenever one of the passengers shifted his weight. Then she stopped again, abruptly enough I almost ran into her.

"So you were married," she said. "Are married. Legally and everything?"

"A civil ceremony," I said. "It didn't take long. No guests. A couple of bondsmen I think were the witnesses."

"And now?" Clara said. "What are you doing about it now? Or is it just the same as ever?"

I looked down at the tops of her shoes, which were less pristine than the rest of her outfit, spotted with mustard-colored blobs of paint, the brightest among clots of different reds and umbers. "I'm getting a divorce," I muttered.

"This is just an idea in your mind?" Clara said.

I got myself to look her back in her cool gray eyes. "Nicole was here—'

on a business trip," I said. "She looked me up. I think she wanted something out of me but I never really found out what. I was worried about it because Stuart told me she had a child, and the age was right, it might have been mine. Conceivably. . . ."

"But now you think it isn't yours?"

"Definitely not. I'm sure of that much now. So once I knew that I asked if she'd divorce me. And I think it's under way, she won't be difficult about it. She'll serve me with some sort of papers when she gets back to New York."

"And after that you want to marry me?"

"I would have asked you a long time ago if it wasn't for. . . ."

"The bigamy issue. So. You want to be married but live apart? Another metaphysical proposition?"

"No, no," I said, spreading my palms against the dampening air. It was getting darker now as the clouds thickened quickly, and there was the faintest trace of a breeze starting up. "I want to be married and live together, both at the same time."

Clara laughed shortly and turned her back on me to face the river. "Honestly, Adrian, sometimes you almost beggar belief."

"Do I?" I said. "It's a sincere proposition, really it is."

"I guess that might explain you being a little preoccupied, though," she said in the direction of the water. "All that intrigue going on, I guess that might keep a person awake at night."

"Oh, but that's not what I think about," I said, like a proper idiot.

Clara made a movement like she meant to snatch me by the collar, but drew her hand back. Across the river, two gulls flew up suddenly from the bank, crying out loudly as they wheeled in opposing circles. The sky was dulling to the color of iron. "What do you think about, then?" she said. "I've often wondered that."

"Nothing much," I said. "A lot of the time I just lie there and look at the ceiling."

Clara hung her head back over the river. A dot of rain fell on her back, dampening the white blouse to her skin, but she didn't seem to have felt it. "Do you think I would want to get married to that?" she said.

"Come back," I said, and cautiously picked up her hand and turned it palm up on my own. Her fingers were slightly rough and reddened and despite the scrubbing, dark traces of paint lined the creases of her palm. A hand that did things, I loved that. "Come back and I'll tell you everything you want to know."

"I don't know," Clara said, and pulled her hand quite definitely away.

"I need you," I said. "I'm fully prepared to admit that I need you."

"You don't need anyone," Clara said, "because you live in a dream world all the time."

"That may be so," I said. "But I need you in my dream world too."

"What for?" Clara said, and shook her head, but the wind had come up and it blew her hair across her mouth again. The sail had bellied out on the boat, which now moved smartly east across the water. Clara twisted her hair down on one shoulder and held it there. "Tell me what you need me for."

"Love," I said. "I love you to death, do you understand that? Let me give just one example. Suppose that a pig, who likes better to turn about in mud than in a bed of linen, were to fall in love with a woman—"

"No," Clara said. The rain was beginning to pat down on her forehead, but when I reached to wipe it off, she pulled away. "I don't want to be a goddess in your mystery cult. I'm not that. I'm only me."

"Yes," I said, hearing the rain begin to rattle on the canopy of leaves. It was waking me up, the thin wet tapping, refreshing that other part of me. "Yes, but what are you? What are you, really?"

"I'm not just a batch of tropisms," Clara said, "and I'm also not just an idea in your mind. If you want to just transfer that whole complex from Whatshername to me—that frightens me more than anything else, do you think you can understand that?"

"But that's really not the way it is—"

"You could love anyone like that."

"Yes, but it's not just anyone—"

"That *is* the sort of thing you think about, isn't it? When your eyes start spinning in opposite directions and you stay up for days and days? You could use a dose of your own treatment, that's what I think, a little something to calm you down."

"Undoubtedly," I said. "That's the proverbial paradox."

"Yes, but I don't want to live inside it. No thanks, there's no way I can stay with that. Once it gets that way, I'm out of there, I'm gone. I can't just be the subject of these crazy inspirations." Clara was still holding her hair down against the gusts; it leashed her head so that she couldn't shake it as far as she probably would have liked. "I'm the pig myself, don't you see?" she said. "If you insist on discussing metaphorical swine—I feel like the pig *myself*. I'm the searcher, not the object, can't you see that? Can't you?"

"Yes," I said. "I've thought of that, quite a lot these last few days. I've been having dreams about it, or visions I guess you'd better call them. . . ."

"Don't," Clara said.

"No, I promise you, it's actual. It's perfectly concrete. There's a way for the whole thing to come together, all the elements. Just give me time to work it out."

"I know, I know," Clara said. "It's an alchemical experiment. I don't like being the material for that."

"It's not a matter of material," I said. "Look—oh hell, I just can't say it. You always came back before, didn't you? Why did you always come back before?"

"I don't know," Clara muttered. "I couldn't tell you, I just did."

"You see?" I said. Just then, I felt like I did understand. "After all, some things can't be talked over. Some things just happen, they get done. Come back, just do it one more time, I know I can work it out—"

"But maybe this time I just won't," Clara said. "And won't be able to explain that either."

"No," I said. "You'll come, you've got to."

"I think not," Clara said. She was giving me the look, the one that bored right through me with its comprehensive power. I wanted to turn my face away from the force of it, but every other time she'd looked that way, she'd found something to attract her.

"You'll come," I said, just barely able to keep meeting her eyes. "It's not just anyone. It's you."

"I don't know," Clara said. "Maybe if you had the sense to come in out of the rain . . . haven't you noticed it's raining yet?" And before I could answer she wheeled away and was running back over toward the bridge. The wind puffed out her blouse like the sail on the boat, which was now coming about and tacking back in the opposite direction. The worn soles of her running shoes were turning up quickly: one-two, one two. The hole I'd envisioned or hallucinated previously winked up at me from her right heel.

I started after her, but I didn't have a chance. My knees weren't up to it, my lungs weren't up to it, and I was too tired anyway. After only a few pounding paces, a pain in my side doubled me up against the rail. The best I could do was raise my head in time to watch her out of sight. Just above me, one of those gulls had banked into the wind and was hanging there like a helicopter, unable to progress, or not wanting to. I often pictured the way she ran but I seldom imagined her running away. Maybe if she ran fast enough she would go right around the curve of the earth and find herself running toward me again.

# twenty-five

Looked like I didn't have enough sense yet; anyway I was dripping wet by the time I had managed to limp back to the tube. All around me people were twirling raindrops off their bumbershoots before folding them away. No sign of Clara, and why should there have been? She'd been in easy running distance of her studio. I was here, and she was there. She was there, and I was in transit. It was cold underground, or seemed so. There was gooseflesh on my arms and it took some force of concentration to keep my teeth from chattering. I felt that people were staring at me as well.

However, I wasn't long on the train. At Fulham Broadway I dismounted and went walking east on Fulham Road. It was still raining, not torrentially, but hard enough. I didn't hurry, being already as wet as I could get, or near it. The black umbrellas went along by me like troupes of uprooted mushrooms with legs. Aboveground, under the pouring sky, it no longer felt so cold, and the pattering of the rain on my skull stopped me being obliged to think.

No lights were on at the house on Slaidburn Street, and no one stirred at the front of the building. There was no regular practice scheduled for Sunday, but still, sometimes. . . . The door folded inward when I gave it a good push. I tiptoed into the gray-green gloom and stopped to listen. From down the stairs I heard something, yes, a guttural flow of unintelligible language, end-stopped by a short brisk bark. Master Kim, with a private student. I put my head in the empty dressing room, then went softly up the stairs. There was only one room up there, long and narrow under the eaves. On the landing stood a coatrack with a few wire hangers dangling empty, and I bethought myself to take my crumpled tux out of the bag and hang it up on one of these. As my bag was alleged to be waterproof, the tux was only slightly damp. I spent a minute or so yanking out the creases, the best I could see them in the poor light. Then I took my shoes off and ducked under the low lintel into the attic room.

The peaked roof was so badly insulated that the sound of the rain was almost as immediate as it had been when it was pounding on my cranium, outside. Now and again a gust of wind whipped rain into the sash windows that were cut through the other three walls of the room. There was more light here, with all the windows: the light of an aquarium's interior. One of them was acrack and water was drooling over the sill and wetting the mat beneath it. I padded sock-foot across and shut it, then set down my bag, away from the wet spot. My shirt was wringing wet when I peeled it off. I squeezed a measure of the water out and scrubbed it over my hair, though it didn't seem to make much difference: no moisture exchanged in either direction.

On the shingles above, the rain slackened its pace, and then redoubled it. I stripped off my trousers, pulled on my gi pants and knotted the draw-string. No need for the top or the belt, no need for much ceremony, no one was watching. My bare torso was cold as stone. I did a set of push-ups to warm up; I hate push-ups. Then side splits, front splits, butterflies. I got up gingerly and did a set of punches, the length of the attic, and a set of blocks back. Front kicks forward. Side kicks back. Reverse punch, forward and back. Back kick forward, roundhouse back. I was putting a lot of concentration into cat-footing every move, stepping so lightly I wouldn't be heard downstairs.

I was breathless when I finished the quick basics, but still quite cold. That struck me peculiar. There was a lingering chill in my limbs, a sort of ague, it felt like. Possibly, with my whole system weakened by the days and nights of sleeplessness, I might be coming down with the flu.

Work it out, then. I did Chul Gi I, once slowly, once at speed. Then Pal Sek, twice the same way. Breathless again, but I still felt miles outside my body, when all I wanted now was to inhabit it completely, exclusively. To be only body. Otherwise—

Work it out. I started forms again from the beginning: Kuk Mu I and Kuk Mu II, Pyong An I through Pyong An V, then Chul Gi I and Pal Sek once again. That was everything I knew, but still, still not enough, though the effort of those repetitions dropped me to the floor at last, flat on my back with my belly blowing in and out like a toad's. My skin was clammy on the vinyl mat, but strangely I still hadn't managed to break a sweat; it was as if my skin were sealed.

I lay there for quite a few minutes, with my knees drawn up. The bad knee was pulsing a sharp bright pain, and that was the only strong signal

I wasn't already a corpse. I tensed for a second when I heard voices below, but they didn't seem to be coming toward the stairs. It must have been Master Kim and his student going out, because after a minute I heard the lock click and then a rattle of someone trying the door from outside. After that there was only the rain.

When another measure of time had drained away, I got up. Contact, that was what I needed. Impact. Shock. The subaqueous light at the windows was shrinking into a deeper dark. Either the clouds were thickening further or it was later than I'd thought. I went to the end of the room where the heavy bag was drawn back out of the way and clipped to a hook above the windows. It swung down trembling and creaking on its chain when I released it. A four-foot-long stuffed sausage, hung about a yard off the floor from its swivel up in the eaves. The dirty white canvas was speckled with brown in the middle-target area, where people had skinned themselves with sloppy punches. I touched the scab between my own front knuckles, then took a short step forward and slugged the bag: right hand, left hand, jab, reverse punch, knife hand, hammer fist. There was a tiny distant pain that grew a little nearer as the cut reopened to its original length. The bag dented in a little, and bounced a few inches back with every blow, but it was a *very* heavy bag and I couldn't start it really swinging, not with hand techniques.

When I was completely breathless I backed away and stooped over with my hands braced on my knees. A sweat had finally started, pocking out all over my skin and burning like an acid. When I straightened up, a little thread of blood ran down the back of my hand from the cut, following the route traced by the vein. All right, no more punches, then. Better not stain the bag too much. I moved a little closer and began to whip it with roundhouse kicks on alternate legs, each contact bringing a broad flat sting across my instep. The bag jounced from side to side, then recentered itself on its swivel, as I backed further away and then stepped behind and struck it dead center with a side kick, leading with the heel. The bag crumpled and flew away; I switched stance and hit it again with my heel's point as it came back toward me on the backswing, stopping it cold. Then again, and again on the same pattern. I wanted to blast it back far and hard enough to break a window, but that was impossible. The arc the chain defined was much too high. Frustrating, that. I began dodging out and coming in again at different angles, which complicated the bag's backswing and made it more difficult to meet it correctly, so that the shock ran perfectly through the frozen fork of my body from my one heel striking the weighted canvas to my other fixed against the mat.

Then I slipped in the puddle where it had rained in the open window and crashed down heavily on my side. Good thing Master Kim had already gone out, because that tumble surely would have been heard below. I rolled away, out of the damp place, and after a moment could ascertain that I hadn't broken or ripped anything much. There was a hot orange glow in my bad knee now, but not much more. However, I was still unsatisfied. I wanted to use my bodily power in some other way, to attack and injure other human flesh, but whose? After all, I had tried that very thing the day before and had small joy of it. But still, I was unsatisfied.

A complete martial art ought to include a workable method for suicide. I have often thought that simultaneous twist punches might do it. Haven't tried it, though, so far. I squeezed my eyes tight shut to derail that train of thought, and saw the mirrored wall of the straight room, and heard my voice telling        something about        . . . .

Work it out. I got up, with divers twinges. Try something I wasn't good at. Try something I couldn't do. I thought it over. Jump spinning back kick, that should do it. That, so far as I was concerned, was the asymptotic approach to the impossible.

I backed off to the far end of the attic and drew in my breath. At the opposite end, the bag was still swaying lightly on the chain. A practice run? No, do it on faith. What faith? I was running, then jumping up as high as I could and doing my best to twirl around in midair and lash my foot out parallel to the floor. But I missed the bag almost altogether, only brushing it with my shoulder as I skidded past and slapped my palms up either side of the window just before my head would have crashed through.

That would be one way to break it, not the best. I retreated and tried again. This time I connected with the bag, but incorrectly, while I was still turning, so that it was really more of a hook kick. My off leg landed in the puddle and I fell down, got up, backed off, and took another running start. I knew when I left the floor I had it right this time and sure enough it was a clean connection. With my eyes jammed open, I saw the bag go blowing away, high above the top window ledges, the chain coming almost horizontal. I landed on my back with a slam, and the bag passed down over me like a great dark scythe.

Try again, for a better recovery. I got up, backed off, and took another running start. *Yes!* The bag disappeared into the eaves, and I came down in a neat back stance and stood there in a glow of self-congratulation, until the bag swung back and knocked me out. I never really felt the impact proper, only felt myself catapulted end over end into the engulfing dark—sweet unconsciousness, at last.

Unfortunately, this recognition woke me up. I came to myself, such as I was, crumpled with my cheek pressed into the sticky vinyl of the mat, sobbing a little, though less from pain than from despair. What had I come here for? To hide out, and prepare myself. But there was no hiding place for me, and probably no enemy to prepare for.

Giordano Bruno went against the established church because, as he said, *they use force, and not love.* Which statement became one of the charges the Inquisition brought against him. They used force on him, no mistake about that. And not love. I had botched it. Bruno botched it also, sad to say. Too many of the magi were not wise enough.

Although my position was painfully awkward, I couldn't seem to move at all, not so much as a fingertip. Maybe I was really broken, this time once for all, but it didn't seem to matter much. It was dark, and the rain on the roof was reduced to a whisper, and I was done for. I had done for myself, I knew that. Out of my farsightedness. From the corner of my eye I thought I saw a huge cue ball reverse itself on the far wall and come rolling back toward me. The arcane symbols chalked in blue along its curves put me in mind of all I had forgotten about where I really had come from, how far I had come away from it. All those ambivalent disappearances of Clara's had been, though I had never noticed it before, my series of last chances, and now I had surely missed the final one. It was her I ought to have been studying, whatever it might be she thought and felt, the mysteries of why she did the things she did. I should never have forgotten her. I should have been attending, but I wasn't, and that's just where the trouble started. That's where I missed my last opportunity for ordinary human love, which is of course the one true element of every transmutation.

Oh, dear me, looks like I blew it. If I could say a prayer to her, or work the spell I'd struggled with—but even if the old crow wings could haul me into the air again, I'd still be solitary as a lone dot on the pale sky. She just didn't want to be prayed to, that was it. And she was right, but I wasn't wrong. I'd got lost in my fantasies of everything our love could become, but that didn't mean the fantasies weren't true. It was a mixture, both sides of the question blending. After all, there's no such thing as merely human. If I could get her back, I'd tell her that.

But no, the paradox hadn't been adequately entertained, and now my incantations wouldn't work. I didn't have the strength required, or enough perspicacity. The most critical ingredient had been allowed to go astray. Well, I wasn't the first to foul up the formula, though it was cold comfort to think so now. Most of the other necromancers had made similar mistakes. The magicians turned themselves into mechanics, then rapists, then murderers. I could feel the world screwing round and round beneath me now, twisting in its final agony under the force of their operations . . . *because they use force, and not love.* I would die with it, symbiotically, according to my helpless faith, but not sleep. I knew now that I would never sleep again, but die with my bald eyes open and watching it all.

There was a movement at the door, I saw. Someone put a head in, then took it out. Then put it in again.

"Adrian?" Terence's voice. "Is it you?"

"Yes," I said. "I think so."

"Oh," Terence said. I watched his sock-feet coming across the mat toward me. "I thought it was a pile of rags."

"Quite," I said. "Thank you. Very observant."

The socks stopped a few inches away from my nose. Bit of a hole by the left great toe, I noticed.

Terence spoke again, from on high. "What happen to you here?"

"The bag got me on the rebound," I said. "I was trying jump kicks."

"Foolish," Terence said. "Best get up, then. It's getting on for time to do your show."

"Right."

And I discovered then that I could sit up, though not without a bright radiance of pain through all my joints. Terence had stretched out his hand to me, and I climbed up the length of his arm to reach my feet.

"Nothing broken?" Terence said.

"Maybe not," I said. "Though I'm awfully stiff."

"That's the damp," Terence said. "So, look sharp now."

I went ahead of him through the door and stooped over awkwardly for my shoes. At the lower landing I remembered the tux and the bag and turned back.

"Go on," Terence said. "I'm bringing the lot of it."

So I went down into the dressing room and stood between the benches with my shoes dangling loose in my hands by their laces. Terence put the light on, making me blink, then walked by me into the showers and turned on a pair of taps.

"Go on," he said. "Get in."

"What's the time?" I said.

"You've got an hour," Terence said. "But don't dawdle."

I slipped the drawstring loose and walked out of my gi pants, into the swirling steam. The hot water fogged instantly on the damp cool air. I let it beat down on my head and shoulders for who knows how long, till Terence called me out again.

"You've been careless with that cut," he said, frowning at the trickle of blood between my fingers. "Wear gloves, won't you, the next few times you work the bag?" He tossed me a towel. "Here, dry yourself."

He went out and I began rubbing myself down, doing my best not to bloody the towel.

Terence came back with a first aid box. "Eh, look at that," he said when he opened it. "Just the thing. Give me that hand." I watched him crimp the edges of the cut shut with a couple of butterfly adhesives.

"Tidy work, Terence," I said. "Never took you for a nurse."

"As need presents." Terence had spread various elements of my tux out on a bench and was peering down at them. "Here's a proper puzzle," he said. "Haven't dealt with one of these since my youngest sister's wedding. You'll be wanting studs for that shirt."

"Try the breast pocket of the coat," I said.

"Very good," Terence said. "Here, put on your trousers, Adrian, and don't waste time."

"What brought you here?" I said, pulling up my pants legs.

"Looking for you," Terence said. "I ran out of other places."

"What for?" I zipped my fly and settled the waistband on my hips.

"I was worried," Terence said, and pulled my arm down through a shirtsleeve. The arm stuck out cataleptically after he let go; with an effort I forced it to lower.

"Why didn't you tell me Karnock's frighteners were after you?"

"I didn't know whose frighteners they were," I said. "But believe me, at the first of it, I came looking for you right away."

"So Maurice told me," Terence said, clicking in my collar stud. "Once he got round to it. But then you never mentioned it last night."

"Slipped my mind," I said.

"So what were they on at you about?"

"A mix-up," I said. "They really wanted Stuart. Karnock was worried about his trade."

"Bit paranoid, that?" Terence said. "Lift your arms, would you?" He lashed the cummerbund around my belly.

"He was talked out of it fairly easily," I said. "Stuart blew him a little smoke, and he laid off. I'm not expecting any more trouble. Not from that quarter anyhow."

"That's for the better," Terence said, as he evened the ends of my bow tie. "An eccentric fellow, Karnock."

"In numerous ways," I said. "Interesting meeting him, of course, but not anything I'd want to repeat."

Terence slipped the tailcoat on over my arms and beat a portion of dust from the shoulders. "I suppose you might pass for a headwaiter," he said, turning from me. "Eh, these shoes could do with a polish. What have you done with your dress shoes?"

"Forgot them," I said. "Give them here, it won't matter. The light's dim there, no one will see." And I sat down to tie my laces.

"Here," Terence said, passing a crumby brown orb by my nose. "Better have this."

"What is it?"

"Scotch egg."

I took the thing into my hand. By God, it was a Scotch egg too, and not half bad when I bit into it. "Did you lay it?"

"Brought it along from the pub," Terence said. "You haven't time for a regular meal. Don't dribble, you're wearing your good suit."

"What's the time?" I said, swallowing crustily.

"We'll get there if we take a cab."

"We?" I said. "Thought you didn't approve of the Empress."

"Can't have you out of a job, though, can we," Terence said, turning away to shove loose bits of my gear into my bag. "Or you'll have no money to spend in my pub. And you look in need of a keeper tonight."

"No man has such a friend," I said indistinctly through Scotch egg.

"Eh?" Terence said, over his shoulder.

I swallowed the last bit of egg white and breading. "No man has such a friend as you," I said.

"I only saw you were in need," Terence said, turning to toss me a long dark garment. "Here, you'd better have my raincoat."

# twenty-six

I brought Terence into the Empress by way of the moat, a kidney-shaped sort of orchestra pit that had a back door letting onto Bridle Street. The door was locked, according to custom, but I could hear the Triple-A trio tuning up on the other side of it, and after I hammered half a minute, someone came over and opened it. June.

"There you are," she said peevishly. "You've got Eric all in a lather."

"What for?" I said. "Hello, dear. We're ten minutes early, what's the difficulty?"

"He starts getting worked up an hour beforehand," June said. "You know that. No one can find Kiki either, and you know what she's like."

"That could be a worry," I said. Terence went around the back of me and I watched him sidle over toward the trio, where Azrael was keeping up a low, insistent line on his big stand-up bass—ba-baum, ba *baump*—ba-baum ba *baump*. . . . I peeled off Terence's raincoat and hung it over my arm. "Hasn't she been in all evening?"

"That's the worrying part," June said. "She came in and changed for her act—all her street clothes are there in the dressing room. Can you picture her doing a bolt in her stage gear?"

"Vividly," I said.

"So can Eric," June said. "We've been combing all over the shop, but no go."

"Try to keep him away from me, then," I said. "Tell him I'm here, but keep him out of my hair. Did you restock my prop bag, by the way?"

"The perishables, yes," June said. "It's in the dressing room."

"Goodo," I said, hooking my hand at Terence, who came back my way out of the shadows. "Look, I've brought my brother down tonight. Get him a nice quiet table, could you? And put whatever he has on my tab."

"You're not much alike," June said, deadpan.

"I had a childhood skin disease," I said. "Terence, June—June, Terence. . . ."

**266**

"Delighted," Terence said, making a yeoman's effort to look her only in the eyes, which was challenging, considering that the rest of her rig was meant to draw your attention elsewhere. Spike heels, fishnet stockings, pin-striped hot pants supported by red suspenders that pinched her two bare breasts together. Her dyed hair was cut and polished in the shape of a Wehrmacht helmet, and crowned with a banker's bowler hat. She did have nice brown eyes, though, if you looked.

"Here, you have your raincoat back," I said, passing it to Terence.

"Right, just follow me, then," said June. And I noticed she slipped two fingers into the crook of Terence's elbow as they went off together. Ba-baum, ba *baump*—ba-baum, ba *baump*. . . . That bass line was so low, it was almost below my threshold of perception. Abdul was tracking the rhythm of it with a pair of brushes on a cymbal. I went over.

"The Wiz is late," Azrael said, pulling the strings of the bass with his long black fingers.

"But not too late." I reached down to a bench to pick up one of a couple of radio mikes lying there. "Will there be any singer tonight?"

"Nah," Aziz said. He was moving with the gentle sway of an underwater plant, holding the tenor sax out from his chest at the length of its strap, with one thumb. Behind him, Frank was bent in a U, figuring inaudible progressions two inches above the keyboard of the black baby grand.

"Just us and the Wiz," Aziz said. "And Kiki if she ever turns up."

"And if she doesn't?"

Aziz touched his mouth to the reed, then drew it back. "The Wiz will have to think of something."

"I'll get on it right away," I said. "Maybe one of you lot could strip." I switched on the mike. "Nuke 'em till they glow—uh-oh, pardon me lay-sungemmun, didn't know this mike was live." My voice, foreign and de-tached, boomed out of the stacked speakers all over the ballroom above. At one of the tables up there I thought I might have heard someone laugh.

"Equipment seems to be working, at least," I said, switching off the mike and dropping it into a pocket of my tailcoat. "That's something. How's the house?"

Aziz shrugged. I chinned myself on the rim of the moat and hung there long enough to count maybe ten pairs of men's shoes under the tables, and six or eight pairs of ladies'. There were Terence's feet about halfway back and on the left, in tai chi slippers, despite the wet. He has smallish feet for

**267**

a man his size. I let myself drop back to the floor. In the old days, when the Empress had been less "variety" and more strictly "burlesque," the moat served to discourage our patrons from storming the dancing girls on the stage. In these later times, a gangplank allowed me to bring people over the gap for my act, but it could still be kicked out in an emergency.

Ba-baum, ba *baump*—ba-baum, ba *baump*. . . . It was strangely seductive for something so simple. I craned my head back in the other direction. The stage was empty except for some chairs. A single red spot glowed on the silver starburst painted on the canvas backdrop. No Kiki— wonder what became of her? Rubbing my neck, I walked over to the drum kit and flipped the lever that brought the springs tight against the bottom of the snare.

"Leave that," Abdul muttered.

"Indulge me," I said, "and I'll make this a night to remember."

"The Wiz will work wonders," Abdul said, still patting the brushes down on the cymbal, a sliding, stirring stroke. The bass, coming along through the floorboards, was making the snare buzz faintly, and when I passed my fingers over the drum skin I could feel the pulse of it there.

"What are you playing?" I said, at large. "A new one, sounds like."

Azrael showed me a row of his teeth. "Don't you know it?"

I shook my head, mildly surprised: it was an affectation of the Triple-As to address me only in the third person.

"The Wiz don't know it," Azrael said, and his smile slid back down his throat.

Frank swung around toward me on his stool. He brought the trio up to quartet strength, but they hadn't given him an A-name yet. He was new to the group, the only white member, and maybe older than the rest, though it was hard to tell for sure. He had silver hair, but his face looked younger, and might have been too handsome were it not for his shark's smile.

"It's Coltrane," Frank said, and struck a string of cobalt chords. "I think you'll like it."

"Thanks for the information," I said, and with a wink I went around the bow of the piano through the stage door, and climbed the iron ladder up into the dressing room. Some instrument cases were piled up in the corner and I saw that Kiki's street clothes were strewn all around the room. Tara sat before the long mirror, fidgeting with her frowsy blond hair and adjusting her suspenders to the outside curve of her breasts.

"How's the life?" I said, strolling over to my prop bag, a moldering leather thing in the shape of an old-fashioned medical satchel, sitting on a stool in the far corner.

"Eric's in a foul humor," Tara said.

"That's what I hear."

June or someone had gone over the worst spots of dry rot on the bag with shoe polish, I discerned. Sweet of her to trouble. I opened it: all was in readiness. I changed the batteries in the penlight—the beam was so bright it burned them up fast. I dropped it in the opposite pocket from the radio mike, and took a glance at myself in the mirror. Terence had really done quite a nice job.

"I hate this bloody stupid costume," Tara said. "I'll be gooseflesh all night, with this damp."

I picked up the cigarette from her ashtray and took a quick drag.

"Leave that," Tara snapped. "I'm not made of brass, you know."

"It's only your health I'm thinking of," I said. "You haven't seen Kiki, have you?"

"No, and don't care to." She snatched the cigarette from my fingers and snubbed it out. "I hope she's gone for good, the crazy bitch." She jammed her bowler hat on her head and flounced out, or would have if there'd been enough cloth about her for flouncing. I followed her, but only as far as the door of the men's. Inside, I crouched to check for strange feet in the stalls and saw none. But as I was washing my hands there was some sound in that direction and when I looked again I saw a gold spike heel had fallen to the floor of the second stall.

The foot spilled out of that shoe looked altogether too graceful to belong to any drag queen. I flipped up the door latch with my card, and when I opened it, there was Kiki, sprawled out over the porcelain throne, with her head lolled back on top of the tank and her other foot still wedged on the paper dispenser—to ensure her greater privacy, that was. She had on only the tassels and the gold G-string, but in spite of these fripperies her body was even more beautiful than advertised by the posters outside. The incarnation of divine light, and what a ruin she was making of it! The needle was still hanging in her arm.

My mind was clicking, thinking where she'd keep the rest if there was any rest, not on her surely, but had I seen her purse back in the dressing room? I hung over her, listening to my heart go bang. Then I put my thumb on the vein and pulled out the needle and snapped it off short against the edge of the tank, to forestall any further temptation. She was leaking, but just a little. When I tightened my grip on her left arm, she moaned and moved her head—good, that meant she was alive. When I let go, there was a thumbprint-size mark that looked more like a bruise than a puncture, and three finger marks too on the outside of the arm. Good job for Kiki she bruised so easily—she hadn't been shooting up for long, but Eric might fire her if he caught her at it here.

"Upsy-daisy," I said brightly. "Hey babe, show time?" But she was still showing the whites of her eyes. When I hauled her up, they came open, like a doll's, then immediately rolled shut.

"Lem'be," she grunted.

I swung her arm over my shoulder and towed her over as far as the sinks, hoping none of our beer-sodden guests would choose this moment to swagger in. Kiki pressed damply into me, warm and soft and wholly useless. I took a palmful of cold water and spread it back over her brow and her hair. Her eyes flashed at me again and then went out.

"Wake up, stupid," I said. "Or it's your job."

"I'm orri. . . ." Kiki trailed off. I set her back on her heels, let go, then caught her just before she hit the floor. When I leaned her against the wall, though, she slipped down only a little way, and stuck there. I dropped the dead syringe in the waste can and tore off some paper towels to cover it up. When I turned back, Kiki was looking glazedly at the bruises on her arm.

"That's right," I said. "You want to hit yourself in the tongue. Or between your toes, or something. Can't be doing it any old where—not when your living's in your skin."

"Wha . . . wha?" Kiki's hand flopped back against the tiles. She couldn't quite focus her eyes on me. "Ay . . . Aydrun?"

I wet my hand again and slapped her once lightly on the cheek, not hard enough to leave a mark, and watched myself do it, in the mirror. Christ, what did that remind me of? It was enough to widen her eyes.

"Come on, love," I said. "You're on in three minutes." But it sounded absurd the moment I said it. I wrapped her arm round my neck again, cupped my hand in her opposite armpit, and snatched her quickly down the short hall into the dressing room, with her toes turned under and dragging on the way. When I adjusted her in the one stuffed chair, she sat up straight for about half a minute, then nodded off again with her cheek against the tattered wing. I pulled the radio mike from my pocket.

"Dressing room, Eric."

The echo from the amps came back at me through the plywood partitions. Eric and June wedged together in the doorway in their rush to come in; Eric was the first to work free. As always, he wore the dirty white raincoat he'd imitated from Columbo on TV. He was a short dark curly fellow, with beady eyes and an agitated manner, who basked in the luxury of his awful temper fits.

"How many times have I told you not to use that thing as an intercom— Here, what's the matter with her?" All in one fast blurt without changing gears.

"Appears we need to rearrange our dance card," I said.

Eric reached up and plucked me by the lapel, putting his head to one side, really exactly like Columbo. "Come on, how'd she get in this condition?"

"She's been taken ill, can't you see," June said sharply. I didn't know why she'd cover for Kiki—if she was on dope herself she was a great deal more discreet about it.

"Food poisoning maybe?"

"Won't kill her, will it, whatever it is?" Eric said. "Look, I can't have her dying in here."

"No fear," I said. "She'll be dancing again in an hour, I'll wager. But I think I'd better go on first."

"Better go on first, Adrian," Eric advised me. "Look sharp too, we're behind the time." And he went dashing off somewhere.

"What a cock-up," June said.

"Try to keep her awake, if you've got time for it. Give her a pinch or a splash of cold water any time you pass through."

June made a face at me.

"What's the matter?" I said. "The house is half-empty."

"It filled out the last few minutes," June said. "You don't think she's really in any danger?"

"She's only having too much fun," I said, swiping up my prop bag by its two handles. "Well, I'd better go do my tricks."

"Right you are," June said. "Do you want anything?"

"Rum one fifty-one, in a brandy snifter," I said. "Better make it a double, I think. Would you cue the band for me as you go?"

**271**

After she had gone out I gave Kiki one more brisk shake, and watched her eyelids flutter. She'd live, I was ninety percent sure of that. Swinging the bag by my left knee, I walked to the wing over at stage left and waited there. The band had started, the same bass line, with Frank lightly marking out chords on top of it, and the drums whispering along as they had been before. When the horn started up I heard the bass walk out from under it all, into something long and intricate—always the undercurrent controlling the rest. Azrael was the leader, and the one who chose the A-names—I wouldn't have picked Azrael if it had been me, but it was none of my affair. It was a good band even when I wasn't quite listening, when I was only wanting to be nodding out with Kiki, rocked in the waves of her poisoned blood. My baggy eyes were blurring down toward the curls of the slut's wool on the stage floor, dyed red by that spotlight. The bass worked back to its original pattern and I heard the Triple-As all begin chanting into a single mike.

A Love Supreme. . . .
A Love Supreme. . . .
A Love Supreme. . . .
A Love Supreme. . . .

Ghost voices, echoing in their ghostly chamber. . . . They went on. When they stopped, the bass continued alone, climbing measuredly almost to its top pitch, and I thought the horn would pick it up then but instead the solo ended with a single cymbal crash: my cue. I put my best foot forward and twirled out onto the stage, as if for a spinning back kick, so that the tails of my monkey suit went swirling out around me. Ape of nature that I was. . . . The white spot came on and I stopped in the center of it, took a bow, and snatched the radio mike from my pocket.

"Ladies and gentlemen," I said. "With this bare stage, and the powers of my mind, I will now present the greatest show on earth." The room was silent, except for chairs scraping and a few conversations I could hear continuing. I couldn't yet see out of my cone of light. June walked onstage with my drink on a tray. I picked up the glass and as she turned her back, I snapped my fingers under the mike.

"Pardon, miss, could you spare me a vesta?"

June lit a long match and I spun the glass under it, watching the blue flame spring from the rim. With a grand gesture, I knocked the whole thing back. There was a patter of clapping, and a couple of hoots. I threw the glass over my shoulder and aimed the mike at the jingle it made.

"That'll do you all sorts of good with Eric," June snipped at me, as she left the stage. But I was already crossing the gangway, the spot following me into the jumble of little round tables. The house had grown, I could now see, to about forty strong. I was cruising for the likely ones—there's a look they have, and you get to know it. Half again as many men as women, and they'd have come for Kiki more than for me—especially that troupe of lager louts lined up behind three tables in the front. Wanted their bit of skin, they did, but they'd have to take what they were given. They were already beginning to stamp and catcall. Do something about that right away.

"Turn our old Bill into a chicken!" one of them cried as I came up. *Hawhawhaw. . . .*

"Give over, Arold," Our Old Bill muttered. The spot was on him now and he didn't seem to like the attention. Arold, a weighty bloke with a face like beefsteak, stuck his hands in his armpits and began to flap his elbows and caw.

"Bugger me, oima chicken!"

I pulled out the penlight and flicked it on. "Careful there, Bill, you've got something in your eye. Be very still, I'll get it out for you." I pushed the light up near his face, and his eye went flinching away from the beam. When I made a looping pass with the light, his eyes came dead center and blinked. *Gotcha!*

"All gone now, Bill, close your eyes, rest them a bit. D'you know how to play the flute? Here try this one—it's a magic flute!" I handed him a piece of air, and his fingers closed twitchingly around it. "Go on, play it. You're the Pied Piper. Have a walk around the room and see how many people follow you." Down in the moat Aziz started up some high thin noodling on the sax, thank you very much, and Our Old Bill's fingers began wiggling in time. I nudged his elbow and he got up and wandered off. Arold's jaw fell into a gape; he looked as if he might call out but I stabbed him twice in each eye with my penlight's beam.

"Follow the Pied Piper, Arold." After a beat of hesitation, he obeyed. The rest of the beerheads were now rather subdued. Two fine young Ox-bridge couples were at the third-row table, on a slumming expedition, I should think. With one brief effort I got a pair of them following the Pied Piper as well. As I went on, a cotton-shod foot stuck out and tripped me.

The rum went white hot and steamed into my head as I lurched forward and caught myself on the tabletop. Terence plucked me by the sleeve. He was sitting in the shadows behind some horrendous fishbowl drink with a gardenia floating at the rim.

"Careful," he hissed to me. "They're here."

"Who's here?"

"Karnock's lot."

I followed his finger flick and discovered it wasn't any of the higher-up partners he meant this time, only Sid and Ted sitting at a rear table. Ted had got his spikes restarched so they stuck up good and proper once again, but it took me a moment to recognize Sid, he having shaved his head for some reason. A pair of young punkettes were with them, with cones of hair dyed white and black.

"They'll be all right," I said. "I think we've reached an understanding."

"I'll stay to walk you out," Terence said. "All the same."

"Appreciated."

The Pied Piper was swinging his following past Sid and Ted's table— holding his flute like a recorder, though that hardly mattered much. It seemed natural for me to head in that direction. I stretched my hand down for two shakes— *Hello Sid, Hello Ted.* The shaved head gave Sid a curious ascetic look. There was a pale pink stripe down the skin of his head, perhaps from the dye in the old mohawk. It was Ted who introduced the girls as Fiona and Vi. It seemed all right—they were only taking a night on the town. They weren't after me particularly, but then again, why not pick off one of them? Not waiting to consider why, I made a downward slash with the penlight and saw Sid's eyes follow the path. With the light I drew a U, an S curve, a circle closing on its center.

"Go on, Sid. Follow the Pied Piper." When he got up Fiona followed.

"You're a rare 'un," Ted said, but he looked fretful.

"Not to worry," I said. "It's all good fun." Over the mike, I gave out a few more instructions, and Our Old Bill piped the rest of the gang across the plank, and sat them down in the row of chairs there. I went after them, took a bow, got my smattering of applause.

"Now shut up that bloody flute, will you?" I said, and made a snatch between Our Old Bill's fingers. On cue, Abdul terminated Aziz's sax solo with another big bang on the cymbal.

"Time to watch the film!" I shouted. And I took the six of them through it all: the chase, the love scene, the death of Little Nell. They laughed, they wept, they bloody well did what I told them to. . . . And between bits, I took another look in the prop bag.

"Bit peckish after the picture show?" I said to the little Oxbridge snot, who was sitting with his lady, on the end. "Here, help yourself to this apple." I gave him a large red onion from the bag. "Better peel it though, for your lady friend. Here, you may use this paring knife." And I handed him a hammer. His efforts won a small ripple of laughter among the tables. The little Oxbridge miss was beginning to look impatient for her slice. . . . I passed down the rows of chairs, stopping behind Arold.

"Why, look what you've got—a rubber nose!" I said, reaching round to give it a tweak. "You'll have a jolly lot of fun pulling on that, won't you? Wish I had a rubber nose myself, I do." I left him pulling it and snapping it back, and went on down the line to Fiona.

"Not afraid of mice, are you, love?"

Fiona gave a little jump—enough to make all the chains shackled round her middle start jangling. She had sharp hips and sharp shoulders under the black punk armor, and a sharpened nose and chin to match. The usual vampire makeup, black lipstick, the whole bit.

"No, no, of course you wouldn't be, a brave girl like you? See that little mouse just there?" I focused the penlight on a bare patch of floor, and Fiona shrank away from the hot bright dot.

"Dear little white mouse," I said. "There—he doesn't mean you any harm. Only wants to be your friend. Now then," I said, moving the penlight nearer the shoe. "If you sit quite still, I think you might persuade him to walk right up your leg." She trembled a bit, but sat there and let the thing transpire. "Over your *this* and over your *that*—right into the palm of your hand!" When I saw that her eyes were transfixed on her bare palm, I shut off the penlight. "There, you see, he's quite harmless. And really rather pretty, the dear little thing. What lovely small red eyes he has, eh? Go on, you may stroke his fur." With kind of a nauseous fascination, Fiona began to make a petting motion with her forefinger, about a mouse's height above her empty hand. "Feed him a bit of this shredded wheat," I suggested. "That's what he likes best, you know."

Sid was cold-cocked, when I moved to him. He'd gone deeper than I knew. His arms were slacked down against the chair legs, and his head hung off his neck like a melon from a vine. Gave me a funny feeling, that.

**275**

He was helpless as a child. I switched off the mike as I leaned over his shoulder.

"Where's your master, Sid? Where's our Mister Kay?"

"Dunno," Sid muttered, voice slurred as a drunk's.

"Don't you really?" I lifted one of his arms into the air; it hung there exactly where I released it. "You can trust me, Sid, you can tell me anything."

"Int'nick, I fancy," Sid said.

"What for?"

"What's it matter? He won't stop long."

"Where'd you take the car last night from Piccadilly?"

"Back t'boat. . . ."

"And after?"

"Nowhere. Dint go back out."

"You didn't drive?"

"I told you. . . ."

"But the car went out, didn't it, Sid?"

"That's as may be . . . he knows how to drive orright."

"And where does he go when he drives out alone?"

But Sid didn't answer that one, and I was spending too long with him. I picked up his other arm and fixed his two hands together in a time-out signal and left them there. Now, what for Our Old Bill? I switched on the mike as I moved in behind him, and looked back over the others on the row.

"Here, that's revolting!" I called to the Oxbridge pair. "What are you eating that onion for?" They both of them went into spasms of spitting. There was considerable laughter from the audience; the Empress draws rather a vulgar crowd. Arold was sniggering too as he watched, but he was still having a jolly good game of his own, pulling at his nose and releasing it. On down the line, Fiona was holding her mouse by the base of its tail, and the mouse bulged up from her hand like a hot air balloon, straining upward, lashing at the vacant air with all four paws, his little jaws wide and gasping. . . .

Oh God. I wasn't supposed to be seeing that.

"You, Sir Cat!" I howled, giving Our Old Bill a poke in the back. "What do you mean letting that mouse run about? We're not meant to make a pet of a mouse, are we? After that mouse at once, I say!"

Fiona hopped onto her chair and stayed there on tiptoe as Our Old Bill lunged at her hands with a loud *rowr!* On all fours, he continued to pursue the alleged mouse round and round the bank of chairs. The commotion gave me time to get control of my trembling.

"Doesn't bear thinking of, where he goes, does it?" I whispered, bending over the back of Sid's chair.

"That's all about it," Sid replied.

"You stay here when the others go," I said. "I've got something special for you in mind, eh? Something out of the ordinary run."

I straightened up and called Our Old Bill to return to his chair, then had them stand to take a bow, all but Sid.

"Ladies and gentlemen, a generous round of applause for a truly . . . exceptional crew!"

Abdul stirred up a dose of enthusiasm with a roll on his big tom-tom. There was some clapping, laughter, and catcalls. With a few muttered deprogramming suggestions, I sent my five subjects back to their tables.

Sid was still signaling time-out to the audience, with his head sunk down behind his hands and his jaws sagging. I crouched down over my prop bag, regardless of my coattails and my putative dignity, and dug all the way to the bottom of it, for something I had had for quite a long time but never yet had occasion or nerve to use. A slim steel rod, about the gauge of a knitting needle, but longer, about two feet long. It was bent slightly to the contour of the bag, but when I took it out, it sprang back straight. I stood up and displayed it to our clientele, whipping it a little; it made a tearing sound, slicing through the smoked air. The spotlight caught the silver shank and purled toward the rubber guard over the point.

"Ladies and Gentleman!" . . . *this might not work.* . . . "This is *not* a trick." I pulled off the rubber guard and let it drop. Taking one bounce, it plopped into the prop bag. Dumb luck that I hoped would continue. I pricked my left forefinger on the needle point and squeezed it for a pendulous drop of blood.

"It's sharp, do you see? Very sharp." I thrust my finger high in the air, feeling a slight draft where the blood dampened the ball of it. "It's perfectly real, as you can tell." Actually only the first row could see it, probably, but maybe the rest of them imagined. . . .

"Come here, Sid!"

He rolled forward, rose into a crouch, then straightened his legs and

**277**

came to me. Kicking a few clots of masticated onion over the lip of the moat, I positioned him so that the toes of his Doc Martens were flush with the edge of the stage, and smoothed his arms down to his sides.

"Here we have a gentleman of rare ability," I said. "A cataleptic—you won't see one of those every day. Observe."

I pushed him forward, forty-five degrees from his ankles, over the moat. When I stepped back, he held the impossible position. I let the effect of that sink in, then pulled him back a couple of feet and turned him sideways.

"He's lost all his sensitivity," I said. "Perfect anesthesia—he's no longer capable of feeling anything, fancy that. Observe."

I cracked him once on each side of his face, considerably harder than I had Kiki earlier, but taking care not to graze the lump of stitching in the middle of the tattooed web. He took it like a fence post—his head never moved.

"And now. . . ." I stepped to the edge of the moat, two fingers on the satin seam of my trouser leg, to cue another drum roll from Abdul. Down there, at least, I had their interest; the Triple-As were all craning their necks to see what I might be about this time. I moved around in back of Sid, whispered a few deepening suggestions into his ear, and took a hard pinch out of his skin just ahead of his jaw muscle. Out there in the hall, it seemed very still. Even Tara and June had stopped pushing drinks to watch; the only one who seemed restive was Ted. I flourished the long spike over my head, as Abdul came down on the cymbal with the full weight of his arm.

"Observe."

I pulled Sid's jaw just a trifle looser, and felt for his last molars with my forefinger, which was still bloody enough to make a red smudge. I set the spike against this point, stood back so that the audience could see my action clearly, and pushed hard. Sid never flinched, didn't move a muscle, he might just as well have been molded in clay. Not a whisper came out of the crowd. The spike went in easily as into wet clay, about three inches, I'd have guessed. I turned him so his profile faced the other way, and reaching my hand around behind I pushed on the butt end of the spike until his cheek bulged out with the point, then fixed the loose skin between my two fingers and pressed harder. There was a long low gasp out there, as the point came through, clean and bright.

I turned Sid to face full front. Eight inches of limber steel stuck out from either side of him, just there under his ears.

"Open," I whispered, prompting him with a tug on his chin, and demonstrated with the penlight. Just where a horse's bit would go, the spike glittered damply against the back of his throat.

"Think it's all done with mirrors, do you?" My voice was shaking, and so were my knees, I didn't know whether from triumph or fear. I closed Sid's jaw back tight again. His eyes were half-lidded, unfocused and blind. With the shaved head and his queer composure, he looked like he might have been a Zen monk—even his tattoo had assumed a certain dignity.

"Think it's all done with mirrors, eh?" I took a long step to the edge of the stage. "We'll see about that. Come up here, please, you and you." I marked out two of the larger louts with the penlight. They rose and came shambling over the plank. Big strapping fellows. I needed their strength. "It's in there solid, wouldn't you say?" I bent the spike down on either side and let the ends of it twang back. "You don't detect any jiggery-pokery?" I stuck the mike at the larger oaf.

"No, guv, not a bit of it," he muttered. Seemed uneasy, stage fright perhaps. I pulled the mike back.

"All right, take hold. You there, you there." I positioned them on either side of Sid. "Both hands firm on the metal, please. All right, now lift. Go on, heave ho!"

These two weren't hypnotized, but buffaloed sufficiently to do as they were told. As strong as bears, the two of them. It took them little apparent effort to press the spike high enough that Sid's shoes dangled a foot above the floor. Without prompting, Abdul began the drum roll. I stopped and bent Sid's knees, for better clearance, and swung them forward with all my force. He looped the loop one time on the pivot of the spike, then hung there, swinging like a pendulum.

"Well done, lads, you can set him down now. Gently, gently, that's the way. Good work, yes. And now you may go back to your seats." When they had filed away over the plank, I set my two fingers around the spike and snatched it out, quick and clean. And bloodless. When I wiped away the smear my own finger had left, I couldn't even see where the spike had gone in. I whipped it at the floor and it stuck there, trembling. With a couple of whispered cues, I brought Sid back to consciousness.

"How do you feel, my boy? All right?"

"Orright, yes," Sid muttered into the mike.

"And what've you been up to, this last little while?"

"Dunno quite." He blinked heavily. "Here, how'd I come on this stage?"

I chuckled a little—but all by myself. "Well then, why don't you tell us your name?"

"Sid Toomer."

"Ladies and gentlemen, let's hear it for a remarkably talented subject— Sid Toomer!"

The whole club was entombed in silence for what seemed to me like a very long time. Then the applause broke like a thunderstorm. I gave Sid a poke to start him over the gangway, switched off the mike, and headed for the wings myself. My legs were so watery I wasn't sure I'd make it all the way or not. I'd heard of stunts like that before, but never tried to do one. Azrael was fingering out that same subliminal bass line, I heard as the clapping slacked off, and just at the moment I reached shelter, the horn snatched the tune and ran away with it, pouring out like blood from a ruptured heart.

Just inside the dummy wall of the stage's molding, I clung to a strip of lathe to hold myself up. That belt of blazing rum was making odd movements in my gizzard, and there was an equally strange twirling motion in my head. In fact everything was topsy-turvy, including the band. The drill was for them to play dance tunes now, and take requests (the Empress had a small dance floor), not this sort of wild weird stuff. As I was pondering this irregularity, a shadow brushed by me, and blocked the spotlight. I saw it was Kiki, blowing her cue, goose-stepping and strutting her way to center stage. She was still in only the G-string and heels, having omitted to put on all the satin and sequined articles she was meant to take off before the public eye. The music was wrong too, but it didn't affect her. She set her feet wide apart, straddling the prop bag where I'd abandoned it, bent her knees, stretched out her arms, and began to twist and undulate, so that her tassels gained speed and rotated in opposite directions—her *pièce de résistance*. Meanwhile Aziz's solo continued unaltered.

"What a cock-up," June mused, bouncing her empty tray off the clips of her garter, as she paused just behind me.

"Going about it backwards, isn't she?" I said. "What if she were to start putting her things back on?"

**280**

"It wouldn't do, I don't think," June said. "She did wake up, though, that's the thing."

"Approximately." I pushed myself away from the partition and found that I could stand without support, and with a fair feeling of security.

"You gave them what-for, didn't you?" June said.

"Ah, but how will I follow it up?"

"That's your look-out," June said. "Oh, and the phone's for you, that's what. Somebody still waiting there. Very persistent. Wouldn't ring back."

"In Eric's office?"

"No, the phone box," June said. "Get it, would you? I've got to get back to the bar."

"Right, thanks."

I found the pay phone where I'd left it, on the wall between the ladies and the gents. June had balanced the receiver on top of the coin box. I lifted it with some trepidation—this wasn't a number I gave out.

"Here I am, and who are you?"

"You're a hard one to get a hold of." George or Sam's voice whirred frantic as a June bug in a jar.

"I do what I can," I said. "What's the trouble?"

"It's Karnock, you see. . . ."

"What about him?" I was wondering how they'd found the number, but doubtless all British Telecom's secrets were as an open book to the Dutchman.

"He's dead. The Head's in a devil of a state about it. Undone years of work, he says."

"Ah, but death waits for no man, so I'm told."

"Quite," George or Sam said testily. "But no one can understand how it happened, you know."

"Heart attack, maybe? Maybe a stroke? They're all hypertensive, all that sort."

"He broke his neck," George or Sam said. "Or his back, something critical, I don't know. We haven't a clue how it could have occurred. He was in a tight cell, not even a window. It's as if someone came in a keyhole and did him and then went out the keyhole again."

"That's the best you've got?"

"We've got nothing at all," said George or Sam. "At the moment, it's presenting itself in the light of an impossibility, yes. The Head thought perhaps you might shed some light on the question. The tape's blank for the last bit of your interview—appears something went wrong with the wiring."

"Oh, you didn't lose anything out of the ordinary," I said. "Only the usual calmness and relaxation sort of thing. The same as on any other session. Sorry, but no help here."

"Mmmph," George or Sam said. "There's another door shut, isn't it? Be a good fellow and forget I called."

He rang off, and I followed suit, resting there with my weight on the phone box, its metal and plastic contours. I couldn't feel it, though; it had become impalpable. No difference of texture or temperature between me and the machine. The shape of the mean hallway shimmered and blurred and I could easily perceive that it was not real, not any part of it. But I went out by the door, out of politeness, since I could as easily have passed through the walls, and returned to the stage to continue my work. I turned sugar to salt, light into darkness, laughter to tears, grief into anger, rage into passion, and passion into nothing at all. I turned men into swine, and back again. I could do whatever my will invited, go wherever my fancy led me, and I found that nothing was beyond me, as I rose on the ascending spiral of my power.

# twenty-seven

Then, after my last show had concluded, I slipped back out by the moat's street door, in order to avoid Terence. A dirty trick after all his kindness, but to do what I was planning next I needed to escape his stewardship. The solution that had become obvious to me needed to be accomplished quickly. Do it now and get it over. Now more than ever, it seemed obvious. . . .

The tubes were long shut, and I was too mean to take a cab. A false economy, considering that I would soon place myself beyond the use of money, but old habits die hard. I went on foot, and indirectly. The streets were empty, except for my dreams.

I had taken no thought of my direction on departure and I was soon undone in the snarl of the Soho streets. Whenever a building interposed itself in my path I halted and waited for it to shift. If it did not, I walked either around or through, depending on what its ontological status proved to be. In this way, I eventually passed into Mayfair, which was deserted also, the streets swept clean, the rich goods all fettered behind iron bars. Only a black girl in an elegant brown leather suit approached and asked me, did I want company? She was solid and warm when I touched her forearm, but being unsure of her, I went on alone.

It had begun to spit a little rain when I reached Hyde Park Corner. I had never intended to arrive there at all, but I went in at the mouth of Serpentine Road. My monkey suit was getting drenched in the rain, but of course that wouldn't matter much afterward. I diverged from the pavement and went across the patchy green, which stuck to my shoe soles with a sucking grip and sound. Halfway across the great meadow, it began to seem as though I were at sea, so very far away from all the landing lights, and even the ground itself was swelling under my feet in waves. Or seismic shocks, from some enormous footsteps. I looked behind me and saw an elephant coming majestically in my direction, briefly silhouetted against the lights beyond Marble Arch, then lost in the long shadow on the grass. It

*283*

was a corporeal elephant, I was sure; I could almost smell the peanuts on its breath, but as long as I waited, nothing arrived, only a slow cold breeze passing over me, blowing south.

Shivering, I turned and walked forward a few more steps. At the far edge of the vague terrain was an irregular lumpy horizon line made by the bushy tops of trees, and above them the dull reddish glow of the city's southern lights, reflected from the cloud. In the way ahead of me was something else, small, dark, bulky, with a white patch in its middle. The thing came closer and resolved: a man in dark trousers and an old-fashioned white ribbed undervest. Great bristles of black hair sprang up from his bare shoulders. He held two little children each by the hand, or maybe they were holding him, like anchors.

"So you're out," I said.

"Yes, I'm well out of it." Karnock's voice, kinder than I remembered, almost avuncular I might have said.

"No fear, my son," he said when he'd come nearer. I suppose I must have raised my hand, or taken a step back. "I don't bear malice to you, you know. I'm better off as I am, may be. Though you couldn't call it anything but murder, eh?"

"Is that for me to say?" I said.

"Who else?" he said. I could see it was Karnock now, through the flicker and pulsation of the strange uncertain light.

"Who else is left?" Karnock said. One of the children made a sudden lunge ahead, tugging on his arm so hard he made a sudden stumble forward. "Eh, well," Karnock said as he righted himself. "I think I'd best be going." As the three of them passed around me, I could feel the breeze turn back, but when a moment afterward I looked over my shoulder, there was nothing there but the empty expanse of tattered grass, and at its border a cab shifting gears higher and higher as it sped east on the Bayswater Road.

I was cold and solitary as a planet circling . . . *those large animals, which are called stars*, august but irremediably distant from one another. I had not expected my apotheosis to take such color or such form. My hair hung in wet hanks from my head, but the rain had stopped now, and the clouds had sunk nearly to the ground. Cloud clung to the milky surface of the Serpentine as I walked along its bank. Up the slope to the northern side, the canny old trees were stirring, improving their positions under cover of the fog. My surroundings were revolving in slow orbits, so that I had to halt to regain my balance, and I saw Nicole carried toward me on a wandering finger of mist.

"You used me," she said sorrowfully, plucking at her lower lip with her nail.

"Haven't you got that backward?" I said. "Wasn't it you that used me all along?"

I saw she was about to respond, but when I moved toward her, her long ellipse took her further away, circling round behind me, and gone.

"That's the way of human life," Stuart said, as his orbit rotated him helplessly by. "We all use each other. It's a fallen world."

"Not necessarily. . . ." I said.

"Will you argue that even now?" Stuart said, as his orbit rotated him helplessly by.

"Of course," I said. "I've come where I meant to. Only I wasn't prepared for the loneliness."

I awaited his answer, but Stuart had already whirled off into silence, and I was alone again in my majesty, floating in the black field of deep space, with stars above and below me too—frigid, brilliant, and unreachable. I could not come near enough to make any of them my sun.

When I rejoined the world of things I saw that I had somehow crossed the bridge and was walking with a staggering pace down a grand alley of chestnuts into Kensington Gardens. Ahead, the Round Pound opened its perfect circle. The fog had lifted, so that the smooth water returned the obsidian vacancy of the sky. I walked into it without breaking stride, waist-deep, shoulder-deep, and over my head. For thirty seconds I thought it was done, but then my reflexes took over, and I discovered I couldn't outwit my resilience. I was floating whether I would or no, couldn't seem to forget how to swim. Even the soaking weight of the tailcoat was insufficient to drag me to the bottom.

So I gave up trying and thrashed my way to the other side. Automatically I had kicked off my shoes, so goose slime squelched between my bare toes as I labored up the concrete bank. The drenched tails of my coat wrapped around my legs and made me stumble as I went, but I was back in the right road now, homeward bound, willy-nilly, and I would make it under my own marvelous power. Power to kill, not make alive.

It was no distance anymore, but once out of the park I had to go gingerly, my bare feet wincing away from the pavement. There was something ludicrous about that, and by the time I had reached my doorstep I was laughing, out of hysterics, and shaking from an ague fit. But I hushed myself, as a drunk would do, and went in stealthily on tiptoe. With great craft I made my way to the bathroom, shut the door, switched on the light. I peeled to my skin and dropped my clothes into the tub. The tux was a write-off, no mistake. There in the mirror was my naked body, in which the universe was rendered. Murder the one, and destroy the other. That thought calmed me, and stopped my trembling.

So I sat down on the rim of the tub and washed the pond muck off my feet. No use tracking up the rugs. Was that important? Hard to say. I wrapped a towel around my shanks and chose a fresh razor from the cellophane packet. It was one of those throwaway jobs, with the silver of metal buried in plastic molding. I carried it into the kitchen, where I stooped under the sink to root through the jumble of tools until I found a pair of needle-nose pliers. My head went spinning toward a blackout when I rose, because I had straightened up too suddenly. I sagged into the sink for support, bracing my palms on the damp enamel. The razor toppled off the edge and hit the floor with a plastic click. When my head recentered I remembered the snake.

Now what, to a snake, would be euthanasia? But perhaps he had died of his own accord over the course of the day. I cinched the towel tighter round my waist and went into the front room to see. Funny thing, he didn't look half so moribund as he had earlier that day. As soon as I had raised the cover, he went slithering vigorously around in the gravel, then interrogatively raised his head. His colors had sharpened; his black eyes looked bright. I picked him up, carefully, and he trained himself around my wrist and gripped with enthusiasm, lowering his head on six inches of neck to quest round the room. A veritable metamorphosis—well, of course that's what it was. I knelt over the tank and saw on the gravel by the big stone the papery heap of his old skin.

Aha, so there, so that was it. It had been stupid of me not to know it. I unwrapped him from my arm and set him in the tank, then picked up the loose shed skin. He'd come out of it almost perfectly, leaving the translucent scaled patterns intact, down to the yellowed scales that had covered his eyes. Now he was hungry—very hungry, undoubtedly. Have to pop out in the morning to Waltham's for a mouse . . . only my present planning precluded that, didn't it?

Always something. . . . I re-covered the tank and went to a drawer to find pencil, paper, an envelope. One more favor to solicit from Terence, and then I'd be done. I sealed my house keys into the envelope, with a brief note about the care and feeding of snakes, and scratched the address of the Tooth and Claw onto the front. The keys made it heavy, so I stuck on a slather of stamps from the roll. Then I stuck it up under the lid of the letter box to be taken away in the morning.

And now.

I went back into the kitchen and retrieved the safety razor from the floor, and went to work on it with the pliers, breaking off shards of plastic and letting them fall into the sink. It was clumsy work, and my hands were unsteady. When I cut into the ball of my thumb, the sting of it brought tears to my eyes. Silly, under the circumstances. I sucked at the cut till the pain eased. It wouldn't hurt much, when I came to the point, and certainly it wouldn't last long. And even a pig could be brought to love death, given the right conditions.

I laid the silver strip of razor blade on the counter, scraped the bits of plastic up from the sink, and dusted them from my hands into the rubbish. I turned the cold tap on full blast, and let it pour over both my wrists, just where the pulse was beating. After a couple of minutes had passed, the water turned a deep artesian cold. I let it run till my wrists were quite numb, then shut it off and turned on the hot. Hot water, to speed things up a bit. Steam rose from the post of water pounding against the blotched enamel of the sink. The bit of razor was so slender it was difficult to get a grip.

"Adrian?"

A ghost voice, from the bedroom. Ignore it. No distractions now. I nicked the corner of the blade into the skin of my left wrist and set myself for the long deep stroke.

"Adrian?" Clara's voice, actual. "Is that you, finally? Damn but it's late."

I flicked the razor blade into the rubbish and reached across to shut off the water. A valve clanked back at me, deep in the wall. Well, God, I nearly did it then. Took your time about it, didn't you? I went to stand in the bedroom doorway. Clara was sitting up in the bed, blinking into the light behind me. The sheet was wrinkled around her waist and her hair ran over her breasts like a waterfall.

"I was at the club," I said. "You remember, the Sunday night show."

"Late even for that, aren't you?" Clara yawned. "I tried to wait up for you, but I didn't make it."

"The tubes were shut. Had to walk back."

"Oh." Clara flipped her hair over her shoulders and back on both elbows. "Forgotten taxis?"

"What's a taxi?" I said. "So, you're back, are you? It isn't a dream or a joke or whatever?"

"Pinch yourself," Clara said. "Or . . . but wait, first you've got a phone call."

"It'll have to keep, surely, at this hour."

"She only called a little while ago," Clara said. "And it did sound like some sort of emergency. One of your patients obviously. Peavine or something she said her name was. Didn't you see the note on the phone?"

"You know it's four o'clock in the morning?"

"Well, you're not asleep, and I doubt she'll be, from the sound of her. She sounded upset."

"Ahhh . . ." I said. But Clara turned over onto her side, winding the sheet back up to her shoulders. I went back to the front room and there was the note right where I'd walked past it. A torn sheet of loose-leaf shouting Miss Peavey's name and number in red magic marker inside a red star. Yes, but then my mind had been elsewhere.

She answered before I'd even heard the first ring. "Yes?" There was a pounce in her tone. "Yes?"

"Eh, hello, it's Adrian Strother here, the hypnotist, you know. Obscene hour to be phoning, I realize, but . . ."

"No, thank you, thank you for ringing me back. I wanted very much to talk to you—"

"—so I gather—"

"—to apologize, really . . ." She hesitated.

"No, no. Apologies due from me, I should think."

"Certainly not," she answered with authority. "You were quite right. I've had a long think on it, and you were quite right."

"If you say so . . ." Reflexively, I wadded the loose-leaf note into a ball. "There's a distinction, perhaps, between right and helpful."

"No, but, er . . ." There was some buggy whistling on the line, and at the other end I thought I heard a door bang. "You did me all sorts of good, you know. It took me most of the night, but I see it plain now.

And . . . I felt I must get on to you right away, never mind the time, because I do want to come back, you see. . . ."

"Oh no, Miss Peavey, I don't think that's a wise course at all. . . ."

"But you—"

"I'm out of my depth with you, understand?" I went on right over her, though she seemed to be raising her voice too. "I meant to be treating your agoraphobia, not your, er . . . your other conditions. In a case like yours, I could make a referral—"

"But you helped me." Her voice bored into my ear. "No one else helped me, only you."

"That," I said, "is a debatable point."

But she wasn't paying any attention.

"And so you've got to go on helping me," she said. "You mustn't just stop."

"No?" I said.

"No, you mustn't," she said.

"All right," I said, holding the phone some little distance from my ear. "All right then, since you put it so strongly. Call round tomorrow, or no, better not. Looks like tomorrow's already today. Let's make it Tuesday. Your usual time?"

"Yes," she said. "Yes, definitely. And thank you, Doctor Strother, thank you so much."

"I'm not a doctor," I said, to the dial tone. It appeared that she had already hung up.

So, how do you like that? All the while I'd thought I was talking myself out of the thing, I was only talking myself deeper in. Looked like tomorrow would be another day after all, whether I'd planned it that way or not. I put down the phone and started for bed, chucking the towel into the bathroom on my way. It bounced off the rack and fell to the tile, but I didn't stop to pick it up, because I was suddenly in a hurry, in a mood of garrulous excitement—so ripe with news for Clara I didn't quite know where I would begin. She rolled over to face me when I lowered myself at full length on the bed . . . but then I heard a slight rasp in her breathing, and felt it stir on the skin of my shoulder, and I realized she'd already gone back to sleep.

Well I'll be a. . . . She was sleeping with such concentration she might almost have been at prayer. It was enough to make me laugh, that light, bright, mercurial feeling, but I held it in, so as not to wake her. She was breathing on my arm. A wedge of street light lay on the wall, watery from flaws in the glass. The light was rippling and waving to me, but then my eyes fell helplessly shut, and I felt myself pulled powerfully down, reorganized, like filings drawn to a magnetic source. There is such a marvelous patience in things that the hope of return cannot be exhausted, and that is the end of the story of the shaikh, I remember now, yawning and stretching, sinking down into my inexhaustible store of sleep, returning, one more time, to the way.